In Zodiac Light

ROBERT EDRIC

LARGE PRINT

Oxford

First published in Great Britain 2008
by
Doubleday
an imprint of Transworld Publishers

Published in Large Print 2009 by ISIS Publishing Ltd.,
7 Centremead, Osney Mead, Oxford OX2 0ES
by arrangement with
Transworld Publishers
a Random House Group Company

British Library Cataloguing in Publication Data
Edric, Robert, 1956–
    In zodiac light. – Large print ed.
    1. Gurney, Ivor 1890–1937 – Fiction
    2. World War, 1914–1918 – Veterans – Fiction
    3. Composers – England – Fiction
    4. Paranoid schizophrenics – England – Fiction
    5. War neuroses – Fiction
    6. Psychiatric hospital patients – England –
    London – Fiction
    7. Biographical fiction
    8. Large type books
    I. Title
    823.9'14 [F]

ISBN 978–0–7531–8244–4 (hb)
ISBN 978–0–7531–8245–1 (pb)

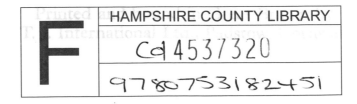

For Bruce Jones
another Gloucestershire boy

I walked midsummer in Flaxley Wood,
And waited through the daylong night;
Attendant of a world not come,
And cast by dark in zodiac light.

Ivor Gurney, "In Flaxley Wood"
London Mercury, 17 June 1921

zodiacal light: a very faint cone of light in the sky, visible in the east just before sunrise and in the west just after sunset. Caused by the reflection of sunlight from cosmic dust in the plane of the ecliptic.

Part One

Dartford Asylum, London

Spring, 1923

CHAPTER
ONE

Because we were an asylum party, the bus driver refused to set off before checking each of the names on the list I'd given him. And having checked the names against the labels on the men's pockets, he then insisted on checking them again. There was considerable malice in the man's actions, but unwilling to delay us further, I refrained from commenting on his remarks.

"That you?" he said to the first of the men — a man called Hartley, already standing on the open platform and gripping the polished rail with both his hands. "That you, is it? That you?"

"This is Hartley," I told him, putting a hand on Hartley's shoulder to reassure him.

"Ought to be alphabetical by rights," the driver said.

There were only six men, and our outing had been arranged late the previous evening, after an hour of special pleading before Osborne, who had only given his permission shortly before our departure.

Hartley looked from the driver to me.

"Your name's on the list," I told him.

"No one's denying that," the driver said. "That wasn't what I said." He slapped the sheet of paper against his steering wheel and looked Hartley up and down, pausing at his hands, still locked tightly around the rail.

We were distracted by a shout from one of the other passengers, an elderly woman sitting close by the door. She demanded to know when we would be moving.

The driver glanced at her, but said nothing.

It was normal procedure on these outings for the patients to be seated together at the rear of the small single-decker buses, and this often necessitated other passengers moving forward to vacate those seats. The timing of the outings was invariably calculated to avoid the fuller buses of the early mornings and late afternoons.

"Are we going to have to move seats?" another woman called.

I told her this was unlikely, that there were only nine of us.

"Nine?" the driver said, slowly counting the six names on the list.

"Six patients, myself and two orderlies," I told him.

I held my hand over Hartley's for a moment and then told him to walk down the aisle.

Hartley released his grip on the pole and started walking. I motioned for those still waiting at the roadside to board the bus and follow him.

"You need my permission to board," the driver said.

We didn't, and both he and I knew that.

"You've got your list," I told him.

"All this tells me —"

I took the sheet from him, held it against the small window which separated us and signed my name.

6

"Plus three," he said. "Write that down. 'Plus three'."

I wrote the words, folded the paper and gave it back to him.

He pushed it into the leather satchel beside his seat. It would be presented to the relevant medical committee at the end of the month and the bus company would be duly reimbursed. Life in and around the asylum was filled with such precise and minutely observed procedures.

The five other patients followed Hartley on to the bus, gathering together as they came. The elderly woman said hello to each of them as they passed her; only Hartley and one other answered her. None of the few remaining passengers spoke. On other occasions I had seen women on the buses surreptitiously cross themselves as the men passed them by — though whether this was done out of any genuine feeling of sympathy for the inmates, I was never certain. Perhaps it was merely some instinctive gesture of self-protection on their part to insure against the possible contagion of the men's suffering. Or perhaps it was some equally inexplicable display of relief that the same had not befallen their own husbands, brothers and sons, lost or returned — a warding-off of malign spirits.

The men finally arranged themselves on the rear seats and sat facing forwards.

"And the rest?" the driver said.

I looked out to where Cox, the senior orderly, and Lewis, a recent appointee, stood and smoked. I called to Cox, but other than raising his hand to me, he made no move to board the bus. Lewis, a youth of eighteen or

7

nineteen, began walking the few paces to the doorway, but Cox held his arm and told him to wait.

"Just finish this," Cox called to me, holding up his cigarette.

"No — now," I said, unwilling to raise my voice.

Cox whispered something to Lewis, and Lewis laughed. Then both men dropped what remained of their cigarettes and came to the bus.

Lewis was the first to board.

"Go to the rear. Sit ahead of them," I told him.

Lewis hesitated, half turning to Cox, who remained on the road.

"Best do as he says," Cox said. He blew out a last mouthful of smoke and then spat heavily into the overgrown verge behind him. All of this, I understood, was for my benefit, asserting his authority over the men under his immediate control. He was an old soldier, a sergeant, and this remained apparent in everything he said and did. Equally evident to me was his resentment at all he had lost upon his return to civilian life. He was in his early forties, and most of the men in his charge were half his age.

Finally boarding, he reached out his hand to the driver, who shook it.

"Give you the list, did he?" Cox asked the man.

"Such as it is," the driver said.

"Go to the others," I told Cox.

Cox drew himself suddenly rigid, saluted me and shouted, "*Sir*." And before I could respond to this, he dropped his arm, slapped the driver on the shoulder and laughed. The driver laughed with him, glancing at me to see if I was finally prepared to share in their cold joke.

Cox then walked slowly down the bus, pausing to look at the elderly woman, who turned away from him as he passed her.

I followed him, and as soon as I started walking, the driver engaged his gears and the bus lurched forward, causing me to stumble and to hold on to the seats as I continued.

Our journey lasted less than fifteen minutes, and when I saw our destination ahead, I rose and returned to stand in the doorway. I pointed out to the driver where we would alight.

"Not a designated stopping point," he said.

Ignoring this, I beckoned the others forward and they came.

Cox, the last to rise, shouted, "Do as he says," to the driver, who drew close to the road junction and then braked sharply, causing the men to collide with each other.

Unwilling to tolerate any further delay, I told Lewis to lead the men away from the bus and off the road.

"Is this the right place?" he asked me.

I showed him the simple map one of the nurses had given me, and he looked at it, unable to make any connection between it and the empty countryside around us.

I pointed out to him the inverted "T" of the road and the lane we were about to follow. "And the river's just beyond," I said, indicating the waving line the nurse had drawn.

"The Thames?"

"Unless there's another," I said.

The men started to move ahead of us and I told Lewis to catch them up and walk with them.

The land around us was open and treeless, a few fences and low hawthorn hedges, a line of telegraph poles and a drainage ditch on either side of the lane.

There were buildings in the distance, and a succession of smoking chimneys, but nothing close by. It was clear to me that we were approaching the river, but it was not yet in sight. It was a bleak, exposed place, planed by a constant wind. It had been my intention to ask the bus driver how frequently the service returned past the asylum, but I had forgotten to do this. Cox would know.

I looked back to where he followed us, smoking again, plumes of smoke forming above him in the cool air. I waited for him.

"Is it far?" he asked me, swinging his arms.

I showed him the map.

"What does that tell you?" he said. He traced his finger to where the lane met the river, and then slid it to the marked cross. "Did she tell you how far?"

I'd guessed the river to be no more than a couple of hundred yards from the road, and if that were true, then the distance from the lane's end to the cross was considerably less.

"And what if the tide's in?" Cox said, his voice low, and his manner considerably less aggressive now that we were out of hearing of the others.

"Above the high-water mark, she said," I told him.

"Makes sense," he said.

We were on our way to see a beached whale. The creature had been sighted a week earlier, already stranded and dead, and since then there had been a succession of reports in the local newspapers, prompting visits by anyone interested enough to want to see it. It was upon reading one of these reports that I'd made my application to Osborne. I'd been reminded of all the other stranded corpses I'd seen, in Orkney, Shetland and the Western Isles before the war, and I'd put up a notice in one of the day-rooms to see if anyone else was interested.

I knew as we walked that those earlier sightings — most of them on the white sands and dunes of the Inner Hebrides — would be considerably different from what we were likely to encounter today.

And almost as though reading these thoughts, Cox said, "You got their hopes up. They're going to want to see it swimming up and down, blowing water from its hole and probably with Jonah standing in its mouth and waving back at them."

I acknowledged this. Even the nurse, who had visited the creature four days earlier, when its corpse was only recently discovered, had told me not to expect too much. She had hesitated when I'd asked her if the visit was worth making. Then she'd said, "How often do you see a whale?"

Ahead of us, the men had stopped walking and were gathering together. Lewis stood beside them. He cupped his hands to his mouth and shouted something neither Cox nor I could understand, his words lost in the wind between us.

"They've spotted the river," Cox said. "They're on a dyke bridge."

I looked at the men and saw that they stood on a slight rise.

"A sluice or something," Cox said. "There used to be brickfields close to the shore. For the clay. They've all gone now, filled up. Look at them — they're like kids, excited because they can see the water." He pointed to our right and I saw a line of distant vessels sitting on the horizon, appearing at that distance to be resting in the far-off fields. Studying a map the night before, I'd seen that the shipping channels opposite Tilbury were called the "Lower Hope Reaches" and the name had made me laugh.

We approached the waiting men and rose alongside them on to the covered drain.

The river lay ahead of us, filling the horizon, its far bank visible across the miles of grey water.

"So where is it?" Lewis said.

The question was echoed by several others.

According to the map, the whale was to our right, towards the mouth of the estuary. I shielded my eyes and searched in that direction.

"Should have brought some field glasses," Cox said.

I still possessed a pair somewhere amid the clutter of my half-unpacked belongings.

"You're right," I told him.

I continued walking to where the lane ended in a field of rough grass. Cattle stood between us and the water, turning to watch us as we approached.

"Anyone scared of cows?" Cox said, and laughed.

Two of the six patients raised their hands.

"You two don't count," Cox said. "You're scared of everything. Always have been, always will be." He then walked towards the cattle, clapping his hands to disperse them. The animals turned at his approach and walked away from him. They were dark, thin creatures, mud-caked and with long, misshapen horns. I searched for the farm to which they might belong, but could see nothing. I urged the men to follow Cox through the open pasture, and within minutes our feet and shins were soaked. Turning to wait for us, Cox called for everyone to follow him single-file, indicating that there was a path of sorts through the morass and that he could see it ahead of him.

A few moments later, he rose from the field on to a low embankment, searched around him and called out that he could see the whale.

Upon hearing this, the others started to run, splashing over the sodden ground and then gathering around him where he stood. He pointed something out to them and they fell silent. Several of them wandered away from him in the direction he pointed. I knew from this sudden silence that there was going to be no spouting water or waving Jonah.

Cox waited for me. I climbed the low bank and stood beside him.

A short distance away, more than half-embedded in the soft, saturated mud of the estuary, lay a disappointingly small shape, a boulder perhaps, or an upturned boat.

A flock of gulls rose from the mound at our approach, shrieking and circling above us.

It was clear that we would be able to approach no closer to the whale than the rise on which we stood, an old flood-defence line curving back and forth along a lost boundary or a straightened curve of the river.

We walked along this until we stood directly above the whale. There was neither tail nor mouth visible to indicate which end was which. A mud-covered protuberance that might have been the remains of a fin had already been eaten away by the birds.

"I wonder what sort it was," Cox said.

"The newspaper reports said it might be a pilot whale," I told him. "Apparently, they're not uncommon at the mouth of the estuary." I looked further to the east, to the dull, unbroken plane of water, its horizon with the sky and distant land already lost.

I told the others this, and some were interested, and some feigned interest. Most of those who were eligible for these excursions seized the opportunity whenever it was offered, regardless of their destination or purpose. One man picked up a stone and threw it at the corpse, missing but cheering his shot. Others copied him. The mud, more liquid than it appeared, swallowed their missiles and then showed no sign of where they had struck. A direct hit raised a louder cheer. Some of the men threw their stones at the circling gulls.

In one of the newspaper articles, the writer had speculated on how the pilot whale had acquired its name, suggesting that it was either because it led other whales to their feeding grounds, or because it led the

14

whalers to where the larger whales might be found and killed.

I repeated this to Cox.

"Why would it do the second?" he said. "Where's the sense in that?"

"Perhaps it led the boats unwittingly," I suggested.

Lewis returned to us. "They think the real whale might be further on," he said, betrayed by his own lack of conviction.

"Tell them to forget it," Cox said. "Tell them they'd have signed up for the outing, whale or no whale." He left us and walked to where the others stood above the corpse. He pointed. "That's its head and that's its tail." There were no clear grounds for this identification, but because he'd said it, then the others saw it too. "And that's its eye, and there's where its flippers are buried in the mud," he added.

He came back to me. "They're happy now," he said. "If you like, I'll tell them to feel free to jump in, run to it and sit on its back for a photo on the off-chance that any of them gets a visitor in the next six months."

CHAPTER
TWO

I sought out my field glasses later that same evening. They were in the third chest I emptied, still in their leather case, their strap wound tightly around them, and the case itself still coated inside with the dust of mud turned dry. I wiped the lenses with my handkerchief. When my mother had presented them to me there had been a small yellow cloth in the case, along with a fine-haired brush and a bottle of cleaning fluid. In addition, she had bought a small can of oil and a tiny screwdriver, both recommended to her by the salesman from whom she had bought the glasses, and both supposedly vital to their operation, though neither ever used, and now long since lost. I searched for them at the bottom of the chest, but they were not there. There was, however, some faint aroma of the spilled oil — it had smelled distinctly of fish, I remembered.

It was beyond me to search further through any of the other chests, packed as they were to the brim, mostly with books — beyond me to take any of these out and study their various inscriptions: to me from others; to others from me, later returned; and to others, also long dead, from their own loved ones.

I sat for several minutes with the contents of the chest strewn around me on the boards of my room, and then I repacked its contents and slid it back into the corner from which I had taken it.

Having cleaned the lenses, I went to my window.

My room was one of the highest in the hospital, on the second floor of the oldest part of the building, Stone House, and looked down over the garden between two of its more recent wings, towards the inner wall and the greenhouses and the land beyond. The outer wall formed my far boundary, higher than the closer wall, and intended as a screen to protect the privacy of those inside. Rooftops and trees were visible beyond this, and from my vantage point I could easily make out the taller buildings to the west.

The focussing wheel was stiff, clogged with the same fine dust, and I wiped and then blew this away. I searched the trees and rooftops, gradually closing in on the outer wall.

A group of nurses sat together at the garden entrance and I watched them for several minutes. There were a dozen of them, perhaps more, and they sat on the benches there, empty now of the men who filled them throughout the day. Some of the women sat with their eyes closed; others walked back and forth and stretched the aches from their arms and backs. It was almost eight; they would have been on duty since midday.

I stood a few feet back from my window, certain I would not be seen by them.

After a few minutes, those sitting rose as though at a signal, and all of them came back into the asylum and entered by a rear door.

I dampened a towel in my small sink and wiped out the leather case, leaving it to dry on the sill. It had been my mother's intention to have the glasses inscribed before my departure from home, but this had never happened.

In the same case I had come across the photographs she had collected for me, and the manuals and illustrated booklets she had insisted on removing from my father's collection for me to take with me. I had tried to explain to her that these would be better left where they were — joking that I would have little time for botany, bird-watching or bee-keeping where I was going — but she had insisted that I take them, conceding only insofar as to remove the heavier of the books. I knew even as I protested that it was never her intention that I should *use* the books and manuals, simply that I should have them with me, and understanding this, I had acquiesced to the remainder of her wishes.

Afterwards, I had spent sleepless nights reading and re-reading the books, searching out my father's annotated additions and critical remarks. Sometimes these were as little and as vague or misleading as a solitary question- or exclamation-mark; elsewhere, he wrote more in the margins than was printed on the pages. I found him there; and after so long dead, he spoke to me again. I also came to understand what my mother herself had gained from these never-fading echoes in the years she had survived him, and, consequently, what a precious gift she had given me.

In each of my letters home — frequently one a day during those weeks when I was afforded the time to write — I remarked on something I had done or seen which allowed me to refer to something my father had already written.

I retrieved other volumes during my infrequent leaves, reassuring her that what I had already taken with me was in safe hands during my short absences. What was never said, of course, was that the whole of this precious library was under strict instructions to be returned to her in the event of the unthinkable happening. That was how we then chose to think of it — "unthinkable". Except that it was never that — unthinkable — after the first few months, and especially not after the death of Charles.

There were hives in the asylum garden beyond the inner wall, and I could see their vague, pale shapes beneath the trees. I had been there a month before I learned of them, sent to attend to a patient who had wandered too close to them, been stung, and who had then developed a strong reaction to the sting. No one had known what to do for the man, and remembering how my father had treated my own childhood stings, I had killed a handful of the insects, collected the venom from their sacs, mixed this with honey, and then rubbed some of this on the man's stung face and neck and forced him to swallow the rest. By then his eyes were swollen shut and he was having difficulty breathing, but after less than an hour this simple remedy started

19

taking effect. Even Osborne had come from his office to watch. The stung man said it was the first honey he had ever tasted and he asked me if he ought to go on eating it to prevent any further reaction to the bees. I told him it could do him no harm. At home, Charles and I had been fed a spoonful of honey morning and night. Later, as we grew, my father gave us other samples, treating us to the new season's crop, and to honey from various sources, quizzing us and then responding over-enthusiastically when we repaid him with our half-guessed answers to all he was trying to teach us.

It was after the incident with the stung man that I had first been taken to the hives.

The garden beyond the inner wall was intended to supply the asylum with its fruit and vegetables. There had originally been livestock — chickens and pigs — but these had been recently removed. Six acres of land were under cultivation, half to cabbages and potatoes — the staples of most of our evening meals — and the remainder to other vegetables — peas and beans, mostly, and to soft fruits in the late summer and autumn.

There had been espaliered fruit trees — apples, pears and apricots — against the crumbling brick wall, but all that remained of these now were their trunks and overgrown lower branches, growing untended in all directions and bearing little fruit. The man who pointed this out to me, a patient who had once earned his living as a market-gardener, expressed his regret that the trees had been neglected in this way. When I asked him why this was, he said he didn't know, unwilling to speculate or to suggest any remedy for the future. He then brightened and told me about the small orchard in which the hives stood. He indicated the tops of the trees at the far end of the plot and led me across the untended ground.

I said nothing of my own knowledge of bee-keeping, and was disappointed by what I was shown: two dozen hives in a state of disrepair amid rank grass and overgrown brambles, most of the structures empty and abandoned, and the remainder half-filled with feeble colonies struggling to survive.

It seemed a pity to me that both the hives and the small orchard in which they stood were not better cared for — and perhaps brought into greater productivity — and I suggested to several of my colleagues that the subject might be raised at our next meeting with Osborne. Few even feigned enthusiasm at the suggestion.

At my father's funeral there were representatives from many local and several national bee-keeping societies. Most of these men and women were by then his friends, or at least his long-term correspondents. His death was reported in their journals, and for months afterwards there were articles about him, all of which my mother collected in another of her albums. It was a life he had lived largely away from her, but it was an absence she had neither regretted nor complained of. He was the chairman and treasurer of our local society, and the vice-chairman for twenty-five years of two of the county organizations; he spoke at gatherings all over the country, and his own articles and meticulously kept records were printed in all those same journals.

His profession as a doctor, a country practitioner, is what led him to his interest in the medical aspects of apiary. And just as my mother had gathered together all those appreciations and garlands when he'd died, so she had also devoted herself to working with him on the articles he wrote, typing them out for him, creating indexes, checking his references, finding illustrations, and in many instances making neat copies of the drawings and watercolours herself.

Later, when Charles and I developed an interest in photography, he worked with us in finding the best ways for our tiny subjects to be captured, buying cameras and lenses for us, and sacrificing countless numbers of his own bees to our scalpels and pinning boards as we became increasingly adventurous in our work.

Upon later receiving all those same journals at the death of my mother, it surprised me to realize that we were still only boys — Charles perhaps fifteen or sixteen, myself five years younger — when he had encouraged us in all of this, treating us as his equals and sharing his understanding and secrets with us as he guided us into the small, arcane world he had already made for himself, and from which we might have been so easily excluded.

Waiting until the last of the nurses had left the garden, I closed my window and went back to the fire. It was a small grate, cleared and re-laid every day during my absence, the brass and walnut scuttle in the alcove beside it filled at the same time.

The mantel above the fire was filled with my possessions, reflected in the mirror which hung there, the varnish of its peeling frame all but gone, and the mirror itself blemished over its entire surface. At the centre of the shelf stood the individual photographs of my parents and my brother, their small smiling faces level with my own. The three people who had once been everything to me, and who were now all gone. I was without them in the world and the holes of their absences would now never truly be filled again. My father was sixty-two when he died; Charles twenty-five; and my mother, dead fourteen months later, had died a month before her fiftieth birthday. It seems an impossible history of endings.

CHAPTER
THREE

I next saw Osborne the following morning. He came to me as I ate my breakfast and told me to accompany him to his office. I hadn't finished eating, but he stood beside me for a moment until I rose and went with him.

"How was your whalefish?" he asked me.

At first I thought he was making a joke by using the archaic name.

"Dead," I said.

"Naturally. And?"

"And a long way from home on a fruitless and hopeless journey, and barely resembling the thing it once was," I said.

He smiled, pausing briefly in his brisk stride, and looked across at me. "I imagine you were the only one truly disappointed by what you found, Doctor Irvine. The others, as I'm sure you now realize, were only there because it meant a few hours away from this place."

It was what Cox had already made clear to me.

"Did you bring back any souvenir?" he said.

"Such as?"

He shrugged. "A tooth, perhaps; a piece of the creature's flesh."

I told him how far we had been kept from the whale by the mud in which it had stranded itself, and into which it was now slowly sinking.

"A wasted journey all round, then," he said.

He left the dining hall ahead of me, holding the door as I followed him.

Osborne's own office was at the entrance to the asylum, above the reception area, and adjacent to the smaller offices of his administrators.

We arrived at his door and he unlocked it at three points. He carried a chain which contained a dozen keys, most of them longer than his fingers.

Inside, he indicated a chair in front of his desk. He unlocked a drawer and took several sheets from it.

"A strange request," he said.

He read from one of the sheets for a few seconds.

"From the Royal College of Music. A woman." He searched the sheet. "Marion Scott. She lists all the initials of her so-called qualifications. None of which means a thing to me."

"What does she want?"

"Apparently, we have a genius amongst us. Man called —" He read again. "Gurney. Ivor." He pronounced both names as though he did not entirely believe either of them. "Gurney. Gloucester man. Delivered to us some time ago from Barnwood House. Apparently — according to Miss Scott, that is — he's something of a poet and a musician. He *writes* music. She doesn't say anything about him playing the ukulele." He laughed at the remark, waiting for me to do the same.

"What does she want from us?" I asked him.

"God knows. To come and see him, I suppose. To see if there's anything we can do to" — he read again — "'to allow him to continue at his chosen tasks'. 'Tasks'? She actually uses the word 'genius'. Our usual stream of do-gooding misses, ministers and mediums are usually content with pointing out that these men are as sane as you or I. Miss Scott, however, seems to be considerably bolder in her assertions. She hopes we might *provide* Gurney with the *means*, the *calm* and the *opportunity* to continue his writing and his music-making. Apparently, it will be his salvation. It will *redeem* him. How often do we hear that, eh?" He laid the papers on his desk and looked at me. "You're a reader."

I had never heard of the man. "Is he a war poet?"

"Of course he's a bloody war poet. They're all bloody war poets these days. A soldier poet and God knows what else."

"I haven't read anything by him," I said, trying hard to remember. It wasn't a common name.

"In addition to which, you play the piano," Osborne said.

In addition to which, I had also played the ukulele at my brother's twenty-first birthday party.

"Not particularly well," I said.

Osborne flicked the denial away. "You're a reader and a musician. I want you to write back to our Miss Scott and tell her that of course we'll do everything within our power to ensure that her darling protégé, her darling I-vor, is given everything he needs in the *pursuance* and *furtherance* of his talents, his *genius*."

"*Is* she coming to visit him?"

"I imagine so."

"Does she say that his coming to Dartford from Gloucester is part of her overall plan?"

"Her what? What plan? All she's doing here is trying to set down a few ground rules. We play along with her. Like we play along with them all. She'll be here for one hour a month, perhaps not even that. She'll see what she wants to see, hear what she wants to hear. And if she turns into another trouble-maker, then *we* point out to *her* that we're not a conservatory, or whatever they call them, and that her boy is in here for a very good reason."

"And that we are the people who best understand his needs and how to proceed?" I did my best not to sound as though I were mimicking him.

"Precisely. I knew I could depend on you. And if she *does* turn out to be a trouble-maker, then send her to me. Otherwise, I'm sure you're more than capable of keeping the pair of them happy and pointing in the same sunny direction."

He rose and went to his window, looking down at the men and women coming and going from the entrance below.

"And if he *is* a genius?" I said, though without conviction.

"Then we shall parade him before the world," he said. "As proof of the effectiveness of our regime here.

27

After which, you and I will hang on to our genius's coat-tails and make our names." He turned back to me. "Do what you have to do, Doctor Irvine. I think we both perfectly understand the situation." He came back to his desk. "Gurney's had time to settle. Him and another man from Gloucester. Name of Lyle, Oliver. The two of them are sharing a room. No one writing on *his* behalf yet," he said. "And nor will they, I imagine. In fact, I imagine we'll have nothing but a grateful silence from any friends or family Mr Lyle might once have had."

"Is he a serious case?"

He considered the remark. "Not in that sense. Though, in my opinion, and for what it's worth where the Board is concerned, he should have been sent to Warrington rather than here."

The Warrington asylum had gained a reputation for the harshness of its routines and its treatments, and was considered by many, myself included, to be more of a prison than a hospital. Osborne had worked at Warrington for two years before arriving at Dartford, and he seldom spoke of his time there except with a note of pride in his voice. He had been there during and immediately after the war. It had been a time of stumbling discovery and urgently devised treatments. Osborne regretted what had passed — what, in the broader sense, had passed him by — and this was apparent in much of what he now said and did in re-creating himself at Dartford.

I asked him what he meant about Oliver Lyle.

"An objector," he said simply. "Did his military service at Durham, Winchester and Pentonville." He smiled at the tired joke.

"And from Pentonville to the Gloucester asylum?"

"From Pentonville to Gloucester."

It was not a difficult route to imagine.

"Via a few other places," Osborne said. He listed a succession of prisons and asylums. "God knows how he ended up at Gloucester."

"Perhaps he was born there," I suggested.

He ignored me. "But all that matters now is that he's here."

"Is there any particular reason why you put the two of them together?" I asked him.

"A conchie and a poet genius? What — you think they're from the same mould?"

"Is there anything to suggest Gurney —"

"Nothing whatsoever," he said angrily. "Except that he left a trail of admissions and transfers a year long while the war continued. Gassed, apparently. Sent home, stayed home." There was the same uncontainable note of scornful disbelief in everything he said. "And, meanwhile, presumably, his genius continued to flower and grow. I daresay you'll hear all this again from Miss Scott."

Presumably when I met her and reassured her with our usual range of well-rehearsed platitudes; when I listened to her pleas on Gurney's behalf; and when I finally understood that everything Osborne was now telling me was true.

"Does she say when she intends coming?"

He shook his head. "Just that she's happy Gurney is at last close to old friends. And that she and they will now be in a position to do a great deal more for him. What does she imagine this place is? What does she imagine we *do* here? Best of all, and I say it again — why does she imagine her — her —"

"Wunderkind?"

"Precisely — her wunderkind is here? She writes as though the place were some convalescent home for retired theatrical folk. Plenty of those on the Downs, on the coast. Perhaps that's what she's aiming at — getting Gurney out of here and back into the clean, fresh air." He paused. "Perhaps I — you — should write back to her asking her to bring some actual proof of Gurney's genius to show us."

"We can't completely —" I began.

"What?" he shouted. "We can't completely *what*? Can't completely ignore the fact that Gurney *isn't* some kind of blighted genius? Is that what you were about to suggest? In which case, perhaps I'm talking to the wrong man. Perhaps I should hand Gurney over to Webster or one of the others."

I felt a sudden and inexplicable pang at the thought of not now being appointed to assess and care for the man.

"I was going to say that he might at least have some talent, some capability," I said.

"I imagine whatever small talent he might once have possessed has long since deserted him. Do you honestly think he'd be here — *here* — otherwise?"

I shook my head. "So how do you want me to proceed?"

Osborne sighed. "Where Gurney and Lyle are concerned, I want you to do exactly what you would do with all your other patients, no more, no less. You may have Miss Scott's over-enthusiastic endorsement ringing in your ears where Gurney is concerned, but I believe you understand your duties and the true extent of your responsibilities as well as any doctor here, and that, as usual, and as with the remainder of your patients, you will undertake and fulfil those duties and obligations to the best of your capabilities." Even he had become bored with this small and often-repeated reminder. It was the thick, dark, official seal stamped on to every uncertain or wayward conversation in the place. A drawn line. A reminder, too, of the division of responsibility and authority. Osborne had made himself Perfectly Clear. Any further complaint, discord or confusion, then I alone was its architect.

Soon Osborne would return the scattered papers to their files and hand them to me, a baton passed, the exact point of exchange.

"I could perhaps take Gurney to a piano and find out what he's capable of," I suggested.

"Or perhaps you could give Lyle a rifle and show him a photograph of his mother, sisters, whoever."

It was a cruel and clumsy comparison to make, and I saw that he regretted it the instant he'd finished speaking.

"Forgive me," he said.

"Perhaps Gurney's playing — if he's still capable of it — might be in some way therapeutic," I said, unwilling to dwell on his remark about Lyle for both our sakes.

"'Therapeutic'?"

It was another of our new and eagerly embraced expressions.

"Perhaps," he said. "I'll leave that for you to determine. Townsend at Barnwood says he's perfectly harmless. Gentle as a lamb. He even goes so far as to suggest that Gurney — by his own admission — was suffering from varying degrees of mental and nervous exhaustion before the war started. He even suggests that his enlistment and service did him some good as far as his health was concerned, that it gave him something other than himself to focus on. Imagine that."

"And afterwards?" I said.

He pursed his lips and shrugged. "Who knows? Perhaps afterwards those same old problems and weaknesses simply returned. I imagine Miss Scott might be able to tell you more on that score." He paused briefly, considering what he was about to say next. "She sounds in her letter as though Gurney were her son." He looked directly at me. "It might be something you'd want to bear in mind when you meet her."

"Or him?" I said.

"Either way, it would certainly be something we might need to take into account if she *did* turn out to be a trouble-maker. The more we know, the better prepared we'll all be. But, as I say, by all means lead the horse to water."

"Sorry?"

"Gurney. Take him to one of our pianos. Let his genius ring out loud and true and clear." He hesitated, remembering something else he had read in either Gurney's file or Marion Scott's letter. "He's also highly regarded by Sir Hubert Parry, Charles Stanford and Walford Davies."

The names meant nothing to me — I'd heard of Hubert Parry, but that was all — and I shook my head at hearing them.

"And by Ralph Vaughan Williams."

The name caught us both by surprise.

"Probably attached to Miss Scott's music school in some capacity, and added to the list to give it some weight, I imagine. He's probably added it to a dozen other appeals on behalf of ex-pupils. I wouldn't set too much store by it, if I were you." But I could hear by his tone, and by the speed with which he made these qualifications, that he regretted the sudden imbalance caused by the name. "Apparently, judging from what she says, Miss Scott is a good friend of Vaughan Williams and his wife. You might clarify the matter with her. For the record, so to speak. Perhaps they themselves — the Vaughan Williamses — might also want to come and see Gurney and convince us of his talents. I imagine the press would love that. War Hero to Asylum Maestro." He was pleased with the remark. "What do you think?"

"I think it will all come to nothing," I said, remembering the countless other appeals I'd seen in the past five years, all of them cast too hard and too insistently against the solid walls of what the men concerned had continued to suffer and endure.

"You think Marion Scott will come here, see Gurney, and quickly realize the futility of her claim?" he said.

All he wanted to hear me say was "Yes".

"It's more than likely," I told him.

But it was enough, and he immediately slid the scattered sheets into their files and pushed these towards me.

"My grandfather was a fisherman," he said unexpectedly.

I wondered if I'd heard him correctly.

"The whale. My grandfather. Up in the North-East. There was a whalebone arch on the clifftop close to where he used to live. We were taken to see it as children. I had three sisters — two now. We were told that walking through it would bring us luck. He drowned at sea. His body was never recovered." He stared absently at the files. "Perhaps I should have come with you to see the fish."

"Then it would have disappointed you more than it disappointed me," I told him.

"They called the bone arch the 'Eye of the Needle'. Imagine that. My grandmother and my parents went out to sea and threw a wreath on to the water. We children wanted to go with them, but weren't allowed."

I rose from my seat and he looked up at me.

CHAPTER
FOUR

I was busy for much of the day with my other patients, and it was late in the afternoon before I was free to visit Gurney and Lyle.

My morning was occupied by routine ward visits, talking to and assessing the progress, or otherwise, of those men already assigned to me. This task was seldom rewarding. Some welcomed my visits and examinations, but many sat in complete silence as I spoke to them, forcing me to turn to their assigned orderlies for answers.

I encountered Lewis again and endured his own banal assessments and recommendations without argument. I still heard Cox in most of what he said.

A few of the men I visited continued sitting and staring and speaking to themselves as though neither I nor any orderly had ever existed, lost to themselves in the worlds they now inhabited.

I measured wasted limbs. I asked simple questions and assessed even simpler answers, usually no more than a baffled "yes" or "no", a nod or a shake where nodding and head-shaking were largely indistinguishable from each other.

Some of the men greeted me like a long-lost friend; and some, having been seen by me almost daily since my arrival there, asked me who I was. I answered all their questions as simply, as openly and as honestly as I could, though all my answers were tempered by my desire to cause them as little distress as possible. As might be expected, my commonest remark was that I didn't know. But this was usually enough for them, and most were reassured by it until they next asked me exactly the same question. Some held my arm as they spoke to me, as though this were some measure of my integrity or honesty; others stood in the corners of their small rooms, their faces to the wall, for the duration of my brief visits. I encouraged men to sit with me, to talk face to face, but few accepted these invitations, preferring to maintain their distance or to cling to the other few failing certainties of their lives.

Examining one man, who insisted on stripping naked to the waist in front of me, Lewis told me that I was wasting my time. I listened to the man's lungs and heart because that was what he wanted of me.

"What do you mean?" I asked Lewis, increasingly impatient of his ill-informed interventions and judgements. The man in front of me relaxed at the touch of my stethoscope.

"He can put it on," Lewis said. "All that breathing stuff. Minute your back's turned, he'll be sitting on his bed and laughing like a girl at having tricked you. Does it every day. I'll prove it to you."

"Does it matter?" I said.

"What do you mean, does it matter? You get through with him, come outside, close his door, and then look back in at him through the glass. That's what he'll be doing. He puts all this on like a stage act." He turned to the man before me. "That right, Billy-boy? All an act? This what got you sent home in the first place? This what's keeping you away from it all now?"

The man grinned at him and nodded vigorously. His heart continued beating at the same excited rate. I made him hold out his arms and then examined his wasted muscles. I pressed his stomach and liver. His ribs and breastbone were clearly marked against his pale flesh. There were bruises beneath one arm. I asked Lewis about these.

"He holds himself," Lewis said, making a clasping motion with his own arms. "Like this. Grabs and lets go, hours on end."

I asked the man why he did this, but he merely grinned at me in answer. As usual, upon finishing my examination, I gave him the stethoscope so that he might listen for himself to his own racing heart. And, as usual, this both pleased and calmed him.

"You're still alive then, Billy-boy?" Lewis said to him, and the man nodded.

I made my notes in his file and then initialled all the necessary pages.

He was my last patient before lunchtime, and the bell summoning everyone to eat, or at least alerting them all to the possibility of eating, sounded as I left his room.

Outside, Lewis held my arm. "Want to see?"

I looked back in at the man, and just as Lewis had said, he was now sitting calmly on his bed, holding himself and grinning. Another day away from wherever it was that he had lost himself.

"See," Lewis said. "Things I could tell you that you'd never learn in a month of Sundays from your examinations."

"I'm sure," I said, and then left him. I went outside, standing for a moment to clear my head. The meal bells rang in sequence through the distant buildings.

I walked to the rear of the block and emerged on to the lawn. The men who had been cutting the grass and edging the borders were now being gathered together and lined up prior to being taken to eat. Orderlies collected the tools they had been using and these were laid out on the grass and counted, and then counted again.

I saw Cox standing at the centre of the orderlies, watching as the mechanical mowers were pushed together, and then insisting on them being perfectly aligned, crouching on his heels to assess this, and then indicating for one or other of the machines to be moved backwards or forwards an inch.

When he was satisfied, he led the men away from me. Many of them, I saw, swung their arms as they walked, and others made the effort to march in step with the man in front of them. Cox encouraged them in this by shouting out, "Left, right, left, right," as he stepped aside to let them pass him. Upon my arrival at the asylum, I had considered this an unnecessary imposition, detrimental even to the men's treatment and recovery, but I quickly saw that many of them appreciated — enjoyed, even — being treated like this. Even the ones who had never been soldiers. When I had remarked to Osborne on Cox's barking of orders, he had told me bluntly to stop interfering. Some things work, he had said, and some things don't. Even then, only a few days after my arrival, I had known not to persist.

Waiting until the lawn was empty, the mowers in their perfect line and the rakes and hoes laid out equally precisely alongside them, I crossed the grass to the far trees. Rhododendrons grew to the lawn's edge, old plants twenty feet high, and beyond these, round a curve in the border, there were seats, unseen from most of the buildings. I went there often for a moment of uninterrupted peace during my busy days.

The grass was short and firm underfoot, dry in the sun, and dotted yellow and white from the daisies which grew in it. Swathes of pure, brighter green showed where it had recently been mown.

Turning the corner, I was disappointed to see someone already sitting on one of the benches, a woman, a nurse, waving a long piece of white material ahead of her, as though unrolling it or perhaps drying it in the warm air. She concentrated on this as I approached her, slowly reducing the length of the material by wrapping it around her forearms.

She saw my shadow first and shielded her eyes to look up at me.

Only then did I recognize her as the nurse who had told me about the stranded whale.

She started to rise, but then sat back down and completed her folding.

The material, I saw, was a length of fine and weightless muslin, which she continued to compact into an ever-smaller piece. There was an open book on the seat beside her. She seemed unconcerned by my intrusion. She closed the book and brushed the wooden slats. I saw the scarlet "efficiency" stripes on her sleeve as she did this.

"Was there anything left?" she asked me.

"Not much."

"I thought you were Sister Kidd. I'm on a break."

Sister Kidd was the senior nursing sister, and breaks, however long or short, were meant to be taken at one or other of the designated Nursing Stations throughout each building.

She patted the seat and I sat beside her. Then she asked me if I had a cigarette and I gave her one. Something else that was prohibited to the women. We sat together in silence for a moment.

"What was the cloth?" I asked her.

"Muslin," she said. "I've been to see the bees."

The remark surprised me and I turned to face her. "My father used to keep them," I said.

"Mine too. That's why I went. Do you know about them, then?"

I told her that I did, and remarked on my disappointment at finding the hives and their colonies in such poor condition.

"No one cares about them," she said. "There were nuns here during the war. They brought the hives with them from their convent in Surrey."

"And never took them back?"

"They were supposed to have been left as a gift. You know — lunatics and honey balm. They probably had as much faith in it as a remedy as anything that's happened here since." She looked away from me as she spoke, towards the orchard and the hives, and I wondered if she had intended the remark to sound as critical as it had.

I introduced myself to her.

"Alison West," she said. She considered me for a moment and then held out her hand to me. "Are you one of Osborne's lot?" I heard a great deal in the way she said this.

"We're all Osborne's lot on the medical staff," I said. "One way or another. Whether we like it or not."

She held my hand for a moment longer.

"I've just spent two hours watching over a man on his hands and knees picking daisies from the lawn," she said.

"No doubt while General Cox pointed them out to him one by one."

"Something like that." She smiled. "I was supposed to be washing him, the patient, but Cox decreed otherwise."

"He came with me to see the whale," I said.

"Only because he imagined he might be missing out on something if he hadn't gone."

I picked up her book and read its title. It was a manual on preparing corpses.

"I know," she said. "Apparently, it's something I need to know about before I can progress any further."

She looked down. "Preparing corpses. As though I didn't know enough on that particular subject already."

I waited a moment for the remark to pass.

"Were you in France?" I asked her then.

"Mendinghe. Then Camiers, then Proven, then Le Touquet." It was a litany and she recited it by heart.

"And since?"

"Alexandria, Reading and here." She drew deeply on her cigarette before dropping the last of it to the ground. I did the same, offering her a second, which she took. "You?" she said.

"Mendinghe, too. Calais, and then Le Havre."

She rested her hand on my forearm for a moment and then took the book from me. She opened it and searched its pages. She cleared her throat and read to me.

"'It is of the utmost importance to afford the recently deceased the standing and dignity of their condition, and every effort must be made to present the deceased in a manner best suited to afford that comfort and understanding vital to the remaining members of the deceased's family.'"

"Don't," I said to her, half imagining what she might have been about to add.

"No," she said, closing the book and laying it back beside her. She breathed deeply for a moment. The scent of the mown grass filled the air. "Cox made the man picking the daisies lay them in a row and then count them. When I complained about this he told me to shut up and to mind my own business. Then he told the man to nip their stems with his thumbnail until they were all the same length. The saddest thing of all —"

"Was that the man was happy to oblige?"

She nodded. "He'd have been happier still if Cox had told me to leave them to it. Perhaps then they could have made a few jokes about me behind my back." She shook her head. "I should be used to all this by now."

"All this?"

"Being treated like a . . ." She waved her hand.

"You imagined things would change? Because of the war?"

"I imagined things might change for people like me, yes."

"Because of what you did, what you saw?"

She looked at me for a moment. "*Things* should have changed for everyone," she said. She looked back over the empty lawn, her meaning clear.

Another distant bell sounded, announcing the end of the first lunch sitting.

Hearing it, she rose from beside me. She smoothed down the stiff apron she wore, patting even flatter the muslin in her wide pocket. "What do you think will happen to the hives?" she asked me.

I shrugged.

"Most of them only need dismantling and cleaning out," she said. "Half of them are clogged solid with rotten cells and dead bees."

I wondered if she was suggesting that it was something she and I might undertake together, or perhaps with a party of patients.

"You know how to do it," she said, prodding me.

"I'll talk to Osborne," I said, unwilling to reveal to her that I'd already done this and achieved nothing.

But even this answer disappointed her. "Meaning you'll wait until I'm out of sight and then forget all about it."

"Perhaps Cox could get someone to lay out the corpses," I said, causing her to smile.

She tapped her book. " 'With all the appropriate and requisite dignity and respect'?"

When the older colonies had failed at home, my father had often dismantled and then destroyed them, killing off their dying populations and establishing new ones elsewhere. "On clean ground", he called it. It was work in which Charles and I had often been allowed to participate. Blighted colonies seldom recovered. We had gathered the turgid and unresisting mounds of dying insects in hessian sacks. We had scooped them with trowels from the rotting wood of their hives, more like soil than living creatures.

"I'll see what Osborne says," I repeated.

She nodded once and began to walk away from me. She stopped after a few paces and came back to the bench. Raising the hem of her skirt, she turned her calf to me and showed me the long white scar there.

"Mendinghe," she said. "We were shelled one night by our own guns. I was in charge of eight men, and every one of them was killed."

"Would they have survived otherwise?" I said.

She considered the question, and then turned without answering and walked away from me again.

44

I watched her until she rounded the corner, noting the slight limp with which she walked, apparent, strangely, only at that distance and not when she was closer to me.

As she was lost to sight, a line of patients appeared, walking towards me, Cox beside them. Several of the men called to her, some whistled. The men continued walking until they reached where I sat. Then they picked up the hoes from the lawn and arranged themselves into a line, each man distancing himself from his neighbours by the length of his outstretched arms, as though they were forming for parade. Waiting for Cox's command, they then started to shuffle the blades of the hoes through the dry soil beneath the rhododendrons.

CHAPTER
FIVE

I finally reached Gurney's room late in the afternoon, only to find it empty. I asked an orderly standing nearby where either Gurney or Lyle were.

"Gurney's with Webster," he said, irritated, as though I had interrupted him at something. "His physical." It was customary for these independent assessments to be made before they were assigned to their own doctors.

"And Lyle?" I looked around the sparse double room, which showed little sign of occupancy other than the suitcases still standing at the end of each narrow bed. These would be left there for a fortnight and then be taken to a storeroom.

"Him? Webster saw him yesterday. Probably be outside somewhere with his nose in a book." He came into the room beside me and went to its window, opening the lower pane through its internal bars. He craned his neck to look out. "What did I tell you?" He stepped back for me to take his place.

I looked out. A young man stood against the wall a short distance away, reading. "Is that him?"

"None other. Want me to shout him in?"

I called to Oliver Lyle myself, surprising him and causing him to search for me.

"Best not to shout at them," the orderly said, grinning. "And especially not at delicate little flowers like Lyle."

I ignored the remark and left the room.

There was a door at the end of the corridor that led outside. It was a low-security wing, and the majority of its entrances and exits would remain unlocked throughout the day.

When I reached Lyle he was again reading from the book he held.

I held out my hand and introduced myself.

"Was it you who called?" he said.

I knew from the details Osborne had given me that he was twenty-four, but he looked considerably younger, little more than a youth in his teens. He was slight to the point of emaciation, and with a thin face and neck. He wore a collarless shirt, buttoned to his throat, and with his cuffs fastened across the backs of his hands, all of which added to his childlike appearance.

He closed the book he held.

"Will you come back inside?" I asked him.

"Have you been sent to assess me? They sent for Ivor earlier."

"It was Gurney I came to see," I told him.

He walked beside me back to their room.

The orderly was still there, stretched out on one of the beds. He rose at our arrival and I told him to leave.

He went slowly, pulling a face at both of us and telling Lyle that he'd be back soon enough. "Not as though he's going to attack you, is it?" he said to me. I said nothing to delay or antagonize him, wondering again at the lack of understanding and the hostility so many of the orderlies continued to show towards the men in their care. It was something I hadn't encountered before, and especially not at Clayburn or Maida Vale. Or perhaps it hadn't existed then because the war was so recently over and everyone was still struggling to stand upright against the last of its aftershocks. Perhaps now, all these years later, those aftershocks were no longer of any account, unworthy of consideration. Perhaps now, with shadows elsewhere deepening rather than lifting, people were unsettled and endlessly disappointed by these constant reminders and tethers.

When we were finally alone, Lyle straightened the blanket on the bed and sat down.

I sat opposite him.

"You were a conscientious objector," I said.

"A Friend."

At first, I didn't understand him. "You're a Quaker?" I said.

"We prefer to use the word Friend. 'Quaker' makes us sound a little *too* holier-than-thou. Not that we aren't — holier than thou, I mean." He smiled at the remark. He put the book he'd been reading on his pillow, and I saw then that it was a Bible. The same book lay on Gurney's pillow. A small wooden cross was fixed to the wall above each bed, adding to the spartan feel of the room.

I read from the notes Osborne had given me.

"You broke your arm," I said. An old injury.

He held out his arm to me. "And seven out of ten fingers."

"How did it happen?"

He shook his head at the question. "To a conscientious objector? Seven fingers and four ribs. Not that ribs counted for much, those days." He stopped abruptly and turned his head to one side, closed his eyes and shook gently for a few seconds. I could hear his teeth grinding; the veins and tendons already clearly outlined on his neck and face bulged a little further. And then, as suddenly as this tremor had arrived, so it subsided and he relaxed, opening his eyes and looking directly at me.

I went on as though nothing had happened, asking him to tell me why he had been transferred to Dartford from Gloucester.

"It's what happens to people like me," he said. "It's a kind of imposed destiny. Or at least it is from now onwards."

"Do you believe you'll never be released from here, from places like this?"

"Is this part of your test?" he asked me. His voice was even and soft, as though he were accustomed to keeping it low, avoiding attention. There was also a formality to it, and the faint remains of an accent. He struck me as someone who might recently have graduated from university rather than someone who had spent the past seven years in either prison or an asylum.

"You and Gurney are my charges," I told him.

He considered me for a moment. "Small mercies," he said, and then signalled an apology for his earlier remark. "Have you not seen Ivor yet?"

I told him I hadn't.

"Then you know nothing of him, nothing whatsoever?"

I shook my head, waiting to see what he might go on to reveal.

"He enlisted only days after the war started. He's a musician and a poet. I've read his poems. Listen to others, they'll want you to believe he's some sort of genius."

"And is he? In your opinion?"

"A long time since anyone asked me for that. Besides, I'm not a great one for poetry, and where 'genius' is concerned in that world, I imagine it tended to get reserved for the officer-poets. What were you?"

I told him and he nodded at my answer.

"He was in uniform for three years. Longer than most, I imagine. He gave me his two books." He indicated the case at the foot of his bed. "Would you like to borrow them?"

I told him I would.

He turned to reach for the case, then stopped. "Or perhaps it would give you an unfair advantage over poor old Ivor. Perhaps you might read them and find it all drivel and then laugh at him like everyone else."

"It's your decision," I told him, and he accepted this. He pulled up the case and opened it. A few clothes fell on to the bed, and among these were several books. He picked up two small volumes. He ran his palm over their covers and his finger down their spines, almost as

50

though he were wiping them clean of something, before handing them to me.

"They broke four of my fingers, all the same hand, in Durham, when they learned what I was," he said.

"You can't have been more than a boy, surely?"

"Perhaps. But you might say the Authorities had had advance warning of me on account of my parents. My father registered his objections on religious grounds and spent two months in Birmingham gaol before his application was accepted and he was released." He paused, remembering. "Not even a single cracked rib. But that was at the very start. He was an old man, almost sixty. They would have had no need or use for him anyway."

"But he still insisted on registering his objection to the war?"

"He believed it was his duty. The more who registered as objectors, he said, then the more likely those of fighting age were to be taken seriously. Or so he believed. Both he and my mother campaigned against the war. He was a lay-preacher, in Evesham. She tried to get various charitable organizations interested in helping refugees. They complied at first, but then as things went on and they better understood the currents turning against people like my parents, one by one they dispensed of her services and disassociated themselves from her."

I made a note to ask about his curtailed education, nothing of which was listed in his details.

"Your father believed he was improving your own chances of being exempted?" I said.

He nodded. "Except he probably made things worse. When I was sixteen I was marched to a recruiting office by two local constables and made to stand there, in front of hundreds, and publicly declare my intention to register as an objector. Sixteen. The war ended eighteen months later. I might have enlisted and then been kept in a reserve unit on home duties for the duration."

"But you didn't?"

"My father was with me, along with half a dozen seventy-year-olds from one of his Meeting Houses. You can imagine the reception they received from all those others eager to grab hold of a rifle and do their bit. Someone went outside and gathered up stones to throw at us when we were finally allowed to leave. I spent a fortnight in prison before being allowed to go home. My mother looked as though she'd aged ten years."

"And your father?"

"What? Did he blame himself for what had happened to me, you mean?" He paused. "Perhaps."

"But his principles always came first?"

He considered this without answering. "Read the poems," he said. "Ivor *needs* someone." It was a strange remark to make, especially in light of all that he'd just told me, and I asked him what he meant. But again he became evasive.

"My father was signed on as a medical dogsbody. Fifty-nine. He was sent to Le Havre, loading the wounded and unloading medical supplies. Him and a dozen others he knew. It always seemed to me that they sent him as a joke. *He* never saw it like that, of course.

To him, it was all part of God's greater scheme of things."

"And did he —"

"He drowned. A month before the war's end. A barge sank in the harbour, or so we were later told. There were stretcher cases in its hold. My father and four other men tried to rescue them, and all of them died, along with the injured men. My mother was told afterwards that the barge had turned bottom-up in twelve feet of water, and that by the time a crane had arrived to turn it upright, everyone inside was dead. She had to make her own arrangements to have his body brought back to Evesham. There was a collection made; she had nothing. She — I —" He stopped talking as another slight tremor gripped him. It was less severe this time and subsided after only a few seconds.

I waited for him to continue. "She died last year," he said.

"Were you able to attend the funeral?"

"What do you think? I was in Winchester gaol. I wasn't even told she'd died until three days after the funeral. All for my own good, of course."

I knew from the file that it was while he'd been in Winchester that the first full assessment of his mental condition had been made. The word "deterioration" concluded most of the simple tests.

"And then, in their wisdom, they moved me to Pentonville."

"Why were you not released at the war's end?" I asked him.

The question surprised him. "Do you think that's how things worked? The war was over, everybody back to what they had once been? Do you think that places like this would exist in such numbers if that were the case?"

"Or people like me?" I said.

He smiled. "Or people like you. Or me, or Ivor."

"When would you have been released?"

"They told me in 1916 that five years was the commonest sentence, and that my case would be reconsidered after half that time. But by then I'd started — they said I needed special attention. Things went from bad to worse."

"With a few broken bones thrown in along the way."

"'Bones mend'. Isn't that what everyone feels so pleased about endlessly repeating to themselves? Well, bones might, but not much else does. Ask Ivor. When they stoned us, me, my father and all those other old men leaving the recruitment hall, my father and the others tried to form a shield round me, to protect me. Not to any good effect, of course, or at least not when the mob saw what they were doing. I suppose they — the men throwing the stones — thought that if I wasn't prepared to go off and butcher Germans, then I had no purpose in living anyway."

"Was anyone hurt?"

The remark made him angry. "Of course they were. All of them were cut and bruised. Some of them were knocked to the ground and helped up again. I think my father believed the police — and they were there in numbers to make sure the crowds waited patiently to sign up — would come to our rescue. But of course *they* saw which way the wind was blowing and waited until the first wave of rage had passed and the mob had drawn blood before stepping in and forcing the stone-throwers to back off. After that, we walked together to the train station to catch the train home. They washed their wounds in the waiting rooms, did what they could. What a sight we must have looked to everyone who had no idea of what had just happened."

And the life he might once have imagined ahead of him had ended there, surrounded by wounded old men and a mob.

"They came and took me away from home less than a month later. They put me in with a batch of new recruits at the Worcester barracks to see if I'd change my mind, but only after telling all those others *why* I was there. My parents petitioned the Commanding Officer on a weekly basis, and each time they came I was singled out at the next parade and everything that had happened was repeated to the others. The sergeants even told them that they could laugh at me if they wanted. Two months later I was taken to Winchester. My mother even approached our Member for Parliament, telling him how young I was and what regulations she believed were being broken. He told her that others among his constituents were writing to him to say how *proud* they were that their own sons had fooled the recruiters."

"Making it clear to her where his own sympathies lay?"

He nodded. "I think both my parents understood by then that their cause was a lost one. There were articles in the local papers. I was taken away from them, and I doubt if any of us truly understood what had happened to us, or what that particular parting meant until it was all far too late." He held up his hands. "So, here I am, Doctor — I'm sorry, I've forgotten your name."

I told him.

He closed his eyes for a moment. "How long will they prod and poke Ivor, do you think?"

"They like to be thorough," I said, wishing the remark hadn't sounded so demeaning or officious.

"Because Dartford's the end of the line for people like him?"

The distinction intrigued me. Almost as much as his continued concern for the man.

"Because this is where men like Ivor end up after everywhere else has failed them?" he said.

There was some truth in this. Dartford did have that reputation. He himself seemed unconcerned by what he was suggesting.

"It's regarded as a long-term institution," I said. "But that doesn't mean men aren't released from here, or that they aren't reassessed and re-diagnosed and sent somewhere more appropriate."

"'Appropriate'?"

"Places closer to home," I said. "Often to recuperative hospitals."

He looked up at me. "Is that what you'll recommend for me or Ivor?" he said, waiting straight-faced for a few seconds before smiling at my discomfort. He apologized for the remark. "I know you're only doing your job," he said. And that too felt like a finger wagged in my face.

I closed the file I held.

"I've disappointed you," he said. "You came for your first look at a genius, and all you found was me. Will they separate us, do you think?"

"Is it what you want?"

He considered the question, gratified that the choice might still remain. Then he shook his head. "He's a good man. If I thought he was any better or any worse than me, then . . ." He tailed off, leaving me uncertain what he was saying.

I tapped the books he had given me and slid them into my pocket.

"He has influential friends, Ivor," he said. "All the time we were at Barnwood House together they wrote to him and visited him there. From London, most of them."

"It's why he's here," I said.

He clasped his hands and lowered his head. "Good," he said, and again his meaning was unclear to me.

CHAPTER
SIX

Within minutes of my father's death, my mother went outside to the hives and informed the bees of their shared loss. She took with her black ribbons to drape around the closest of the structures, and having done this, she stood alone in the garden and said a prayer for her dead husband. She wore her veiled hat as she did this, her hands ungloved and her arms exposed. And as she prayed, the bees came and went around her, adding their own low humming to her murmuring.

Charles and I watched her from the kitchen doorway. Charles had insisted that he and I should accompany her to the bees, but she had told us to stay where we were. I remember I cried upon being told my father was dead. My mother held me for a moment and told me that I needed to be strong. For her, for all of us. I did my best to stop crying, but this was difficult, and as she left us and walked outside, donning her wide-brimmed hat and pulling down its veil, Charles punched me on my arm and told me to stop being a baby. I told him I couldn't help it, and he punched me again. Even then, I knew that he too had wanted to cry, to draw her to him as I knew she would soon be drawn to me, holding and comforting me, a focus for her own sudden,

58

weightless grief. He left me, and I heard him running up the broad staircase, followed by the deeper note as he ran along the carpeted landing to the room we shared.

My father had been ill for only a fortnight, confined to his bed for most of that time. He was attended by two of the town's other doctors, both of them colleagues and old friends; both of them, like him, local councillors, and one of them a fellow bee-keeper. They diagnosed a heart attack and prescribed rest and a succession of drugs for him. Most of all, they reassured my mother that everything possible was being done to ensure his recovery.

They came to see my father, often together, at least once every day, and often two or three times. They told my mother they had been passing the house or treating someone else in the neighbourhood, but it was evident to us all that they had come especially to see him and to confer on his ongoing treatment.

Our home stood almost a mile beyond the town, across open country, and with little beyond it to bring them in that direction. My mother accepted their kindness, expertise and concern, and after seeing my father in his bed, the two men often sat with her for an hour or so. She served them tea, and occasionally, when they called at the end of their day's work, stronger drink. They accepted everything she offered them. They were both old men, older than her sick husband, and they treated her like a favourite daughter.

She moved to a room across the landing from my father, leaving him to sleep alone. She spent most of the day with him, talking to him, reading, occasionally listening to the gramophone with him.

She plumped up his pillows and turned the bed so that he might see out of the window overlooking the garden and his precious hives, and to the pasture and water meadows and river beyond.

Following the attack, he appeared to recover and then grow stronger for a few days. Strong enough to walk the measured paces from his bed to a chair at the window, where he would sit swathed in blankets and watch the world beyond.

When this happened, Charles and I were told to go outside and busy ourselves, either in the garden or amid the bees, and to signal to him to let him see that whatever he might have believed was being neglected in his absence was now being taken care of by his two devoted sons.

The closest of the hives were situated beneath our fruit trees, and immediately beyond these a dozen structures had been placed in a patch of rough pasture on common land. They were here to take advantage of the wildflowers that proved so attractive to the bees. It was important, my father insisted, to keep the grass around the hives cut short. He said that this kept the rats and other predators away, and that the cleared space was an aid to the returning bees. I never truly believed either of these reasons, but I was happy, during his confinement, to meticulously cut the grass and to be watched by him as I did this. He pointed to the hives I had yet to attend to, and then sent out messages of encouragement and gratitude via either my mother or

Mrs Bierce, our elderly housekeeper, who often slept at the house to help my mother. It was frequently Mrs Bierce who woke and fed Charles and myself, helping us prepare for school, while my mother attended to our father, or as she slept briefly on the bed beside him.

My mother told me afterwards that each time she woke in the night she would leave her own room and silently cross the landing to check on him. She cleared a bookcase, took this in to him and then filled it with favourites from his library.

With the help of Mrs Bierce, she bathed him daily, although this frequently amounted to little more than wiping his face, arms and chest with a damp flannel.

On one occasion, mid-way between the attack and his death, and at a time when everyone was growing increasingly optimistic about him making a full recovery, I went in to him to show him a dragonfly I had caught amid the hives. The creature was still alive and sitting on a twig in a jar, magnified by the curved glass. I knew my mother was already in the room with him, and that he would in all likelihood be awake. We had been told not to disturb him without first checking with either my mother or Mrs Bierce. But on this occasion, I went quietly up the stairs and opened the door.

My father was sitting propped up by his pillows, the sheets bunched at his groin. He was slumped forward, an enamel bowl of water on the bed beside him. His eyes were closed and his mouth open. Saliva ran from his lips to his chin, where it hung in a viscous string to his chest. He was breathing in a succession of hoarse rasps. I stood in the doorway without moving, my hand on the polished handle, the door only a few inches open. My mother stood with her back to me, over a radiator, upon which she had draped a towel. She held her palms against the wall, her fingers splayed, as though she were about to fall, and she was crying. Beside her, the window was open and a warm breeze filled the room. I saw that her hands had left damp prints on the wallpaper. Steam rose from the towel on the radiator. Her own breathing was convulsive, and she made an effort to stifle any noise she might make. But she was unsuccessful in this, and her muffled gasping filled the room. I looked from her to my father and wondered if he too could hear this. I wondered if it was why he was sitting with his eyes closed, letting her know that he could not see her, and thus somehow denying her presence in the room and all that her unstoppable tears might have suggested. And from the two of them, I looked to the dragonfly in its jar, motionless, its metallic green body and iridescent wings, its eyes the size of bilberries.

And then I stepped back and silently closed the door before my mother turned and saw me there. Or before my father finally wiped a hand across his mouth and opened his eyes. Despite the globe of his pale stomach and his breasts resting on this, I had never before seen him looking so frail or so vulnerable. And I knew then, in that instant, as I pulled the door shut, careful not to let its catch sound, that the treatment and encouragement and reassurances of his colleagues would come to nothing. I am not saying that I knew he would die —

that was still too far beyond the imaginable — but I am saying that whatever happened to him following his hoped-for recovery, however fully he recovered, and however long he afterwards lived, he would never be the same man again. I understood that a divide had been crossed, and that he and my mother understood this better than anyone.

I went silently back along the landing and waited for several minutes at the top of the stairs. Mrs Bierce appeared at the bottom and called up to ask me what I was doing. I held up the jar to show her. She said she hoped I wasn't making a nuisance of myself and I told her I wasn't.

After five minutes I ran loudly back to my father's room, knocked on the door and called in to him.

My mother told me immediately to wait where I was, and I stood there for five minutes more.

After this, she opened the door and told me to go in to him. She sang to herself as she carried the bowl from the bed to the sink.

My father was again wearing his pyjamas, and he sat upright in his bed, his sparse hair wet and plastered to his head and the sheets drawn taut across his chest. He beckoned me to him and asked me what I wanted. I showed him the dragonfly and he called for my mother to fetch him his Hendrick from the bookcase.

Hendrick was an authority on dragonflies, he told me. He smelled strongly of the bay-rum lotion my mother rubbed on his neck and cheeks. I saw the line of bristles along his jaw where she had missed with the razor. With her back to me, searching for the Hendrick, she warned me against leaning on my father's chest. My father winked at me and took the jar. I gave him his spectacles and he inspected the dragonfly more closely.

He asked me about the bees, about school, and about what Charles and I had been up to in his absence. My mother turned at hearing the word and told him that he wasn't absent, that he was still among us and still central to everything that happened in the house. She grew frustrated at being unable to find the book she was looking for, and he whispered to me to go and help her, telling me exactly where on the shelves the volume was.

I left the bed and went to her. Her handprints were still visible on the wall above the radiator, and steam still rose from the towel that hung there. She knelt with her finger already on the spine of the Hendrick, and as I came close to her, she pulled it from the shelf and held it to her chest. With her other hand she cupped my head and kissed me on the forehead. Then she gave me the book and told me to take it to my father, caressing my head for a moment longer before lowering her hand.

I was reluctant to leave her and return to the bed.

Through the open window, feeling the warm air on my face, I could see Charles at the far side of the pasture, his veiled face looking up at me. He held a long cane, which he brandished like a spear at me. He shouted something, but was too far away for me to hear him clearly.

I took the Hendrick to my father and sat beside him while he searched its illustrations for the dragonfly I had caught. Finally identifying the specimen, he told me to take the book to my own room and to write the name out. Then he suggested that I released the creature close to where I had netted it.

I told him I'd been after butterflies. And then I lied to him and said I'd seen wasps coming and going from one of the hives. Even now I cannot properly explain why I did this, other than to perhaps attract attention to myself in a room so crowded with its other dramas; or perhaps to create a sense of *purpose* now that Charles and I had taken over his lesser, routine duties among the hives. He considered what I had told him, smiled and told me not to worry. It was the wrong time of the year for the wasps to be making inroads into the hives; the colonies were at their strongest and any stray wasps that did succeed in penetrating the combs would be quickly dealt with. He asked me how many wasps I'd seen, repeating the figure to my mother. She, too, showed little concern, but I could sense her irritation at my lies.

My father sat without speaking for several minutes, and then he told me to keep an eye on the situation and to report to him daily. He told me to search the cut grass around the hives for the corpses of the wasps, and to take these to him so that he might examine them. My mother complained that I had more important things to be attending to, primarily my schoolwork. I see now how complicit the pair of them had been in acknowledging my deception and all it implied.

I left them and went outside to release the dragonfly. I searched for Charles, but he was no longer in the pasture. The cane he had held was stuck into the ground beside one of the hives, and I pulled this out and carried it with me for the rest of the day. In the afternoon I set out traps for the wasps so that I would have something to show my father.

Three days later, at two in the morning, he suffered another attack, and an hour later, having been sent for by my mother, the two old doctors arrived together and went with her to his room. I learned from her afterwards that she had been lying alongside him when this second attack had occurred. He had woken gasping and choking, clutching at his sheets and then inadvertently striking her as she had tried to calm him.

The attack was long over by the time the two doctors arrived, and they sedated him further. Charles and I, accompanied by Mrs Bierce, stood on the landing outside and listened to their muted, muttering voices through the door. Mrs Bierce tried to persuade us to return to our room but we refused to go, and for once she acceded to us. She made warm drinks for us, knocking to ask if my mother and the doctors would like one too. It was half past three in the morning and the full moon filled the upstairs rooms with its pale, cold light.

Eventually, the doctors emerged with my mother and they saw us standing there. The elder of the two men came to Charles and held his hand out to him, and the instant Charles reciprocated, uncertain what was expected of him next, the man told Charles that he must take charge of me and that he must do without protest anything his mother told him to do. I saw by my mother's face that she immediately regretted the remark and all it uncertainly suggested; but she thanked the man anyway and then ushered us all downstairs. I asked her what had happened, and she told us that my father had had another attack but that he had survived it and was now sleeping peacefully.

He died four days later, in his sleep, alone and undiscovered until my mother woke in her own bed and went in to him at five in the morning. She then went downstairs, where Mrs Bierce was sleeping, and afterwards she woke Charles and me and told us to go with her into my father's room.

She told us simply that he had died and that he was now in Heaven. She kissed him on the cheek, and thus prompted, Charles and I did the same. When this was done, she pulled the lowest sheet over his face and let it settle over his features.

And then she told us to leave the room while she went out to the hives.

Mrs Bierce stood at the door with us and watched her.

I asked her why the bees needed to be told, what good this would do, and she told me to wait and to ask my mother when she returned to us.

I watched my mother unrolling her black ribbons, knotting them and draping them over the hives. It was too early and too cool for the bees to be active, and that was why she walked among the hives wearing only her veiled hat.

When she came back to us she asked Mrs Bierce to call the doctors and tell them what had happened. I kept my questions to myself. My mother said she felt hungry — "ravenous" was the word she used — and she asked Charles and me if we felt the same. We both told her we did and she started preparing a large, early breakfast for us all, telling us that the house would be filled with people for the rest of the day.

Eventually, as we ate, Charles, and not I, asked her what good telling the bees had done. She stopped eating and bowed her head for a moment. She seemed suddenly lost, unable to speak, to bridge those few seconds that would draw her forward into her life ahead.

I told Charles that she'd told the bees because now *they* would know to spread the news of my father's death. It was something I had known all along, something my father had told me after a recent funeral. Charles shook his head at my intervention and at the simple answer and made a noise behind his hand. My mother raised her head, looked at me and smiled. She reached out, as though to caress me again, or perhaps simply to touch my cheek, but then she turned to Charles and laid her hand on his shoulder instead. He sat motionless for a moment, as though paralysed by the gesture, and then he pushed her hand away from him, rose and ran from the table, his chair falling to the floor behind him. She watched him go, her eyes fixed on the doorway as a succession of slammed doors and receding footsteps marked his departure from the house.

CHAPTER
SEVEN

I read Gurney's poetry that same evening. *Severn and Somme* and *War's Embers*. I was surprised by what I found in the two slender volumes. Uncertain what to expect, I had imagined something more formally structured; barrack-room ballads, perhaps, as much song or limerick as poetry. But instead I found a variety of verse considerably more than competent in its structures and rhythms and in its range.

Of the two volumes, I preferred the first. Not because the second was any less accomplished — in fact the war poetry it contained seemed to me to be considerably more potent than the earlier work — but because the first contained Gurney's poems of the Gloucestershire countryside, of the Severn Valley and the Forest of Dean. I was familiar with the places and the landscapes he wrote about from my own boyhood holidays. My mother's family came mostly from Tewkesbury, and her sisters had lived at Ross-on-Wye, immediately north of the Forest of Dean. Charles and I were taken there for an annual holiday until a few years before the outbreak of the war, when my uncle died.

I recognized most of the places Gurney wrote about, and was struck by the depth of his own affection for them. I looked forward even more to meeting him, and to being able to discuss with him this common history and geography.

As children, my mother had often read poetry to us. Charles had been less enthusiastic than myself, but for her sake he had sat and listened to her recitals — often the day's final ritual as we both prepared for bed — and later, he and I read the same poems back to her. After that, as we became more proficient in our readings, and when I, at least, gained some pleasure from the exercise, we were brought out to recite at family gatherings. My father compiled several volumes of poetry and prose, all connected to bees and bee-keeping, and nothing gave him greater pleasure than hearing the two of us recite his favourites. Our own pleasure in these performances was greatly enhanced by — and solely dependent on in Charles's case — the money my father secretly paid us after each recital. Occasionally, one of us would read the poem or short passage and the other would make a background noise of bees, a rising and falling buzzing or droning in keeping with the drama of the words.

My mother and various of his apiarist friends tried to persuade him to find a publisher for these anthologies, but he invariably rejected the idea, insisting that he gained more from the poems and the readings because of the *private* pleasure they afforded him. When he died, my mother found poems that he had written himself. She copied several of these out for me — the ones containing both the bees and his own sons — and gave them to me on the eve of my departure overseas.

70

Her own favourites were those poets she herself had read and declaimed as a girl — Tennyson and Browning chiefly — but she also had what my father referred to as "a fine ear" for more contemporary work — Hardy, Masefield, Bridges, de la Mare — and she read these to us, too. The bamboo-and-lacquer bookcase in her dressing-room attested to this lifelong interest.

I felt certain she would have enjoyed and appreciated Gurney's work, and I regretted that the two sets of poems collected in his first volume — his poems of the Severn and those of the Somme — had not been published as separate collections. And realizing this, it struck me as both a perverse and a brave thing for him to have done, especially before the war's end, to have combined the two sources of his inspiration in the same book.

Having read the work, I slid the poems into Gurney's file and laid this on the table beside my bed, hoping for a more successful visit the following day.

CHAPTER
EIGHT

The next morning, as I was washing, there was a knock at my door and Osborne appeared. He considered me for a moment without speaking. He was agitated and out of breath. He came into my room and sat down.

"Barstow," he said.

Barstow was another of my patients, and I waited for him to explain, wiping the last of the shaving cream from my unshaved neck.

"He's attacked one of the orderlies."

Barstow was sixty-seven years old and had lived in one institution or other for the past fifty years.

"He wants to see you. He's insisting on you going to him." He crossed the room and sat beside my cold fire, all urgency suddenly gone.

"Do you know why?" I asked him, buttoning my shirt.

"You told him his mother was coming to visit him today. Apparently, he woke up this morning, realized you'd lied to him, and now this." He picked up an old newspaper, scanned its front page and dropped it.

"Barstow killed his mother fifty years ago," I said.

"You know that and I know that." He smiled.

"I told him his *sister* was coming. His sister. According to his file, she comes every three months. She lives in Northampton. She comes every three months, sits with him in almost complete silence for two hours, complains about the length, complexity and discomfort of her journey, and then leaves. Usually after putting in a new application to have him transferred to the asylum in Northampton to make her own life easier."

"He was sent here from there," Osborne said.

"She thinks that because he's growing old and infirm — because they *both* are — he ought to go back to her."

"It's not very likely," he said. "The Boards here and there have washed their hands of him. He's here for the duration."

I knew all this.

"Is there no possibility that he might be sent somewhere else, closer to her? On compassionate grounds?"

He laughed at the phrase. "Why? Because it would be the *humane* thing to do?" He laughed again. "From what I hear of Barstow, he spends days on end sitting motionless and in complete silence. He's a complainer, like his sister. She's older than he is. Besides, it's an hour, less, on the train. Some charitable foundation or other will be helping her with her fares. She could cut her visits to one a year and I doubt he'd notice."

I put on my white coat and went to the door. "Shall we go to him?" I said.

"We? I'm merely the messenger. These things happen all the time. I'm sure you're more than capable of dealing with this yourself. Cox and one or two others are already with him." He looked around my room as he spoke. I had no authority to ask him to leave, and he showed little inclination to do so just because I was going.

"What about the man he attacked?" I said.

He shrugged. "They know the score. A couple of cuts and bruises perhaps."

"Cuts?"

"Bruises, then. He's sixty-seven, for God's sake, heavily medicated, hardly a muscle in his body. You've seen him." He slapped his palm on the arm of his chair, as though about to push himself up from it.

I picked up my briefcase and slid several files and loose sheets into it.

Osborne finally rose, considered himself in the mirror for a moment and then came to stand beside me at the door. I was still uncertain why he'd come to see me himself instead of sending someone else to fetch me.

As I locked my door, he said, "I take it you've seen Gurney." He waited for my answer.

"Not yet. But I've read his work."

"His work?"

"His poetry."

"Oh. That's 'work', is it? And?"

I told him what I thought, and everything I said either annoyed or disappointed him.

"You're probably giving him more credit than he warrants," he said. "Probably because of everything that's happened to him since, him being here."

"Perhaps," I said, knowing that to contradict him then, not yet having spoken to Gurney, would have served no purpose other than to disappoint him further. And to have argued on Gurney's behalf would certainly have done neither of us — Gurney or myself — any favours.

"Give you the poems himself, did he?" he asked me.

"Lyle had copies. Like I said —"

"Lyle?"

"He was there when I went to see Gurney."

"And what do you make of him?"

"I only spoke to him for a few minutes." I was reluctant to reveal anything else to him until I'd spoken further with Lyle, and perhaps until I'd seen the two of them — Lyle and Gurney — together.

"Did he tell you he volunteered to come with Gurney from Gloucester?"

He hadn't.

"Thought not. Apparently, him and the genius Ivor have become *close friends*." He invested the two words with a cold emphasis, and though I understood what he was suggesting to me, I didn't share his own uncertain belief.

"Lyle was due to sit his Board in a month's time. I spoke to Townsend up at Barnwood House. Model patient, by all accounts. The Board would have ticked every line on the sheet."

"Meaning he would have been released?"

"Sent somewhere else prior to that, most likely. Kept there for two or three months longer just to make sure, and then sent home to get on with things. He's still practically a boy."

"And has he jeopardized any of that by coming here with Gurney?"

He shrugged. "Perhaps, perhaps not. His application for his Board has followed him here. He can sit it just as easily here as there, and to the same end."

Both of us knew that this was not true. The doctors, visitors and independent assessors in Gloucester would already know Lyle and the progress he had made since being released from prison. They might send on their recommendations to the panel assessing him here, but it would still not be the same thing. I tried hard to think of a single patient who had been recommended for release after his first Dartford Board.

"So he was taking quite a risk," I said. "In coming here with Gurney."

"Oh? Perhaps he thought that volunteering to come with his *friend* would do him more good than harm. Especially if Gurney *is* what they say he is. Besides, now that you're his doctor here, you'll no doubt get to have your say when the time comes." He walked ahead of me along the corridor and down the stairs, our footsteps echoing on the metal staircase and off the tiled walls.

I followed him to where Barstow had been secured.

Approaching the doorway, I saw Cox and several others standing there, including Lewis.

Cox saw Osborne and came to him. "You took your time," he said, surprising me with the insubordinate and aggressive remark.

"Doctor Irvine wasn't quite ready," Osborne said. I'd expected him to reprimand Cox, especially in front of these watching others, but he seemed unwilling to do this. "Where's Barstow?"

"Where you left him. In there. Sitting in a corner and crying like a baby." He beckoned one of the orderlies to him.

The man came.

"Show the doctors your bruises," Cox told him.

The man turned his face from side to side. He had a slight bruise on his cheek and another on his forehead. They were not the marks of a serious assault and needed no treatment.

"There's more," Cox said, and he grabbed the orderly's arm and pushed up his sleeve. A third bruise, equally minor and barely coloured, showed on the man's wrist. Prompted by Osborne, I examined this, prodding it, and then the one on the man's cheek to judge any pain he still felt. I told him that all he needed was to keep them exposed to the air, that they would have faded to nothing in a few days.

Cox turned to me with a look of exaggerated disbelief on his face. "And that's it, is it? He practically gets strangled by that old bastard and all you tell him is to go away and forget about it?"

"That wasn't what he said," Osborne said.

The orderly, I saw, still held by Cox, would have been happy to have done as I'd suggested.

Cox ignored the remark. "And now you'll go in to Barstow and spend an hour with him trying to convince him that everything's all right, that he's not to blame for any of this."

"Of course I'll go in to him," I said, glancing at Osborne in the hope of some support. Turning back to the bruised man, I said, "If you are feeling any other pain from the assault" — the word seemed too much and I'd used it deliberately — "then go to the dispensary and tell them what's happened."

"And then what?" Cox said. "They dab some iodine on it and tell him to stop complaining?"

"In all likelihood, yes," I said, unwilling to endure his provocations any longer.

"Perhaps we might *all* just return to our duties," Osborne said.

Cox turned his back on us and mimicked the words.

And again, Osborne let the remark pass without comment or reprimand. "I'll see you later, Cox," was all he said, and he turned and walked away from us.

"You can count on that," Cox called after him, just as Osborne turned a corner. It was unlikely that he would not have heard the remark.

I considered asking Cox why he'd addressed Osborne like that, but knew that this would only prolong his tirade, and that it would add to the pleasure he took in this, especially in front of all these subordinates.

Instead, I told the bruised man to come and see me the following day if any of his bruises had failed to fade. "Either that, or go back to Cox and tell him. I'm sure *he* has your welfare at heart." My meaning was clear to the man and he smiled at the words.

Seeing this, Cox finally released his grip on the man and told him to get back to his work.

The man saluted him, said, "Yes, *Sir*," and then walked away from us.

Cox waited where he stood for a moment, watching me closely, and then he too left us.

I asked for the door to be unlocked and went into the wing in which Barstow had lived for the past eight years.

I found him in his room, alone, sitting on his bed, crying, his hands held palm-upwards on his knees.

I went over to him and he looked up at me. At first he appeared not to recognize me — prior to the previous day, I'd seen him only once or twice during the past month — and so I told him again who I was.

"I did a terrible thing," he said.

"I know. But no one was harmed, or only slightly."

"I mean my mother," he said. "That's why I got so upset, see? I got set to dreaming about her last night. Had it in my head" — he struck his forehead with the knuckles of both hands — "that she was coming to see me today. Had it in my head that it was her — my mother — and not that miserable old bag of a sister coming here to sit in her funeral clothes and talk all about how hard everything is for her."

"I told you she was coming, yesterday," I said.

"Did you?"

"Perhaps you misheard me?"

"I doubt it. Would me not hearing you right bring my mother back to me after all these years? She'd be" — he made a quick calculation — "nigh on ninety by now. People like us don't make old bones." He looked up again. "I hit that bastard, didn't I? He had it coming. He pushes us about like we were cattle. I should know. That's what I was, see — a farm hand."

I let him talk, and he went on for a further twenty minutes, re-telling me the story of his life, his work, his brothers and sisters, the woman who might have been about to become his wife, the children he might have had, the profession he might have followed when he finally stopped working on the land. A perfectly remembered and rehearsed story. Right up to the night he killed his own mother. After which, the abyss opened up and everything fell into its unfathomable darkness.

After twenty minutes, he fell silent, the story over.

"What now?" he said after a minute.

"I don't know," I told him. "It's probably up to you."

"She lost her husband of forty-five years last Christmas," he said. "My miserable old bag of a sister. He visited me once, with her, soon after they were wed. I was still in Northampton, then. I told him that him and me would soon be swapping places, that living with her would soon drive him mad. He laughed about it at the time. *She* never did, mind, but he found it funny enough. At the time. And that was the last I ever saw of him. No kids. Three born, not one living past six months."

I put a hand on his shoulder.

"If you were strong enough to attack a man forty years younger than yourself, then I might need to reassess your medication," I said. I was only half joking.

He raised his arms, bent them at the elbow and flexed his non-existent muscles. "I still got it, boy," he said. "Comes from all that hard work I did. Farm hand, I was."

And before he could begin to tell me the same story all over again, I rose and told him I had to leave.

He came to the door and held out his hand to me. "It was good of you to take the trouble to come," he said. "Never get a proper doctor anywhere near the farm."

"Any time," I told him, as though the choice existed for either of us.

CHAPTER
NINE

"I owe you an apology."

The voice caught me unawares. I was sitting on the terrace with my eyes closed, feigning sleep, listening to the men around me.

I opened my eyes.

Alison West sat beside me.

"Oh?"

"My wound. Showing it off to you like that. It was insensitive."

"Is that what you were doing — showing off?"

"I said showing *it* off." She shook her head, exasperated. "Don't," she said. "Don't make it into a joke."

At the time, it had felt closer to an intimacy, a genuine revelation.

I pulled my shirt out of my waistband a few inches and showed her the waxy mark across my stomach.

"And round here" — I patted my side — "I've got a constellation of small white stars, twenty-seven to be precise, pinpricks. Sometimes they look like a hand, and sometimes — and not entirely inappropriately — they look like a gun, a pistol."

Beside her stood a large wheeled wicker trunk on which the word "Laundry" was stencilled in white.

"I see they're still finding work for you commensurate with your skills, talents and abilities," I said.

"'Commensurate'. That's a big word. First I push this all the way *to* the laundry, and once there, I hang around for an hour until someone gives me another one to push all the way *back* again to the linen store. The sick and the maimed and the mere lookers-on part at my approach and then close back around me when I've gone."

"It looks heavy," I said.

"It is. At least I've got some help." She looked to one side of her and was surprised to see no one there. A man stood at some distance from her, his back to us. "He was there a minute ago," she said. She shouted to him and I was just as surprised to hear her call out Lyle's name.

The man turned to us and I recognized Oliver Lyle.

"I know him," I told her. "He's one of mine."

"I know. He told me."

Lyle came to us and she asked him affectionately why he'd abandoned her.

"I didn't abandon you," he said.

"One minute you were pushing, the next . . ."

He clasped his hands together and moved them in a repeated pattern. Alison West reached out and held him for a moment.

"It doesn't matter," she told him, but the reassurance did little to calm him. "You know Doctor Irvine," she said.

Lyle acknowledged me, and I him. I told him of my second thwarted visit to see Gurney earlier in the day.

He stopped wringing his hands at the mention of Gurney's name. "Ivor's had a bad morning," he said. "Doctor Webster came back to see him. He sent me out." He looked from me to Alison West.

"It's why he came to help me," she said. She cast me a puzzled glance.

"I wasn't told," I said. "As Gurney's doctor, *I* should have been sent for, not Webster. Or at least notified."

"It was over as fast as it came," Lyle said.

"What was?"

He hesitated before answering me. "People talk to him," he said.

"What people?" I asked him.

Beside him, Alison West looked at me and shook her head slightly. I understood what she was telling me.

"Sorry," I said to Lyle. "I wasn't trying to get you to betray a confidence."

Lyle considered this. "He hears voices," he said.

"They — we *all* hear voices," Alison said. She held his arm.

"What happened?" I asked him.

"He started shouting. Something about one of his compositions, a proper argument. He wouldn't quieten down when they told him to. They had to restrain and then sedate him." He became anxious again, and Alison took one of his hands in both her own.

"I should have been told. No one told me," I said uselessly.

84

"It happens twenty times a day in here," she said. "Perhaps it was just one of those things and no one considered it serious enough to inform you."

"I still ought —"

"It's over," she said sharply, exasperated by my insistence in front of Lyle.

"He was asleep all morning," Lyle said. "They locked our room and told me to make myself useful somewhere else."

"Which is how he found me," Alison said. "His guardian angel. His angel of the laundry room."

"I enjoy it," Lyle said. "Keeping busy. I'm used to it."

"Because the devil makes work for idle hands?" I said.

"It's true," he said.

"He makes it for all of us," Alison said. "Idle or otherwise."

A group of men, orderlies and patients, approached us, and Lyle became nervous as they drew near.

Alison lifted the lid of the basket and pretended to search through the dirty linen inside, handing a ball of sheets to Lyle. He held this to his chest, covering his face as the men arrived beside us and then passed us by. When they had gone, Alison retrieved the sheets and pushed them back into the basket.

Lyle acknowledged the gesture with a simple nod.

To me, she said, "We call it an 'expedient'. That's another big word."

"Is Gurney all right now?" I asked Lyle.

"I saw him an hour ago, through the window. I asked him how he was and he couldn't remember what had happened. I told him he'd been arguing with one of his musician friends and he laughed and said it happened all the time. I saw the same thing before, in Gloucester. He said his only regret was that he couldn't remember who it had been. I made a few guesses for him, but he saw through me and told me not to."

"I read the poems you gave me," I told him.

"Poems?" Alison said to him. "You write poems?"

"They were Gurney's," I told her. "Two published volumes."

"I thought he was a musician. He *is* a musician: I've heard him play the piano." She looked from Lyle to me. "Are the poems any good?"

"Very," I said, and Lyle could not resist smiling at the judgement.

"He's written many more," he said.

"To be published?"

He shrugged. "They're as good as anything in the first two books. Better, according to Ivor. Said he wanted to call the collection *Rewards of Wonder*. The publishers didn't even want to see it, said there's no appetite for the kind of thing he's writing about these days. Or at least not from people like him."

"And he still writes?" I said. "Here? Now?"

"Of course he does," Lyle said matter-of-factly.

"'People like him'? You mean because he's in here?" Alison said.

"That doesn't seem to bother him," Lyle said. "According to Ivor, it's got more to do with the fact that he was an ordinary soldier. That, and then because of everything that's happened to him over the past five years or so. He says it's the last thing people want to go on hearing about. I bet if you asked him when his sedative wears off how many people there are out of work in this country, he could tell you to the nearest hundred."

"He's probably right about people not wanting to continue hearing about all that," I said, more intrigued than ever about the man in our midst whom I had yet to meet. And angry again at Webster for not at least affording me the professional courtesy of telling me what had happened.

We were interrupted by another nurse walking swiftly across the lawn towards us. She was a young woman, a colleague of Alison's. She was overweight, and stood for a moment with her hands on her knees to catch her breath.

"They're looking for you," she said to Alison. "They're damping down the boilers for the day. Anything that isn't in the wash now will have to wait until tomorrow."

"And if that happens," Alison said, "then the whole world will run a day late and everything will start to unravel."

Both Lyle and I understood her, but the woman only looked at her, mystified, and said, "What are you talking about? What's a day late?"

"I was held up by this lunatic," Alison said, indicating me.

The nurse looked at me and gave a slight, awkward bow.

"He's not royalty," Alison said to her.

"Sorry," the nurse said. "Is this the laundry? Is this what they're all waiting for?" She started pushing the heavy basket along the path. Lyle went to help her, looking over his shoulder at Alison in the hope that she would join them.

"Tell them I insisted on stopping you and talking to Lyle," I said to her.

"And it'll sound like nothing more or less than the excuse it is. Why does everything have to run to such a rigid timetable? What does it matter, a few minutes here or there? Some of these men have got their entire empty lives ahead of them."

"Most of them, in fact," I said.

She looked at Lyle, still struggling alongside the nurse. "Including him?"

Knowing what I now knew of Lyle, his imminent Board, the reason for his commitment in the first place, and the reason for his being here now, I doubted this.

"I don't know," I told her, uncertain why I was neither more truthful nor more explicit with her.

"I hope not," she said.

Lyle and the nurse moved slowly along the path towards the laundry, and I saw that he was becoming increasingly anxious the further away he walked from Alison West.

Alison saw this too. "I ought to go," she said, then paused. "It's probably more of a hand than a gun," she said. "Your scars. Being a brain doctor, you're more likely than not equating the marks with what made them."

"A 'brain doctor'? Besides, it wasn't *that* kind of gun."

"Whatever kind of gun it was, you survived," she said quietly, closing her eyes for a moment.

"I know," I said. "And whatever kind of gun it was, I never heard it coming, and didn't have even the faintest idea of what had happened to me until three days later."

"Good," she said. And then she left me to go and join Lyle and the struggling nurse. I watched the three of them manhandle the unwieldy trolley up the steps of the laundry room.

CHAPTER
TEN

On those days when he held no surgery and had no patients to visit, my father spent whole mornings and afternoons amid his hives. It sometimes seems to me now that in every photograph I possess of him, and of my parents together, the bees are in some way involved: countless poses of him alone and of the pair of them wearing their gauntlets, their faces hidden by the gauze of their hats. His was the usual headgear, but my mother adapted old hats of her own. I never thought of her as a woman in thrall to the fashions of the day — as she often accused her younger sister of being — but looking at those pictures I can see that with her bee-keeping outfits she stamped her own personality on this shared pursuit. I say "shared", but hers was never a true passion. Not like my father's, and certainly not like Charles's later came to be.

Once, as a boy — I can have been no older than nine or ten — I was badly stung on my hands and forearms while trying to scrape honey from an exposed rack. The hive was a new one, and the early honey more liquid than solid. I was clumsy in my theft, or perhaps my father had not subdued the hive sufficiently with his smoke, and the bees had reacted angrily. My fingers had swollen to twice their normal size and, alerted by my screaming, both my mother and father had come running to see what had happened. My mother had brushed frantically at the bees still on me until my father had pulled her gently aside and had then plucked the insects from me one by one and dropped them to the ground where I stood. It was a cool day and the bees were sluggish. I remember them falling without attempting to fly. I remember looking down and seeing them crawling around my feet.

I lied to my father and told him the bees had attacked me for no reason, but in reply to this he simply ran his finger through the honey which still coated my palms. My mother continued to make a fuss over my swollen fingers and he told her sharply that she was doing no good — that, on the contrary, she was scaring me, herself and the bees alike. He went inside and returned with a jar of balm. He made this himself, and it consisted of poultry grease into which he had mixed an extract of venom. He tried to explain to me then — though I took little notice of what he said through my tears, my tantrums and my need for attention — that being stung like that so young would later increase my resistance to the poison. If I was going to suffer any genuine or serious allergic reaction, he told my mother, then I would already be having difficulty breathing and would be close to collapse. He counted ten stings. I insisted to my mother that I *was* having difficulty catching my breath and she grew even more concerned. My father, however, understood what I was doing and remained unconvinced. He examined my eyes and my throat and told her I was making up these symptoms. My fingers, he pointed out to her, were already less swollen than only a few minutes earlier, and I could not refute this.

All this time, Charles had stood to one side of us, his face hidden by the gauze of his own hat. We were told almost daily to wear the hats and gauntlets when going anywhere near the hives, regardless of the time of year or the activity of the bees.

Even then, Charles showed a far greater interest in the upkeep of the hives and the lives of their inhabitants than I ever did, and he and my father spent whole days together away from the house as the various operations vital to the well-being of the bees were carried out. My father believed that bee-keepers were born and not made. He also believed — though he was careful never to make this explicit — that there would only ever be one true bee-keeper in any generation of a family. Even then, at that age, I knew that this was a ridiculous notion. Not least because we were the only proper family I knew who actually kept bees.

The bond between Charles and himself was further strengthened when Charles announced his decision to attend medical school and become a surgeon. The celebrations lasted a week, family members came from all parts of the country, and I doubt if either father or son had ever been happier.

Perhaps understanding how excluded I came to feel, my mother consoled me with talk of what *I* would become, of all *I* would achieve in the world. But later, when it became clear that any aptitude I possessed also lay towards medicine, but of a kind anathema to both my father and to Charles, it became difficult for even her to remain genuinely enthusiastic about my chosen course. And though she never once tried to deflect me from this, I saw what a disappointment I had become to her too.

Regardless of their own thoughts on all these matters, our parents treated us equally, and both Charles and I followed our slowly divergent paths and grew apart, separated as much now by our individual interests and ambitions as by our ages.

Upon my return to Stroud at the end of the war, I was unable to suppress the unexpected and perverse satisfaction I felt at discovering that the hives had been abandoned, and that they had fallen into disrepair and rotted through neglect, and that the few that were still occupied — like those in the asylum orchard now — were filled with weak and sickly colonies at the ends of their lives. Along with this neglect, disease, overcrowding and predators had also done their work. Without either my father or Charles to care for them, the bees had been unable to survive. These strong and perfectly organized societies had depended wholly on the men who protected them and cared for them, and without those God-like men, anarchy had ruled, and death and loss and ruin had prevailed.

In fact, the whole of the garden was irretrievably overgrown after only four years of neglect, and many trees had been uprooted by the winter gales. The surrounding farmland was also rank with abandonment, and the few crops that had been planted and tended were sparse and pocked with the blight which came in that wet summer after the war, grown more through impulse than the expectation of a profitable harvest.

CHAPTER
ELEVEN

I finally encountered Ivor Gurney for the first time two days later, after tea, behind the greenhouses in the far garden. He and Lyle stood together, examining something Gurney held. Both wore spectacles and looked closely at whatever was in Gurney's hand.

It was a warm evening, and whenever the spring weather now permitted, those patients allowed unattended out into the grounds were given the freedom to walk and gather outside for an hour after tea. The evening meal was served at five, allowing time afterwards for those who required medication or treatment to be seen. The remainder were afforded this extra degree of freedom in the hope that either the evening air or whatever gentle exercise they took might help them sleep better.

A round was made of all the external gates and doors, and all those inner doors which needed to be kept secure, before the bell was sounded to end the meal and announce this freedom.

This evening time was regarded as a privilege by Osborne and was frequently withdrawn from those men who were deemed by him to have abused this privilege. A further bell would sound at seven, and later, at the height of the summer, at eight, to announce a general return to rooms and wards.

Lyle was the first to see me, and he considered me for a moment before speaking to Gurney. Then he too looked up and considered me.

My first instinct had been to leave them alone, but having seen me, Lyle beckoned me to them.

"Meet Gurney, Ivor," he said formally as I reached them. He held out his hand to me and I took it.

He nudged Gurney to do the same, which he did, withdrawing the instant our palms had touched. He seemed embarrassed by the gesture, as though it committed him to much more now that we had finally met.

"Doctor Irvine has been assigned to us," Lyle said to him. "Or we to him. He's our doctor. He's assessing us."

"Is that what you were doing watching us?" Gurney asked me. There was neither anger nor suspicion in his voice; he seemed genuinely curious.

"What's that?" I asked Gurney, indicating his hand.

He revealed the stems and leaves he held. "Wood anemone," he said. "Smell it." He held the leaves to my face and I took a deep breath.

"I recognize the smell," I said, unable to place it.

"Apple blossom," he said. "Probably to attract the same pollinating insects."

I took a second deep breath. It was exactly the scent of apple blossom.

"We found it by the greenhouses," Lyle told me.

Gurney pressed the leaves to his face and closed his eyes. "What do you need me to do?" he said. "For your assessment?"

I told him there was no urgency. I wanted to ask him what Webster had already done to him and perhaps told him.

"He means you'll be here for a long time," Lyle said to him, and laughed.

Gurney, too, was more amused than concerned by the remark and all it implied. "Suits me," he said, his eyes still closed.

"I'd like to talk to you," I said. "Not much more. A few tests."

"I've had enough of those over the past few years," Gurney said. "Now?"

"I only came out for some fresh air," I said.

"Will things be much different from Barnwood House?" Gurney asked me, opening his eyes and watching me closely, his eyes magnified by the small, thick lenses of his spectacles. I knew from his notes that his first attempt to enlist had been thwarted by his poor eyesight.

"Perhaps, perhaps not," I said, unwilling either to speculate or to mislead him. "Have *you* changed much since coming here?"

"Careful, Ivor," Lyle said. "It might be one of their trick questions. And knowing you, you'll probably say too much and back yourself into a corner."

"No one's going to do anything against your will," I told Gurney, and the remark surprised him.

"I went to Barnwood House voluntary," he said, his Gloucestershire accent even more pronounced. Sometimes he spoke with it, and sometimes without. It was something I looked out for at each of our subsequent meetings. Just as I noticed his proper or improper use of words — "voluntary" for "voluntarily", for instance — and his use of both slang and the vernacular. I saw even then, at that first encounter, what small but cherished pleasure he took in all of this, in presenting and then concealing these different facets of himself. I saw, too — or perhaps I only imagined I saw, knowing what I already knew of him — the loss and the growing confusion behind these slender, brittle surfaces.

"Perhaps," I said. "But that doesn't necessarily mean you could just have left when you'd wanted to."

"I know that." He seemed suddenly disappointed.

"'Necessarily'," Lyle said. "A bit mealy-mouthed. There was a lot of that at Barnwood House."

"It's a fact," I told him. I began to wish that I'd encountered Gurney alone, that this filter of their friendship did not now exist between us.

And as though sensing this slight tension, Gurney threw the few leaves at Lyle, who batted them away from himself, scattering them in the grass at our feet.

"He's prone to sudden outbursts of violent behaviour," Lyle said.

Gurney turned back to me. "They told us at Laventie that the Germans might be about to use gas, and that we'd be able to tell if this was in the air because it would smell of garlic."

"I was at Laventie, briefly," I told him. "A mile behind the front."

"We were in reserve. Second Battalion, Fifth Gloucesters, Company B, reserve battalion to the First. They were in it from the very start."

It was a common thing, this brief recital of military service, a foundation upon which everything afterwards might be built.

"We went up on the tenth of June. Beautiful weather. We had Garrison reserve posts at Laventie, Masselot, Fort Esquin and Wangerie." He smiled as he told me all this, as though he remembered the places fondly.

It surprised me to hear how easily he remembered the places, and how correctly he was able to pronounce them. Most others took a pride in deliberately mispronouncing them.

"Billeted in houses, bright-red brick, and a church. I saw brick like that stacked around the brickfields at Longney and at Allingham."

"There are brickfields close to here," I said, remembering what Cox had told me on our excursion along the estuary.

"Oh, where?"

I told him, but he was momentarily lost in his remembering, following his course through an old world; all here was new to him.

Lyle, I noticed, continued to watch him closely, clearly encouraged by the effort Gurney was making.

Gurney went on. "There was a fifteen-inch railway gun and four batteries of eighteen-pounders. Day and night they kept firing. We were up that time for a week.

The Buckinghamshires relieved us in the middle of the month. A week." He fell suddenly silent and his expression changed in an instant. "I went off for signal training after that. A week in the line, week in reserve, week at rest, same old routine. Fatigues, parades, duties. Standing to and standing down." And as he said this, his voice slowed and deepened slightly and I heard an echo of several of his poems, as though he might even perhaps have been reading from one of them.

Lyle, I saw, had stopped listening to him and was peering up into the sky.

Gurney stopped talking. He reached across and picked one of the stems he had thrown from Lyle's hair.

"You were talking about the gas," Lyle said, his face still turned to the sky.

"They told us it would smell of garlic," Gurney said. "'Stink' is what they said."

"I remember," I said.

"Except that nobody in my Company had ever smelled garlic, let alone tasted it. Only me."

"I daresay —"

"I used to pick the wild stuff down at Fretherne and Saul," he said, going on as though I hadn't spoken. "Wherever there was dog's mercury growing, or pennywort or wild arum, the wood garlic would never be far away. I used to sleep out nights in the woods at Saul." He looked beyond me as he spoke.

"Tell him what you did," Lyle said, gently drawing Gurney back to us.

"Did?"

100

"About the garlic, the gas."

"I bought a few bulbs from a French farmer and gave a clove to everybody. All they had to do then whenever there was a gas-call, was to crush a piece and keep sniffing at it on their fingers. Some of them refused to do it. You'd think *it* was poison to hear them talk."

I knew from Gurney's medical records that he had been evacuated from the St Julien front fifteen months later suffering from the effects of gas. I had hoped to avoid all mention of this at our first encounter.

He stopped speaking again and concentrated on buttoning up his shirt, struggling with the awkward collar stud until Lyle intervened and did this for him. Gurney stood perfectly still, his neck craned, as Lyle manipulated the stud. And again I was reminded of a mother attending to her child.

"I read your poems," I said when Lyle had finished. "I thought them very accomplished, powerful." I immediately regretted the way the two judgements seemed to cancel each other out. "I'd like to see more if you have them."

"I sent them all to Marion when I came here," Gurney said. "For safe-keeping."

"Marion Scott?"

"She acts as a kind of agent for him," Lyle said, glancing at Gurney as though he were uncertain how Gurney might respond to him revealing this. "When he was overseas," he went on, "she kept everything safe for him. She made copies and —"

"She's better than a mother to me," Gurney said suddenly and loudly. "I mean that."

"That's what I was saying, Ivor," Lyle told him. "That's what I was getting to." He put a hand on Gurney's shoulder.

"She's written to Osborne," I said, uncertain whether or not Marion Scott's application to visit Gurney remained confidential.

"I know," Gurney said. "She wanted to come the day I arrived. I asked her to stay away until I was properly settled. I didn't know how I'd be. There were some awful rows back in Barnwood. My brother, family, all that. I didn't know how I'd be. I didn't want Marion coming when I was at my worst. She's seen it all before, mind, but I didn't want her seeing me here, in London, her home, like that."

"We thought a month or two, didn't we, Ivor?" Lyle said, his hand still on Gurney's shoulder.

"She said she'd contact Doctor Osborne to see how things were progressing," Gurney said. "Was that what she said — 'progressing'?"

Lyle said it was.

"Did you think the move from Gloucester would distress you?" I asked Gurney.

He considered this. "Had to be done," he said simply. "Up there, I was too close to everything; everything on my doorstep, so to speak; everything that ever mattered to me. They thought it would help me if I was able to make the break. And what use was my family to me? They never cared, not one bit."

"Ronald cared, Ivor," Lyle said. "Your brother, he —"

Gurney shook his head. "Not about me, he didn't. Only that I was a burden on him and *his* family. He'll write to someone here, in London, you'll see. He'll write telling them what a burden I was to him, what I owe him, what I will always owe him. He reckoned he wanted to become a medical man, but that any money to spare had been spent — wasted — on me."

I waited a moment for Gurney to calm down and then said, "It's why I'll make my own assessment. After which, we'll work out together which treatments might benefit you the most."

"Are you listening, Ivor?" Lyle said.

"My father — he was the only one who ever had any time for me," Gurney said absently. "Called me his misfit boy."

I knew from Gurney's notes that his father had died of cancer.

"He died," I said.

"May tenth, first year of the peace," Gurney said. "I don't want to say any more about it, him, any of them."

It was also mentioned in his notes that since his arrival at Barnwood House, Gurney had refused all contact with his family.

"You're honoured," Lyle said to me. "That's as much as *I've* ever heard him say about any of them. All *I* ever hear is Marion this and Marion that." He said it with some amusement, watching Gurney closely and gauging his possible anger at the remark. Gurney, however, read his friend's intent perfectly and grinned

103

with him. I began to wonder then how much Gurney had transferred from his family to the woman, and about the precise nature of the burden that now rested on her shoulders.

"Did the garlic trick work?" I asked Gurney.

"One of the sergeants said it was the Germans we had to look out for, not vampires. And some of them didn't even understand that." He paused briefly. "No — I doubt if it helped a single one of them. Most of them were lost in a barrage at Guemappe, and then after that at Buire au Bois, outside Arras. What was left of us was finished off with the Oxfords and Bucks at Pond Farm. Heard of it?"

I hadn't and I shook my head.

"Buysscheure. Three days in support trenches at Warwick Farm and then they sent us up against a concrete fort. You think a bit of garlic on your finger was going to do much good against that lot? I doubt half of them ever even knew if they were in France or Belgium most of the time. Besides . . ." He hesitated, and Lyle and I waited for him to go on. "Besides, by the time I got my gas at St Julien, it smelled of nothing. 'New Gas', they called it. It was the chlorine stuff that smelled of garlic, not the new gas." He stopped again, looking around us.

"Tell him about the cards," Lyle said, tugging again on those same invisible reins.

"We had cards handed out to us," Gurney said. I knew what he was going to tell me, but I let him go on. "'Useful French Phrases'. Apparently. Depends what you mean by 'Useful', I suppose. How to ask directions, say 'Thank you'. That kind of thing. On the asking-for-directions card they left a blank space for the name of the place you were headed for. '*Excusez-moi, est-ce que c'est la route au*' and then dot dot dot. Except on the cards they gave us some wag had written 'Berlin' over the dots. You can imagine how hilarious we all thought that was after spending months moving just as far backward as forward. I spent hours trying to teach them to say it in French."

There had been a collection of similar cards returned to my mother among Charles's belongings. The same three dots filled in with the place-names of his own back-and-forth wanderings. We had learned our own French accents by singing songs with her at the piano, little realizing then, ten years beforehand, that any of what she taught us would later be of such practical use.

I was lost in these thoughts for a moment, and when I looked up, I saw that Lyle was considering me closely. Gurney, too, had fallen silent.

"I sent my work and all my compositions to Marion because no one at home would have shown the slightest interest in them," Gurney said eventually. "They said I was bringing down the Gurney name by doing what I did, by the things I wrote."

"The London critics didn't think so," I said.

"You think *they* count for anything back in Gloucester? You think whatever *they* had to say about me didn't only confirm what everybody back there already thought and said?"

"Then it's a pity," I said.

The remark caught him unawares and he considered it. "It is," he said. "A true pity. Except that pity doesn't really count for much any more, does it? Not these days."

"*I'd* still appreciate seeing more of your work," I told him. "Are you still writing? Here? Because if you are —"

"I'm not," he said bluntly, contradicting what Lyle had told me. "At least not yet." He pressed a finger hard into his temple, leaving a white spot when he removed it.

Both Lyle and I looked at this, watching the flesh grow pink again.

"I slept out in Saul woods and other places — May Hill, Dymock, Maisemore — for days on end. Saw a speckled bird, a crow, being attacked and killed by others up on May Hill. That's what they did to *their* misfits. Big bird, it was, bigger than two of the black ones put together. Killed it and then tore it to pieces where it fell. I could take you to any one of those places and show you where the garlic grows."

"Of course you could, Ivor," Lyle said. "You could show us all of those places."

CHAPTER
TWELVE

I awaited the arrival of another of my new patients. A man called Clayton, twenty-three, who had been committed to the Bedford Asylum at the age of twelve, and who had then been sent to Dartford a decade later with the recommendation that no further assessment of his condition was required. "F.R.P.", one of the Bedford doctors had written at the head of the file. "Final Resting Place". It was my first encounter with the man.

As I read Clayton's file there was a knock at my door and Alison West appeared there.

"I'm expecting someone," I told her.

"I know," she said. "You don't imagine I'd be brazen enough to come here on my own initiative, do you?"

I started to answer her and then stopped as she guided a young man into the room ahead of her, holding and steering him by his shoulders. His head was turned rigidly to one side, his eyes fixed on her as she did this. She closed the door behind them, released her grip on the man and came to stand in front of him.

"Meet Philip Clayton," she said.

The man nodded slightly at hearing his name.

"I saw he was rostered to see you; I was rostered to take care of him this morning; and so here we are — two for the price of one." She drew up two chairs, guided Clayton to one of them and then sat down beside him. Clayton held out his arms as though he were driving a car and she lowered these to his side. The sleeves of his jacket were too short for him and his forearms showed below them.

I told him I was pleased to see him and he turned immediately to Alison.

"He's pleased to see you," she said to him. To me, she said, "It's partly why I came: he's not much of a conversationalist, our Philip."

This time Clayton grinned at the mention of his name. He raised his arms again, and again she lowered them, into his lap this time.

"Contact and guidance," she said. "Otherwise . . ." She left her own hard seat and went to the armchair in the corner of the room, as though to remove herself from whatever happened between Clayton and myself. Clayton watched her go, and then continued staring at her as I spoke to him. Nothing I said to him solicited even the simplest of answers and I gave up. In Bedford he'd attempted suicide by gathering up as many mothballs as he could find and then swallowing them.

"He's been institutionalized since he was twelve," I told her.

"Stop using stupid words like that," she said immediately. "Another one of Osborne's edicts, is it? Think of a word and then make everything fit? I know what he's *been* for the past ten years. I probably know more about it than he does. Giving it one of your stupid names doesn't make it any more —" She waved a hand at me in frustration.

"More knowable?" I said, disappointing us both.

I turned back to Clayton and asked him if he knew why he'd been sent to see me.

And for the first time, he appeared to be considering what I'd just asked him.

I waited.

"Oh," he said. It sounded more like a prelude to a considered answer than a reflex of surprise.

I continued to wait.

"Oh," he said again.

After a minute of silence, Alison said, "That's it. You might think there's more coming, but there isn't. Is there, Philip?"

The man turned to her, half raised and then lowered his arms.

"There's nothing else you want to say, is there?"

"Oh," Clayton repeated.

I asked her how long he'd been like this.

"I've been here seven months and he's been like this all the time I've known him."

I regretted not having known more about the man before his arrival.

"It says he started showing signs of mental distress from the age of six or seven," I said. "He seems to have attended rather a lot of schools." I looked over the sheet to her and she shrugged.

"Boys, I suppose," she said. "Look how slight he is now. I can't imagine he looked any more robust as a six- or seven-year-old."

Clayton was only a little over five feet tall. His hair was badly cut — the asylum barber — and stuck out from his ears, giving him a comical appearance.

"You should have seen him before I smartened him up," Alison said. She came to Clayton and wiped his mouth. "He hasn't had a single visitor all the time he's been here," she said to me, her voice low. "According to Webster, you're all wasting your time in trying to do anything for him." Having wiped his mouth, she tried unsuccessfully to flatten his wayward hair. She cupped his chin and turned his face from her to me. "Are you going to break the habits of a lifetime and say something to the nice doctor?" she said to him.

"Oh," Clayton said.

"He hardly eats or exercises," she said.

"Oh," Clayton said.

She returned to her chair. "That's right — oh, oh, oh."

There was no indication in his file when Clayton had actually stopped speaking. I'd seen this same condition before, at Netley and then Maghull, where I'd worked under Ronald Rows, and mostly it was a temporary condition, easily cured. It was one of the symptoms most effectively dealt with by hypnotism, and the vast majority of men treated like this — over nine out of ten at Maghull — quickly retrieved their power of speech, often along with a great deal else.

110

Again, there was no indication in Clayton's notes that anything had been attempted to remedy the problem.

"If he can say 'oh', he can talk," I said.

"Tell *him* that," Alison said.

"You can talk," I said to Clayton.

He sat calmly and in continued silence, his gaze unblinking.

I left my desk and went to crouch in front of him. I felt his pulse, which was slow and even, and then I pulled down his lower eyelids to examine his eyes.

My face was only a few inches from his as I did this, and I continued to talk to him, reassuring him.

"Are you hypnotizing him?" Alison asked me sceptically.

"It works," I told her, my eyes still on Clayton's. "Osborne might not have much faith in it, but it does work. With certain conditions." I took off my watch and held it close to Clayton's ear so that he would hear nothing except its ticking. His eyes flicked briefly from side to side at the sound.

"Do you hear that?"

"Oh."

"You can hear, you can speak. Tell me your name," I said. Usually, and always when treating shell-shock cases, this had been followed by a list of further reassurances — that the recovery of speech wouldn't lead to a return to Active Service, that other assumptions would not be made, that no one would accuse the patient of deliberately remaining silent. In the past, I had usually encouraged the silent men to

111

recall the names of their wives, sweethearts and other family members. Often, a photograph or letter held in front of them had been sufficient to persuade them to do this. And once the barrier was broken, so great was their relief at speaking again that they had been unable to stop for days on end, repeating everything over and over to anyone who would listen to them as their relief and uncertainty faded.

A few eventually fell silent again, but the procedure was easy enough to repeat, usually with longer-lasting results the second time. Only a very few failed to respond in some way to being hypnotized, and they had often been the ones who had remained completely silent — not even crying out when pain was inflicted on them — and who displayed a range of other conditions, of which their unwillingness or inability to speak had been considered a relatively minor one.

I went on talking to Clayton for a further ten minutes, attempting to solicit a variety of responses from him, but only ever receiving his "Oh"s.

After five minutes longer, Alison West said, "Has the mumbo-jumbo failed, then?"

I ignored the remark and she apologized for having made it.

"You were trying to appeal to him using his parents and family," she said. "From what I know of Philip, that isn't exactly going to endear you to him."

"You think it might even be having the opposite effect?"

She shrugged.

"Perhaps I should have used your name," I told her, realizing only afterwards how cruel the remark must have sounded to her. Her concern for the man was genuine, and her understanding of his condition and all he had endured surpassed my own.

"I've been talking to him for months now," she said, "and I've never had more than an 'Oh' in reply." It seemed a kind of apology for her earlier remark.

"I wish I'd been able to see him when he first fell silent," I said.

"I took him to see the bees last week," she said. "Speaking of which, have you seen Osborne about them yet?"

I hadn't, and told her so.

I expected her to be disappointed, but it was what she'd expected me to say. I told her I'd mention the hives the next time I saw him.

"Of course you will," she said. She rose, as though about to leave. "I made a few veils," she said. "From the muslin."

Clayton watched her as she went to the door, but made no attempt to rise and follow her.

"You can stay for another twenty minutes," I told her, holding up the watch I still held.

"What good will it do Philip?"

"Twenty minutes of peace and calm and intelligent conversation?"

"Oh," she said.

"I'm sorry about the bees. I'll do my best to persuade Osborne."

"You could try hypnotizing him," she suggested.

"After today?"

She looked at Clayton. "Nothing was ever going to get him to talk. Was it, Philip?"

Clayton remained silent.

"Not even an 'Oh'?" she asked him.

"Oh," Clayton said, and she applauded him.

I offered him a cigarette and he took it and gave it to Alison. She, in turn, took a second from my box, lit it and gave it to him. She sat beside him again and yawned, covering her mouth and then rubbing her face. "I've been on duty all night," she said. The hand she held over her face was tanned slightly and I saw the pale band of skin around her wedding finger. All jewellery was forbidden, either removed at home or kept in a safe in Sister Kemp's office. None of the junior nurses were married, and it surprised me to see the mark.

She opened her eyes and caught me looking. She held her hand closer to me and splayed her fingers.

I occupied myself gathering up Clayton's few papers.

"I was married," she said.

Clayton said, "Oh."

Alison laughed. "'Oh' indeed." To me, she said, "He was killed in Mesopotamia. A place I only ever thought existed in the Bible."

"I'm sorry," I said.

She shook her head. "It's not what you think. We'd known each other since we were children, neighbours. He enlisted on his eighteenth birthday and was then sent home for six weeks to await his call-up. I understood well enough then why we did what we did,

114

but it doesn't make much sense to me now, looking back. My parents were surprised — shocked would be a better word — but had the good grace to say nothing. He only had his mother and an older sister, and both of them thought it was the greatest thing ever. We all just got carried away. Engaged and then married inside a month. Lowestoft. And then a fortnight later he was gone. We lived with his mother all that time. I think we were both regretting what we'd done even before we walked into the church."

"Too late to turn back?"

"Probably not, but it was a strong tide, and we were barely swimmers. He was killed three months later. First missing, then confirmed dead. And me the supposedly grieving widow. I stayed with his mother for a further three months and then left her to start my training. She died a year later." She turned to Clayton. "Are you getting all this, Philip? Are you listening to what fools we all are?" To me, she said, "They sent me his belongings — my husband's — nothing personal, just a few bits and pieces that could have belonged to anyone. No photos, letters, nothing like that. I got a letter two years after the war telling me where his heroic death was to be commemorated, and asking me if I wanted to go and see whatever monument they were erecting to him and a few thousand others. Cut-price travel arrangements. I never answered and they never wrote again."

She cupped Clayton's upper arms and he rose obediently from his seat.

"Time for us to go," she said. "Say 'Goodbye' to the doctor."

But Clayton now stood with his back to me, rendering me invisible. I doubted if he even remembered the ticking of my watch.

CHAPTER
THIRTEEN

"I came last week, but Doctor Osborne forbade me to see Ivor, even through one of your trick mirrors. I suppose he had his reasons. A little too much like Bedlam, otherwise, I suppose." She looked around her as she spoke. Marion Scott.

"Sorry?" I didn't understand her.

"An excursion to see the lunatics," she said. She drew off her gloves and pulled a long pin from her hat. "Something to make the rest of us feel a little better about ourselves. Our sanity. Our own good fortune and capabilities. Though I assure you, you'd be making a great mistake in considering Ivor one."

"One?"

"A lunatic."

"I see," I said.

She was younger than I'd expected — forty-five or -six, perhaps — and certainly not the mother-figure Gurney himself had suggested to me. But though not old enough to be Gurney's mother, she did appear at least a decade older than she probably was — an impression created in large part by her clothes, which seemed to me to be twenty or thirty years out of date. She laid her gloves in her lap and smoothed them flat.

She held her wide-brimmed hat until I motioned for her to rest it on a pile of books and papers on my desk.

"We only use the mirrors for purposes of observation," I said. "It's sometimes useful to be able to do so without the patients knowing we're there."

"Because you think some of them put on an act?"

"Not an act, necessarily, but the presence of others — especially doctors — sometimes alarms or confuses them."

"And do you think that of Ivor?" She held my gaze as she spoke. "What little you actually know of him, I mean."

I ignored the remark. "I've only spoken to him once," I said. "It was why I wanted to see you before you went to visit him."

She pursed her lips, as though I might have been asking her to betray a confidence. "Do you have his records from before all this?"

I slid the file across my desk to her. It was held shut by a slender elastic band. She ran her finger along this, but did nothing to remove it.

She had arrived unexpectedly a few minutes earlier, two days after my first, and so far only, encounter with Gurney. She had gone first to Osborne, and he had directed her to me. I imagine she was disappointed to discover that Osborne himself had not taken on Gurney as his own patient.

"His doctor in Gloucester referred often to his 'neurasthenia'," I said. "I see the term as early as 1904, when Ivor was only —"

"Fourteen. Yes. His doctor in London was my own. Even as a child, Ivor suffered from bouts of strange behaviour, eating and digestive disorders."

"Depressions?"

"While he was at the College, certainly. Deep depressions. He was unable to work for weeks on end. He sometimes disappeared and left no word of his whereabouts. 'Ivor the Wanderer', we used to call him." She smiled. "Sometimes he stayed in London, sometimes he went back to his beloved Severn. Have you read any of his work?"

I told her I had.

"The published volumes are the least of it, believe me." She paused. "Ivor himself has always harboured uncertainties and doubts over his work and talents, believing himself some sort of exception to every rule, a fluke almost. He displayed emotional instability, shall we say. Not uncommon, I imagine, in young men possessed of his capabilities — or perhaps 'sensibilities' is a better word. But with Ivor it was always something more, always something to struggle against. Others might accept their gifts, be grateful for them and develop them to the best of their capabilities. But with Ivor it was always a source of conflict, of self-doubt and extreme effort." She spoke swiftly to prevent me from interrupting her, and her remarks, though convoluted, seemed rehearsed, leading me to wonder how many times she had said exactly the same thing to others elsewhere.

"And you concur with the other doctors?" I read out the list of evasive, vague and all-too-common assessments. "You agree that it was this emotional instability which culminated in his increasingly serious nervous breakdowns?"

She shook her head, though more in uncertainty than disagreement. "You — they — made it all seem so inevitable," she said. "Sir Charles said to me after his first meeting with Ivor that we had a prodigy on our hands. A prodigy already verging on genius. Someone who possessed an artless spontaneity — those were his very words, and I have never forgotten them — and someone who strove for greatness whilst never fully recognizing or appreciating or properly harnessing his own unique talents."

"Sir Charles?"

"Stanford. One of Gurney's chief examiners. Sir Charles Stanford, Sir Hubert Parry, Doctor Davies, Doctor Charles Wood." She was pleased with this same barrage of names — the plinth they already built beneath Gurney and all the unspoken doubts and arguments they destroyed. "I'm sure they will all confirm whatever it is you need to discover or establish for yourself about Ivor's capabilities."

"You believe he still possesses these gifts?" I asked her.

"I do," she said, but only after a second's hesitation. She looked beyond me to the window, and then to the tops of the trees outside. "When he returned to the College the year after the war, everyone could see that he was a changed man. He possessed a great distaste for the city and everything he attempted to achieve there. Having said that, however, the latter part of that

120

year boded well for him. He recovered from most of his ailments — the most obvious ones, at least — and was able to create a period of calm and stability for himself within which to work. Even the start of the following year, 1920, was a productive time for him."

"But, nevertheless, you noticed a change?"

Again, she waited before answering me. "I believe we all did. He started disappearing again, forever longing to be elsewhere. And I use the word advisedly, Doctor Irvine — longing, that's what it was, a kind of elemental need, a restlessness."

"To be back in Gloucester, the place of his childhood and youth?"

"Again, it all sounds so simple, so straightforward. The difference this time was that he tried to avoid his family completely and started living the life of a tramp, walking everywhere, not eating, living rough, sleeping outdoors. When he next returned to London, we barely recognized him."

"And yet he was still able to compose music and to write his poems?"

"He was."

There was a knock on my door and an orderly brought in a tray of tea. I cleared a space for this and he poured us each a cup. We both waited for him to leave before continuing.

" 'Neurasthenia'," she said hesitantly as I passed her a saucer. "I imagine it's a much overused word nowadays."

"And covers a multitude of conditions and symptoms," I said.

121

"Still?"

It had interested me to see the term used so frequently before Gurney's enlistment. Or perhaps one provincial doctor had come across it in a journal, used it because he preferred the modern sound of it over "nerves", and had then been copied by others reading over the same notes.

"You were the Secretary of the RCM union when Ivor first came there," I said.

"In 1911, yes. Autumn."

"He speaks very highly of you."

"We have a great fondness for each other, a great attachment. We exchanged letters every few days while he was on Active Service. He sent me all his poems and what few compositions he was able to write. I made good copies and kept everything safe for him." It was a proud achievement and she smiled as she told me of it.

"They wouldn't have been published without your efforts on his behalf," I said.

She considered the remark and all I might have been hoping to suggest or test by it. "If not me, then someone else would have done the same for him. Someone else at the College. None of us — none of the people who *knew* him — was ever in any doubt about his talents or the lasting value of his work. *Our* only doubts were about Ivor's own ability to properly engage and express himself. It may interest you to know that Ralph Vaughan Williams was Ivor's composition teacher and that he considers Ivor to be one of the finest composers and practitioners of contemporary English music at work today. Adeline — Mrs Vaughan Williams

122

— telephoned me only last night to enquire whether she too might come to visit Ivor in the near future. I told her that, in this instance, I would prefer to see Ivor alone. I'm sure you can understand why."

"Of course," I told her.

She had been too emphatic — too self-congratulatory almost — in what she had just said and we both understood this. Neither of us spoke for a moment.

"I had no idea," I said eventually, "about his musical capabilities."

"Then I shall show you some of his compositions. The College possesses performance-ready copies of a great deal of his work."

"Made by you?" I said.

"At my insistence, yes. In addition to being the Secretary, I was also the editor of the College magazine and president of the Society of Women Musicians. My official title, I suppose, is musicologist" — she pulled a face at the word — "though I would much prefer to be known for my virtuoso skills as a violinist."

"Oh?"

"My apologies. I was making a poor joke. A joke possibly as poor as my violin-playing."

"Have you performed any of Ivor's work?"

"A great deal. I truly do wish you could have seen the Ivor I — we all — saw then. 'Oi Be Gurney', he used to call himself. He mocked his own accent. He can turn it on and off. 'Ivor in Waiting', I used to call him. He had such a life ahead of him, such a career and reputation."

"And you believe that all that is now gone?"

She considered her answer before speaking, and for a moment I imagined she was going to say nothing. She put down her cup and saucer.

"Something changed," she said. "Before, and certainly before he enlisted, there was always a vigour in him, a strength of hope — does that make sense to you? Always a notion that his work and his own need to undertake that work would somehow sustain him, feed him, provide a way forward. I never knew a man so bound to his work, so inseparable from it, as Ivor once was. Even afterwards, when he was sent home, even then I could still see the same fire burning in him."

"And more recently?"

She looked at me, unable to speak, unable to put her belief into words for fear of what that simple utterance might accomplish.

"You believe that same flame has started to consume him?" I said.

"At the risk of sounding even more like one of my melodramatic library books, yes, something like that. He seems lost to himself. As though all the energy he once put into his work he is now using against himself."

"And do you believe he does it deliberately, consciously, with some goal in mind?"

She shook her head. "I don't know. He committed himself to Barnwood House voluntarily. He must surely have understood *something* of what was happening to him, what was now consuming him."

"After which, he agreed readily enough to leave Gloucester and come here."

124

"At my urging — mine and others'; he still has many friends at the College; people who still believe in him — in his — his —"

"His salvation?"

She smiled and nodded. "You must think me a fanciful old woman, a dreamer." She held up her hand. "I know. Forty-five. But it sometimes seems to me that I have always been old beyond my years."

"Just as Ivor has perhaps been younger than his?"

"'The Gloucester Lad', Will Harvey calls him. Housman, you know. Ivor used to play up to it, said it made him sound endearing, worthy of charity. He was never short of others like me to take him under their wing. It might be something for you to consider in your care of him."

"Perhaps they were substitutes for his own family," I suggested.

"I don't wish to speak of them," she said quickly. "As you might imagine, there have been dealings. None of them — not a single one — has the slightest idea."

"Which was another reason for you wanting Gurney brought here." And again the remark sounded considerably more critical of her than it was intended to be.

"You think I was wrong to do that? I discussed everything in detail with Doctor Steen beforehand."

Steen had recently been seconded to the newly formed Greater London Mental Health Authority as its senior advisor, leaving Dartford before Gurney's arrival. The Health Authority was planning a massive expansion of its establishments around the city, and

Steen was now involved in the planning of these. His contract allowed for him to be absent from Dartford for at least a year, and possibly two. Osborne had been promoted to Acting Superintendent in his absence. No one considered it likely that Steen would return once the new hospitals had been built and as they became operational. Osborne understood this better than most, and he knew too that in all likelihood he would very soon be appointed on a permanent basis to Steen's position merely by ensuring the smooth running of the place during Steen's absence.

"Doctor Steen used to attend a great many of our concerts," Marion Scott said. "He and I were, if not friends, then associates. We share a passion for Beethoven. I believe he was in attendance at the performance of several of Ivor's shorter, interval pieces."

Another severed connection, then, I thought.

"I don't know whether Doctor Osborne has any interest in music," I said.

She was unconcerned by this. "Perhaps it might be for the best."

I told her of my own limited musical interest and knowledge, and she repeated the words. "And before you feel the need to avoid saying it, Doctor Irvine, yes, of course I shall consider myself responsible if being here proves not to be what Ivor needs or wants." It seemed as much a denial in its vagueness as an admission.

"He might always return to Gloucester," I said, knowing that this would not be as simple as I was suggesting.

126

I offered her a second cup of tea and she accepted. Holding out her cup and saucer, she knocked her hat to the floor.

"I ought not to have worn it," she said. "It's ancient. Look at it. It looks like something my mother would have worn." She laughed at herself, at this simultaneously sad and pleasurable revelation.

She asked me how old I was and I told her.

"Everyone seems so young," she said. "Either that, or old beyond their years. Is that the fate of us all, do you think? I mean now, after all that's happened?"

I didn't fully understand the confused remark, but understood enough of what she was trying to say to agree with her.

"There were some," she went on hesitantly, "some of my colleagues who imagined that I carried a torch for Ivor — you know, as a sweetheart — but it was never that. There were even those, I imagine, who might have mistakenly believed the same of him. I *did* carry a light for him, and he for me, and although those lights were founded in our friendship, in our fondness, admiration and affection for each other, it was never anything more — or less — than that."

"It seems more than enough," I told her. I knew how important she'd been to Gurney while he was overseas.

"Thank you. It was. I would not have sacrificed, denied or disowned a single moment of my affection for Ivor for anything — not to save face, not to protect myself, not for anything." She paused. "I'm rambling again."

And I told her again that I understood what she was telling me.

We had been together an hour, and I asked her if she wanted to go and see Gurney.

She immediately smiled at the suggestion.

"He said you were a mother to him," I said.

Her smile broadened. "That's what he used to call me — 'Mother Hen'. Forever clucking after him, asking him what he needed, sending him the wrong things. You must also understand that he had no real relationship with his own mother. Close to his father, who loved him, but never her."

"His father died."

"Eighteen months after Ivor came home. If *he* were still alive, then Gloucester might have remained an option." She retrieved her hat from the floor and rose. "Will you come with me?" she said.

I told her I had other patients elsewhere.

"Will I be able to walk with him in the grounds?"

"I see no reason why not." It was a warm, dry day. I told her about Oliver Lyle and she listened intently to everything I said. I told her nothing of Lyle's condition or of his history prior to arriving with Gurney, just that the two of them were now close, that Gurney seemed dependent on the man, and that in turn Lyle was protective of him. I wondered as I said all this if she might not now consider Lyle to be in competition with her for Gurney's affection or trust.

She held out her hand to me and I took it. "Gloves," she said. "Who else would wear gloves on a day like this?"

In the corridor, I called for the orderly who had brought us the tea to take her to Gurney. I gave him the form authorizing this.

"Will I see you again before I leave?" she asked me.

I told her I thought this unlikely. I would be in the secure part of the hospital most of the day.

"Then until next time," she said, adopting some of her initial formality in front of the orderly.

"Don't sit near any mirrors," I said to her, and she laughed.

CHAPTER
FOURTEEN

Alison West stood amid the hives. The uncut grass and brambles grew to her waist, and she was further hidden from me by the low branches, their early blossom starting to fade and drop, their leaf buds already opening.

I went through the doorway to her. Behind me, a group of orderlies worked in the greenhouses, gathering up the tools of earlier working parties.

She saw me and raised her hand at my approach. She wore gauntlets and a wide-brimmed hat with a veil that fell to her waist and obscured her even further. At that distance, and in the early-evening light, she looked exactly as my mother had looked on the countless occasions she had accompanied my father to the hives.

She came to the edge of the untended orchard and raised her veil.

"I came early," she said, pulling off her gauntlets. She clasped the tall stems beside her and ran them through her hand.

I'd finally been to see Osborne earlier in the day to raise the subject of the hives again.

Entering his room, I'd found him there with several of his cronies — there was no other word for the men

130

— sitting around his desk. They were all smoking and a cloud had formed against the high ceiling. One man was holding the parts of a fishing rod and telling them all about his weekend's angling.

Impatient at my interruption, Osborne had asked me what I wanted and I'd told him in the vaguest of terms.

My request surprised him. Several of the others added their own comments, mostly to the effect that I was wasting my time. But Osborne saw that I would not be so easily dissuaded, and he acquiesced to my request to get rid of me. I said nothing then of Alison West's interest in the hives, or of the possibility of afterwards engaging our patients in their restoration.

Since the departure of Steen, others in the hospital hierarchy had also risen to positions they were ill-equipped to occupy, and to my mind Osborne was already buttressing himself with these others.

"And next time," he said as I was about to leave, "please knock before barging in. As you can see, we are *in conference*." He gave the phrase an undue emphasis. At first, I thought he was making a joke — several of the others laughed at hearing him — but I saw from Osborne's sudden look of displeasure that he was being serious.

"My apologies," I told him.

"He sends his apologies," one of the laughing men mimicked, prolonging their amusement.

My proposal would no doubt be discussed among them long after my departure.

I told Alison West what had happened. She was unconcerned at my treatment, puzzled only by my own lack of understanding. She said that my being ridiculed by Osborne in front of these others was the price I'd had to pay for him sanctioning the work on the hives.

"I don't think he actually 'sanctioned' it," I said, realizing how official this now sounded, what freedom and scope it might appear to afford me, us.

"He said yes. It's enough. If he'd had a rubber stamp in his hand saying the same, then you'd have had it in writing."

I asked her if she'd been there long. She wore trousers tucked into her socks, and a kind of shapeless craftsman's smock with a broad leather belt at her waist.

"I came off duty an hour ago. I didn't know if you'd be able to come." She motioned to the hives behind her. "They're in a pretty bad state. They're all Langstroths. Most of the frames are sound, but not much else." She walked to one side of the small orchard and brought me a hat and gloves of my own. "I doubt if we're even going to need them," she said.

I took off my white coat and laid it on a stone bench, grey and yellow with lichen.

"Before we begin," she said, hesitating slightly, "my middle name is Melissa."

"After *Melissae*?" I said.

"My father insisted. His only concession was to stick Alison on first."

"It embarrasses you?"

"As a girl it did. It always sounded like the name of someone I was striving *not* to be. Does that make sense?"

132

I told her that my father had joked with my mother — though half-serious in his intent — that had she given birth to a girl, then Melissa would have been one of her names, too. My mother, or so she later told Charles and myself, had agreed only because no one beyond his close, bee-keeping circle of acquaintances would have fully understood the significance of this.

"Are the hives diseased, infected in any way?" I asked her.

"Foul brood? I don't think so. Just congested and in a poor state of repair."

She led me back to the scattered structures.

We counted thirty frames, half of which were already beyond retrieval. The grass and brambles grew up the stands of most, and some had long since had their openings obscured and blocked by the undergrowth.

The first hive we inspected together still contained its small colony. The bees were sluggish, mostly gathered together in the lower third of the frame. The bee-spaces were clogged with debris and uncleared wax, and by the desiccated corpses of dead insects. The living creatures had made new passages and moved slowly along these.

Alison lifted off the roof and took out several supers.

"They're all stiff with old wax," she said, shaking the frames free of the few bees which still clung to them. She wiped at these with her fingers, flicking the dirty, brittle wax to her feet. She took a long-bladed knife from her pocket and did this more cleanly.

"The floor's rotten," she said, indicating where the wooden tray at the base of the hive had fallen away at her disturbance. "It's a wonder they haven't all drowned or frozen to death."

One of the orderlies had told me earlier that honey had been gathered from the hives throughout the war, when sugar had been in short supply, but that little had been done to them since then. He said that the nuns who had temporarily taken over the running of the asylum had had their own hives at their convent, and that they had later dismissed the asylum bees as being considerably inferior and hardly worthy of their attention.

I'd asked him if any keepers' equipment still existed, and he'd shrugged. All he knew was that anything to do with the hives would have been undertaken in one or other of the potting sheds close to the greenhouses. I'd passed the structures on my way to meet Alison West. I'd intended investigating them, but had then decided otherwise upon seeing the men congregated there.

"The brood box," Alison said, laying the frame in the grass at our feet and pulling out the box. "It's heavy," she said. "Probably full of more corpses." She tapped the sides of this. The wood was soft there, too. A few bees emerged from the remaining slats and hung above us in the air. Most, however, fell to the ground and disappeared in the long grass.

"Are they all like this?" I asked her. I was beginning to doubt the advisability of what we were attempting, but kept the thought to myself.

She pointed to a row of a dozen hives closer to the orchard wall.

"They're in much better condition," she said. "They look as though someone's been tending them. Some damage, mostly to the casings and stands, but I daresay we could replace everything that's beyond repair with parts salvaged from the other hives."

"You sound optimistic," I said.

"I am," she said. She took off one of her gloves and pushed a finger into the tight spaces of the brood box. It was clear to me that her expectations in all of this exceeded my own.

"I think this is all that remains of the excluder," she said, holding up a slight wooden square, which then crumbled in her hand. It was what had once kept the bee brood separate from the honey.

I remembered my father telling me that it was the most important part of the hive, the greatest part of Langstroth's discovery. For reasons I didn't then understand, the excluder not only kept the bees from the honey, but it also meant that the bee eggs did not have to be destroyed when the time came to harvest the honey. It meant, my father said, that the keeper was now in a position to control his bees. Control, he repeated emphatically. It made every difference in the world. Before this explanation, I'd always assumed that every bee-keeper had always exercised complete dominion over the small worlds in his care. Before the excluder, he tried to explain to me, the broods were often killed off each winter. Now, if the keeper wished it, they could be saved, allowed to survive, to struggle through to spring. Life and death, life and death. I remember at the time being more interested in the notion that the bees "hatched" from eggs, and that their produce — the honey and the wax — could be "harvested" like crops in a field.

The lost mesh of the excluder, and now its crumbled frame, could be easily replaced, and if no ready-made replacements could be retrieved from the other hives, then I was certain that either I or a more accomplished carpenter among our staff or patients could produce them. After my earlier doubts, I grew more optimistic.

Alison West threw the pieces of flimsy wood she held against the wall.

"We need to make a proper examination," she said. "An inventory. What can be cleaned and re-used, and what can be salvaged and repaired."

I agreed with her, and for the next hour we walked from hive to hive, inspecting them all.

Some were rotten and collapsed beyond retrieval; others had merely been abandoned and then fallen into disrepair. These latter could be dismantled, disinfected and made sound.

The hives along the orchard wall were in the best condition of all, and most of them might easily be made habitable again. All we would need to do was replace broken parts and then clean everything.

"It's only wood. Wood, nails, a bit of mesh here and there," Alison said at one point during our inspection, when five hives in succession had been declared to be beyond all hope.

After that hour, and more encouraged than disappointed by what we had discovered, we returned to the stone seat and sat there.

"The first thing is to get the grass cut and to take off a few of the lower branches," I said. Some of the bees had followed us to our seat and we batted them away from us with the backs of our hands.

"They'll sense what's happening," she said seriously. "They'll know someone's interested in them again."

"Will they respond?"

"They can't do otherwise. We'll have to search for any surviving queens. It's probably the wrong time of year to be doing all this. Winter would be better." She understood as well as I did that neither of us might be there in six months' time. She knew, too, that at least a dozen of the hives would have to be destroyed completely, along with their failing broods.

"I once saw an old keeper use a puffball instead of smoke to stupefy his bees before taking their honey," she said. "Popped it over the roofless hive and then blew its spoors in."

I remembered my father telling me about the same thing.

"Did it work?" I asked her.

"It seemed to. He said he'd been doing it for decades. He gathered the toadstools in the wood and kept them dry for when he needed them. My father always used smoke."

"Mine, too," I said. And I remembered something else he'd told me — that the smoke was believed by most to deaden some instinct in the bees by which they might otherwise have become defensive and aggressive. The smoke numbed and then confused them regarding whatever was threatening the hive. His own belief,

137

however — and he told me this in that same emphatic hush — was that even the most cultivated and domesticated of broods remembered the smell of the smoke from when they had lived wild in the tree canopy or in hollow trunks. They *remembered*, he said, and because they knew that surviving the forest fires was impossible — that in some instances it was even impossible to flee from the flames — they *remembered* and then they submitted to the fires and awaited their fate. I told Alison all of this.

"What do you believe?" she asked me.

I told her I preferred the latter theory, that I appreciated its romantic drama.

She disagreed with me, though more, I imagine, for my reasoning than for the choice itself. She'd heard the same theories from her own father.

"My father used to be called out to help in the destruction of wild bee colonies," she said. "No one wanted the wild colonies mixing with their own broods. They stupefied the bees with so much smoke that most of them died in their nests. And those who didn't were burned alive. If they'd learned anything from the smell of smoke or the approaching flames, then it didn't do them much good."

I told her I'd go back to Osborne and tell him what we'd found.

"This time make sure you have a plan," she said.

I told her I'd also search the outbuildings for whatever might remain of any of the original equipment, assuming it had been there in the first place.

We sat by the hives for a further hour.

She lived in a house on the London road with three other nurses, twenty minutes' walk away. I offered to walk with her, but she said she'd prefer to go alone.

A solitary bee came close to her face and she held her hand in front of it until it settled on her palm. I watched it closely.

"We stink to them," I said. My father used to rub his hands with either rosemary or lavender when working at the hives. Pots of both grew around the garden, available to him all year round. When the lavender was at its ripest, he cut the stems and dried them in his workroom. I remembered Alison running her hands through the tall grass earlier.

"According to Milton, the bees fled Paradise in disgust at the fall of man," she said, still mesmerized by the solitary creature in her palm.

"And settled here?" I said.

She cast the bee above us and then watched it as it rose and fell, faltered and then gathered momentum on its slow flight away from us.

CHAPTER
FIFTEEN

I next encountered Marion Scott two days later, in the day room with Gurney, the pair of them looking out over the lawn. A second man sat with them, a bowler hat and furled umbrella at his feet, both his hands clasped around Gurney's. The two men sat leaning forward and Marion Scott sat beside them. From the doorway, they looked like conspiratorial children in the company of an aunt. A briefcase stood beside Marion Scott.

I was about to leave them to their visit when Marion Scott saw me and called for me to go in to them.

I had known nothing of this second visit so soon after the first until only a few minutes earlier, when I had encountered Oliver Lyle at the front of the building. I started to make small talk with him, but he showed no interest in what I said and then told me at the first opportunity that Gurney had visitors and that he, Lyle, had been told to stay away from them. He was unable to disguise the resentment he felt at this, and I reassured him that it was the usual thing for patients to be visited alone. But this only served to frustrate him further and he turned and left me.

Marion Scott introduced me to the man sitting with Gurney. He rose and held out his hand.

"Frederick William Harvey," he said. "Will. A good friend of Ivor's."

"Ivor and Will were at the College together," Marion Scott said. And again she said the word as though it were the only college in the country, or as though everyone would have heard of it and shared her own high, all-encompassing admiration of the place.

"I went up a year after Ivor," Harvey said.

"Are you a musician?" I asked him.

He grinned. "A musical solicitor," he said. "Ivor's the only true musician amongst us."

"Composer," Gurney said, still sitting, his head bowed, his clasped hands resting on his knees.

"Composer," Harvey said, reclaiming his hold on Gurney. Gurney, I saw, relaxed as he did this. "Ivor was one of the family," Harvey said to me. "We lived at Minsterworth, on the river. Never away from us, Ivor. I swear my parents and sisters would have traded him for me any day of the year. All the girls were in love with him, you see, every single one of them. Compared to old Ivor here, I was a bit of a dull, leaden thing. In addition to which, of course, though none of us was astute enough to realize it at the time — him being the bumpkin that he was in those days — I never possessed as much as one per cent of his talent." He continued grinning as he said all this. And from anyone else it might have been easily dismissed as exaggeration or flattery, but from Harvey, the words sounded the two true notes of affection and respect.

"Two per cent," Gurney said, and the three of them laughed.

To me, Harvey said, "I'm serious. I'm not here to flatter him. He flatters himself enough without me adding to the chorus. He might be a raving lunatic, but he's his own very particular brand of raving lunatic." Like Marion Scott before him, everything Harvey said revealed the depth and nature of his attachment to Gurney.

"I asked for Doctor Osborne to be informed of our arrival," Marion Scott said. "I wondered also if you might want to see us. I see the message reached you."

I nodded, wondering why Osborne hadn't seen fit to pass on the message.

"Ivor and I were together at the very first performance of Vaughan Williams's Tallis Fantasia," Harvey said, and I knew by the way both he and Gurney awaited my response to this arcane remark that the occasion was of great significance to them both. I wasn't familiar with the work — I hadn't even heard the title before — but rather than expose this ignorance, I nodded and said, "I see."

Gurney started to hum and Harvey joined him, both of them stopping on the same note a few seconds later.

"And the Sea Symphony," Gurney said. He paused to think, and neither Harvey nor Marion Scott interrupted him. "February, 1913."

"Exactly," Marion Scott said, smiling at her clever child, and knowing that her other clever child knew the date too.

142

"The twelfth, a Saturday night. City of London Concert Hall," Harvey said.

"You wore that same suit," Gurney said, indicating Harvey's jacket.

"Perhaps I did, old pal, though I've got a dozen like it, these days. Probably put on an ounce or two in the past ten years."

"Ten years?" Gurney said.

"Since the 'Sea'." To me, Harvey said, "We used to walk the length of the Severn and back, all over the Forest of Dean. Maisemore, May Hill, Redmarley, Dymock." The litany of names was again for Gurney's benefit, drawing him back to this shared past. His eyes registered every place he recognized and remembered.

"I used to walk to Maisemore with my father," Gurney said. "Four miles there, four miles back. Used to do it for a stroll, see his relatives. Saw my first black ouzel on one of those walks to Maisemore."

"And boating," Harvey prompted. "The *Dorothy*."

"At the lock," Gurney said.

"We walked and sailed every inch of that country," Harvey went on, his own sense of near-rapture growing alongside Gurney's at the distant recollections.

"And did you serve together?" I asked him.

The smile fell from his lips for an instant and then returned.

"With Ivor here? No — I was in with a proper lot. The Fifth Gloucesters? Playboys, they were. All they were good for was sitting on their backsides in cushy billets three miles behind the lines, drinking their rum ration and making love to any mademoiselle unfortunate enough to come within reach."

"I'm sure that's not true," Marion Scott said, uncomfortable with the suggestion.

"Tell them, Ivor. As God's my witness."

"It's true," Gurney said. "It's all we were good for. Not too many willing mademoiselles, mind."

It encouraged me to see how easily and enthusiastically Gurney entered into this teasing banter, how capable he was of understanding and then responding to the subtleties of what was being said. I regretted only that Marion Scott was with the two men. I knew this was an uncharitable thought, but I also knew that without her watchful presence, they would have talked even more freely and openly of their shared past.

"I was stupid enough to get myself taken prisoner," Harvey said to me. "August, 1917. Douai. Went out to patrol some supposedly empty trenches, next thing I knew I was surrounded by people pointing rifles at me and whistling *Lieder*."

"What did you do?" I asked him.

"Heroics, you mean? None of that. I'd taken four others with me. My fault. I told them to put their rifles down and stick their hands up. I spoke a bit of German so I put it to good use."

"You should have joined in the whistling," Gurney said. "You probably knew the song."

"Funnily enough, I did," Harvey said, causing more laughter.

"And you were all taken prisoner?"

"We were. For a year." To Gurney, he said, "It was a month after your five pieces were performed at the College, remember?"

Gurney nodded.

"He was able to compose, even there," Marion Scott said. "He sent the compositions to me and I arranged a charity performance at the College. They were the most remarkable pieces."

"'In Flanders' and 'By A Bierside'," Gurney said. "Two of my favourites."

"Masefield," I said. "'By A Bierside'."

We were all gratified by my identification.

"I had hoped to arrange for a repeat performance once Ivor was safely returned to us all," Marion Scott said. "But, alas, it never happened."

"Alas," Gurney said, bowing his head and then raising it and grinning directly at Will Harvey.

"We tramped for a fortnight, outside every night in the summer before you enlisted," Harvey said. "Elmore, Arlington, Bollapool."

"We went eeling," Gurney said. "With the eelers."

"So we did," Harvey said. "I'd forgotten about that. And the haymaking."

"At Ledbury," Gurney said.

And again, both Harvey and Marion Scott caught my eye to ensure that I understood the significance of these recollections, and of Gurney's ability to remember.

"We sang together as boys in the All Saints Church," Harvey said. "Then in the cathedral choir, though I didn't last long there."

"Ivor was at the King's School," Marion Scott said, and again this was intended to impress me. "Attached to the cathedral," she explained.

She was about to say more when we were interrupted by a sudden argument at the far side of the room. Two men rose from their seats and stood facing each other with their fists clenched. Others rose around them, encouraging them to fight. An orderly stood by the door, making no effort to intervene, laughing at what he saw. I shouted to him and told him to go to the men. At my call, Gurney withdrew his hands from Harvey's and covered his ears. Marion Scott laid a hand on his shoulder.

I apologized to them for having shouted, and then I watched as the orderly went to the two men and pushed them back down into their seats, where they sat without speaking and without even looking at each other.

"It happens all the time," I said to Marion Scott, hoping to make light of the incident. "They seldom actually fight."

Harvey continued watching the two men. The orderly wagged his finger at them and then pretended to slap each of them on their faces.

"The Orpheus Society," Gurney said suddenly, drawing us back to him.

But the incident had intruded on our privacy, and Harvey kept glancing back at the two men, concerned, I supposed, that they might become violent again, and that the four of us might in some way be drawn into the conflict. The orderly left the room, leaving us even further exposed to their intrusion.

"You used to meet at the Palace Library," Harvey said.

"The Orpheus Society," Gurney repeated.

"That's who I mean," Harvey said. "Then you had a stint playing the organ at the Mariners' Church down in the docks. You enjoyed that, but your mother soon put a stop to it. Mind you, I doubt if there was anything you did that she *didn't* have her reservations about."

It was what Marion Scott had already suggested to me two days earlier.

"Were you treated well as a prisoner?" I asked Will Harvey.

"Fair enough, I suppose. And compared to the few months beforehand . . ."

"Where were you?"

He glanced at Gurney before speaking. "St Eloi, and then the Messines Ridge. I was with Ivor at Arras." He shook his head briefly, as though to clear it of a bad memory. "I worked as an orderly most of the time I was a prisoner. In a hospital."

"Like this one?"

"No. A good old blood-cut-and-stitches place. A bit of a cushy number, really. And I swear I only got that because I could sing a few songs in German." He sang a line from one of the songs.

"William's repertoire extends to hundreds," Marion Scott said.

"I used to sing to request," Harvey said. "Ivor did the same. Tell him, Ivor."

Gurney looked at me. "I sang," he said. "When we were far enough back. They all knew the songs. They sang themselves. You might think a farmer's boy wouldn't know, but they all did. Used to beg me to sing for them. I heard songs from some of those boys I'd never even heard of. I used to write them down."

"And send them to me," Marion Scott added.

"Not that they had any idea of history or provenance," Gurney went on. "And when I asked them about music or composers, they used to laugh at me and say there was never any such thing, that they were just songs. Songs that only existed, see, in the mouths of those farm boys. I doubt if many of them will be singing still."

"There's still you and me, Ivor," Harvey said. "We'll walk back up the Severn one day, singing all the way."

I thought for a moment that Marion Scott was going to say something to endorse this hopeless plan, but instead she remained silent, watching Gurney even more closely as he absorbed what Harvey had just suggested.

After a moment's silence, I told Gurney about my visit to the ruined hives, hoping to solicit his interest in the resurrection of the colony.

"Your uncle had bees," Harvey said. "Up in —" He clicked his fingers in an effort of remembering.

"Maisemore," Gurney said.

"You used to help him out with the bees and the honey." He looked from Gurney to me.

"They *all* had hives," Gurney said. "And poultry, and pigs. Up in those hills. Like a separate world up there."

148

"If you know something about bees . . ." I said, waiting.

But this time Gurney's enthusiasm was short-lived, and after his remarks about him singing in the trenches, he seemed unable to concentrate on what was being discussed around him.

"We sang songs from *Elijah*," he said. "At the Three Cities festival. And from the *Messiah*, the *Creation*." He looked to Harvey, his eyes moving swiftly from side to side.

I wondered for a moment if he weren't having some kind of small seizure.

"*The Apostles*," Harvey said. "*Gerontius*."

Gurney scratched his forehead violently, and after a few seconds of this I took his hand and lowered it to his lap, where he pressed it into his leg.

"*The Apostles, Gerontius*," he said. "You weren't singing then," he said to Harvey. "Not good enough for the Three Cities festival." He smiled at this seemingly malicious remark.

"Never good enough for the Three Cities," Harvey said. "All *I* was ever good for was singing for my supper."

Marion Scott touched my arm. "Talk to him again about the bees," she said, unheard by Gurney. "I'm sure he'd appreciate being involved. I think it was an uncle on his father's side." She said this as though she believed it would be of some use in persuading him. I promised her I'd raise the subject again.

I'd spent longer with them than I'd intended and I told her this.

I rose from my chair and both she and Harvey rose alongside me. I guessed there were questions they had both wanted to ask me, but which they would now leave unspoken in the presence of Gurney.

Gurney himself continued to list the pieces he had performed at the festivals, oblivious now even to our presence.

Harvey was the most alarmed at seeing this and I tried to reassure him.

"I haven't seen him for a couple of months," he said. "Work, everything else."

"Is he much changed?"

"More than I'd hoped," he said, adding quickly, and mostly, I suspect, for Marion Scott's benefit, "But it's still old Ivor."

"I would never consider your remarks a sign of disloyalty," I told him.

"No, well . . ." He looked down at Gurney as he spoke.

Marion Scott picked up her case and took a thick folder from it. "I brought you copies of some of Ivor's compositions. I thought you might like to look at them. It might help you in . . . in all you have to do."

"Thank you. Of course." I took the folder from her.

"What *will* you do for him?" Harvey asked me.

"All I — we — can," I said, the answer as dismissive and as reassuring as all such answers were. Regular visitors quickly learned not to ask, and always more for their own sakes than for those of the people they were enquiring about.

"I see," Harvey said.

150

Beside us, Gurney started singing. Both Harvey and Marion Scott recognized the song and Harvey told me its title.

"'The Disappointed Man'," he said.

As Gurney's voice grew louder, Marion Scott leaned down to him and told him to sing more quietly.

His voice fell immediately.

Marion Scott and Harvey left a few minutes later, and I walked with them to the asylum entrance, where a taxi waited to take them back to London.

Harvey and I said little on our short journey through the grounds and along the corridors, held in check by Marion Scott's own silent presence.

At the entrance, Harvey shook my hand and said he'd return soon. I assumed he meant alone.

"He was so changed," he said to me, and I could do no more than acknowledge this concern with a nod.

Marion Scott pulled him gently away from me and into the taxi.

I stood on the street and watched them go, the high wall on either side of me.

Returning to the day room, I saw Gurney entertaining everyone else there by walking up and down in Harvey's forgotten bowler and swinging his umbrella in perfect mimicry of Charlie Chaplin's tramp, cheered and applauded by everyone around him.

CHAPTER
SIXTEEN

"Should we give grief its due, do you think, Doctor Irvine?"

Lyle sat with his eyes closed and his hands pressed hard together, as though in fervent prayer.

I'd encountered him unexpectedly in the corridor outside my consulting room. I asked him if he was waiting to see me.

"Should we afford it all it demands of us?" he said. He opened his eyes and looked at me.

"I don't understand what you're asking me," I told him. "The usual line is that there are as many ways for grief to be endured, accommodated and got rid of as there are people to suffer it. Are you talking about yourself, Gurney, or what?"

My answer disappointed him, and my impatience clearly annoyed him.

He rose from where he sat. "I'm wasting your time," he said.

I opened my door and held it for him. He hesitated a moment and then followed me inside. I was due to begin my rounds of the nearby wards in an hour. I had hoped to spend the time until then catching up on my reports, but I knew that if I turned Lyle away now, he would very likely remain unresponsive to me in the future. He was already more forthcoming than Gurney, and we both understood that he, Lyle, was vital to any understanding I might gain of the other man.

"When I first started practising this branch of medicine, I was met with something approaching disbelief bordering on contempt almost everywhere I went," I said. "Even my mother was unable to completely disguise her uncertainty and then disappointment at my choice. We were called Nerve Doctors, and everybody has nerves. We — me and all my other deluded co-conspirators — were accused by others in our profession of only telling the military authorities what we believed they wanted to hear — that, for whatever reasons, and based upon whatever vague and spurious 'nervous' diagnosis we might make, a man was either fit or unfit for service. There was a conflict of interest, you see, right from the very start."

"Between the individuals and the Army," he said.

"Precisely."

"I'm sure you made all the right decisions," he said. It was the same veiled criticism others had already levelled at me. I waited a moment and asked him again why he had come to see me.

He took an envelope from his pocket.

"From the Board at Barnwood House. The members want to know if I'm going back there for them to do their job."

"I think you should," I told him. "The Board here don't know you. How many other objectors are still locked away in prisons, hospitals? Not many, surely?"

"Probably more than you realize," he said. "I imagine we come under a lot of other headings these days."

I told him he was guessing, and he conceded this. Only those men — like Lyle? — whose mental instability had been *caused* and then exacerbated by their imprisonment and subsequent treatment would still have been incarcerated. It was a subject I was unwilling to discuss with him; everything I said would fall more readily on his side of the argument than my own.

The simple fact that he possessed this understanding of his own chances of parole and release made me even more convinced that staying at Dartford was wrong for him. Back in Gloucester he would be assessed for what he was by people who had assessed him before — in all likelihood by people who had themselves grown increasingly uneasy at the reason for his imprisonment — and there was every justification now for him to be transferred to a convalescent hospital prior to his eventual release a short while later.

Here at Dartford, often four or five Board meetings were considered necessary, and frequently at six-month intervals. The very fact that a man had come to Dartford was enough to persuade most of the panels that both transfer and release were unsafe decisions. And after those four or five prevarications, it was often too late, and even the men who might once have been considered worthy of rehabilitation were no longer regarded as such.

Perhaps — as Alison West had already warned me — there was too much talk of men becoming "institutionalized". But I saw it to some lesser or greater degree in

154

every man I examined or spoke to. I saw men pacing back and forth over the same few yards of ground for hours on end while awaiting an appointment; I saw men burst into tears at a meal bell sounded thirty seconds late, anxious that they might now starve.

I began to explain all this to Lyle, but he stopped me by telling me he'd heard it all before.

"Then it's clear you should return," I said. "It's clear cut. If I were on the Board, I'd have no hesitation in —"

"In releasing me? You didn't know the man — boy — who was first locked up. I've changed, Doctor Irvine."

"And the people at Barnwood House will see that change and *still* consider you worthy of your parole."

He shook his head at this.

"In 1913 there were a hundred and sixty-five thousand registered lunatics in this country. A hundred and sixty-five thousand."

"And you weren't one of them," I said.

"Neither was Ivor. But you've seen his record. I bet there wasn't a single write-up that didn't mention his nerves."

I was again uncertain about the point he was hoping to make.

"Gurney was never committed. Nor was it ever suggested to him that he admit himself voluntarily," I said firmly. "Is it solely because of him that you're insisting on staying here? He'll survive without you. One way or another. Some of them are brought here by their parents, or wives. They all bemoan their losses to begin with, and then imagine it's the end of the world.

155

But they all survive. They all settle down to their treatments and go on living, go on being cared for. And those same wives and families come back again and again to see them. Life goes on." I knew as I spoke that everything I said was working against me.

"They'd be the men over in Stone House," he said dismissively.

Stone House was the original name of the hospital, and the building itself, away from the road, was still in use for the care and treatment of the more serious cases. Men were confined to individual rooms there; most spent their days either heavily sedated or restrained, sometimes both. The building, though now connected to the newer parts of the hospital, was kept separate by a succession of permanently locked doors and a series of equally secure ante-rooms, in which the inmates of Stone House were held when being moved in and out of their rooms during treatment elsewhere.

"The patients I'm talking about are all over the hospital," I said unconvincingly, angry that he was deliberately misconstruing what I was telling him. I tried to remember how many men were currently being held in Stone House, and if any of them were there as a consequence of illnesses brought on by Active Service. It was unlikely that there were any of these, but I resisted telling him this in case he already knew better and my argument was to be finally lost at this simple, avoidable turn.

"Ivor's worrying about his 'electricals' again," he said. He sounded conciliatory, concerned, suddenly unwilling to prolong this small conflict.

156

"I've treated hundreds of limbs with Ajax dry cells," I said, sounding as though I were endorsing the batteries.

He cupped his hands around his head. "Not spasms. In his head," he said. "When he's at his worst, he says they're all around him."

"'They'?"

"Currents. Electrical currents, waves. All aimed directly at him. Sometimes it's music, sometimes just voices. Mostly he says it's just a kind of noise, like static."

"I've never seen him like that," I said.

"Then you should."

"Why? Because it would better convince me of your own misguided reasons for wanting to stay with him? What do you imagine you're doing for him — looking after him, protecting him from something that only you know about?"

He smiled coldly at the remark and all it revealed. "He even talks back to some of them," he said. "To the ones he knows."

"Knows how?"

"Musicians. Famous people. He gets some big names coming through some days." He smiled again as he said this.

"When I worked in the Base Hospital at Le Touquet," I said, changing our direction yet again, "the first man I treated walked back and forth across the ward with his arms held out by his sides, feet one in front of the other, heel to toe, his chin up, eyes forward, as though he were walking on a tightrope. Back and forth, hour after hour, grasping on to the bed frames at either end of the room as though he'd just crossed a chasm a hundred feet up in the air."

He listened to me intently, raising his own arms in the manner I'd described.

"I cured him in five minutes flat," I said. "Less. A weak current to his muscles. First fingers, then forearms, then biceps and triceps. I even ran a current over his shoulders for good measure. And all the time I was doing this, I told him that the treatment was working perfectly and that he would soon no longer have to go on with his performance. I did it in front of everybody else on the ward, and when I'd finished and the man had settled down to read a newspaper, everyone applauded him. He returned to Active Service a week later."

And again, whatever point I believed I was making to him decreased in impact the more I said.

"What happened to him?" he said.

I told him I didn't know and he apologized for the remark.

"Are you telling me you can do something similar for Ivor and his 'electricals'?" he said.

"I can try. I can ask Osborne what *he* thinks might work best."

"Osborne is happy to let him rot," he said, raising his voice. "Osborne thinks Ivor's only here to make life a little more convenient for his clever friends to come and visit him. Gloucester's a long way off in the back of beyond. And how long do you think *that* would have lasted, them traipsing up there month after month?"

"And is that what Gurney believes?"

"Ivor says 'So what?'," he said reluctantly. "Easy come, easy go, that's our Ivor. According to him, everything's always for the best."

"Hardly," I said.

"No, well . . ."

"Your own records contain nothing very specific about your treatment at either Durham or Pentonville," I said. Another diversionary course.

"That's because no one saw the need to write any of it down. Probably had other things to worry about. Besides, it's a mania, all this record-keeping. What does it ever achieve? What does it prove?"

"You could have insisted on a full account being kept. The Governors have a duty to —"

"To what? They had no duty to people like me, no duty at all. In Durham, a month after I arrived —" He stopped abruptly, agitated, lowering his head to his chest and pressing his hands back together.

"Tell me," I said.

"They stoned me and two other objectors from the edge of the exercise yard. Usually, we were taken out alone for an hour here and there — nothing regular, as specified, nothing to ever actually look forward to — but on this occasion the warders took us out when there were twenty or thirty others still out there, waiting to go back in."

"And they threw stones at you?"

"They *stoned* us. My parents' neighbours threw stones at *them* when everything came to light — broke every single pane of glass in the house and garden;

159

threw clods of soil at my mother in her Sunday best on her way to the Meeting House. In that prison yard, me and the two others were stoned."

"And the warders?"

"They stood and watched and laughed at it all for a few minutes before stepping in. The three of us huddled together in a corner, our backs to the stone-throwers, trying to protect our heads. We must have made a very easy target. One of the other boys was knocked out. I had three of my ribs cracked. I bled from my ears for a week afterwards. And all the time it was happening I could hear the cheering and the shouts of encouragement from the windows overlooking the yard. It was clear enough to everybody else there that we were getting exactly what we deserved."

"You ought to have —"

"I was seventeen. Seventeen. Look at me."

I could think of nothing to say to him.

"I watched my mother walk down the street of a village she'd lived in for almost fifty years, pelted with mud by her neighbours. I saw the children run up to her and throw their sods, encouraged by their parents to get as close as they could to her. And she ignored it all, just kept her head up as best she could and carried on walking. She *forgave* them, you see. That was her nature, her way, her belief. It was all she could do — forgive them. I wanted to go out and throw the sods and the stones back at them, but she wouldn't let me. And there's no record of any of that, either, Doctor Irvine. No record whatsoever."

He caught his breath for a moment, his head still bowed.

"Suppose that Board back up in Gloucester could see me now," he said eventually. "Are you still so convinced they'd send me off for a rest-cure up in the hills somewhere?"

"Being angry at what you endured is probably as good an indicator of sanity as anything else," I said.

"I still wanted to wring their necks for what they did to her. And to my father. I still wanted to do something that might make me stop feeling so bloody useless." He apologized for the profanity. It was an offence throughout the hospital, usually punished by a brief withdrawal of privileges.

"And is that why you're looking out for Gurney now?" I asked him. "Because you're doing something *useful* for him?"

He shrugged. "I imagine all his friends are better placed to look out for him than I am," he said. "I'm a lunatic, remember? Whether by nature or design, I doubt if anybody — you included — can properly say, but it's still what I am in the eyes of the world."

"I spoke to one of the men applauding the cured tightrope-walker," I said, remembering the incident for the first time. "He had a wound in his chest, over his heart, still open. None of the surgeons who'd operated on him could believe he'd survived, but he had. His heart was scarcely touched. Most of his ribs were smashed up, one of his lungs, and he still had shrapnel embedded in his spine that they were waiting to take out. I went to him after the tightrope-walking

161

exhibition and he told me the reason he'd survived was because when the shrapnel hit him and knocked him twenty feet through the air, his heart had been in his mouth."

Lyle smiled at the anecdote. "I wonder how many times he's told the same story since," he said.

"You can ask me what happened to him."

"Meaning he survived and was sent home?" he said.

"Both of those things," I said. "He even walked again. After a fashion."

CHAPTER
SEVENTEEN

I made a start on clearing and re-building the hives two days later.

Osborne agreed for Gurney, Lyle and several other interested inmates to participate in the work, but only on the understanding that Cox and a pair of his orderlies were also present. It was a small concession to make.

We began mid-afternoon. The sun was out and the ground beneath the trees was firm and dry.

Our first task was to cut away the tall grass, weeds and brambles, and we did this with scythes. Both Gurney and Lyle were adept at using these, as were the other volunteers — three elderly men — and I soon abandoned my own clumsy and ineffectual cutting and turned my attention instead to the boxes.

The bees were not yet fully active, and succumbed easily to the little smoke I gave them. I wore the hat Alison West had made for me. I told the others to wrap lengths of the muslin around their heads if they came close to an active hive.

Alison came out to us an hour after the work had started. She brought us drinks. She was on duty until six, and said she would return to the orchard then.

Osborne had insisted that the patients finished their work an hour earlier, in good time for their evening meal.

I told Alison my plan for the afternoon, and she asked me how I intended capturing and confining the bees. I showed her the sacks I'd brought with me. They were small and torpid broods. I had also gathered a collection of cardboard tubes, sealed at one end, in case I came across any surviving queens. If I was able to capture a queen, then wherever I placed her in one of the refurbished hives, her brood would follow and congregate around her.

Alison examined the tube I showed her. She recalled, as I had, the sealed tubes in which queens had been sent to our fathers. Each one with its block of sugar attached to keep the bees alive during their journey. The insects had been known to survive in transit for up to a month in these containers. My father's favourite source of new bees had been the Berlin Academy, and Charles and I had fought for the stamps these held. It seemed strange to us both that the bees should come from so far away, but my father was convinced that they were the best he could acquire, and so he persisted.

Having distributed her drinks, Alison left us, saying she regretted that she couldn't join us sooner in the work.

She took her jug and glasses to Cox and his orderlies, Lewis included, none of whom showed any inclination to join us in our labours, and who instead sat on a low wall away from the hives, occasionally calling to me or one of the others that we weren't working hard enough.

164

One of the older men took these remarks to heart and I told him to ignore the calls. He told me he was convinced he'd seen a queen enter one of the hives and he pointed it out to me.

Having cut the grass and undergrowth, we stacked this against the wall. Cox said he'd burn it, but I stopped him from doing this, knowing that the smoke would drift back to the hives and further disturb the already agitated bees.

"What's that, then?" He indicated the smoke can I held, its rag smouldering at the spout.

"I need to use the smoke carefully," I told him. "Too much, everywhere, will only confuse and then panic the bees. I need to be able to control it."

This rebuttal made him angry and he turned his back on me and walked away.

My priority, having cleared the ground, was to remove all those hives rotted beyond repair to eliminate the possibility of infection from them. The structures were filled with earth and debris and other insects, and I couldn't take the chance that there were any hive beetles or varroa mites among these; or, worse still, that the dormant spores of foulbrood were present.

I laid canvas sheets beneath these structures and tumbled them to the ground, crushing the larger pieces of the rotten frames with my feet. The debris was carried beyond the orchard wall and dumped there. I called to Cox that if he still wanted a fire, then he could burn this mound of wood later. He ignored me, glancing at me briefly before turning back to his

165

subordinates. They smoked and shared jokes, relieved to be outside and doing so little in such fine weather.

I went with Gurney and Lyle to the first of the sound hives and Gurney examined it, pronouncing only its stand to be beyond repair. He took off the lid and lifted out several frames. I could see immediately that he had done the work before and that he was not alarmed by the bees. There were few insects, and he allowed these to rise around him and then disperse. Lyle took the dirt-encrusted frames from him and laid them on the ground. Four of these were sound and re-usable; the remainder would be made up from elsewhere. Gurney scraped the inside of the frames with a long blade, wiping what he collected over his sleeve and leaving black lines there.

Lyle scraped the individual frames, revealing the wood beneath. The hives had once been bleached and then whitewashed, but this had not been done for many years — not since their abandonment by the nuns, most likely — and the white flakes of desiccated paint fell to the ground like blossom. We were all encouraged by most of what we discovered.

My only true disappointment during that first hour was to realize how few of the bees themselves still remained. I searched for the queens that might have survived, but found none of these. Even the hive in which the old man said he thought he'd seen a queen was empty. I bagged the bulk of several small broods in the sacks and left these in the shade of an old pear tree. I had hoped to find more healthy communities, however small. But I was at least encouraged by the knowledge that once the hives were ready to receive them, then any new or replacement broods I introduced would quickly multiply and build up.

Alison West had wondered aloud at the advisability of keeping *any* of the bees that remained, especially considering how dilapidated the hives were, and how exhausted their colonies. I had told her how swiftly the redistributed bees would form their own self-sufficient colonies, but she'd remained sceptical. I knew from my father's hives that seldom had any of them been empty and unproductive in the summer, however hard and destructive the previous winter had been. She said I was looking too far ahead — two, perhaps three years. She made this sound impossibly distant.

Gurney, I noticed, worked largely in silence, whereas Lyle spoke endlessly, questioning him, asking his advice, answering his own remarks when Gurney's answers were not forthcoming. On occasion, Gurney would pause in whatever he was doing, stand upright, his face raised, his eyes tightly closed, and he would murmur or hum to himself, perhaps composing something new or remembering an earlier composition; or perhaps simply remembering an earlier time when he had undertaken similar work elsewhere. I wished I could have spoken to him then, asked him what he was remembering. But I knew that if I had interrupted him, he would have said nothing, or at best made some excuse, keeping these necessary, sustaining secrets to himself. Lyle, too, I noticed, fell silent at these times, and pretended to busy himself in his own work while keeping a watchful eye on his friend.

After an hour, I told everyone to stop their work and to rest. The three older men went immediately to where Cox and the orderlies sat and asked them for cigarettes.

I sat with Gurney and Lyle beside the gently humming sacks. The bees inside would remain calm in their restraining darkness. Occasionally, one or two insects would emerge from a hole, rise into the air, hover a moment and then return to the others.

"My uncle always said that if you must buy bees, then you should always pay silver for them," Gurney said. "Or, better still, barter for them. Buy them with comb or honey." He watched Lyle as he spoke. "When I was a small boy there was always a psalm-singing ceremony in front of the hives each year, the whole congregation." He paused. "As many as six people sometimes, and not one of them under eighty." Both he and Lyle laughed at the remark. "And when he gave a brood or a queen to another smallholder, he always insisted on a written contract from the man, promising to take proper care of the insects. He used to write these up himself; all the other man had to attach in most cases was a muddy thumbprint."

"And no bad language," Lyle said suddenly, surprising us both.

"That's right," Ivor said. "No blaspheming in front of the bees." To me, he said, "It upsets them, see. They can't abide profanity."

It was something else I already knew, but I said nothing, happy to indulge myself alongside them.

I knew, too, that Achilles, Alexander the Great and all the Earls of Southampton had been embalmed and then buried in honey.

My mother had sent Charles to turn those hives closest to the house away from the door on the day my father's body had been taken out. She had then pointed out to us how silent the bees had fallen while this was happening. I had heard the usual background drone of the creatures across the garden, but had said nothing. She and Charles had stood together, their hands cupped to their ears as though straining to hear the same thing.

"We gave them gifts," Gurney said. "Wedding cake, christening buns, funeral biscuits dipped in wine. You forgot the hives at your peril. *You* might forget, but they never would, the bees."

And Marionne, Herod's wife. She was preserved in honey, too. Executed and preserved. My mother had put a cake of honey into my father's coffin. Food for the Afterlife. His finest white honey. The willowherb honey that few others appreciated.

"Willowherb," I said involuntarily.

"Fireweed," Gurney said, looking directly at me. "Bombweed. Light a fire, let it burn down, and the fireweed always comes."

"My father's favourite honey," I told him.

"You won't beat borage," he said absently. "My uncle up in Maisemore used to swear by milkweed and golden rod. They had wild balsam growing on the Frome. Said it had come from seeds washed out of

Spanish fleeces imported to the mills at Whitminster. The bees went for that like it was nectar."

It grew warmer, even in the dappled shade of the trees, and I sensed that they were impatient to return to work. The old men sitting with the orderlies kept looking across at us, unhappy, perhaps, that I would soon signal them to return to the hives. Cox raised his hand to me, said something to the others, and everyone in the small group laughed.

"Jokes at our expense," Lyle said, and then rose from where he sat. Gurney followed him, and the two of them returned to the hives. I waved to let the others know that we were resuming, but several minutes passed before they returned to us.

We worked for a further two hours, and at the end of that time, when Lyle and I returned the bees to their refurbished homes, we had salvaged a dozen hives. A few of their bases would still need to be rebuilt, but this was a simple enough task, and would not unduly delay the overall rebuilding of the colonies.

The honey frames and brood boxes in some of the hives would need to be removed again and repaired further, but that too was straightforward. What mattered now was that the structures were mostly weatherproof, and that all the vital bee-spaces had been cleared, allowing fresh air to circulate with the insects. All rot and detritus was gone, and the bees that remained could be left to their own devices until the opportunity arose to increase their number. The absence of queens remained my only true concern.

170

"Put an advert in the local paper," Gurney suggested. "There's always queens going begging."

It seemed a simple solution and I told him I would.

Lyle asked me if he and Gurney would be allowed to return to the hives without supervision, during their usual free time in the grounds. I considered this unlikely — especially in light of all my other hard-won concessions from Osborne — but did not tell him this.

"Of course," I said.

He could not have missed the note of forced conviction in my voice, but he said nothing.

"Hear that, Oi Be Gurney? We'll be back down here filling up on honey this time next month."

But Gurney, despite his earlier bout of reminiscing, was now largely silent, occasionally standing with his face to the sun and humming to himself, a note not entirely dissimilar to that of the bees themselves.

Lyle continued helping me return the bees to the hives, unrolling the sacks into the open structures and then leaving them as the first of the creatures dropped into the spaces below. Gurney held the roofs ready, carefully placing these over the empty sacks as they were pulled away.

Shortly before five, Cox came to us and looked around him at all we had achieved.

"Doesn't look much different," he said dismissively. "You two don't look to have done much. Ask me, Osborne made a big mistake in letting you take this on."

Angry that the remarks were made in front of Gurney and Lyle after all their work, I told him to shut up, adding that he didn't have the slightest idea about what we had or hadn't achieved because he knew nothing whatsoever about the hives. Beside him, both Gurney and Lyle smiled at the remark.

Cox turned immediately to Lyle. "Think that's funny, do you? Funny is it, you bloody coward? Think I'm not going to go straight to Osborne and tell him what a bloody waste of time all this has been? Think this is the start of something, do you? Another cushy little billet, out here in the fresh air and sunshine, swanning about and doing bugger all all afternoon?"

Lyle bowed his head to avoid Cox's eyes. But Gurney, I noticed, looked hard at Cox, and his mouth trembled, as though he were summoning up his own small store of courage to answer the man back. And knowing what response this would immediately solicit from the all-powerful Cox, and what being amid the hives had meant to both Gurney and Lyle, I held Gurney's arm, tightening my grip until he turned to me, understood my intent and grew calm. Lyle, for his part, was content to remain the target of Cox's anger, if it meant that by this simple expedient, Gurney was spared.

Eventually, Cox stopped shouting, turned and walked away from us.

"You ought to go back inside," I said to Lyle.

He looked down at his hands, which were shaking in anger, clenching and unclenching by his side.

"Ignore him," I said. "Don't rise to his provocation. You know how he works."

172

He glanced at Gurney and then reached out and held his arm. "Come on, Ivor. They'll know if you're upset and then they'll come sticking their noses in." He went closer to him. "And as for your balsam honey, I wouldn't take it off your hands for free."

But Gurney remained deaf to these gentle reassurances, still staring to where Cox and the other orderlies awaited us.

I walked with them back to the dining hall, ensuring that Cox was given no further opportunity to continue haranguing them.

And afterwards, waiting until I saw Gurney and Lyle sitting with their meals, I went back to the orchard and waited there for Alison West to return.

CHAPTER
EIGHTEEN

"It appears there are one or two things our budding Tchaikovsky's seen fit not to tell us." Osborne sat back in his seat, his legs splayed.

"I wasn't aware that Gurney had said much of anything to anyone," I said.

"Perhaps with good reason." If he'd heard the scepticism in my voice then he was careful not to respond to it.

"I should have smelled a rat when the application for him to come here arrived. Who in their right mind would actually *apply* to come here?"

I wondered if he'd intended the poor joke, and then if the remark was intended to solicit a specific response from me. I remained silent, waiting for whatever revelation he was building up to.

"And if he didn't apply himself, then he didn't put up much of a fight to prevent others doing it on his behalf."

He meant Marion Scott.

"Has something happened?" I said eventually.

"Happened?"

I was about to say "To upset you," but thought better of the remark. "Has Marion Scott said something about Gurney's treatment?"

He slapped his hand on to an envelope on his desk.

"She's already complaining to me that we aren't creating" — he took out a closely written sheet — "that we aren't providing her Dear Little Ivor with 'a sufficiently relaxed or stimulating environment for him to continue his work'. 'Environment'? What's that supposed to be? What does she think this place is? 'Relaxed'? 'Stimulating'?"

I waited until he'd calmed down. Again, it seemed to me to be a crisis entirely of his own making.

"I'll deal with her, if you like," I told him. It was why I was there, what he wanted to hear from me, another unspoken part of the contract between us now that Gurney was my patient.

"Why? Because you agree with everything she's saying? Because you're as convinced as *she* is that we're harbouring another Mozart or — or Shakespeare in our midst?" He slid the letter back into the envelope and flicked it towards me. It fell to the floor and I retrieved it.

"I'm making no allowances," he said. "No concessions, none whatsoever. Gurney's here for a reason. And the sooner *she* understands that, the better. She treats this place like an Eastbourne hotel. She's coming back again. What's that, three times in hardly a week? Apparently, she left some of Gurney's scribbling with you. You might have afforded me the decency and courtesy of telling me."

"I didn't think it —"

"Didn't think it what? Relevant? Important? In future, I want to know every stunt she tries to pull. Besides . . ." He trailed off, smiling to himself.

175

I waited.

"As it happens, and strictly *entre nous*, our little genius Ivor might not be all he makes himself out to be." He looked at me, again prompting a reaction, wanting me to urge him to go on.

"In what way?" I said. Whatever the revelation, it would no doubt contain some further implied criticism of my own response — or, so far, lack of it — to Gurney and his treatment.

"I was up in town last night. The Savoy. Dinner with an old colleague. Professor Poulson. You might have heard of him."

I had. "Of course," I said. I'd worked with the man briefly at Maghull, when he'd tried unsuccessfully to get Ronald Rows dismissed and discredited for his work on the hundreds of shell-shock patients we were then treating. Results, common sense and necessity had finally prevailed, and eventually it was Poulson who was "retired" and returned to the London Health Authority.

"Anyhow, Poulson was at Bangour War Hospital outside Edinburgh when our Ivor washed up there straight from Ypres or wherever."

"He was gassed," I said. "And wounded."

"Gassed? Not according to Poulson, he wasn't. Hardly affected at all. 'Gas and Nerves' it said on his docket. Poulson said that right from the start he could see that Gurney was swinging it, a malingerer. He wasn't the first and he wouldn't be the last. They had him down for a month's rest and then back to A.S., where —"

176

"G.O.K.," I said, interrupting him, the unexpected memory expressing itself before I could even consider it.

"What?"

"G.O.K. God Only Knows. It's what they used to write on some of the labels attached to the wounded men sent to us."

He looked at me for a moment. "As I was saying . . ." But by then he'd lost his train of thought.

"Besides," I said, "whatever happened then, it was six years ago. It surely has no bearing on his condition now." It was a weak and uncertain argument, and my own lack of conviction was clear to him. Once again, the only true conflict between us now was my own, seemingly misguided defence of Gurney.

"No? They didn't even have a record of *where* he was supposedly gassed," he said. "That doesn't strike you as strange? Another man sent from the Gloucesters who washed up at Bangour the same time as Gurney said they were always falling into ground where the gas was held in pockets in the churned-up earth and water holes. He said Gurney had probably just fallen into a pocket of this, breathed it in, got it in his eyes and throat, and had then got himself sent back from the front complaining of worse effects than he was actually suffering."

"We don't know any of that," I said, already sensing the gathering force of all that might be about to follow. I remembered what Gurney had told me about the smell of the gas.

"He's shown no symptoms since," Osborne said. "None whatsoever. According to Poulson, the first of Gurney's books was published the day after his arrival in Edinburgh. If that hadn't happened, they'd probably have transferred him even sooner. Even then he was a bit of an oddity, a misfit. And that's not all." He was getting into his stride now, and was clearly relishing each new revelation. Nothing he'd said so far had convinced me.

"There was a nurse. In Edinburgh. Caring for Gurney. According to Poulson our boy formed an 'unsuitable' — or was it 'inappropriate' — attachment to her. Stricken, apparently, besotted. Poulson even told me her name. Something Scottish. A few years older than Gurney. He made a fool of himself with her. Letters, poems, presents; music, even. She felt caught up in it all and then told her superiors. Moved her away. According to Poulson, it looked like Gurney's first fling. What was he, twenty-six, -seven? His first romance. If it was ever that, anywhere except in his own mind. I bet the blessed Marion never once mentioned *that* to you when extolling his virtues."

I tried to remember. "She didn't," I said. "But it's surely not uncommon, especially among men fresh from the Front, men recuperating."

He looked at me for a moment. "You ought to listen to yourself sometimes, Doctor Irvine. Everything you say sounds like an excuse or an apology for the man."

I let the remark pass.

"Poulson says they packed Gurney off fast enough after that. Back to a command depot in Northumbria.

Gave him an All-Clear. Fit for ordinary training again. I bet that put a rod up him."

"And so Poulson was confirmed in his view of Gurney as a malingerer?"

"Of course he was. The man was a bloody liability. Otherwise why not send him straight back to France?"

I knew from Gurney's medical notes that he'd been in Newcastle General Hospital early in 1918 with stomach trouble. That, too, had been attributed to the after-effects of his gassing. And after that he'd been sent to Durham for further training, where he'd had the first of a succession of breakdowns. The notes were no more specific. By May of that year he'd been admitted to Lord Derby's War Hospital in Warrington. It was there that the most complete notes of his condition had been made.

Gurney had come under the supervision of George Robertson, with whom I'd afterwards worked at Warrington, and whose judgement I rated as highly as Ronald Rows'. Robertson was convinced that Gurney had suffered a delayed, but complete nervous breakdown as a consequence of both his gassing and of shell-shock. Apparently, Gurney had attempted suicide while in Robertson's charge, and had afterwards asked to be transferred to an asylum where he might be properly treated for his suffering. He'd gone from Warrington to the Napsbury at St Albans.

"Apparently, even after he'd been discharged, Gurney went on writing to this nurse and sending her gifts. He inscribed his book to her. Whoever she was, she can't have been much of a reader, or at least not of

179

verse. She gave it to Poulson. She wanted nothing to do with Gurney. At least *she* showed good sense in that direction. He had his regimental badge gilded with cheap gold and sent that to her, too."

"And did she give that to Poulson?"

"Naturally. Everything's probably still sitting in the Bangour storeroom. Not much of a one for poetry himself, Poulson. A bit of Kipling, perhaps, but not the shoddy stuff Gurney was spewing out." He waved his fingers to suggest the insubstantial nature of Gurney's poems.

There were no notes in the file following Gurney's transfer from Warrington to St Albans.

"What happened at Napsbury?" I said.

"They did what Poulson said *he* should have done sooner. Examined Gurney properly, found nothing wrong with him and then sent him home."

"To Gloucester, back to his family?"

"That's what Poulson said. After swinging it to stay in Blighty, it seems he was now swinging it for a proper discharge and a better pension. He was up for the Pensions Committee three times in a month. Sent him back to Gloucester to chew straws with the rest of them there."

I made a mental note to ask Marion Scott about Gurney's time back at home following his discharge. By my reckoning, he'd left St Albans less than a month before the end of the war. If Osborne or Poulson were right in suggesting that Gurney was a malingerer, then what would have been the point of any further pretence from Gurney? There would have been no need. No one

180

would have sent him back to France. No one would have allowed his previous three years of exemplary and conscientious service to count against him. And surely no one would have accepted what Poulson was saying and use this to reduce his pension, especially not in light of Gurney's previous service history.

"So you see," Osborne said, locking his fingers and sitting back in his chair, "considerably more than meets the eye, wouldn't you agree? Played any of his music yet?"

I hadn't. "I —"

"Thought not."

It would only have encouraged him to continue if I'd told him again what I thought of Gurney's poetry. Our interview was over. It had achieved nothing. He was more confirmed than ever in his prejudices. And I, in turn, had wrested another small part of Gurney away from him. It was clear to me that he was still intrigued about what might yet be revealed about Gurney — or, more precisely, what Gurney himself might reveal of his talents — but he was even more concerned now, and especially considering all the possible changes about to take place in the asylum, to close the file on Gurney, to have both his diagnosis and treatments confirmed and then to let Gurney fade into the background, one of hundreds, a distant figure on the lawn, standing with his back to the building and waiting for a bell to sound.

I started to tell him what progress we had made with the hives.

"Cox told me all about it," he said. He yawned. "I asked him to come and let me know when you'd finished."

"I wanted to talk to you about Cox," I said.

"What about him? As I've already told you — he's good at what he does. If you're about to make an official complaint against him, then I advise you to reconsider. Officially or unofficially, Cox has my full support."

"He bullies the patients," I said, caught off-balance by this opening salvo in defence of the man.

"'Bullies'? He's firm with them, that's all. It's what they need, most of them. It's what most of them *expect*, what they respond to best."

"And he shows no respect whatsoever to his superiors."

"Meaning yourself? What do you expect?"

"And you," I said.

"Me what?"

"He shows no respect, no deference to you, either."

"Says who? You? I think I'll be the judge of that. Besides, if *I* felt that, then surely it would be up to *me* to say something to him. I think you're making assumptions, Doctor Irvine."

"After the assault by Barstow," I said, "ten days ago. He was rude to you. In front of others. He does only what he wants to do. And he treats the orderlies under him like he's still their sergeant-major."

Osborne smiled at the remark. "And that's a bad thing? I don't hear any of *them* complaining."

"Only because they're terrified of him."

"I'll ask you again, Doctor Irvine, where do you think we are? What do you think this place is? If you've got a genuine, supportable complaint, then make it.

182

Make it through the proper channels and let it get dealt with through those same channels. That's what they exist for." He paused. "Well?"

"All I wanted —"

"The proper channels. If you're committed to —" He stopped abruptly and smiled. "Oh, I see — is this in connection with Gurney, too? What's happened? Has Cox raised his voice to *him*? To him or his pathetic little friend? Has he told them to do something they didn't want to do? Something to make them get their hands dirty?" He paused again. "*Is* that what all this is about? Did Gurney get stung or something? Because if he did, Cox never mentioned it to me."

There was no answer to this barrage, and any genuine complaint I might have had against Cox had now been undermined by Osborne having added Gurney to the uncertain tangle of conflicts and allegiances. I was still surprised, however, by his insistent defence of Cox, especially in light of how he, Osborne, sometimes treated his own staff.

He considered me for a moment, and then relaxed.

"I hear what you're telling me," he said. "Let's just say that Cox has his ways, and that he sometimes overreaches his authority on certain matters. But he gets things done. And sometimes those things can only get done by men like Cox. You're not the first to sit in front of me and tell me all this. But most of those others are long gone."

"And Cox is still here?" *Doing your dirty work?*

"He says you all made a good job of clearing the trees."

"It's an orchard."

"Trees, orchard, whatever. I was wondering if it might be a good idea to have them felled. It's a fair-sized piece of land. Might come in handy for more greenhouses or a field of potatoes. It's not as though we aren't going to need all the space we can get in the future, not with the way things are going here. Our numbers seem to go up every month. I was only saying to Webster last night . . ."

I stopped listening to him, wondering if the remark about the orchard had been a threat or a warning, and if it hadn't just been maliciously made on the spur of the moment to add a final emphasis to everything else he'd just warned me against.

I put Marion Scott's letter in my pocket and rose from my seat.

He stopped talking.

"I'm boring you," he said. He shook his head slightly, and then dismissed me with an even slighter wave of his fingers.

CHAPTER
NINETEEN

"You wrote that Death was a small thing, as long as no dishonour was attached to it."

Gurney sat alone in his room. I'd been with him almost an hour and so far he'd said very little.

" 'Death is a very little thing, so long as dishonour does not lie there,' " he quoted, correcting me, clearly intrigued and perhaps encouraged by even my imperfect memory of the lines. His voice became sonorous, perfectly pitched in both tone and pace to the words.

"Do you remember the rest?" I asked him.

He recited the poem in its entirety, all eight lines, and when he'd finished I felt a chill in the room, as though a door elsewhere had been silently opened and all the warmth had been sucked from it.

"I first wrote the words in a letter to Marion," he said.

"You were talking of the war dead."

He considered this and shook his head. "All men. Death itself conveys no honour."

"But the means of dying might?"

He shrugged, but held my gaze, as though encouraging me to go on speculating.

185

When I said nothing, he said, "They put the wrong initial on my identity disc."

"Common enough, I imagine."

The offhand remark annoyed him. "A 'J' instead of an 'I'. How many Gurneys did they have? Me and my brother, that's who. They should have got it right. They should have known to get it right. They never understood nor cared what that might do to a man. Not to a man on Active Service, not with people scanning all those lists in the newspapers."

I waited for his anger to subside.

I was there to continue my assessment of him. Two days had passed since all of Osborne's tainted revelations. It was, I realized, my first meeting with Gurney alone. I'd encountered Lyle in the dining room on my way through, and discovering my destination, he'd wanted to accompany me. But I had insisted on seeing Gurney without him. "I'll come in an hour, then," he had said, as though my time with Gurney were a concession he alone might grant me. I told him I'd come back through the room when I'd finished. "An hour," he'd repeated, as though he had neither heard me speak nor understood my intent.

"You spent four years back in Gloucester," I said to Gurney. "After your discharge."

He put on his wire-rimmed spectacles, again making himself look even younger. They were cheap glasses, probably Army-issue, with flat lenses and circular frames the size of pennies. They left a faint line across the bridge of his nose and from his eyes to his ears because they were too tight for him.

186

"I was never right," he said. "Is that what you've come to find out? Never right. Never right from Edinburgh onwards. I went back to my family. I should never have gone back there, not to them."

"Because you felt at odds with them?"

"Them with me, more like. Ronald had had his compassionate discharge by then. He was wounded. Welsh Guards. It hurt him that, being put in with that lot. He wanted the Gloucesters, like me. My father was ill. He would have had me home, and no problems. Cancer. My mother was never the same, and she made Winifred's life one long bad childhood."

"Your sister."

"We were never close. There was another." He stopped talking and held a finger to the bridge of his nose.

"Another child?"

"Between me and Winifred. She was eldest. I was next. Four years. A boy. Baby boy. Born and buried and that was the last anyone ever spoke of him. My father tried, but he was the only one. A dead birth. Is that what you're asking me all these questions for? Will it all play some part?" He looked from side to side, as though realizing only then that we were alone in the room.

"I need to know how best to proceed," I told him. It was at best an evasive answer, and I regretted it. "Your treatment and medication."

"I'm happy with whatever I get," he said, his anxiety rising. "This is where I want to be. I've seen other men cause nothing but trouble. Madmen who swore they were sane to their bones. You looking to send me back to Gloucester? You won't hear the same from me."

"You appear to have had a succession of breakdowns, some only minor, but all of them taking their toll on you one way or another," I said, avoiding his eyes. "Is that how *you* see it?"

He considered his answer carefully; unhappy, I suspected, of saying anything to dispute my own barely formed notions of his suffering.

"Depression," he said. "Always that."

"You've always suffered from it?"

"They always wrote it."

"It was usually only used as a form of shorthand to encompass a great deal more. There are men in here who insist that being here is the only thing that depresses them."

He smiled at this. "Was it a full four years? Back in Gloucester?"

I looked at my notes. "You were discharged from Napsbury in October — eighteen, and committed to Barnwood House in the same month — twenty-two."

"I was never back home for all of that time. After my father died, I tried my luck in London again."

"Back at the Royal College," I said.

"Before that, I tried for work on the boats at Beachley Docks. I traipsed up and down the river. Bristol. I tried for work at the docks there, too, and on the ships. That's what my father used to say of me — 'Always got his face to the sea, that boy.' He said I'd be better for a long spell on the boats. America, Canada. He said I'd need Liverpool for that, or Southampton.

That's the way I always went, see? South. Always downriver. You know what they gave me, what pension? Twelve shillings a week. That was why I went back to London. They sent the police looking for me in Bristol. It was them who took me home. I was looking for Will Harvey. I thought he'd be at Crickley. Crickley, I went to. Then Birdlip and Lydney. I was a healthy man, then. Healthy enough to walk all day and then sleep in a field. I walked back and forth to London from Gloucester."

He paused at the happy memory and then savoured it, licking his lips as though he could taste it.

I doubted if he had any idea of his scattered, staccato delivery of all this. But in all the time I'd spent with him, it was the most loquacious I'd heard him, and I considered telling him this, hoping he'd appreciate the remark. But I knew too that it might just as easily prod him back into his usual suspicious silence, believing that I was again setting my small and unavoidable traps for him.

"Were you still writing during all that time?"

"Marion was collecting everything together. I destroyed a lot of it. At St Albans. They said I was selfish. Some of the chargehands mimicked my accent. How was I selfish? How can three years' service be the mark of a selfish man? I had such dreams at that time. They put it on worse than I ever used it, that accent."

I remembered another phrase from one of his poems. "You wrote about 'faithful dreams'," I said.

"I tried to remember them. I wrote some of them down for Marion in my letters home."

189

"Did you never write to your parents, to your family?"

He shook his head. "Everything *they* wanted to hear they got from the newspapers. Or from Ronald. Now *there* was dirt and coarseness. An old French farmer at Amiens once came into our billet and asked me why we English went to so much trouble to remember our dead. All the others laughed at him when I told them what he'd said."

"You speak French?" I asked him.

"Enough to work out what he was asking me. Sometimes it seemed the dead were all we had. I went into what was left of Amiens Cathedral. Pitch black. We were all living like poor savages then. We might have done something afterwards for the dead, but we always emptied their pockets first. I helped a lad who'd been a joiner spell out their names for his crosspieces."

He bowed his head and we sat in silence for a few minutes. The voices of men working outside came in to us.

"You went to a convalescent home for neurasthenics," I said. "Near Bristol."

"Bristol docks? Was I down there again looking for work, then?"

"It doesn't say."

"'Always got his face to the sea.'" And then he seemed to remember. "It was a magistrate in Gloucester sent me there. Doctors I'd never seen before. And magistrates who always sided with the police, who'd already listened to the doctors. I suppose

190

there'd been the usual complaints. Was it Bristol? Outside, then. Somewhere in the country."

"You were only there for a fortnight before going back to Barnwood House."

"They put my pension up to two pounds. There was other money, too. Ronald took most of it. My father was dead, otherwise he'd have sorted things out for me. Was it only a fortnight? Nobody minds their own business, see? What's wrong with wanting to be left alone? What danger was I ever to anyone else? What danger was I ever to myself? I had a stint at the tax office in Gloucester. I couldn't write much. Probably why I intended going back to Marion in London. Or was that earlier? Earlier. The tax office was later. And only then because someone at the Employment Exchange felt sorry for me. I saw *that* in London — men in spinal carriages like giant prams, men with pawn tickets pinned to their chests where their medals ought to have been. Protesting. Is that what I was doing in the tax office?"

His time there had lasted twelve weeks.

"There's already millions unemployed. People like me drowned in that sea. '*Après Le Gore*'. You heard that one? I walked to May Hill one clear night just to see Arcturus. Went back the night after. That constellation was so clear to see. I know men who carried telescopes and tripods up that hill just to see the same. Like machine-gunners. Not me." He lifted the spectacles from his eyes. "Not too good close-up, but all those millions of miles I could see clear as day. Some dreams I never saw the purpose of. No comfort in them. Old ground. Others seemed to me to be like smoke from dying fires. Embers, living but dying. Marion told me I should write them down. That's your stuff, isn't it? Dreams. Is that what you're asking me all this for?"

I hadn't asked him a direct question in half an hour.

"Your return to the College wasn't successful," I said.

He thought about this. "There was always too much petrol in the air. You can taste it on the road here."

"Here? Surely not."

"On the road outside. Petrol. All I could smell on May Hill was that apple blossom. Same in France — petrol. The fighting season was always the worst. Petrol and cordite and gun-cotton. We all had black-lung from that stuff. I used to joke and say we'd all need dipping. I used to help in the dipping, out Dursley way. And sometimes at Moorslade. Always a day's work and three meals on those farms. They'd have children working when there weren't the men. I've seen them fall into the dip and go completely under. You'd hear the men laughing at it all. '*Après Le Gore*'."

I made a succession of notes as he told me all this, but it didn't add up to a reliable plan of his journey through those mapless years. All I knew for certain was that he had wandered in a maze, and that its passages, diversions and dead-ends had confounded him and unravelled inside of him as well as out. What little of his work I had read revealed a different life completely. And I daresay what Marion Scott had managed to gather together so far would reveal another life again.

"Do you write much still?" I asked him for a second time.

"Of course I write," he said angrily, contradicting his previous answer, again pinching his nose and then relaxing just as suddenly. "I'm sorry," he said.

"There's no need to apologize."

"I failed my F.R.C.M. exam," he said. "Back at the College. Me — Ivor Gurney. Marion told me that all I needed to do was to submit my compositions from the past few years. It was a certainty. I had no peace, then, you see? No calm. I was at my very worst. I was muddled, inconsistent. That was what they wrote. New examiner. If I'd had old Charlie Stanford, or even Walford, then I'd have been all right. Marion said then that they were all concerned for me. Never enough, though, is it — concern?"

"You published your second book of poems around that time?"

"I should have kept them to myself. No taste for it, see? Not then. They turned a third volume down without even asking to see it. Marion told me I needed to get away from everything."

"Back to Gloucester?"

"Back to the Severn. You ever hear of Whitcombe?" He went on before I could answer him. "Cold Slad Cottage, Dryhill, close by Whitcombe. I stayed there. I would have lived there the rest of my life, left to my own devices. Farm work, harvesting and planting and picking. I even worked winter fields stone-picking. Keep the farrow tines working properly."

193

"And it was work you were happy to do? After London?"

"Will Harvey said we were like animals. He came to find me. I knew Cold Slad was only another one of those dreams. Never any money, see? We picked the stones into sacks and then tipped them into a trailer. I could take you back there now and show you where all those stones are still piled. Like burial mounds, ancient, those lesser kings and princes. I once lay in a field at Vermand — I call it a field — I once lay in a field and listened to a man call out for help all day and all night before he was quietened."

"You have a good memory for the names of places," I said.

"Some places. Places wiped away. I'd forgotten Bristol, mind. You saw that. Remembering places that no longer exist and then forgetting Bristol. I'd have had my face to the sun dawn till dusk if I'd lived in Bristol."

"You could go out and walk along the estuary here," I suggested, hoping the idea might appeal to him, that perhaps he and I might walk there together when the privilege of leaving the asylum was finally granted to him.

"What, you think this is the same as that?" He laughed. "The Thames is no proper estuary, not compared to the Severn."

"Did it not worry — concern — you, to be leaving behind all those places that were once so precious to you?"

"Precious? And come here, you mean? It was for my own good. Even the magistrates probably thought that.

194

And if the police told them to think it, then they definitely did. You come to a point when it's best to listen to other people, and to do what they tell you. If my father had been alive then things would have been different. Ronald never looked out for me. And the girls were always too busy cutting apron strings to care. We piled some of those stones as high as a man. Like giant eggs, those mounds. I expect the long grass will have grown up through them by now. It always started growing early in those parts. And wherever I was working, I always knew what direction May Hill stood. I might not have been able to see it, but I could always turn to it. Always that. It never once lost —"

He was interrupted by someone knocking loudly on the open door and we both turned to see Lyle there.

I was unhappy at this intrusion.

"An hour, you said," he said to me, holding up his empty wrist.

"Where you been?" Gurney asked him, his voice changing slightly.

"Only sitting in the dining room," Lyle told him. "You all right, Ivor?"

I wondered how long Lyle had been standing at the open doorway, out of sight and listening to everything Gurney told me.

"I was telling him about May Hill and the stone-picking," Gurney said. But already he seemed less certain of himself, subservient almost, constrained, the released memory slipping from him.

"They should bury you on top of that blessed place," Lyle said.

Even without his confusion, it was evident to me that Gurney would be reluctant to continue talking to me now that Lyle was present, and I rose and held out my hand to him.

"Marion's coming soon," he said. "I got a letter." He glanced at the empty chair. "Shall I tell her to see you?"

"I'd appreciate that," I said.

"Bury you on May Hill and then put a bloody big cross up there telling everybody who's under it," Lyle said.

"Better than I'll get otherwise," Gurney said.

"There was a bee," Lyle said to me as I passed him in the doorway. "In the dining room. A right royal commotion. I tried to catch it, but someone else got there first." He slapped his palm hard against the door-frame.

CHAPTER
TWENTY

Marion Scott returned the following week. She brought with her more copies of Gurney's musical compositions. She sought me out before going to Gurney and gave me the folder of his work. She asked me not to mention to him that she'd done this. Before I could ask her why, she asked me what I thought of the previous batch of compositions she'd brought to me.

I'd hardly looked at any of these — let alone attempted to play even the simplest of them — and I was considering how best to tell her this, when she went on.

"I've brought 'Severn Meadows' and 'Even Such Is Time', the pieces Ivor wrote in Belgium," she said. "Remarkable. In the midst of all that and he was still able to produce such — such wonder." She looked at me to ensure I understood and believed her. "I made good copies of everything for safekeeping. And then I arranged for a performance. Everyone who attended expressed their true appreciation of all he'd achieved. I value the original scores of those pieces — Ivor's own — above all else he's given me. You can imagine their condition, the creases, the marks, the water stains, the erasions and amendments. In the midst of all that, and he was still able to compose."

She closed the folder, securing its wonder and surprise until I was better able to fully appreciate it and concur with her own opinion.

"My apologies," she said. "I'm mother-henning again. It's just that there were so many men — boys, really — who left us and who never returned, all with their own talents and promise. We could afford to tell our farmers and miners to stay where they were, but not our musicians or artists." She shook her head. "Listen to me. I'm starting to sound ridiculous. Of course Ivor had to follow his conscience."

I told her of my long conversation with him five days previously.

"He never talks about his family to anyone who knew them or of them," she said, unable to disguise the note of envious curiosity in her voice. "I've had dealings with the brother, of course." She tensed and pulled a face. "None of them have even the faintest idea . . ."

"Part of the comfort of strangers, I suppose," I said. "They know only *you*, nothing of what made you, of why you —"

"None of *them* made him," she said angrily. "All *they* ever did was undermine and undo him."

I wondered if I'd insulted her with my remark.

"I'm gathering together everything I can of him now because they — the brother, at least — will probably want everything destroyed. Or paid for at extortionate prices later on."

"When Gurney's reputation starts to rise?" I'd almost said "If".

"When he is finally acknowledged for what he is, yes."

Her judgement on Ronald Gurney seemed a harsh and so far unfounded one, but I let it pass.

"Sir Hubert sends his regards," she said. "It had been his intention to accompany me today, but College business intervened."

I fully understood the purpose of the remark, all it was intended to confirm and endorse.

"Perhaps soon," I said.

"I'm sure."

She sat uncomfortably for a moment, looking at the pictures on my walls, at the books and other half-unpacked possessions still scattered around me — all proof, still, of my own unsettled existence.

"I'm trying to get a better, a fuller picture of what happened to Ivor after he was sent home," I said, hoping to divert her along this more profitable course.

"After Edinburgh, you mean?"

I knew by the way she said it that she already understood something of what had happened there, and this made her wary of what I might now be about to ask of her. In her mind, she was still the wall beyond which Gurney stood unseen.

"There was a nurse," I said.

"Who stole from him," she said abruptly.

"There was never any charge of theft, nor even a suggestion of it."

"You won't have heard of any of this from Ivor," she said confidently. "Then who?"

"A doctor who was working there at the time of Gurney's arrival."

She relaxed slightly. "So — another piece of hearsay, another twice-told tale blown this way and that with cold whispers."

I wondered if she were quoting something to me — Gurney himself, perhaps. I had little doubt that she knew by heart every word he had written.

"Something like that," I conceded. "*Did* she steal from Ivor?"

"Probably nothing so straightforward. She led him on, that's all. She was older than Ivor."

"Only by three years." Three to her twelve.

"Still older. In the ways of the world. I don't know what happened, not for certain. Just that he was badly let down by her."

"Do you think she was the first —"

"First what?" She knew exactly what I had been about to ask her.

I said it anyway, unwilling to accede to yet another of her dismissals. "His first romantic encounter, imagined or otherwise?"

She smiled at my own evasiveness. "What I believe is that he was in a very vulnerable position and that she took advantage of him. I think, if she had chosen, the woman might have done a great deal to create some measure of calm and stability for Ivor, but that instead she — she —"

"I didn't mean to imply anything," I said.

It was a lie and she didn't believe it.

"No, well . . ." she said, allowing us both a step backwards. "You will, however, be once again wondering about my own — what would you call it? Over-protectiveness?" She held my gaze for a moment. "Ivor, before I met him, had a tendency to be attracted to other mother-figures. Hardly surprising, I suppose, in light of his own mother's only too obvious disregard for him. There were music teachers in Gloucester, others." And if she knew the names of these women, these other mothers, then she pretended otherwise and kept them from me, kept them vague and shadowy figures in another time and place, far beyond the beam of her own intimate understanding of the man. "He was also attached — if that is the word; and I hope you don't deliberately misconstrue my meaning, Doctor Irvine — to Will Harvey's sisters, girls, young girls."

"Another surrogate family," I said.

"I suppose so. Perhaps. God knows he deserved one." She paused and put a finger to her mouth. "May I tell you something in the strictest confidence?"

I wondered what that might mean in such a place.

She, too, understood this, and added, "I don't want anything of what I reveal to you to work against Ivor in any way, to prejudice what you yourself might think of him, both as a man and as your patient." The remark seemed unnecessarily formal to me, and I simply nodded for her to go on.

"He once confided in me that he had apocalyptic visions." She kept her finger over her lips. "In France and Belgium. And again when he came back, at Warrington and then St Albans."

I'd heard the same said of other men and told her this.

She took her finger from her mouth and relaxed slightly.

"They altered him," she said. "He was convinced by them. Visions and visitations. He spoke to other great musicians. He believed he was being singled out, chosen by these others."

I wondered if these were the same "voices" Lyle had referred to.

"To what end?" I asked her.

"I wish I could tell you. It was clear to me when he finally returned to the College that he was not the same man. He never truly settled again after that. It was why I was happy for him then to go back to Gloucester. I thought it was where he needed to be to go on working, writing and composing."

"And instead it unsettled him even further?"

"He went for a time to High Wycombe, played the organ at Christ Church there. He seemed content. He was composing a great deal, a great many new songs. I showed him all I'd collected, all he'd achieved. I'd tried to interest a number of music publishers in his work — myself and Sir Hubert — but all to little avail, I'm afraid. All anyone wanted then were music-hall pieces. I told Ivor that his time would come, that all he needed to do was to be patient and to continue writing."

"He told me about the farm cottage at Cold Slad," I said.

202

She shook her head. "He looked on that place as a kind of Paradise. It was never that. For one thing, he could never afford to pay the rent. Nor could he work the land well enough, not properly, and certainly not alone. He had an argument with the owner and stormed off, owing him money and leaving the place open to the elements. It was after Cold Slad that he — that things —" She turned away from me briefly.

"Did something happen?"

She breathed deeply for a moment before continuing. "He wrote to me apologizing for something he said he was about to do, something to harm himself."

I realized only as she spoke that she was talking about another suicide attempt. There was nothing of this in Gurney's notes.

"Go on," I told her.

"I lived a day in a panic, waiting to hear from someone what had happened to him. Waiting to hear that he'd succeeded, that he'd . . . Well. And then I received another letter from him saying that whatever he'd attempted had failed, and that he regretted any torment he might have caused me. That was the word he used — 'torment'."

"Did he ever tell you any more explicitly what he might have attempted?"

"I believe he tried to hang himself. Somewhere in one of his blessed woods. I don't know. I don't know if he tried but failed, or if he decided against it at the last minute. He spoke of his shame, of a mark, of something that would never leave him. That was in the late summer."

"And he was declared of unsound mind by the Gloucester doctors and magistrates shortly afterwards?"

She nodded. "To be honest, everyone who knew him and cared for him was so relieved that he was to be taken care of at last."

"Because you believed he would have tried again?"

She nodded once. "At least in Bristol, and then in Barnwood House he would be properly looked after."

"And actively prevented from making another attempt on his own life?"

"I don't think any of us knew for an instant what course we were setting him on, how easily and unknowingly we were about to let him slip away from us into all those other hands — there, here . . ."

"And how difficult it might afterwards prove to regain him?"

"'Regain him'? I don't believe any of us ever truly considered that a possibility. It's why —"

"It's why you're here now," I said to her. And I wondered then — the thought as sudden as it was unexpected and alarming — if Gurney resented her visits to him, dragging with her all he himself might have now been attempting to jettison.

And almost as though reading these thoughts, she said, "He still writes, almost every day."

"To you?"

"Poems, songs, letters. He still composes. He never stopped. Some periods are more productive than others, but I imagine that is the case with all true artists. He shows me everything. I still make copies; I still catalogue everything for him."

"And is it good?"

"'Good'?"

"The work. Is it — I don't know — is it competent, comparable to what he was writing before his first committal?"

Her hesitation told me more than her answer. "It's still *him*," she said. "It's still Ivor. And *I* can still see that even if others can't."

"Have you shown this recent work to others? To people at the College?"

"Some of it." She was again suspicious of what I might have been asking her to reveal.

"Lyle did say something about Ivor still working," I said, waiting.

"What would *he* know?" She looked at her watch, indicating to me that she had perhaps already said far more than she'd intended, and that she was now anxious to see Gurney.

I suggested this and she rose immediately from her seat.

"Will you look at them?" she said, indicating the folder of music she'd brought.

I wondered if she was now having her doubts about me, about the advisability of leaving this later work because of what it might suggest to me after all she'd just told me.

"Of course," I said.

"There's nothing too recent. Perhaps next time." Meaning I would only be shown what she considered to be worth showing. "I'm hoping to gather together a collection of testimonials — from people who understand more fully, and who truly appreciate Ivor's achievements."

Not people like myself; not those people who did not fully understand everything Gurney had once possessed, but which he might now have lost for ever; not people who harboured doubts and who were not prepared to accept unquestioningly everything she now insisted upon.

"To what end?" I said, and again the remark must have sounded like a rebuff to her.

"To make people aware of what a remarkable man he is," she said. "And because, hopefully, once they realize that, then they might be better able to care for him, to allow him to go on working."

We both understood how unlikely this was. We understood, too, and she much better than I, that Gurney's salvation — however vague or unlikely or as distant as this might now seem to all of us, Gurney included — did not depend on anything so simple or straightforward as his ability to continue writing and composing.

Unwilling to speculate any more openly or honestly on any of this, I told her where Gurney would be waiting for us and we walked there together.

He sat at a window overlooking the kitchen and laundry room. Alison West sat beside him. She rose at our approach and I introduced her to Marion Scott, conscious as I did this of the nurse in Edinburgh and everything Marion Scott believed of her.

"I was talking to Ivor about the bees," Alison said. "He thinks they've started building new cells."

"Very interesting, I'm sure," Marion Scott said, her gaze fixed on Gurney, who remained sitting, not even glancing up at her.

I signalled to Alison not to respond to this rudeness.

She looked at the older woman for a moment. Then she crouched beside Gurney to say goodbye to him, and left us.

"She served in France," I said to Marion Scott when Alison was long out of earshot.

"And I'm sure that counts for something," she said. "Or that it once did."

I pulled up a chair for her and she sat beside Gurney and held both his hands. Gurney remained reluctant to face her. He didn't resist being held by her like this, but neither did he respond to her gentle caressing, her fingers back and forth over his own. She started talking to him, telling him about recent events at the College, about whom she had seen there, the men and women who had enquired after him. She made them sound as interested in him as she was. But it was another world now to Gurney. He occasionally repeated one of the names with which she prompted him, but little more. It was difficult to believe he was the same man I'd spoken to only five days earlier.

I sat a short distance from them, clearly to Marion Scott's annoyance.

When she released his hands, Gurney turned to me and said, "They've been after the old honey. You'll have to get rid of it, scrape it out. The wood's saturated. They want it. They'll take everything back into the new hives if you give them the chance. You'll not want that."

"We ought to have burned them straight away," I said. I remembered telling Cox about the smoke.

"You let them bring anything into the new hives and you'll have everything to do over again. I saw wasps hanging around."

The threat from wasps and other insects was always exaggerated by most keepers.

"Not much we can do about them," I said, gratified by his interest and the lucidity of his reasoning. "It's not a bad sign, a few wasps. Shows there's something for them to be interested in."

"Perhaps. But you'll be happier once the colonies are better sorted, once the drones and the workers find their place."

"We were talking about Dryhill," Marion Scott said to him, unhappy at her brief exclusion. "About Cold Slad cottage."

Gurney turned to her. "A wasp in a strong hive and they'll see to it in seconds. But a wasp will always have the advantage in an open space. We saw them on the setting fruit. Some of it already forming. Nothing a man could eat, mind."

"I showed Doctor Irvine some of your work," Marion Scott said. "I showed him 'Severn Meadows' and 'In Flanders'."

Again Gurney looked from me to her. He closed his eyes for a moment. "I whistled every piece of those two a hundred times over to get them right. Whistled and banged on an empty shell case. I saw an aeroplane coming down on the day 'Meadows' was finally done. I don't know what had hit it. German. Came down like a sycamore seed. Got the air beneath it. Round and round. And then the pilot jumped out of it. We all watched him climb out of his seat and then balance himself on the wing. That's how slow the machine came down. And then he just jumped. Came down faster than the aeroplane. Just fell and landed without a sound. He never stood up. His machine came down close by. The day I finished writing 'Meadows'." He hummed for a few seconds and then fell silent.

Marion Scott, who had joined him in this, continued for a few seconds longer, and Gurney watched her closely as she did this.

"You wrote to me about the aeroplane," she told him. "I didn't know it had happened when you were working on 'Severn Meadows'." She was pleased to have made the connection. "You said it looked like a kite, the aeroplane, a toy."

"That's all it was," Gurney said absently. "What did you tell him about Dryhill?"

"Just that you were happy there."

"Happy?" He smiled. "I sometimes doubt if I was ever that."

"Oh, you were. At Cold Slad. You wrote to tell me how content you were, how well you felt and how hard you were working. On the land, on your work."

"I might have *written* it," Gurney said, and I wonder if I alone heard the deliberate malice in his remark.

I regretted Marion Scott's mention of the place, wondering how close Gurney's own memory might now come to his failed suicide attempt. I watched him closely, but saw no suggestion of this.

"You said you were happy and that you would be content to live in the cottage for the next fifty years," Marion Scott insisted. She looked from Gurney to me and quickly back again.

"Happy to be away from London, perhaps," Gurney said.

I wondered if he was going to add, "And you."

"Did the pilot not have a parachute?" I asked him.

He shook his head. "Just jumped. We saw others with parachutes. Some opened, some didn't. This one just worked out his chances, waited and then jumped. We used to shout up to them, 'Jump, you bugger, jump.' They were observing us, see? Writing down where we were, what we were up to, give their guns some proper targets. Always trying to work out where we were going next."

I don't know what kind of conversation Marion Scott had hoped to have with him, but I doubted if this was it.

"I saw a piano," she said. "Here. I wonder if Ivor couldn't be persuaded to give a recital. Perhaps even 'Severn Meadows'?" She sounded hopeful, but I could see that the idea did not appeal in the least to Gurney himself. It didn't frighten or intimidate him as I thought it might, but having considered the suggestion for a few seconds, he shook his head.

"All I'd see would be that falling man," he said. "That poor bloody bugger falling out of the sky like one of Lucifer's bad angels." He started humming again.

"I'm sure *something* could be arranged," Marion Scott insisted. "I'm sure the piano could be brought up to scratch. Perhaps I could persuade Sir Hubert to send along one of our own tuners to look at it." To me, she said, "Perhaps you could suggest the idea to Doctor Osborne. Or would it be better coming from me, do you think?"

Neither Gurney nor I responded to this, both of us hoping, I imagined, that her proposal might evaporate and disappear in our collective silence.

"It's certainly something to think about," I said eventually.

"Then I'll leave it to you," she said. "In the first instance. Excellent."

Gurney turned back to the view over the yard and the men there.

I wondered if Lyle was among them, and if this was why he now seemed so intent on watching them.

"You get a wasp in a hive and he'll sit in some dark corner for days on end, feeding up. I've seen wasps come out of a hive bigger than my thumb, fit to burst with what they've eaten. I've seen a wasp eat a butterfly. Up at Chaxhill, that was. A first-hatch wasp and a cabbage-white. No one ever believed me about that, but I saw it. Everything but the wings. Seen a wasp take a butterfly and then an eft take a wasp."

I looked to Marion Scott.

"A lizard," she said, still the keeper and compiler of these minutiae, these footnotes of a life.

CHAPTER
TWENTY-ONE

I saw Alison West again later that same day. She called to me from beside the greenhouses as I was about to enter the orchard. She was off-duty and came to me across the recently cleared ground.

"He hardly said a word to her after you'd left him," she said.

"Gurney?"

"Is she always so rude?"

"She's concerned for him."

She remained unconvinced.

"You think I'm making excuses for her?" I said.

She considered this. "Not necessarily. But I think she expects everyone to share her own high opinion of him, and that she has no time whatsoever for those who might express the slightest doubt."

I heard her veiled criticism of me in this.

She punched my arm. "Perhaps if Gurney gets sent somewhere else, then you can become her next lost cause."

"Too late," I said, and she laughed.

We reached the first of the hives.

"My father used to say that bee-keeping suited certain types of people more than others," I told her.

"Such as?"

"He said the bees preferred people of a solitary disposition; people able to love what they might otherwise fear; people who were self-possessed and contemplative. It was all to do with temperament."

I could see she was not convinced by this.

"He was talking about another world, another age completely," she said. "*My* father used to give me wax and honey mixed together as a laxative. Raw honey as a laxative, and then boiled honey as a cure for diarrhoea. Where's the sense in that? I once ate some laurel honey as a small girl and poisoned myself."

"Did you live?" I asked her.

"Just. What does the Scott woman expect of you? Does she want you to help her save him?"

"I'm not sure what she expects. Besides, whatever she wants, I'm not sure if Ivor himself wants the same thing."

"I'd like to be there when you pluck up the courage to suggest *that* to her."

Moving out of sight of the greenhouses and the men working there, she took off her headscarf and shook her hair loose, gathering it back into a band.

"I think Oliver Lyle's taken a liking to you," I told her.

"Him and a hundred others. Why shouldn't they? As far as they're concerned, I'm second only to a ministering angel. Besides . . ."

"Besides, what?"

She left the question unanswered.

"I'm hoping Lyle will get himself sent back to Gloucester," I told her, and then explained why.

"Too harmless for this place, then?" She lifted the roof on one of the hives and looked inside. A few bees rose slowly from the frame, dropping back down when they collided with the lid.

We walked further beneath the trees, towards the asylum's far boundary.

"I think we've attracted a new brood," she said. She pointed to one of the hives we'd repaired. A sparse ball of insects hovered above it.

"Following a queen?"

She nodded. "I think I saw her earlier this morning."

I followed her to the hive, stopping ten feet from it and the agitated bees. I could hear their noise even at that distance.

"There are a lot more already inside," she said. "They sound very active."

"Have you definitely seen the queen?"

She shook her head. "But listen. They wouldn't be so agitated if there wasn't something happening. There are plenty of keepers in the countryside around here."

"And perhaps one of them will notice some of his bees have swarmed and come demanding to retrieve them."

She laughed again at this and turned in a full circle. "Here? To a madhouse? What if the bees became mad as a result? He wouldn't want them back then."

It had been my father's opinion that once a brood had swarmed it was better either left where it was or gathered up and taken to a completely new location.

Anything but returned to the hive it had just abandoned. Returning swarming bees to their starting point, even if a new and empty hive had been prepared there for them, was all too often a wasted operation.

"And I've sent away for some," she said.

"Queens?"

"Two. The Kent Apiarist Society. We've probably already got whatever else we need by way of workers and drones. Once the new queens settle, the others will soon build everything up around them."

"I'll ask Osborne to reimburse you," I said.

"I don't want his money. They weren't expensive. Besides, he cares for none of this, not really. All he's doing is humouring you, waiting to see how everything turns out. If the hives succeed, he'll take the credit, for what it's worth; if they fail he'll point his finger at you. He'd be happier with a field full of potatoes or poultry."

I almost told her about Osborne's own veiled threat to this same end, but thought better of the revelation.

"I wish more of the patients were interested in getting involved," I said.

"It's to be expected. Bees sting. It's all most of them know. And how long do you think Osborne would go on sanctioning everything once that starts happening?"

The bees around the hive became even more agitated, perhaps at the sound of our voices, and we walked backwards a few paces, turning to skirt the trees along the wall. I was more convinced than ever that there was now a queen settling in the darkness of the hive and that her subjects were already busy around her.

"You can pay for one of the queens when they arrive," she said as we sat by the bricked-up gateway. A galvanized barrel of water stood by the abandoned entrance, green with growth, and with a sharp odour in the rising heat. Insects skated across its surface.

"I meant what I said about Lyle being attracted to you," I said. I told her about Gurney's "attachment" five years earlier in Edinburgh.

"Is that another reason for the Scott woman not to like me?" she said, smiling.

"Probably. My father used to give honey to some of his more elderly patients because they believed it cured gout and rheumatism."

"Is that what he believed?"

"I never knew. Probably. The rest of us ate it every day."

"Your brother?"

"Charles. Yes."

She put her hand on my arm briefly. "*My* father used to tell anyone who would listen that Charlemagne cured himself of everything that ailed him by eating honey. I doubt if any of them had even the faintest idea who Charlemagne was."

"Just like you and me," I said.

"Speak for yourself. I'm an educated woman." She paused briefly. "I lied to you. About my husband." She took her hand back, and I felt its absence acutely. She breathed deeply. "When he was killed, afterwards, after the war, two years, I went with my sister-in-law — his older sister — on one of Thomas Cook's Pilgrim Tours. What a ridiculous name. Women, mostly, as you might imagine. Women and old men. Four pounds for four days. It was Mary's idea. She'd lost her own husband. I suppose she thought it connected us in some way. I only agreed to accompany her because I knew what it meant to *her*. Or at least that's what I told myself. That, and because she was too scared to go alone. They had everything ready for us. Buses to all the places we'd need to see. All the cemeteries. It was beautiful countryside where her own husband had been killed. I doubt if even Thomas Cook could wring a profit out of Mesopotamia. It was high summer and everywhere was planted up, corn mostly. You could still see a lot of what had happened there, but time, as they say, had passed." She spoke quickly, knowing that if she faltered in what she was telling me, she might not be able to continue. "It was a kind of test, I suppose. A way of making my own uncertain amends. Mary kept telling me that she was certain I felt exactly the same as her. I wasn't brave enough to tell her otherwise."

"But she knew that you'd been nursing out there? That you'd seen it all?"

"I doubt it counted for much. Not in her eyes. She said I was just grieving differently. She said it would be good for us. Pilgrims. Christ. Me."

"You still went with her," I said. "You did what you did for *her*, not yourself."

"I know. But it still sounds like another excuse."

"Were you able to find her husband's grave?"

"I don't imagine it ever existed. Not really. We found the monument with his name on it. Nothing splendid in marble or granite as such; that was all to come. Just a great banner, something regimental, with all the names painted on it. Gold. It was enough for her to see it there and to know that one day it would make it on to the marble."

"It must have brought back some terrible memories for you," I said, immediately regretting the banal remark.

"It did," she said. "The hardest part was keeping it all from Mary, joining in all her pointless speculation about how it must have been for her husband. Talking to the others. Listening to all their tales of their own brothers and fathers and sons and husbands. Drinking tea and eating cakes. Buying our souvenirs, our postcards. Pretending to speak what little we understood of the language. Pretending we'd be going back the following year and the year after that. Telling everyone on the tour that we'd see them all again when the proper monument was finally unveiled. I shared a room with Mary and she cried for an hour every night before she fell asleep. And afterwards, usually, she laughed and told me to ignore her, that the same thing had happened ever since she'd learned of her husband's death."

"She probably took some comfort in it," I said.

"I know," she said. "She told me the same."

My mother had cried for a week after learning of Charles's death. The postman had cycled to the house chased by a neighbour's dog. He'd been stroking its head and talking to it when my mother had opened the door to him. She, too, had patted the animal, telling him it was friendly enough, that it wouldn't harm him, and all the time looking at the telegram he held, waiting as he took off his cap to hand the envelope to her.

I'd been in the kitchen at the time, on leave, with two days to go before I returned. My mother had thanked the postman and given him some money, and then he'd cycled away from her, taking the excited dog with him. I could hear the animal's barking for the full minute my mother stood in the doorway, unable to come back in to me, the unopened telegram in her hand.

"She wrote to me recently," Alison said. "Mary. I think she wants to go again."

"Does she want you to go with her?"

"Not this time. I think she already knows that. Perhaps she's found someone more willing to endorse her own feelings. Besides, I haven't seen her for almost two years."

It sometimes seemed to me as though we were all still adrift one way or another, adrift and uncertain of our bearings and waiting for the horizon to settle to its solid and dependable line.

"Do you want me to say anything to Lyle?" she asked me.

It had been my intention in raising the subject of Lyle to ask her the same thing.

"I'll keep an eye on things," she said when I didn't answer her.

"I think Marion Scott is hoping for a recital from Gurney." I told her about the music I'd been given, about what Marion Scott had suggested earlier in the day.

"Is he up to it?"

"I don't know. I don't even know if it's something he should even consider doing."

"Then why can't *she* understand that?"

"Perhaps she does. Perhaps she wants to shock Gurney into responding. She means well. And Gurney still trusts her and has a great affection for her."

"So what?" she said. It seemed to me to be another harsh and unwarranted judgement on the woman. "You could always ask *him* what he wanted," she said in a more guarded tone. "Perhaps Lyle could even turn the music for him. Gurney and Lyle. They already sound like a music-hall turn. You and Osborne and the Scott woman could sit on the front row and lead the applause."

"I think she intended some of Gurney's old professors and teachers from the Royal College to come and listen."

"God. *That* serious? Osborne would lap it up. You should try and persuade Ivor to say yes."

"I doubt he'd have much say in it either way," I said.

"Something else you have in common," she said, and laughed.

I was about to respond to this when we were interrupted by voices from the far side of the trees. A group of men had come into the orchard from the greenhouses, half a dozen orderlies and the same number of patients. The patients pushed wheelbarrows, which they tipped against the wall. The men called back and forth to each other.

"It's Cox," Alison said. "What's he doing?"

"Dumping rubbish from the greenhouses."

I doubted if the men would come any closer to the hives. But then one of the patients spotted us and stood pointing to us where we sat. Cox came to him, peering through the trees until he too was able to see us. He shouted to ask what we were doing there, and then he said something to the men around him which caused them to burst into laughter. Only the pointing man remained silent. Cox hit his arm several times until he lowered it.

"Not interrupting anything, I hope," Cox called to us.

Neither of us answered him.

"Ignore him; he'll go away," Alison said to me.

But I knew this was unlikely. I saw only then that one of the patients standing beside Cox was Lyle himself.

"Watch out for the bees," I called to Lyle, but this only provoked more laughter. And in defiance of what I'd said, Lyle came closer to the active hives. Several of the others followed him, always a few paces behind him, and then stopped as they encountered the first of the insects. I called for Cox to take better care of the men in his charge.

Cox shouted for them all to go back to him, away from the hives, and the men were happy to do this. Lyle, I noticed, was the last to turn and walk away.

"Happy now?" Cox called to me. He started walking around the hives to where Alison and I sat. He was followed by two of the orderlies and by Lyle.

Arriving in front of us, Cox said, "Lyle here was telling us what a good job you all done on the bumble-bees. And *I* was telling *him* that one hint of trouble from the buzzing little bastards and I'd see to it that every one of them got squashed and burned along with all those brand-new houses you've built."

"Hives," Lyle said.

Cox shouted at him to shut up and Lyle turned away from him.

To me, Cox said, "Is that what you two were up to, then, gathering honey? I bet she tastes sweet enough without it."

Accustomed as I was to the man's provocations, this last remark was too much, and I rose and told him to get back to work, that this time I was definitely reporting his behaviour to Osborne.

Beside me, Alison tugged at my sleeve, wanting me to sit back down.

"You do that, bee-keeper," Cox said, holding my gaze. "You do that."

She pulled again and I sat back beside her.

"Next you'll be appealing to his better nature," she said loudly, looking directly at Cox as she spoke.

"That meant to be funny, is it?" he said. "Because if it's —"

"There's a new brood," Lyle said unexpectedly, interrupting him.

"What?"

"A new brood. Listen." He pointed to where the bees still hovered over the restored hive.

222

Cox and the others watched the insects for a moment.

"Are we safe here?" one of the men asked Cox.

"Not really," I told him, unsettling them all.

Cox turned and walked away from me, careful to move in a wide arc around the hive. The others, uncertain what to do, followed him. Again, Lyle was the last to leave.

"You'd better follow them," Alison told him. "Otherwise Cox will take it out on you."

He accepted this and turned and left us, following the others; except that unlike them he walked in a direct line, bringing him close to the hive and its bees. He paused to watch them for a moment before continuing back to the wall.

"You shouldn't have mentioned Osborne to Cox like that," Alison said when we were again alone. "Everybody knows that the two of them are as thick as thieves, that Cox has got something on him."

The remark surprised me.

"What do you mean?"

"You mean you haven't noticed how Cox struts about and takes his time doing whatever Osborne tells him to do?"

"I thought he was like that with everyone," I said.

"Only because he gets away with it where Osborne's concerned. Only because he knows he can pull a string and make Osborne jump. Do you seriously think he'd be given this much leeway otherwise?"

I considered all this in silence.

At the far side of the orchard, the men with the wheelbarrows finished emptying them against the wall, helped now by Lyle. A succession of bottles and small panes of glass were thrown against the wall and smashed there, the pieces falling into the pile of other rubbish.

CHAPTER
TWENTY-TWO

I intended confronting Osborne over Cox's behaviour the following morning, but upon my arrival at his office, I found him surrounded by his usual coterie. Because of them, he was suspicious and guarded, and I knew he would be dismissive of whatever I said to him, more concerned instead with the light in which my complaint might cast him in front of these others. Everything he said to me reinforced my growing conviction that there was some truth in what Alison West had suggested to me the previous day.

It was a little before noon and there were already glasses of whisky on Osborne's broad desk and on the chair arms of the others. A cloud of thin smoke had settled high along the ornate cornices of the room.

I knew all of the others present, and seeing them there, I at first told Osborne that I would return to see him later.

"No, come in now," he insisted.

"Sit down. Join in the celebration," Webster said to me.

I knew from my infrequent dealings with the man that he was Osborne's friend and ally. I'd already twice asked him to let me see the reports of the physical examinations he had made of both Gurney and Lyle, but so far he'd shown me nothing. I was a long way below him in the hierarchy of the place; my request would most likely have been considered an impertinence by him.

He kicked the door shut from where he sat and handed an empty glass up to me, motioning for a burns specialist called Marston to fill it. Marston did this and then slid his chair to one side to allow me to join their circle.

"What's the celebration?" I asked Webster.

"Oh, you know . . ." He looked at the others.

"A clean bill of health from the Lunacy Commissioners," Osborne said.

"And a Highly Recommended from the Ex-Servicemen's Mental Welfare Society," Webster added, raising a laugh.

"For what they're worth," Marston said.

I knew Marston from my short time at Claybury. Both his legs had been badly burned as a child, and it was why he had chosen to practise that speciality. I was never entirely certain how he had ended up being appointed to an asylum, but I liked and trusted him more than most in the room. I felt him to be something of a kindred spirit, especially amid the slow-moving and conservative huddle of these others.

"The point is," Webster said, "none of them are going to go running to the Lunacy Board to rock any boats. They need *us* — all of them — more than we need them. Perhaps now they'll leave us alone to get on

226

with things and stop interfering with all their plans and changes and whatever."

Osborne, I saw, listened to all this with a strange mixture of both pride and discomfort in his eyes — pride at whatever commendations had been given; and discomfort at the casual and near-mocking manner in which all this was now being discussed.

"To the City of London Home for Waifs and Strays," Webster said, raising his glass.

The others saluted the toast. Osborne sipped at his whisky.

"And good riddance to sexual psychoanalysis," another man said. It was a common joke in the place, a test of sobriety.

"Nothing much there in the first place," Webster said. "We all know what sex is in these places."

Several of the men exchanged glances.

"What are you talking about?" Osborne asked him, unable now to disguise his concern, all of us wondering what Webster might have been about to say next.

"Stop worrying, Alistair," Webster said to Osborne. "Lost personality. Spent nature. We can leave all that mumbo-jumbo to the shining lights up at Maida Vale."

There was more laughter.

"What was it you wanted?" Osborne finally asked me. "Was it anything pressing?"

I heard the note of warning in his voice and thought better of raising the subject of Cox's behaviour.

"I saw Marion Scott again," I said. "She wanted to know if there was any possibility of a recital of Gurney's work."

"Here? Here?"

"Is this our Mad Mozart?" Marston said to me. "They were talking about him." He mimicked playing a piano.

"And she wants *what*, exactly?" Osborne said.

"To organize a performance of some of Gurney's work."

"By him?"

"Possibly. Most likely by others. She's done it before." My uncertainty and my lack of both enthusiasm and preparation was evident in everything I said, and I regretted having raised the subject in front of these others.

"Is he any good?" another of the men asked me.

"Supposed to be," Marston said, his own interest rising. To Osborne, he said, "You should give it a shot. Put on a show."

"Marion Scott thought that Gurney's old teachers from the Royal College might come down for it," I said.

"Lady teachers?" Webster said, pulling a face. "Spinster piano teachers?"

"Perhaps even Sir Ralph Vaughan Williams," I said, more for effect and to silence them all than out of any true conviction that he would be persuaded by Marion Scott to attend.

A moment of silent reassessment followed.

"You should do it, Alistair," Webster said to Osborne. "Think about it. If this Gurney chap *does* turn out to be even half of what they say he is, you could adopt him as your own pet patient. Get your own name up in lights. Madness and genius and all that."

"He's Irvine's patient," Osborne said quickly.

Webster glanced at me with a cold smile. "You're not listening to me, Alistair. I've heard of these cases elsewhere — poets, painters, musicians, book-people. Take him on. Find out what's still in there. What would you have to lose? If someone like Vaughan Williams is interested in him, then —"

"We only have the Scott woman's word for all that," Osborne said.

"Who is she?" Marston asked me, and I told him.

"She sounds a regular Xanthippe," he said, causing everyone to look at him. "Xanthippe. For God's sake, are you all Philistines? Xanthippe was the bad-tempered, older wife of Socrates."

I still didn't understand what point he was making.

"She isn't Gurney's wife," I said. "Only his —"

"Sounds as though she might as well be for all the pushing and pulling she does on his behalf," Webster said. "Perhaps there's more to her and old Gurney than meets the eye." He made a suggestive motion with his clenched fist.

"She's more of a mother to him," I said, wishing I hadn't.

"Well, there you go then. Even better. Socrates *and* Oedipus."

"You're being ridiculous," I told him, hoping Osborne might now intervene to support me and bring an end to this wayward and malicious speculation.

"Of course I am," Webster conceded. "My apologies. I didn't realize it was such a touchy subject." He raised his glass and grinned at those closest to him.

"See," he then said to Osborne. "Irvine here understands the value of taking this Gurney on. He knows what a leg-up it might be for *him*."

I shook my head at the remark. And then I saw that Osborne was watching me even more closely, perhaps finally considering all that had just been suggested to him.

"What would the Scott woman want?" he said to me. "I mean what would she expect of us?"

"I don't know. I'll find out." I was reluctant to guess any further. I still wasn't entirely convinced that Marion Scott's suggestion about the recital had been a serious one in the first place.

"Have you heard any of this stuff, this music?"

I told him I hadn't.

"I'm a dab hand on the old ivories myself," Marston said. "Perhaps I could open the show."

"We could even bring in a troupe of dancing girls," Webster said. "Why on earth do you imagine they keep holding all these medical conferences in Paris?" He refilled his glass from the bottle on Osborne's desk.

"We could perhaps get the Lunacy Commissioners to attend," Osborne said hesitantly. "Let them see what we're achieving here."

"What *you're* achieving here, you mean," Webster said, theatrically tapping the side of his nose. "I can't imagine that would do your chances of a permanent promotion any harm."

"That's nonsense," Osborne said, but it was clear that the idea had appealed to him and that he was already imagining his coming good fortune.

Concerned at how swiftly the discussion had moved beyond my grasp, I said, "It will all take time. I haven't even spoken to Ivor about it yet." It was only a half-lie; I doubted if Gurney himself had believed that Marion Scott's suggestion would ever come to anything. In all likelihood, he had probably never grasped what she had suggested about the recital in the first place, or had already forgotten about it.

"'Ivor', is it?" Webster said. "Christ, they saddle these poor buggers with some queer names. Probably only called him that when they discovered he was a genius."

I said nothing to correct him, letting yet another chorus of laughter and remarks rise and fall around me.

"Oh, come on, Alistair," Webster said to Osborne. "Where's the harm? So what if *Ivor* turns out to be a genius? He's still a lunatic. He's still going to be in here. Nothing's going to change any of that. And especially not half an hour of tinkling the ivories. And even if it does turn out that he's no better or worse than Marston here, then there's even less been lost. No one's going to throw up their hands and say a terrible mistake's been made in sending him here. And certainly no one's going to be to *blame* for snuffing out his — what is it? — his spluttering flame of genius." He looked around him as he said all this. "I'm not up on these things. Is that what they call it these days, a flame?"

"He's right," Marston said to Osborne. "You've nothing to lose."

I knew by the way he spoke that he was saying this in support of me rather than Webster.

"Especially if old Irvine here is going to do all the leg-work with this Scott woman for you."

No one spoke for a moment. Osborne rocked his glass on his desk, backed into a corner from which he was finding it difficult to escape.

"I'll talk to Gurney," I said to him, offering a way out of all this. "If *he* doesn't want it, then it's unlikely that Marion Scott will persist." I wished I'd sounded more convincing.

"And Cox," he said unexpectedly, causing me to wonder if he'd misunderstood me, or if he'd perhaps had some advance warning of my real reason for wanting to see him, and the name was yet another warning to me.

"What about him?" I said.

"If anything *is* going to happen, then Cox will need to know. All the arrangements, that's his department. He'll need to know, to be kept informed of everything that needs to be done."

I knew by his tone that this condition was not open to further debate.

"Let the Scott woman take the load," Webster said. "Seems to me this is as much for her benefit as poor old Gurney's. Makes you wonder what she's trying to prove by parading him in front of everyone like this. That she was right all along? What's the word — protégé. That this Gurney's a genius *and* her protégé? That he's everything she says he is and she deserves some of the credit and reflected glory before he's lost for good? He's *here*, for Christ's sake. She must have at least *some* idea of what's likely to happen to him." To Osborne, he said, "It's an hour's diversion, nothing more, nothing less. All we're doing here is making a mountain out of a molehill. Gurney probably once had a bit of a talent. He's a bloody yokel, for God's sake, from the back of beyond. No wonder everybody thinks he's something special. Added to which, he might have gone through a bit out there. It all adds up and puts a bit of a shine on him." To me, he said, "What was he?"

"He was in the Gloucesters."

"No, I mean what *was* he? What rank?"

"Private," I said.

Webster pursed his lips and held up his palms. "I rest my case," he said.

I wanted to tell him about Gurney's published poems, about the poems he might still have been writing there, in the asylum, but I knew that this would only be further fuel to his amusement and mockery.

"Talk to Cox," Osborne said again to me. "He's already complained to me about the bees, about all the extra work involved. See what *he* says. And get the Scott woman to put her request in writing. Get her to submit it on some kind of official notepaper, make the thing —" He waved his free hand. "Was there anything else?"

Both Webster and Marston looked at me.

It was all Marion Scott would need to convince her that she now had Osborne's approval for the concert.

"You haven't touched your drink," Webster said to me. "He hasn't touched his drink."

I drained my glass and put it down with a loud knock.

"What?" Webster said, feigning surprise. "You got what you came for. Now what's bothering you? Don't tell me you've also got a budding Constable on your hands as well?"

The remark defused the room's awkward tension, and most of the others laughed.

"We're all friends here," he went on. "If there *is* anything else, then tell us. I'm sure it'll go no further. Something to do with the bees, perhaps?" He grinned at Osborne. "Or perhaps it's something to do with the pretty little thing who's also been giving you a — shall we say a helping hand — down there in the long grass."

The laughter this time was long and loud.

I rose and went to the door.

"Oh, come on," Webster said. "Where's your sense of humour, man? Don't be so touchy. All right — my apologies. I apologize. I didn't mean any offence." But everything he now said he said with the same malicious intent and there was nothing I could say to counter this.

I left them, pausing outside to compose myself and to listen to them, and hearing Webster say loudly, "Well, we certainly touched a nerve there."

Part Two

CHAPTER
TWENTY-THREE

By the time of my father's death, his library of bee books consisted of over twelve hundred volumes. Less than a quarter of that number were original titles, and these were supplemented by new editions of the same volumes, and by foreign editions, American and German mostly, especially where there were additional variations in printing and illustrations.

Catalogues from booksellers arrived at the house weekly. When he finally completed Cotton's Bee Book List, compiled sixty years earlier, adding each of its nine pages of listings to his collection, he threw a party, inviting all those others in his associations and clubs embarked upon the same grail-like quest.

I remember Charles and I spending the morning with him, arranging the volumes in the order listed by Cotton in the glass-fronted cases my father had had constructed for that purpose by a local joiner. My mother was also invited to contribute to the setting up of this display, but she declined, saying that "her men" would make a better job of it. I realize now that she probably also considered this to be a kind of unnecessary and vulgar showing-off. But whatever her reasons, Charles and I were happy to participate, unwrapping each of the more precious volumes from their protective tissue and arranging them in the cases, ready for their admiring and covetous inspection.

As we grew, and as we were allowed to participate more and more in the keeping of the bees, so Charles and I came to know the authors and titles of these volumes by heart, and they became as familiar to us as the works of any great and long-lived writer.

Cowan's *Beekeeper's Guide* was a particular favourite of mine, reissued almost annually, and invariably with some changes or added illustrations to make it endlessly desirable, revised and enlarged until it was almost doubled in size. I admired and copied its full-page illustrations, seeing bees the size of my shoes in all their intricate details.

The rarest of his books, and a volume neither Charles nor I were ever permitted to handle, was Butler's *Feminine Monarchie*, a book first printed at the beginning of the seventeenth century, and far beyond the means of most collectors. My father's edition, printed a hundred and fifty years later, copied exactly the first printing, right down to its misspellings and strangely spelled words. The volume took pride of place in the most central of his cases — the only one ranked non-alphabetically — and was not only protected by its tissue, but was also held by padded brackets and then carefully angled away from the sunlight. A thermometer was kept in the library, checked daily by my father; the windows were regularly opened and closed, and the small fire in the room was never lit.

It was a privilege to be trusted to care for this collection. Likewise, it was a privilege swiftly withdrawn when either Charles or I incurred my father's displeasure. We were never beaten by him, seldom even slapped in admonition even as small boys, and the withdrawal of these library privileges was by far the most keenly felt of our punishments.

I remember sitting on my bed and crying for a whole day when I was sent out of the library for creasing the title page of his Morse due to my lack of attention. I remember the occurrence, and every detail of the book itself, vividly. To add to my anguish, Charles was then instructed to remain with my father amid the books, and was then shown how creases and other marks and stains might be removed. I remember hearing my father's voice as he instructed Charles in all of this. I anticipated that my mother might appear to comfort me — I can have been no older than nine or ten — but when she did finally come an hour later, telling me that I was required to go downstairs for lunch, she said nothing about what had happened.

The following day, my father explained to me at great length what damage I had caused by my carelessness. I promised him fifty times over that it would never happen again. And then, just as I imagined I might be about to be banished from the library for weeks to come, he took me in there and put the Morse back into my trembling hands, showing me the vestiges of the damage I had caused. He left me alone briefly, pretending to attend to his work elsewhere. When he returned he pointed out several mistakes Morse had

239

made — allowing me to laugh with him — and then he took the book from me and asked me to help with the restocking of the shelves elsewhere.

Not all his volumes were treated like this. Many, including his later Maeterlinck editions, were used by him as working guides and reference books. He subscribed to over twenty journals, and when a dozen of these had collected he would send them to be bound in covers of his own design, a small golden bee embossed on the spine of each volume.

In addition to these specialist volumes — always "Bee Books" to my father, and never any of the titles other collectors tried to force into common usage — he also collected books relating to agriculture and rural pursuits in general, but which invariably contained chapters on bee-keeping. These included Pepys and Evelyn — he owned a specially reprinted edition of Evelyn's manuscript on bee-keeping from *Elysium Britannicum* — Dryden, Gay, Goldsmith, White, Cobbett, Darwin, Edwards and, of course, de Mandeville. All of these authors kept his more specific collection book-ended with the wider rural economy and the world at large. He owned many editions of White's *Natural History* — one of the first books I remember him reading aloud to me — along with at least a dozen copies of de Mandeville's *Fable*, another of his personal favourites.

A great many of these writers, he pointed out to us, were not only bee-keepers, but also parsons and doctors. There were "affinities", he told us, between these followings and the work involved with bee-keeping. A man who kept bees, he insisted, was attached to Nature, dependent upon it; and a man dependent upon Nature was often forced to reshape his own personality and temperament accordingly. I cannot remember him being any more specific on any of these points, but I believe both Charles and I understood perfectly what he was telling us.

Every birthday, Christmas and anniversary, my mother would strive to present him with something for which he was searching. She wrote to his booksellers and club secretaries with the lists she copied from his Acquisitions Book. I suspected that these men then corresponded secretly with my father and that he made his own surreptitious recommendations on her behalf. She often told him that she did not care about the rarity or the cost of these presents, only about their value to him, and that she was the one able to acquire them for him. But in truth she understood considerably more about all this than she ever admitted, invariably going to great lengths to acquire those books which she knew would mean the most to him.

I remember he once burst into tears upon unwrapping a tenth edition of Moses Rusden's *Further Discovery of Bees*, reprinted a century after the original. Having corresponded with his dealers, he had been expecting something else, and seeing the Rusden so suddenly and unexpectedly in his hands like that, his other gifts and cards already scattered amid the food and crockery of the breakfast table, he had been unable to contain or temper his surprise and joy.

His own gifts to her usually comprised jewellery. At his funeral, and attending his coffin beforehand, she had worn at her throat the gold-and-diamond brooch he had had made for her to celebrate their tenth wedding anniversary, and which he had copied in every detail from Swammerdam's *Nature*, always joking with her afterwards that what she wore was Figure Four from Plate Sixteen. It wasn't much of a joke, but between the two of them it came to seem like the most perfect of intimacies. As intimate as my father rubbing the queens' jelly into her small cuts and grazes; as intimate as the pair of them going together to tell the bees of the birth of their sons; as intimate as her act of putting a piece of honeycomb in his grave with him.

It was after reading Thorley's advice on the use of puffballs to stupefy the bees that he had experimented with this method on several of his own hives. It was not a successful experiment, and he afterwards railed at Thorley's incompetence, completing his argument against the man by saying that he, Thorley, had in any case simply stolen the method from Gerard's *Herbal*. He showed us both references, and then made Charles calculate the number of years — everything being printed in Roman numerals — between the two authors.

In addition to his collecting, my father also wrote numerous articles on the specifics of practical bee-keeping, publishing these in the various journals to which he subscribed; he was already well-known by their editors, most of whom he counted among his friends.

He wrote a series of articles entitled *The Enemies of the Bee*, outlining the damage done by the various pests and diseases, and then how best to tackle these. When I first read these remedies I was disappointed by their simplicity, by how obvious my father made everything seem, by how straightforward and quotidian his prose seemed. He was capable of much more, possibly even of a piece of work which would itself one day become a classic and collectable. Only much later did I understand his true purpose in these simple guides. Any bee-keeper faced with the problems my father outlined in his articles would know how to deal with those problems themselves, quickly, effectively and cheaply. And when one solution was either out of reach or unsuccessful, then another was offered; and after that, another.

Almost a decade after his death, I met a man in Belgium, in Nieuport, Captain Turner, who said he had corresponded with my father, and who, owning an estate in Derbyshire, had bound the articles into pamphlets and then issued these to each of his gamekeepers and gardeners.

We spent ten days together, Turner and I, out of the line at Nieuport and at bathing resorts along the coast. Two days afterwards, and less than a month before he was due to return to England to practise at Manton, he was killed in a barrage and his body was never recovered. I wrote a letter to his wife of two years, explaining who I was and what he and I had shared. But I never sent it to her, knowing how painful it would have been for her to have received this while her husband was officially listed as "Missing", and while the faintest glimmer of assiduously shielded hope might remain. I was still in possession of Turner's oilskin cape and his celluloid goggles, untouched since his death.

After my father's death, the booksellers' catalogues and other journals continued to arrive at our home, and whenever a subscription lapsed, my mother renewed it, explaining to the editors who wrote to her that she saw no reason why these important ties should now be severed. They wrote far less frequently to her, of course, than they had written to my father, but their letters, and her own careful answers to them, were no less precious to her in keeping her husband's memory alive.

But gradually, and equally predictably, their correspondence had dwindled over the years, and finally it had ceased. I imagined some of them believed they were a burden to her, taking advantage of her good nature — of her grief, perhaps — in continuing to take her money. Or perhaps they believed that she had none to spare now that she was alone in the world with her sons.

Occasionally, one of the dealers would write to her cautiously enquiring about the "disposal" of my father's collection, and she was invariably fastidiously polite and firm in her reply, pointing out only to Charles and myself that she would no more scatter her husband's volumes than she would dig up his bones and scatter them on the Common or the public road. We laughed each time she added this macabre detail, and the more she repeated the story, the more she embellished it, keeping us the three secret sharers of the tale.

CHAPTER
TWENTY-FOUR

I approached Gurney the following day. He was with Lyle, the two of them in their shared room.

I started to tell Gurney what more had been said concerning the proposed recital, but Lyle quickly interrupted me.

"He already knows," he said. "One of the other doctors came last night to look at him."

"Which one?" I said, angry at this interference. "Doctor Webster?"

Lyle shrugged. "No one we'd seen before."

"Not Osborne himself, then?"

"We know him," Lyle said.

I wondered if he was again being deliberately evasive, and to what end.

He sat with his hand on Gurney's shoulder.

Gurney sat with his head down, trembling slightly.

"He's not had much sleep," Lyle said, lowering his voice, as though Gurney wouldn't hear him even though sitting so close. "He's been" — he sought for the word — "anxious."

"About the performance, about performing himself? He needn't participate." I crouched in front of Gurney. "You needn't participate yourself, Ivor. Marion just wanted to give us the opportunity to hear some of the music you'd composed." I also wanted to suggest to him what unexpected support and momentum Marion Scott's proposal had now gained, and how far beyond our control — his and mine — it had already moved.

"We had tame Germans building roads," Gurney said absently, his head still down.

"Sorry?"

"At Laventie. We came across a warehouse of three-inch-thick beech slabs. A joinery, carpenters. We laid them as roads. You never saw such good cut wood. Not on the mud, on the chalk. Wooden roads. They were chatty-looking men, every one of them, but glad to be out of it. Card schools morning, noon and night. Brag and pontoon, mostly. Hundreds of tons of that beech was stored, God knows what it was for. You wouldn't believe so much of it could just lie there, unused. Worth a small fortune. We laid it straight on to the ground, butted it with soft hammers and drilled pegs through it to stake it." He looked up at me. "I won't be able to play," he said.

"You might," Lyle said encouragingly. "Just not today, not now."

Gurney held out his hand to show me the severity of his shaking.

"That's just today, Ivor," Lyle said. "It'll soon stop."

Gurney looked at him, surprised.

I was again shocked by this change in Gurney's appearance and behaviour. Only a week had passed since I'd last been with him in the orchard.

"The doctor who came to see us told us it was your idea," Lyle said. "Said *you* were the one insisting on it."

"It was Marion Scott's idea," I said. "Ivor knows that."

"I know," Lyle said. "He told me as much as soon as we were alone again."

"No one will insist on anything happening at all if it distresses Ivor," I said, knowing that this was at best a half lie.

"He played the other day," Lyle said. "In the day room. Pity you weren't around to hear him. For an hour. Not a note wrong. Nothing I recognized as such, so I imagine they were his own compositions. Not a single note out of place. It was a warm day and all the windows were open. He had quite an audience out on the terrace. Played like he did it every day, as though —"

"The old moon had gone," Gurney said, again unexpectedly, and Lyle and I waited for him to continue this separate, unconnected conversation.

When he said nothing, Lyle prompted him. "And the new one not yet come?" Like turning the handle on a cold engine.

"Still three days away," Gurney said eventually. "That's why they'd started the bombardment. Pitch dark, you see. Even in July."

"Ypres," Lyle mouthed to me.

"We sat and listened back in Laventie. Peaceful enough there. A month before Will Harvey went missing." Gurney pressed a palm to his ear and I saw a sudden look of concern cross Lyle's face.

"What is it, Ivor?" I said.

"Electrics," Lyle again mouthed to me. He touched a finger to his lips.

We waited like that for several minutes, none of us speaking, Gurney with his hand to his ear and trembling more vigorously as whatever imagined charge or force passed through him.

Eventually, he took his hand away and slowly turned his head from side to side, listening intently to the silence around him. There was nothing to hear, only the muted noise and voices of men outside. A gramophone played in the distant day room, but I doubt if any of us would have been able to recognize its distorted tune through so many walls and funnelled along so many corridors.

"Has it gone?" Lyle asked him.

"I'm writing again to the Superintendent of Police about my pension," Gurney said, and then, one fractured conversation rupturing another, added, "Epancourt, Croix Moligneaux and Caulaincourt. That's where we laid the roads." He looked at Lyle and myself and then tutted loudly, as though we had somehow misunderstood him. "And after that I was at Vermand and Bibecourt. Wounded on Good Friday." He tapped his shoulder. I'd seen the small scars where the bullet had gone in and come out.

"I think Marion Scott was hoping to get others — musicians from the College — to perform," I said. "The recital."

"They'd come," Gurney said, now seemingly unconcerned by what I was suggesting.

248

"What do you hear?" I asked him. "Anything specific, or just noise?"

Lyle shook his head at the question.

"The electrics?" Gurney said. "You tell me. It's all part of my treatment. You might not want me to know about it, but I do. Trained to be a signaller, see? When I was home for good. They had me for a gunner, but that was never a safe mark. Cushy enough billets when you were out of it, but not much else going for it. They see you lugging those guns around and they're on to you straight away. Signaller, that was better. It's how I know about the electrics. D Mark Threes, we had. And Fullers. Only as good as the cables, they used to tell us. And the stunts put paid to most of them. That's how I know."

"You hear voices, music, noise, what?" I said.

He looked at me as though I'd tried to trick him, smiled and then tapped his nose.

"He thinks you're asking him all this so that you can match what he hears with whoever's doing the transmitting," Lyle told me. "That right, Ivor?"

"It's how they did it in Barnwood," Gurney said. "Another thing we hated carrying — pickaxes and shovels. Strap them to your pack and it was impossible to walk at a crouch. Made you stand up straight, see? Not much future in that. Before we went up at St Julien, we met a wounded digger sitting by a horse trough. Know what he was telling everybody as we walked past him?"

"What?" I said.

"'Go back, turn back, there's a war going on up there.'"

Our laughter was forced and short-lived.

"Is it painful for you?" I asked Gurney. "The electrics."

"Sometimes," he said, already suspicious of my reason for asking him.

"And at other times?"

He shrugged. "Sometimes it's almost quiet. I get the same voices, the same questions."

"The voices of people you recognize?"

"People I might know *of*, but who I never met," he said.

"He means other musicians," Lyle said, exasperated, already having told me this.

"Are the electrics getting worse?" I asked Gurney. "Louder? More frequent?"

He nodded.

"They've been bad the last few nights, haven't they, Ivor?"

"Kept me awake," Gurney said. There were dark rings around his eyes; I'd imagined this was a consequence of his medication.

"We can give you something to help you sleep," I suggested.

"You already do," Lyle said.

"Ivor?"

Gurney didn't answer me.

"He thinks you've altered his medication so that the transmitters can do their job more effectively," Lyle said.

250

"We haven't," I said. "There are no transmitters, no electrics of any sort. All that's in the past. Electrotherapy for muscle spasm, that's all. Not like Ivor means."

Gurney remained unconcerned by these rebuttals. "I know what line you've got to take," he said. "I don't blame you for it."

"Is there any comfort to be gained from what you hear?" I asked him.

"Comfort? Sometimes," he said. "I sometimes hear people from back in Gloucester, from when I was a boy, good people. Herbert Foster, John Haines, Alfred Cheeseman; I hear Emily and Margaret Hunt. I wrote music for her when I was scarcely grown out of a boy. All good people."

The names meant nothing to me. I made a note to ask Marion Scott about them when I next saw her. The women, I imagined, were the unnamed surrogate mothers she'd alluded to.

"And they talk to you now?" I said.

"Sometimes. Rarely. I try to put the same notes together in my head, but they never fit — they knock heads, as Margaret Hunt used to say."

"And that's painful for you, something you regret not being able to do any longer, something you regret losing?"

Gurney considered all this. "It's not all the time," he said. "Sometimes it comes, sometimes."

"Show him your writing," Lyle said.

But Gurney immediately shook his head.

"I only meant —" Lyle began.

"We had horse shows," Gurney said. "Field days. There was an Australian brass band. Filthy instruments. Not one of them polished. We told them they'd all be on a charge in the Gloucesters, but they only laughed at us. They said we were stupid to do all the things we did. Beautiful instruments, mind, only filthy. You could taste it on them." He licked his lips, his finger running back and forth across his bottom lip and teeth.

Lyle and I waited for this to stop before Lyle said to me, "I've decided — I'm going back to Gloucester."

The remark surprised me. "For your Board? Have you made an application?"

"Not yet. But I'll do it soon."

"Does Ivor know?"

"Told him yesterday. He said I was doing the right thing."

"You are," I told him.

"None of us knows anything for certain," he said. "I still don't like leaving him."

"A few months and he may not even recognize you," I said, knowing how blunt and uncaring the remark sounded, but wanting my meaning to be clear to Lyle.

"He's thirty-four," he said.

"So?"

"Nothing. I just don't want to abandon him like everybody else already has or soon will do."

"You think Marion Scott's going to stop coming?" I tried to make it sound like a joke.

He smiled. "No, I suppose not. The doctor who came last night said there were new treatments that Ivor might respond better to."

"What treatments?"

"He never said. Just that he'd come back and see him to work out what might best suit him."

"I doubt if —"

"I know all that. He was just being nosey and humouring us. I'm a lunatic too, remember?"

I looked at Gurney and saw how far he had now retreated from us, and how swiftly this had happened.

"What made you decide to apply to return to Gloucester?" I asked Lyle.

"Something Cox said."

"Cox? What did he say?"

"Just that he'd worked here long enough to know that some people fitted and that others didn't. And that those people who didn't fit to begin with, but who stayed too long, always fitted in the end."

"And that there was then no way out for them?"

He nodded.

"Cox has got a big mouth and doesn't know what he's talking about," I said. "Things — treatments, medicines — are changing all the time."

"There was still a lot of sense in what he said. What changes are there down here, in these rooms, in the places me and Ivor live? No one down here ever sees much sign of these changes. Everything down here is still one long day after another. This is still Cox's little kingdom, remember. You might think it's yours, but it isn't."

Having already endorsed Cox's remark about his transfer application, it would have been unwise now to dispute whatever else the man was saying.

"Three more days for the new moon," Gurney said suddenly. "We buried the dead of Aubers Ridge and then we went back to Laventie. Pitch black it was, but always with that light of the coming day, always that. I used to go up Huntley way to see that. Whitminster and Hempsted. Every constellation in the heavens up there, and always that light at the rims."

He drew a broad half-circle with his arm. And then he rubbed his eyes and looked hard at me.

"They want me to perform some of my songs," he said. "They're getting up a concert."

"I know," I said. "Will you do it?"

"No reason not to, I suppose. Margaret Hunt said she never knew a day when I wasn't glued to a piano or an organ. She died two months before my father. Third of March. I wanted to go to her funeral, but they said I ought not to. Influenza. They were dropping like flies of that. People who never knew my father assumed it was the same thing carried him off. But that was the cancer. That's a cruel thing, that is. He was pared back to a skeleton by the time his number was called. Ronald said I shouldn't have been at that funeral, neither."

"You went back to London soon afterwards," I said.
"Did I?"

"Back to the College and your music."

Gurney smiled. "Course I did. They want me to give a concert here. You hear that?"

"Here?" Lyle said, feigning surprise. "A concert?"

254

CHAPTER
TWENTY-FIVE

Will Harvey called me two days later and asked if he could see me alone. Marion Scott had contacted him, he said, but was then unwilling to add more until he saw me.

I met him that evening, at the main entrance, and we walked together along a field path running towards the river.

He'd been in court all day and was staying in London that night. He looked exhausted.

On the telephone, I'd suggested meeting in my office or room, but he said he'd prefer it if we could meet outside the asylum, and that I didn't tell Gurney of his visit.

We spoke for ten minutes before he finally referred to Marion Scott and the recital.

"You think it's a bad idea," I said, having guessed the cause of his concern. I'd seen during his previous visit that not only was his friendship with Gurney built on separate foundations to that of Marion Scott, but that his understanding of Gurney's currently deteriorating condition, and his own concerns for the man, also differed from hers.

"I just think that it should have come from Ivor himself, to be something *he* needed to do, something *he* needed to prove."

"Before everything's finally lost to him?" I said.

"If that's what's happening to him, yes."

I told him about my earlier confused conversation with Gurney. I also told him what Lyle had mentioned more than once now, about Gurney still writing, and regularly.

"I know," he said. He stopped walking. "But have you actually *seen* anything of what he's writing?"

I told him I hadn't.

"I have. He sends it to Marion. She showed me some after our last visit. Whatever it is she shows you — and God knows who else — you can bet she'll be a little more circumspect about showing anything Ivor might currently be producing."

"Is it not as good?"

"Whatever it is or isn't, it's simply not the same."

"In what way?"

He considered his answer. "Let me send you some. She made me copies. Look at it and decide for yourself."

"Does she know how you feel about this, the recital?"

He shook his head. "I truly believe that without Marion Scott, Ivor wouldn't have achieved half — less — of what he already has done. She saw something in him and then championed him from the very start. It was a blow to her when he returned to London and was then unable to take up where he'd left off."

"She gave him encouragement — a kind of faith, perhaps? — to do what he did?" I saw immediately how simplistic and misleading this suggestion was.

"It was more than that. Everyone says she mothers him. But it was always much more than that. You might just as easily say he was a brother to me as a son to her."

I listed the names I could remember from my conversation with Gurney and he told me who the people were and what part they had played in Gurney's musical upbringing.

"That's how I sometimes see myself — as his brother," he said. "Believe me, if I didn't believe that, I wouldn't be here now."

"You think there's too much resting on the recital?" I said.

"And you don't? It's the last thing Ivor needs. Surely you can see that much?"

I began to better understand what he was telling me.

"He's being treated like a performing dog," he said, deliberately overstating the case. "His achievement, especially his music, is above what even *I* can sometimes appreciate." He saw how pompous this sounded. "And I'm a member of not one, but *two* choral societies and one mostly-in-tune choir."

We stopped at a gate and looked out over the open land to the water, visible in part where it showed beyond a line of low buildings.

"When I was taken prisoner," he said, "when Ivor thought I was killed, he wrote a letter to my mother telling her what he thought of me, what I meant to him.

She treasured that letter. He told her what she — what we all — meant to him, how content he'd been in our company, how he wished we were his true family instead of the one he'd got. He told her he would rather lose one of his own arms than lose me. My mother told me she read that letter — all nine pages of it, written while Ivor was at the front — a hundred times over. She said that she formed a belief that for as long as she was reading it, listening to what Ivor was telling her from his heart, seeing me there, in those pages, in those words, for as long as she could do all of that, then she knew I couldn't be dead. She said he had me to perfection — I know: a mother's son — and that it kept alive her hope."

"And all of that belief was justified when she later discovered you'd been taken prisoner?" I said.

"The pity of it all is that it was such a small percentage of us." He paused. "It's strange. I was taken to a place called Neuweid, on the Rhine, a repatriation centre. Gütersloh, Krefeld and then Neuweid. All through the war, we were sending home German lunatics, and they were sending home ours. A kind of great, terrible balancing act."

"I know," I told him.

"I was put to work at the Neuweid railway station, helping them on to the trains. Lunatics and basket cases. Pitiful, pitiful. When he knew where I was — God knows how; I was shifted from pillar to post — Ivor wrote to me, sent me his poems and songs. He wrote a poem for me — 'To His Love' — thinking I was dead. My mother read it once and wept for a day afterwards. He made no reference whatsoever to me about the letter he'd written to her. Instead, he went on about everything *he* was doing, the things and places he'd seen, all our mutual acquaintances. Deaths, mostly, all those acquaintances who'd died or been injured."

"Do you think he didn't mention the letter because he didn't want to admit to you that he might have believed you were dead?"

He shrugged, unwilling to reveal his true belief. "It hardly matters. All I know is that without him, without Ivor . . ." He trailed off, and neither of us spoke for a moment.

Out on the river, a ship sounded its klaxon, and this was followed by the clamour of the gulls disturbed on the muddy shore.

"He called me Lazarus when he knew I was alive," he said fondly. "The resurrected man. He set two of my own poems to music. 'In Flanders' and 'Severn Meadows'."

I remembered Marion Scott talking about them in his presence.

"I didn't know you —" I began.

"Didn't know I was a poet?" he said. "One volume. The folly of youth. Probably. Nothing to compare to Ivor's work."

"Still . . ." I said.

"Exactly," he said, smiling. "Still . . ." He closed his eyes briefly.

"'And who loves Joy as he
That dwells in shadows?

Do not forget me quite
O Severn Meadows.'"

I understood perfectly why he'd recited this and I remained silent.

"When I saw him after his discharge," he went on, "and after I'd been repatriated, we got drunk together and he declared his intention of marrying one of my sisters."

"Was it a serious suggestion?"

"From him, perhaps. I imagine he made the same offer elsewhere. He always needed someone to keep him on the straight and narrow, Ivor."

"Which is what the Army did, the war?" We were talking about Gurney's health.

"Took to it like a duck to water, he did."

"Did he ever make an actual proposal to one of your sisters?"

He bowed his head, unwilling to answer. "Everything changed," he said.

Taking a risk, I said, "Do you know if anything happened to him at any of the places he was treated following his discharge?"

"You mean Napsbury. Has he said anything himself?"

"Not to me."

"I don't know, not for certain. His records will tell you one thing, Marion another."

I told him what Marion Scott had already revealed to me about Gurney's failed suicide attempt.

260

"None of us wanted to believe it," he said. "First Napsbury, then Warrington. We were walking at Lydney once, Ivor and I, when he told me out of the blue that he'd once tried to drown himself, that he'd filled all his pockets with stones and walked into the Severn at Longney Crib. He asked me if I could think of a more fitting end for him — him and that river."

"What happened?"

He laughed. "He said he'd walked into the water, but that at its deepest it had only come up to his waist. If he'd walked any further, he'd have found himself on the far shore. He hadn't realized how low the flow was. When he was over the worst of things — his depression; his 'possessions' he called them — he said he took the unnaturally low water as a sign."

"That he was meant to go on living?"

"Or that he just wasn't meant to kill himself that way. He seemed to recover more of his old self in the months after that. I was too often away from home, attending to my work; I saw less and less of him. He went to my mother, and she saw what he'd done, what was happening to him. She wanted him to stay with her at Minsterworth, perhaps even to live there with them."

"And he refused?"

"He told them he was too unwell, too unpredictable. He said it was why he preferred to wander alone, among strangers, in places that were unknown to him, in London."

"Do you think there were other attempts at suicide?"

"I should imagine so. Is provision made here to keep an eye on that sort of thing?"

"He shares a room," I said. "His medication will suppress most violent urges."

"Most?"

"He seems content."

We continued walking, eventually turning back towards the road, the estuary at our backs. Harvey picked flowers from the path and from the raised bank of a drain.

"It's what we used to do," he said. "Me and Ivor, grown men, picking flowers and then identifying everything we came across. He had a passion for it. And anything he couldn't identify immediately, he'd make a point of looking up. Even in France. I remember being with him just before Richebourg, in a copse filled with burdock, woodruff, campion, late celandine — creeping-Jenny we called that — and columbine. He picked them and put the flowers in his pockets and buttonholes. When the sergeant told him to take them out, Ivor calmly told the man that they were there as camouflage for when we next went up to the front. 'Flowers?' the sergeant said. 'You think there are going to be flowers where you lot are going?' " He smiled at the memory.

After an hour of walking, we arrived back opposite the asylum entrance. Harvey stood and considered it from the far side of the road. We sat on the blue bench there — painted to alert passers-by that it was intended primarily for the use of the patients.

"Do you want me to try and put a stop to the recital?" I asked him.

"Will you be able to?"

262

It was unlikely, and we both understood this.

"I don't want to do anything to offend Marion," he said. It was where his defeat lay; just as mine lay in the self-serving calculations of Osborne, Webster and the others.

"It shocked you to see him last week," I said.

He nodded. "I'd become accustomed to his . . . changes. But seeing him here, like that . . . I almost didn't recognize him."

"And he you?"

"He once told me that he believed the war and the Army were making him fit for a higher task."

"His music, you mean? His poetry?"

"I'm not sure. When I asked him to explain, he said he couldn't. I think he expected me to understand what he was telling me."

"And you disappointed him by not knowing?"

He considered this in silence for a moment. "He told me the Army was like a proper family to him, that he no longer felt the odd-man-out once he was in, that no one cared about any strangeness he might possess, that it was tolerated. God knows, there was enough strangeness elsewhere in the world."

"Come and see him alone," I suggested. "Soon."

"I will." But he said it quickly, looking away from me as he spoke.

He asked me about the buses back into the city centre and told me about the work he still had to do before his appearance in court the following day. I calculated that he would have a further ten minutes to wait.

"Back in Barnwood, Ivor once told me that he felt he'd been betrayed," he said hesitantly.

"By whom? What?"

"Everyone, I suppose. Everything. He felt that all his suffering — in France and afterwards — should have brought him some reward, some recognition." He looked at me to ensure I understood him.

"But instead all it brought him was more suffering?"

"That's what he believed."

Neither of us spoke for a few minutes afterwards.

When the bus finally appeared in the distance, he rose and shook my hand.

"At Napsbury," he said, calculating how many seconds until the bus arrived, already holding up his arm to signal to the driver, "I think that after whatever he attempted, he was severely punished for what he'd done. He told me he'd been kept in complete isolation for ten days. He didn't tell me why."

"It wasn't uncommon practice," I said. "Especially if —"

"No — that's not it," he said, lowering his arm as the bus approached and slowed. "He told me that he was kept in isolation, but that he wasn't alone, that there were others in there with him, talking to him, keeping him company."

"His voices?"

He was relieved I was already aware of these. "It wasn't the first time he'd heard them. He said they made the whole thing bearable for him. Nobody saw him for a month after he was released from St Albans. When I next saw him and asked him what had

264

happened, he refused to acknowledge in any way whatsoever that he'd even been there. We walked from Wainlode to beyond Aust and he said nothing at all about it except to tell me about the voices. I didn't know what to say to him."

The bus finally arrived and he climbed on to its platform, standing there as it pulled away, looking back at the long, high wall of the asylum as he passed it by, and when that was finished, back to me.

At the bend in the road he raised his hand, waved for a moment and was then lost to sight.

All those ripples of false hope, of loss and disillusionment, and all of them moving back and forth from the man slowly disappearing at their centre.

CHAPTER
TWENTY-SIX

I saw Gurney almost every day during the following week. Little more was said of the coming recital, however, except for his own speculation on which pieces Marion Scott might choose to have performed. I doubted if she had spoken to him directly on the matter, and when I asked him for his own choice of music, he told me flatly — all his previous speculation either forgotten or instantly dismissed — that he was leaving everything to Marion, Miss Scott, that he trusted her judgement, and that her choices would be the right ones. I heard in this unquestioning acceptance a further indication of his unwillingness to contradict her; a deeper understanding by Gurney, perhaps — although again this might have been little more than wishful thinking on my part — of the true nature of his reliance on her, and of the increasingly tragic nature of this overloaded dependency. There was no longer any talk of Gurney himself performing at the recital.

Lyle was frequently with us when we met. He understood my reservations and concerns, and on the few occasions I was alone with him, he, like Will Harvey, asked me repeatedly why the recital was going ahead at all, what purpose it was truly meant to serve. I asked him if Gurney shared these doubts, and he merely looked at me, disappointed, perhaps, by my own complicity in the matter. I eventually lost my patience with the man and told him that perhaps none of us fully understood what Gurney's music still meant to him, and whether or not it might yet prove to be his salvation. I regretted using the word the instant I'd said it, and Lyle laughed at me. To prop up my failing argument, I added that neither he nor I still properly understood what Gurney and Marion Scott were to each other. He refused to respond to this, too, and when I tried to explain myself he simply turned and walked away from me.

In truth, I was growing increasingly tired of Lyle's manipulative behaviour where Gurney was concerned, and I looked forward to his departure, after which I would be able to talk to Gurney without his constant mediating presence.

On one occasion towards the end of that week, I met the two of them together amid the hives, working there with others, once again cutting the grass and pruning more of the lower branches.

I had gone there with Alison West, who had sought me out earlier in the day with the news that the two queens she had sent away for had finally arrived. She had them with her, secure in their card tubes, and she said she intended introducing them to the hives later that afternoon. It was the best time, as the day's heat started slowly to fall, and as the light faded and the bees settled. It ensured the queens would stay where they were, giving off their scent all evening and night, and attracting new colonies to establish around them.

She also told me she had spoken to a farmer in Bexley, who said his own overcrowded bees had shown signs of swarming during the past few days. If we were able to make all the necessary arrangements, then the bees were ours for the taking. It was early in the season, and the swarm would not be a large one, but sufficient alongside the new queens to double the size of our own small colonies.

I asked her what she needed to gather the bees and she told me. I asked her to let me know when the farmer contacted her, knowing how important it was to contain the swarming bees before they flew too far and started to disperse.

"He thinks three or four days," she said. "After the cloud, when some real heat arrives."

Light rain had been forecast for the next few days, and this would delay the bees' departure. My father always referred to it as "damping" them. And when the rain stopped and the sun returned, then the bees would "steam" away from the hives.

She showed me the queens and their certificates. They were as fat as plums in their tubes, barely moving, pulsing slightly and occasionally producing a low and resonating hum.

Shortly before the men in the orchard were due to be called indoors, she took the queens to Gurney and handed one over to him. He held the tube to his eye and peered into it through its pinched slit. He told her he'd never seen one packaged like that before. He told us about the man he'd once encountered on his wanderings who had produced a queen from his waistcoat pocket, tethered to him by a slender cotton thread, like a watch.

"Said he was laying her scent between hives to make sure all the others moved in the right direction. Walked back and forth with her ten times a day."

"My father would have done it only once," I told him.

"Then you had clever and obedient bees," he said seriously. He shook the tube gently and the queen buzzed more loudly. He looked around us for the most suitable of the vacant hives.

I told Alison which I considered to be the soundest.

"Let Ivor choose," she said, and Gurney appreciated this, pacing among the hives, kicking at the freshly cut grass which surrounded them, and shielding his eyes to see where the sunlight lay. Eventually, he chose an empty structure close to the greenhouses and we followed him to it.

Alison showed him how to squeeze open the tube and to scrape out the sugar residue, placing this into the hive, where the queen might then be left.

Gurney and Lyle slid out several of the restored frames and the excluder, revealing the brood box. Alison pulled this out too, and blew through it to clear the last of its dust. She upended it and tapped out any dirt before reassembling the floor and the box. Then she stood back while Gurney took out the queen and put her close to the sugar, watching her rub herself against this before laying the fine mesh of the excluder

269

over her and then re-hanging the frames. Alison gave him the roof and he set this back over the hive, shaking the frame and then cocking his head to its side as though listening to ensure that everything inside had settled back into its proper place. It was something I'd seen my father do a thousand times.

Within only a few seconds of this rebuilding, several bees from the other structures approached and explored the entrance. We all watched them, relieved when the first of them went inside.

Only Lyle was less than enthralled by this procedure, unhappy, I guessed, at the attention Alison West was now paying to Gurney and not to him.

I told Gurney about the probability of acquiring the swarming bees and repopulating more of the hives.

But Gurney was not listening to me; instead, he stood with his ear still pressed to the hive, a finger to his lips.

Eventually, after several minutes of this intent listening, he stood upright.

"They're talking to her," he said.

Beside me, Lyle shook his head.

"What are they saying?" Alison asked Gurney.

Gurney looked at her and shrugged. He turned to me and winked. "I hardly know what half of the over-educated people in here are saying to me most days; surely I'm not expected to understand what bees might say to each other?"

"They probably talk more sense," Alison said. She gave the second tube to Lyle, and told him to choose a hive, but Lyle told her that he had no interest in doing this, and handed the tube to me. Alison glanced at me, quickly assessing the true nature of this refusal.

Only Gurney looked surprised at Lyle's behaviour.

"What is it?" he asked him, raising his hand to Lyle.

Lyle seemed suddenly and briefly embarrassed by his own petulance, and he began to stammer.

Alison took the tube from me and put it back into his hand, telling him again to choose a hive. This time he held on to the queen and started to look around him at the remaining structures. He chose one beneath an old plum tree, more dead wood than living, and which appeared not to have fruited for years. Gurney congratulated him on the choice, and the two men walked ahead of us to introduce the queen to her new home.

"I think Lyle's —" I began to say to Alison when the two men were beyond hearing, and as they talked to each other.

"I know," she said firmly, unwilling to hear what I might have again been about to suggest about Lyle's attachment to her. "And if anyone else thought the same — Osborne or Cox, for instance . . ." She stopped talking and looked at me, ensuring I understood what she was suggesting.

"Is it a common thing?" I asked her. "You . . . the men here?"

She smiled at my awkwardness. "Am I devastatingly attractive to lunatics, do you mean?"

I laughed at the remark.

"Exactly," she said. Then she called to Gurney and Lyle, who waited for her at the chosen hive.

We went through the same procedure of tapping out the queen and placing her at the heart of the structure, settling her in the warmth and the darkness there, close to the last of her sugar. And there, too, the bees were quick to arrive and investigate, and we stood back at their approach.

"You going to listen to them gabbling away again, Ivor boy?" Lyle said to Gurney.

Gurney shook his head. "I was just making it up. They don't talk. Just all that humming, like a faulty wire."

"Him and his electrics again," Lyle said to me. To Gurney, he said, "Electrics coming out of the hives now, are they? You'll need to watch that, Ivor."

I wondered how Gurney might respond to this, but he only laughed.

"I heard bees humming all my life," he said. He turned to Alison. "When you go for the others, you'll want something to tang with."

"What do you suggest?" she asked him.

"Seen my Maisemore uncle use an old bucket or the back of a shovel."

"Tanging" was the act of making a gentle and repetitive noise — usually metallic — which was supposed to calm a swarming brood while it was gathered up in a sack. The sound waves were intended to both mesmerize and confuse the bees, making it impossible for them to communicate their alarm until they were safely collected.

My mother had always brought out a copper-bottomed saucepan and a ladle for the purpose when

272

our own bees swarmed, standing at the far end of the garden as my father prowled around his departing brood, telling her where to reposition herself, how close to come, how loudly or quietly to strike the pan. He had had every faith in the procedure.

Gurney explained the process to Lyle, and this time, rather than dismiss or disparage what Gurney said, Lyle listened intently, speculating further on how it might work.

We were still discussing the best implements to use when we were interrupted by shouting voices from beyond the garden wall. I recognized Cox's above the others, and I immediately regretted that our peaceful interlude had again come to an end.

Now that summer was approaching, more work than previously was being undertaken in the gardens and greenhouses. More of the patients had been found work there, and this in turn necessitated the presence of more orderlies. These orderlies, I noticed, and with Cox frequently among them, used the garden details as an excuse to do nothing. They were supposed to work alongside the patients in a supervisory role, but more often than not they congregated in separate groups and merely sat and watched, or smoked and played cards while the inmates did all the work, little though this often was.

Gurney alone grew concerned at the shouting voices.

Alison mouthed, "Cox" to me.

"Come over here," I said to Gurney and Lyle, indicating the path beneath the trees leading away from the wall, where, unless the shouting men now entered the orchard, we would be neither seen nor overheard by them. Alison led the two men away from the wall.

I followed them.

Looking at my watch, I was surprised to see how long I had spent there, how quickly the time had passed. I had an appointment elsewhere for which I was already late.

"I have to go," I told her, unhappy at having to leave them like this. "Wait here, stay together. I'll tell Cox and whoever to stay away from the hives, that the bees are restless. I'll say I was here alone."

"He won't believe a word you tell him. You know what he's like. If he wants to come in here, he'll come in."

"And me telling him to stay out —"

"Exactly."

Beyond the wall, the shouting grew briefly louder; it sounded as though the men there were actually fighting.

I indicated Gurney's growing concern to Alison and she went to hold him, her hands on his shoulders.

I told them again to stay where they were and then I went alone to the gateway, looking back to where the three of them were now almost invisible in the shifting mix of light and shade beneath the trees.

I left the orchard and walked into the land beyond.

Cox and three other orderlies stood against the far wall. Cox held one of these men against the wall, his forearm pressed against the man's throat, his fist against his face. The man was struggling for air and Cox was shouting at him, his face only inches away.

The other two men stood on either side of Cox and slightly behind him. One of these saw me appear and told Cox.

Cox looked over his shoulder at me, surprised by my sudden appearance. He lowered his fist but kept his arm across the man's throat.

I walked closer to them.

At my approach, Cox finally lowered his arm, now holding his palm against the man's chest. I saw then that the man against the wall was Lewis, the recent appointee who had visited the whale with us. Cox finally withdrew his hand and Lewis leaned forward, coughing, his hands on his knees. Lewis then spat heavily into the grass, stood upright and glared at Cox.

Cox finally took several paces back from him, his palms now held in a placatory gesture.

"What's happened?" I asked Cox.

"Happened? Where? Here? Nothing."

"I could ask him," I said, indicating Lewis, who was now rubbing his throat.

"Ask him what you like," Cox said, unconcerned. "And he'll tell you what I'm telling you — that we had a little misunderstanding, that's all. He's new here, didn't understand all the rules properly. One or two things I had to put him straight on. A few things needed putting right, so to speak." He grinned broadly as he said this, confident that Lewis would not contradict him and reveal the true nature of their argument. He turned to the others, who nodded their agreement with him, and who then avoided me when I looked at them directly.

"Besides," Cox said to me, gesturing behind me. "What you doing prowling around in there all by yourself?"

"I went to check on the bees," I said. "I had a few moments to myself."

"And so you thought you'd check on the bees?"

"Are you all right?" I asked Lewis, who was now wiping his face with his sleeve.

"Course he is." Cox pinched Lewis's cheek, causing him to flinch and then to pull away. "Like I said, just a little misunderstanding."

"About what?"

Cox looked hard at Lewis. "You want to tell him?"

After a minute of silent consideration, Lewis said, "About nothing. It was my fault. I'm new here."

"And lucky to have got the work in the first place, isn't that right?" Cox said.

Lewis nodded.

It was clear to me that he would reveal nothing more to me in front of Cox and the others, and that I was only prolonging his pain and embarrassment by being there.

I saw Cox looking back towards the orchard.

"I want you to come with me," I said to Lewis, hoping this would distract Cox.

"What for?" Lewis said anxiously.

Cox pushed himself between us. "He's under my supervision," he said. "He goes nowhere without my say-so. You're making this up; you don't need him for anything."

"I'm not answerable to you," I told Cox.

"No?"

I realized I was backing myself into a corner, and both Cox and Lewis saw this too.

Behind us, in the main building, the bell sounded to signal the end of the afternoon's work.

Cox grinned again at hearing this. "Looks like we've *all* got to be somewhere else." He started to push Lewis along the wall towards the gate, and for all that the youth was clearly terrified of the man, he still seemed happier to go with Cox and the others than to remain with me.

I did nothing to prevent him from leaving, relieved only that Cox was now more determined to get away from me than he was to investigate whatever I might have been doing in the orchard and whoever else might still be there.

I walked behind the four men, joining the others on the lawn. I watched as they went inside, and then waited a few minutes until Alison West came out of the garden with Gurney and Lyle. She saw me and raised her hand to me. Gurney and Lyle did the same. And then the three of them disappeared into the impenetrable shadow of a doorway.

CHAPTER
TWENTY-SEVEN

Each summer the gypsies would arrive and set up their camp somewhere on the common land beside our house. They usually came in either late July or early August, depending on their work elsewhere, timing their arrival to coincide with the harvest starting to get under way all around us.

My father always regarded their presence with suspicion, and with warnings to Charles and myself to stay away from them. But my mother always looked upon them with a kind of envious and benevolent wonder. In particular, she had an affinity with the gypsy women, and during the ten months of their absence she would save all our old and worn-out clothing for them, awaiting their arrival at our door, dark-skinned and swathed in heavy shawls at the height of summer, and invariably bringing with them their new babies and their own growing children to show to her. Elsewhere, I imagine, this was done in an appeal to charity, but these women knew my mother, and knew that she genuinely looked forward to their arrival.

They sat with her in our kitchen, told her of their year, its profits and losses, and Charles and I would wait outside with the older children, admiring the snares they made and used, watching them climb the trees we were forbidden to climb, listening to them perfectly mimic birds and animals.

Whatever it was that my mother envied in those women, then what Charles and I admired most was the wildness in the boys, their unregulated lives and freedoms. And what we admired, they dismissed. We showed them our toys and made gifts to them of everything that was either broken or no longer in favour.

My father's suspicions and prejudices were largely ill-founded, and my mother invariably warned him of his behaviour when the gypsy men were nearby.

They came to us as usual during the first full summer of the war, when Charles was already in France, and the last summer I myself would be there other than during my subsequent fleeting and unhappy visits.

They usually set up their camp on the far side of the Common, against the woods and the rising land to the west. The river curved there, and they arranged their caravans and few motor vehicles in a line along this, skirting the macadamed road to Stroud. They tethered their horses on the Common, moving them each morning and evening to fresh pasture. The animals were on long ropes, though most seemed hardly to move from where they were first staked.

As usual, the women came to my mother, but that year most of the talk was of their own brothers and sons who had already enlisted. She showed them the silver-framed photograph of Charles in his uniform that she kept in pride of place on our mantel, and they in turn pulled from their jackets and shawls the smaller pictures of their own boys and men.

Some of these had already been wounded and killed, and one man — younger than Charles, I remember — was back at home with a foot and a hand missing. He had been discharged because of his injuries, and now made a living begging in the streets with his service ribbons taped to his begging tin.

My mother spent hours with these women. She made them tea, which they drank by the pint, adding herbs and leaves of their own to my mother's Sheffield-plate pot. My father showed her how these concoctions were tarnishing the metal, but she refused to polish it until the women were finally gone in the autumn.

The summer I remember most vividly was one six or seven years before the war, when, a few weeks before the arrival of the gypsies, my father had relocated a dozen or so of his older hives on to the common land beside the road. They were busy and thriving, making "wild" honey which he sold at a premium in the local markets. He told me to keep an eye on these bees, to guard them. I asked him if he meant from the predations of the gypsies, and he told me again all the tales he had heard of them stealing honey. When I asked him how they did this, knowing how fraught with danger any intrusion into the hives was, he grew angry and told me simply to do as he asked. He apologized to me afterwards, saying that he was more concerned about the recently located bees being disturbed than with the loss of their honey. I tried to explain to him that I was no longer a child, and that most of the gypsy children scattered anyway at my approach. If I was no longer a child, he countered, then I could protect the hives from the gypsy men. Charles, I remember, was away for much of the summer, staying with friends in Worcester.

I knew a number of the gypsy men, and I considered it unlikely that they would steal from us. Most respected the bond their wives and sisters had with my mother. They brought her fish and rabbits, the occasional bunch of flowers and bowls of wild fruit, always leaving these at the door when there was no chance of being invited in to sit with her.

I had little true idea then of my mother's growing sense of loneliness or isolation, or of the losses — real and imaginary — she already bore.

Chief among my father's concerns was the pack of dogs which accompanied the gypsies — terriers and cross-bred hounds, mostly, and most kept for hunting. This was prohibited on the open common land, but was carried out in the surrounding woodlands. The dogs came uncontrolled to the hives, cocked their legs on the frames and disturbed the bees with their sniffing and barking.

When he saw the dogs from the house, my father would run across the road shouting and waving his stick at them, scaring them away briefly and making himself look ridiculous in the process. My mother would wait at the door for his return, her silent gaze fixed on every step he took. He tried to explain to her,

281

but she would simply turn her back on him and refuse to listen. And so instead, and in Charles's absence, he explained everything to me, making me his willing accomplice in keeping away the dogs and protecting the hives.

In every other respect, he treated the gypsies fairly, visiting their encampment at my mother's urging to examine and treat their sick children. And it was she who urged him to take gifts of wax and honey as a sign of his goodwill. And to keep them looking in another direction, he whispered to me. When my mother was not present, he called the gypsies "muggers". It was the name his own father had used.

My most enduring memory of that summer was of the morning my father woke me from my sleep at five o'clock and urged me to get dressed and to follow him outside. He shook me and spoke in an urgent whisper, clearly unhappy at the prospect of also waking my mother.

I dressed quickly and followed him downstairs, where he waited for me in the doorway, searching the brightening horizon. I asked him what was wrong, imagining he'd woken, looked outside and seen someone stealing from his hives.

But the road and the Common beyond were both empty, wet with dew and mostly in shadow as the sun, not yet risen, cast most of its early light into a cloudless sky above the bordering woodland.

I asked him again what was wrong, but he told me to be quiet.

I followed him to the road, waiting at our wall. The hives stood in a staggered line ahead of us, near-luminous in their whiteness, silent in the darkness. "Listen," my father told me, and I cupped a hand to my ear to prove to him that I was doing this. I turned my head to where he pointed.

In the distance, thin lines of pale smoke already rose from the encampment fires. There was nothing unusual in this; some fires were kept burning continuously.

And as I listened, I heard the far-off barking of dogs, and the shouting of men.

"They're out hunting," my father said, "lamping," unable to disguise the alarm he felt. I asked him what concerned him about this, and again he refused to answer me, simply shaking his head at my lack of understanding, at the slowly widening chasm already opening between us in Charles's absence.

He crossed the road, paused at the line of hives, and then continued walking on to the Common, stopping amid a cluster of gorse.

I followed him. Ahead of us were the rusted metal posts of an old fence, most missing or broken, the remainder tilted at angles in the soft ground, and with only a few strands of the wire which had once stretched between them.

My father beckoned for me to go closer to him. The night air was chilled, but already with a promise of the coming day's heat. There had been no rain for several weeks and the ground was dry. The grass at the edge of the Common was all but burned off. Starlings chattered in the distant woodland, and occasionally the birds rose like further trails of smoke into the sky above.

The noise of the dogs and the men grew louder, confirming my father's suspicions that the hunters were heading directly towards his hives. I tried to persuade him that the men would have more sense than to come this close to the road. But nothing I said reassured him.

He looked back at the house and shook his head. I turned and saw my mother standing at her bedroom window, watching us where we waited, already making her own guesses at what was happening, and doing nothing to draw us back to her. The slightest gesture from her and I would have returned to the house.

I was about to suggest turning back, even if only to let my mother know what was happening, what fool's errand we were engaged on, when my father took several more paces ahead of me. "They're coming this way," he said absently, turning and repeating the words to me. And again I considered this unlikely, especially with the vast expanse of the common land and the woodland stretching in every other direction, but again I said nothing to contradict him.

I went to stand beside him.

For the first time, I saw moving lights where the woods fell to the river. The water was shallow and slow-moving at that time of year, and the men and their dogs would have had no difficulty in crossing it.

I searched among the distant lights for anything I might identify, guessing that soon whatever they were chasing would turn back at the open land and re-enter the sanctuary of the trees. There were deer in the woods, small herds with their spring and summer fawns swelling their numbers, and I guessed that the men were in pursuit of one of these. At that distance the endlessly moving lights and barking and occasional shouting suggested only confusion, but I knew that there would be a method in the hunters' seeming disarray.

For a moment, both the noise and the lights faded, and I was about to announce that I had been right in my guess and that the hunt had returned to the woods, when I was startled by the barking of a dog suddenly much closer to where my father and I stood.

We both turned at the noise, and I saw a hound quartering the ground to our right. Other dogs raced towards it, and the men with their lights formed a semi-circle a few hundred yards behind the animals. I searched hard in the half light for the object of all their attention. There were places on the Common where the grass was high and the bracken dense, and I knew how small most of the deer were, few of them any larger than the hound which now raced towards the hives.

Seeing this, my father walked swiftly towards the dog, waving his arms and shouting at it. The hound paid him little attention, pausing briefly to sniff the air and to look around before turning back on itself to join the other dogs.

It looked to me as though it had made a mistake, coming too far ahead of the pack in its eagerness to catch whatever it was chasing. And then it turned again and resumed its loping run towards us, this time accompanied by several smaller dogs.

Individual men revealed themselves, and I felt suddenly foolish, standing there in the night, watching them, waiting for them to reach us. We were the intruders in that world, I realized then, my father and I, not them.

I turned back to look at my mother, hoping perhaps that I might wave and signal to her. But she was no longer at the window, and there was no sign of her standing back from it in the darkness of her room.

"There," my father shouted suddenly, and he pointed to where a doe and her fawn ran to our left, away from the dogs. The adult deer was little more than two feet high, barely clearing the vegetation with her frantic leaping. Her fawn, small as a hare, was visible only when the two creatures crossed open ground. They ran towards the road, the dogs and men quickly closing on them.

Some of the approaching men finally saw us and I heard them calling to each other that we were there, watching them. Some paused to look at us, identifying us before continuing with their pursuit. My father shouted to them, embarrassing me even further, but no one stopped to answer him.

"At least they're moving away from the hives," I told him, and he conceded this and relaxed a little, content to watch in silence as the deer, the dogs and the men ran off.

And then, just as the night's drama seemed about to end, the hind turned away from the trees and approached again where he and I stood. Her fawn continued to run behind her. Both creatures were now clearly exhausted and slowing, and the dogs would soon be on them. The hind, I knew, could have escaped easily by crossing the road, and in all likelihood she had turned away from this only because her fawn, in its own blind and stumbling panic, had already turned away, jeopardizing them both by shortening the distance between themselves and the men. I wondered, too, if the deer had seen my father and myself standing there in the poor light, perhaps posted as lookouts to prevent them from crossing and escaping.

Several of the men came to within only a few yards of where we stood, but still no one spoke to us as the chase approached its end.

The two small deer were practically encircled by then, and seeing this, the men began to call off their dogs.

I told my father that we ought to walk back as far as the hives, to leave them to it, and he came with me.

As we neared the road, a louder call than usual went up from the men, and I turned to see that the fawn had at last been caught, snapped at by the dogs and cast up into the air, falling back to the ground perhaps already dead; or if not dead, then killed a moment later as the dogs tore at it where it lay. I heard its frantic shrieking for a few seconds, and then only the snarling and barking of the dogs as they fought over its tiny, disintegrating carcase. Few of the men paid any attention to this; the hind had always been their true quarry.

Barely pausing to register that her offspring was now dead, the small deer zigzagged back towards the road, and just when I believed she might be about to cross it and enter the gardens, she leapt into the air and seemed to strike something invisible there, falling to the ground and scrambling quickly back to her feet. She had collided with one of the few remaining strands of rusted wire between the posts, invisible to her in that light.

She landed closer to the men than the dogs, and one of them, a man as old as my father, portly and out of breath after his exertions, leapt on her and caught her by one of her hind legs, holding her up to the others and calling to them, seemingly oblivious to the creature as it struggled feebly to escape from him.

My father shouted to him and the man came to us, securing his hold on another of the hind's thin legs, showing off his exhausted trophy.

Around him, the other hunters finally contained the last of their dogs, most of which had at least had a bloody mouthful of the fawn, and which were as slow and as silent now as they had been frantic and baying beforehand.

The man with the deer reached where my father and I stood, and the others joined him, most still carrying their burning torches. They admired the small deer. Someone told the man holding it to kill it. The chase was over, and some of them turned away and started walking back to their encampment.

The man holding the deer seemed disappointed that his skill — though in truth it was never more than luck — in catching it had not been more admired and praised. He swung the creature across his legs. The doe's face was covered in a froth of foam and her tongue hung from her mouth.

The departing men walked away in silence, and it surprised me to see how quickly they had lost all interest now that the chase was over. In that respect, they were little different from their dogs. I told my father I was going back to the house, and he asked me to wait for him.

Seeing that he was about to be abandoned completely, the man holding the deer lowered it to the ground, where he crouched over it, his hold on its legs still secure. And as we watched him, he deftly switched both his hands to a single shin, raised this to his thigh and then broke the leg-bone over his knee. The deer squealed in pain, and the man did the same to the other foreleg, leaving the deer incapacitated on the ground, still squealing and driving itself in a circle with the convulsive kicking of its hind legs.

The man rose from it and wiped his brow, watched the others walking away from him for a moment and then shook his head. A moment later he lifted the hem of his jacket and pulled a broad knife from his belt, wiping it clean across his sleeve as he knelt back down to attend to the deer.

CHAPTER
TWENTY-EIGHT

I next saw Lewis two days later. He stood by the main entrance, close to the locked doorway, and beside him stood a pair of inmates. He was in charge of the two men, though neither of them appeared to be there for any specific purpose. It occurred to me that he was accompanying them on an outing, and that they were waiting either for the door to be unlocked or for the arrival of their transport.

I went to him, anticipating that he would attempt to avoid me, or that, if unable to do this, he would refuse to talk to me.

Instead, when he finally recognized me, he grinned, drew hard on the cigarette he smoked and blew a plume of smoke between us.

"Wondered how long it'd be before you turned up sniffing around again," he said.

"You weren't this brave when Cox had you up against the wall."

Beside us, the two patients laughed, and one of them repeated my words in a whisper to the other.

"Shut it," Lewis shouted at them, but neither of the men responded to him.

Seeing that he showed no signs of trying to avoid me, I turned my attention to his charges. I recognized the two men as Webster's patients. I spoke to them briefly, and they both responded as though I'd said something amusing, laughing and then repeating in the same urgent whisper most of what I'd just said.

I went back to Lewis and asked him why he was there.

"Waiting for a bus," he said dismissively, meaning it was none of my business. "They're off to a clinic. Don't ask me what sort. Not that you can't imagine. They're a pair, they are." He looked at the two men and pulled a face of disgust. One of the men, I knew, had been emasculated during the war; the other was a compulsive masturbator.

"Did Cox send you with them?"

He looked from side to side. "So?"

"More punishment?"

"What you talking about now?"

I'd been right in my guess. "He'll go on doing it until you —"

"Not to me he won't," he said with more enthusiasm. "I'm leaving. I was only ever here temporary, and now things have been sorted, I'm off."

"What things?"

"Joining the Black and Tans. They signed me up last week. My brother's already in. Durham Lights. He put in a word for me. Crying out for blokes like me, they are."

"To serve in Ireland?"

"Where do you think?"

"I thought they only took on regular soldiers," I said.

He looked suddenly uncertain at the remark. "I told you — desperate for men, they are. My brother's pulled a few strings, told me what to say, all the right things. He's already well in, he is. Bit of a hard-case. Reckons they only took him on because of the things he'd already seen and done over there. Said he'd already been . . ." he hesitated, searching for the word. ". . . brutalized. Said he'd been brutalized by what he'd already seen and done. It's what they want for taking care of the Micks. He's told me what to say. By his reckoning, I'll be here another week at the most."

"And does Cox know all this?"

He grinned again, lighting another cigarette from the stub of the first. "He's got that surprise coming."

"So what was the other day all about? If you're leaving, you shouldn't have to put up with —"

"You haven't got the faintest idea, have you?" He began to relish his power over me.

I'd deliberately prompted him with the remark, hoping that he would want to settle scores during the time remaining to him.

"About Cox?" I said.

"About any of them. Cox, Osborne, the lot of them."

This sudden inclusion of Osborne made me wary, and he saw this.

"That's right — Osborne," he said. "You think Cox gets away with all he does because Osborne doesn't know it's happening? You need your eyes tested, mate. Cox practically runs this place, and you and all the other bloody whitecoats know that." The profanity pointed to his growing confidence.

"I know Cox treats you lot like his own subjects," I said.

"And all with Osborne's blessing. Now, why do you think that is?" He looked across to the two inmates, both of whom had come closer in order to overhear what was being said. "Getting all this, are you?" he shouted at them, and both men nodded vigorously. I saw that they were now holding hands.

"You're telling me Cox knows something about Osborne that allows him to get away with everything?" It was a vague but obvious understanding.

"What do you think? Cox has got a marker on Osborne that Osborne doesn't want to risk being made public."

"And was it because of this that Cox assaulted you?"

"Assaulted? He just pushed me about a bit, that's all. It's what he does. Assaulted? You call that an assault? Where you been? You see any blood on me? No, me neither."

I waited for him to go on, to make a concrete connection between Cox's behaviour and Osborne's compliance or duplicity.

"So tell me what it is," I said. "For all I know, you're making all this up just to save face."

"What, when I'm a week away from joining the Tans and getting out of here and going overseas? Hardly likely, is it?"

"They don't take children like you," I said, provoking him further. "And all you're doing here is telling tales

293

out of Cox's hearing. You can barely do what's expected of you here. They'll laugh in your face when you turn up in Ireland."

He started breathing heavily, unable to control his anger. He took a step towards me, and then a step back.

"What?" I said. "You were thinking of assaulting *me*? Perhaps you are braver than you look."

Beside us, the two men giggled like children, turning in unison every few seconds between the two of us.

"You don't know sod all about it," Lewis said, regaining his composure.

"If you say so. Perhaps I should go to Cox now and tell him what you've just told me."

"If you —"

"Or perhaps if you told me what you know, I'd wait until you were off taking pot shots at republican rebels before letting any of it out."

He considered this and then beckoned me further away from the two men towards the empty gatehouse.

When we were beyond hearing, he told me to give him another cigarette, which I did.

"This gets back to Cox before I've gone . . ." he said.

"It won't."

"And I'm only telling *you* because that arrogant little bastard's got it coming. That clear?"

I nodded.

"Osborne was on a tribunal. During the war, down in Maidstone. Military Court. He was the medical officer."

"What sort of tribunal?"

"I'm coming to that. Besides, you *know* what sort of tribunal. The war was only half done. For all anyone knew, it could have gone on for another ten bloody years."

"A court martial?"

"A bloke sent to Maidstone by mistake. Tried in France, but then shipped home by mistake. Someone marked up his docket wrong. He should have been sent to a hospital in France. But instead someone messed things up and he ended up in Maidstone."

"Where it was then up to Osborne to examine him and determine whether or not —"

"To see if he was what he was claiming to be, or if he was as sane as you and me and right enough to be put up against a wall and shot. Apparently, he was a bad 'un right from the start. He'd absconded before, even made it back across the Channel on one occasion. *He* was a Paddy. Something O'Donnell. I can't think that that helped his chances much. Apparently, it took the authorities a month to realize where he'd ended up. They thought he'd absconded from the jail in France. He had a chaplain on his side, and there was other stuff. Truth is, nobody was keen, even then, to put him up against that wall."

I asked him how he knew so much, already beginning to doubt what he was telling me, uncertain of his own embellishments to the story.

"You calling me a liar all of a sudden?"

"You weren't even a soldier," I said.

"Exactly. But my brother was. And this O'Donnell bloke was in the Durhams. I got all this from him, my brother. He was one of the men who felt bad about what was happening to the lad."

"He was a deserving Paddy a minute ago."

"Yes, well . . . My brother said they all felt good about him having disappeared like that, having escaped, like."

"When all the time —"

"When all the time he'd been handed over to Osborne with the paperwork still attached."

"And you're saying Osborne then took it upon himself to finish the work of the medical authorities in France?"

"Got it in one. Had him in Maidstone for a month and then sent the poor bastard back with a letter saying he was perfectly sane, swinging the lead, but that was all."

"And *was* he shot, O'Donnell?"

"My brother says not. Says they were getting a bit itchy about things like that by then — the authorities, that is. He says the doctors in France — the *proper* doctors, the ones who knew by then what was happening — he says they were ready to swear to the court martial that this lad was suffering properly from his nerves, and that he was a case for being discharged, sent home and looked after there."

"But by then Osborne had already come to *his* decision, and his decision was final?"

"Something like that. Apparently, he was senior to the other doctors. The court had to listen to him. The lad was put back in the dock and somebody decided to send for Osborne to tell them all in person what he thought. According to my brother, it was the only time Osborne ever spent in France. A week in Paris."

"And was the execution eventually carried out?"

"My brother says not. Says there was enough of an outcry by then for the lad to be discharged and then put in a prison over here. Probably still there, for all I know. Or perhaps even a place like this."

"Here, even?"

"Nah." He laughed at the suggestion, but I saw the flicker of doubt in his eyes.

"None of this explains why Osborne gives Cox such leeway," I said. "Or why Cox then takes everything out on people like you."

"Cox was Osborne's orderly at Maidstone. The two of them were hand in glove even back then. Cox went overseas a few months later. When the war ended he went to Switzerland, to a military hospital there. There were still real soldiers up on charges and awaiting trial. Cox reckons he was sent to keep an eye on them for the authorities. But, like I said, that was after the war — not much of an appetite for all that kind of thing then."

"And Osborne?"

He shrugged. "What do you think? A few years climbing up the greasy pole. I don't imagine *he* spends much time talking about O'Donnell and how he did his level best to get him shot. Especially not now that he's waiting for his promotion to come through to put him in charge of this place. I daresay all that Maidstone paperwork is still floating about somewhere — under ten feet of mud, probably — but I bet you won't find it within a hundred miles of Osborne. A bit of a black mark, that, don't you reckon, him being what he is, and everything?" He looked over my shoulder at the two inmates, who were again huddled together and whispering to each other. "What do you reckon Osborne would do to those two, given the chance?"

"It was a long time ago," I said. "He might have changed."

He laughed. "You don't believe that any more than Cox does. It's what gives Cox his —" He held up his fist. "And even if Osborne has changed, even if he believes all this brain-and-nerve mumbo-jumbo now, he's still not going to want that dirty little story getting out and hanging over him like the stink it is. Not now, not with all this at stake. Nobody on the Governing Body or the Board of Control would stand for having him, not knowing all that. According to Cox, Osborne even appealed against the rejection of the death sentence on O'Donnell. Imagine if that particular docket ever came to light."

"Just another war story," I said absently, more to myself than to him.

He reacted angrily to this. "Of course it's just another bloody war story. That's all everything is these days — another bloody war story. What do you think this place is?" He nodded to the two men. "What do you think them two poor buggers are? War stories, that's what. And who do you think really cares; who do you really think gives a toss? Osborne? Cox? Me? You? You think *they* even care?" He lowered his voice. "I'm telling you, the sooner I'm out of here and taking that pot at the Mick, the better. You think anyone's ever going to get the better of Cox in this place? All I had to do the other day in the garden was mention my brother to him, the Durhams, and he went crazy. What does he think *I'm* ever going to be able to prove? He's a bloody liability, I'm telling you. You want to watch yourself with him."

"Especially if Osborne's position is made permanent?"

" 'If'? Grow up, mate. They've got that, this, everything stitched up between them. Try and upset that particular apple-cart and you'd be out on your arse faster than you ever believed possible. Who are you? Nobody, that's who."

Neither of us spoke for a moment.

Then I asked him if he could find out from his brother more details of the court martial, other names, places, dates.

He looked at me disbelievingly. "Why? So you can try and do something about it? What? It was seven, eight years ago. You've got all you're getting from me, mate. And any whiff of this and I'll deny everything."

"Osborne's done you no favours — any of you — by allowing Cox to go on treating you all like this," I said.

"I don't give a toss about Osborne. But with Cox, you never know. Supposing he's got mates in the Tans. He's a bastard, and by all accounts they're the biggest bunch of bastards on God's earth. It's not a chance I'm going to take."

"There might still be a man in prison or an asylum somewhere who deserves another hearing," I said, already knowing it was a useless appeal.

"O'Donnell, you mean? Just one less Mick for me to have to shoot at."

He was distracted by a porter arriving at the gatehouse. The man called to us and held up a bunch of keys.

"The bus will be waiting," Lewis said to me, and then, "Everything I've just said, I — you —"

"No one will know," I told him.

I thought at first that his hesitant words might betray another threat, but I heard by his tone that he was relieved to have told me everything he'd just revealed.

"I don't really care," he said, doing nothing to disguise the lie.

The porter opened one of the high doors and shouted again.

Outside, a bus stood at the roadside, its few passengers peering in at us.

"I'd better go," he said.

"Why aren't they being treated here?" I asked him, indicating the two men, who came even closer to us.

He shrugged. "Some special doctor in town who knows about this sort of thing." He held his crotch briefly. "Makes you wonder how many there are like them to make it worth his while. Jesus Christ, who'd want to come back alive and go on living like that?"

I wondered which of the two men he was talking about, or if they both fell into the compass of his disgust. If there was even the slightest hint of pity or even concern in his voice, then it was buried deep. I imagined his reunion with his brother.

"Just another two of those war stories," I said.

"They're not even men," he said, doing nothing to prevent the two patients from hearing him.

But he was wrong: it was a world composed almost entirely of men, and every one of them, or so it now sometimes seemed to me, was living on a hostile planet.

CHAPTER
TWENTY-NINE

"Word from Gressingham." Osborne took a sheet of paper from the envelope he held. Another of his small, calculated dramas. Gressingham, a much disliked man, was the Chief Superintendent of the recently established London Mental Health Authority.

This impromptu gathering of his senior staff had been called only a few minutes earlier and we had all been summoned from our work elsewhere to attend. Webster, Marston and the others arranged themselves around me.

Osborne waited for silence before going on, clearly relishing what he was about to reveal to us. "Doctor Steen has been appointed by the Lunacy Commissioners and the Mental Welfare Society to lead an inquiry into mental-health provision and regulation with regard —"

"More red tape?" Webster said.

"And interfering politicians," Marston added. "Is this another of Thurtle's hobby-horses?"

Others began speculating, causing Osborne to rap on his desk. "Please, allow me to finish."

"You've already told us all we need to know, Alistair," Webster said. "Steen's been kicked upstairs.

And now the same thing's about to happen to you, here. Better get used to calling you 'Sir', I suppose."

Those around him laughed at this.

Osborne wanted to deny everything, but could not do this with any real conviction.

"Does that leave you our *official* unofficial C in C for the time being?" Marston asked him.

More laughter.

"I suppose —" Osborne began.

"Of course it does," Webster said. "Congratulations."

"My position as Steen's stand-in during his absence stays much the same," Osborne said. "Any further recommendations or promotions the Commissioners might see fit to make . . ."

"Nonsense," Webster insisted. "It's in the bag."

"I shall of course endeavour, during this period of uncertainty and transition, to undertake —"

"Period of what and what?" Webster said. "Is this turning into a speech, Alistair?"

Osborne clearly regretted the remark, forcing him to abandon what he had been about to say, and extinguishing the glow in which he had been about to bask.

Webster started applauding and the rest of us joined him for a few seconds, until Osborne held up his palms and motioned his thanks to us.

Two days had passed since Lewis's revelations.

"This will all be on account of the bloody pensions people playing up again," Marston said. "Saving public money. Pensions for lunatics. Whatever next?" More laughter. It was an old argument, another unwelcome diversion for Osborne.

"Does Steen's letter imply that your position here *will* become permanent?" I asked him.

Osborne looked quickly at the sheet he held, probably calculating by how far he had already overstepped the mark in making his announcement.

"Not as such," he said, though still hoping to suggest considerably more.

"But we'll take it as read, anyway," Webster said. "You're being far too modest, Alistair. You have every justification to believe, blah blah blah."

"Does that mean a celebration is called for?" another man asked.

But even Osborne could see how presumptuous and premature this might seem to anyone who did not fully accept how justified he now was in his expectations. "Later, perhaps," he said. "And, as I say, nothing is official . . . yet. I shall need to enquire further of the Governing Body." He slid the notification back into its envelope and then put this in his desk.

"It'll mean changes," Webster said, already calculating his own advantage in Osborne securing the post. Similar guesses and estimations were taking place all around the room.

When Marston had mentioned Thurtle, Osborne had looked at him and then quickly looked away. The Labour politician, while an advocate of full and properly regulated care for mentally injured soldiers, had also recently agitated for a review of all executions carried out during the war. This had achieved little, and almost everyone drawn into the inquiry had been only too pleased to see it swiftly lose momentum and then disappear. I wondered if Osborne had been contacted, but considered this unlikely. One of the reasons the inquiry had never really got under way was because of the absence of a great many records and much of the paperwork relating to war trials and sentences.

"Then I propose *we* formalize arrangements," Webster said, distracting me from these thoughts.

"Arrangements?"

"Our celebration of Osborne's well-deserved good fortune." It seemed a calculated remark to make, and caused me to wonder who else beside Cox might already know of Osborne's secret.

A chorus of "Hear, hear"s rose around me, which Osborne did nothing to discourage.

I'd spent most of the previous day considering the implications of what I'd learned from Lewis. But I knew now, watching Osborne slide Gressingham's letter back into the safety of his drawer, that whatever conclusions I might have come to would count for nothing. And more than anything else, perhaps, I had come to understand my own helplessness in the situation, knowing that I had gained no personal advantage over Osborne, and that there was nothing I could do that would in any way threaten his authority. And when his promotion was finally made official — as it surely soon would be — then even the smallest advantage — even the advantage of *knowing* — would finally be lost to me.

All I would achieve by confronting him on the matter would be to jeopardize my own position. With Osborne in absolute control, I would become easily disposable, transferred elsewhere at his recommendation. Every asylum in the country was filled to overflowing and crying out for trained and capable staff.

Soon Osborne would wrap Webster, Marston and the others around him like a protective fence, with Cox and all his minions still in place to do his bidding.

"Is that all?" I said, half raising my arm as I spoke.

"All what?" Osborne said.

"I mean, can we all return to our work now that you've passed on your good news."

"I hardly think my own likely —"

"I meant the news about Steen's appointment," I said.

He looked at me suspiciously.

"There's always somebody ready to spoil the party," Webster said loudly.

"Too true," someone else added.

I rose from where I sat. I was about to say something more — something, perhaps, to put Osborne even further on his guard, when there was a sudden loud knocking at the door and one of the junior doctors came into the room, stopping in surprise when he saw us all there. Someone ran past him in the corridor outside. The doctor, a man called Kemp, was uncomfortable at having disturbed us like that.

"I didn't realize," he said. He looked around us, stopping at me. "It's Oliver Lyle," he said. "He's one of yours?"

306

"What about him?" Osborne said, diverting Kemp from me.

"It's our own little Salieri," Webster said, and those few who understood him laughed.

"What's happened?" I asked Kemp. I went to him in the doorway.

"I believe I already asked Doctor Kemp that question," Osborne said.

"He's attacked a nurse," Kemp said, looking from me to Osborne and back again.

I held his shoulder. "Are you sure it's Lyle we're talking about?"

"This sounds interesting," Webster said. "You wouldn't think he'd got it in him to attack a crossword."

This time, only Osborne laughed, stopping abruptly when he realized he was alone.

I stood between Kemp and the others.

"Badly?" I said. "How badly?"

"He was outside with her," Kemp said. "I wasn't there. An orderly came into the day room. I said I'd find you. All he told me was that Lyle had attacked a nurse. Cox and a few others are there now. I think it's bad. It sounded bad."

"Attacked her honour, you mean?" Webster said, continuing to make everything sound like a salacious joke.

"I don't — I think —" Kemp stumbled. He finally looked at me. "That's what the orderly said."

"That Lyle had attacked her in that way?"

Kemp nodded.

I pushed him out of the room. Others rose behind me. Osborne called for calm, telling everyone to remain where they were, telling them that I was Lyle's doctor, that I would deal with it, whatever *it* turned out to be. I could already hear that growing distance between us, those same carefully measured degrees of detachment.

As I left the room, Osborne called after me that he wanted a full report on the incident as soon as possible. To the others, he said, "If Cox is already there, then I'm sure he'll have everything under control and that there's nothing to worry about. This isn't the first time —"

I stopped listening to him, holding Kemp's arm as he and I walked quickly along the corridor.

"Where are they?" I asked him.

"In the garden somewhere. Somebody had to pull him off her."

"Who is she?" I braced myself for his answer. Back in Osborne's room, the others would already be speculating towards their own conclusions.

"No idea," Kemp said. "Just a nurse. I don't even know why she was out there."

"Were they at the hives?"

"No idea."

We descended the stairs and emerged outside. Men had gathered in small groups on the lawn. A line of inmates was already being shepherded out of the gateway beside the greenhouses.

I stopped an orderly who passed us and asked him what had happened.

At first the man shrugged, then said, "Cox is in there now. Apparently, this Lyle character tried to have his way with her."

"Are you sure?"

"It's what I heard. She's a bit of a looker, by all accounts. Cox said she probably led the poor bugger up the garden path." And again it sounded like the punchline to a joke.

Kemp and I reached the entrance and went together into the garden.

A dozen people congregated at the far side of the space. Orderlies and nurses, mostly, and a few others, patients, standing apart from these. I searched for Alison West, Lyle or Gurney, but could see little at that distance.

It was only as Kemp and I approached that I saw Alison sitting on one of the stone benches, surrounded by other nurses. Sister Kidd stood beside her. Another woman wiped Alison's face. Looking up, Alison saw me and raised her arm to me.

It was only when I reached her and looked into the orchard beyond her that I saw Lyle there, pinned face-down to the ground by several orderlies, a man for each limb, another with his hand cupped to the side of Lyle's head. Cox stood over the men. I searched for Gurney, but he wasn't among the nearby inmates.

"What happened?" I asked Alison.

"She was attacked by that randy little bastard," one of the other nurses said. I recognized her as the woman who had pushed the laundry basket with Lyle. Having said this, she glanced at Sister Kidd and immediately covered her mouth.

Sister Kidd, whom I had known at Le Havre, and afterwards at Maida Vale, let the remark pass. And then she urged the gathered women away from Alison and took them to the inmates.

I thanked her.

"Probably a lot more to it than meets the eye," she said to me, her voice low, her eyes on Cox and his orderlies as she spoke. She held my arm briefly. "Cox doesn't really need an excuse these days." She went to her nurses, most of whom were now leading the remaining patients through the gateway.

I shouted for Cox to call his men off Lyle.

"You make them sound like hounds," he called back. "This is necessary restraint. You saying otherwise?"

I knew I would achieve nothing by persisting. I told Kemp to go to Cox and ensure that no further harm was done to Lyle, and that he was able to breathe more easily.

I sat beside Alison West.

"What happened?" I asked her. There was a bruise on her forehead and another starting to show on her wrist. She rubbed this as I spoke.

"This is it," she said matter-of-factly. "No blood, no broken bones, no you-know-what."

"What are you asking *her* for?" Cox called to me. "You want witnesses — *I'm* your witness."

Angry at the remark, I shouted back, "It's what you're good at — standing back and watching other people do all the dirty work, keeping your own hands clean."

The remark, and all it might imply, caught him unawares and he said nothing for a moment.

"What's that supposed to mean?" he shouted eventually.

I turned back to Alison.

"Is there any point me asking you the same question?" she said.

I drew back her cuff to look more closely at her wrist and to ensure there were no other injuries.

"They're saying Lyle attacked you," I said, my voice low.

"Attacked?"

"Did he?"

"Not the way Cox is making it sound. He lost his temper, that's all. A few seconds, less. He just exploded and took me by surprise. He was close to me. I don't even think he meant to strike me, just throw out his arms to keep me away from him. We were at the edge of the bees, the long grass where we dumped the broken hives. I stepped back to avoid him and fell over. I hit my head on a brick or something. When he saw what he'd done, that I'd fallen, all Lyle could say was that he was sorry, over and over, and then he tried to grab me and pull me up. I couldn't get my balance. The ground's full of rubble. He might even have thought I'd knocked myself out for a few seconds. He was pulling at me, making things worse. I told him to let go, but you know what he's like. He just kept on trying to pull me upright, still saying over and over how sorry he was.

Eventually, because he was pulling too hard, trying too hard to get me back on my feet, and because I couldn't find my footing, my balance, *I* ended up pulling *him* to the ground."

"And that was what Cox saw?"

"Cox? I doubt it. One of the other orderlies, perhaps. It was all over and done with in a few seconds. I think Cox was in one of the greenhouses. Someone shouted to him. The next thing I knew, Lyle was helping me to this bench when Cox and a few others grabbed him from behind and threw him back to the ground. I tried to tell them what had happened, but no one was listening to me, too concerned with supposedly subduing Lyle."

"Did he need subduing?"

She considered this. "He started to struggle as they pulled him away from me. It probably looked like it to them."

"And especially with Cox's urging?"

"I shouted to them that nothing had happened, but by then no one was listening to me. Cox even called over to me that I was safe now and that I should keep away from Lyle in case he escaped from them and tried to get back to me."

The mark on her face was as much dirt as bruise. The skin was lightly grazed and she wiped at it with a handkerchief.

"Did Sister Kidd see nothing?" I asked her, knowing the woman's account of what had happened would count for considerably more in Osborne's eyes than Alison's own.

She shook her head. "She was busy. She only came with the others when Cox sent someone running for help. Everything just seemed to get out of hand after that."

"Because that was what Cox wanted," I said.

She signalled over my shoulder and I turned.

"That my name I hear being taken in vain?" Cox said, now only a few feet behind me. "She all right? Looks like we got the vicious little bastard off her just in time." He smiled. "At least that's what I'm hoping. Miss?"

Alison refused to be drawn.

"Nothing happened," I told him. "At least not what you're suggesting."

He feigned surprise. "Oh, and you were here, were you? Saw it all, did you?"

"No more or less than you did," I said.

He pointed to the gateway. "I was standing right there. Saw the whole lot. So don't tell me what I did or didn't see."

I looked at Alison and she shook her head once, making Cox even angrier.

"What?" he shouted at her. "You and him in this together, are you? What about you and the conchie over there? Leading him on, were you? You and him good friends? What was it, a lovers' tiff? Not what I saw, darling. And not what I'll be telling Osborne when he asks me."

"Go away," I told him. "Go back to Lyle and make sure he comes to no harm."

"I thought you'd sent the other one for that." He motioned to Kemp, whose own efforts on Lyle's behalf were proving equally unsuccessful.

"This will all get out of hand," I said.

"Already did," Cox said.

"Lyle's going back to Gloucester to sit his Board there soon."

"That official, is it? I've seen nothing in his records."

"That's because you're an orderly and not a doctor," I said. "It's what I'm telling you now."

"Oh, I hear what you're *telling* me," he said. "And what I'm telling *you* is that, as far as I'm concerned, the little bastard's going nowhere until all this gets sorted out. Perhaps Osborne might change his mind after this little lot. Perhaps the conchie just proved that here's where he belongs. Perhaps we've got him for good now."

"Just go," Alison said to him.

He looked at her. "And is that all the gratitude I get, all the thanks? You want to think yourself lucky that I was close by. Another minute, and who knows what might have happened. And it doesn't bear thinking about what might have happened if Lyle had been with that other freak when he decided to attack you."

He meant Gurney, and he'd made the remark solely to goad me.

One of his orderlies called to him — something about there being blood on Lyle's face.

"Hear that?" Cox said to Alison. "Perhaps you managed to scratch him while you were struggling to get him off you. Any blood on your hands? Make sure

314

you leave it there. Perhaps it's something else Lyle's Board might want to consider."

He finally left us, and as he went Sister Kidd returned.

"Is she all right?" She sat beside Alison and put an arm around her shoulder. "She told me what happened," she said to me. "I'll go to Osborne and tell him what I know."

I told her about the letter confirming Steen's appointment.

"Ah," she said, then fluttered her hand. "It could be weeks yet before anything is made final. And Osborne might not want anything to upset the otherwise peaceful equilibrium of this place until that happens."

I understood what she was telling me.

She looked to Cox and the others. "He's getting up," she said, meaning Lyle.

Lyle was finally on his feet, surrounded by the orderlies, two of whom still held him. There was blood around his nose and on his chin. Cox brushed the dirt and grass from his chest and shoulders.

Lyle looked to where we sat. "Is she all right?" he shouted. He was about to repeat the question when Cox hit him on the side of his head.

"Of course she's not all right," Cox shouted at him. "How can she be all right after what you've just tried to do to her?"

"I'm sorry," Lyle called.

And this time, Cox raised his hand but didn't strike him.

"I'm sorry," Lyle repeated.

The orderlies started pulling him further away from us.

I rose from where I crouched in front of Alison and stood watching as the men left the orchard. I started to follow them, but Sister Kidd held my arm.

"Leave him," she said. "All you're doing is antagonizing Cox. Let me go to Osborne. Think about it — he won't want anything to happen now to jeopardize everything that's about to happen. He might not like me, but he'll listen to me. I'll give him a way of smoothing all this out, and he'll take it."

"And Cox?"

"The two of them will have to sort that out between themselves. Despite what Cox thinks, there's every chance that this will speed up Lyle's transfer back to Gloucester."

Again, there was a good deal of sense and truth in what she said, and I was grateful for the clarity with which she, at least, was able to see all this.

"I'm looking forward to our musical evening," she said.

"The recital?"

"A step up from our usual visiting missionaries with their magic-lantern shows. Are you familiar with any of Gurney's musical work?"

The question caught me by surprise. "No. Only some of his poetry. You?"

"A little," she said. "My brother was at the College. Before Gurney's time, of course, but he still keeps in touch with the place, attends as many of their concerts as he's able to." She looked at Alison and smiled. "Still, time for all that later, eh?" She helped Alison to her feet.

"I'm fine," Alison told her.

"*Was* Gurney here, with Lyle?" I asked her.

"I know you are," Sister Kidd said before she could answer me. "And if I thought for one moment that what Cox was saying was true, then I'd be doing something about it myself, right now."

She walked a few paces ahead of us and waited.

"Lyle was alone," Alison said to me. "He'd gone with me to see if the new queens had settled and their colonies were starting to establish." She paused. "It was when I suggested to him that we might go and find Ivor, and that the three of us might visit the hives together, that he lost his temper."

"I can imagine," I said.

The remark both angered and disappointed her, and she left me without speaking and went to where Sister Kidd awaited her. I called after them, but neither woman answered me as they passed through the gateway and out on to the lawn beyond.

CHAPTER
THIRTY

I found Gurney alone in his room, nothing of the commotion outside having found its way in to him yet.

He sat at the window, clutching a folder of loose sheets. Ribbons hung from the folder and I recognized it as being similar to the one in which Marion Scott had presented his song scores to me.

"There's been some trouble with Lyle, Ivor," I said, waiting, wishing I'd said "Oliver".

He raised his head but did not look at me.

"Marion said she'd make all the choices. I thought Will Harvey would have talked to me."

"They're saying Oliver Lyle attacked Alison West."

"I was always clever at putting things in code for Marion, at not saying things outright. The censors, see? In my letters. I couldn't say. I'd let her know where I was, but I wouldn't ever say. She said we were leading them a merry dance. Never needed any stamp, see, not then. What about Lyle?"

"Cox is accusing him of attacking Alison West. They were at the bees."

"He's attacked her? Some would always write 'O.A.S.'"

"On Active Service."

"That's right, that's right. And then there were some of us who were later entitled to write 'W.S.L.'"

I struggled to remember.

"Wounded Soldier Letter." He wrote the letters on the folder with his finger.

"Is that your music?" I asked him.

He looked down at what he held.

"I once worked for a farmer at Tiberton, siding land, too close to the river for much but wet pasture and soak. Planted his big field with potatoes. October time. And neither he nor I nor any of the twenty other men he hired picked a single one that wasn't home to leatherjackets, wireworms or slugs. Slugs you can pull out, and save the tuber for eating. Not the others. I've heard potato merchants on Gloucester Dock crying with laughter at the sight of a single wireworm in a sack. Halves the price, see?" He tapped the folder. "Lyle said I should give it to Marion, let her take care of things. She'll want other pieces performed. She had it all marked up for instruments, see?"

"And this is new stuff, more recent? Pieces you've written here?"

He nodded.

Writing of any sort in the asylum was a considerable rarity. I could count on the fingers of one hand the men who even read out of choice, and then rarely anything but newspapers and magazines, and then only for minutes at a time.

"May I see?" I asked him.

"Lyle told me I should take charge. He didn't really understand. I would have said to Will Harvey. He would have known." He handed the folder to me abruptly, lodging it in my lap and then immediately withdrawing his hands, folding his arms stiffly across his chest and turning to one side, every gesture distancing him from both me and what I now held.

"And up at May Hill," he said, his eyes fixed high on the window.

"May Hill?" I'd lost track of what he was saying.

"Thin winds," he said. "Always blowing. On a curve see, that hill? I worked two late summers, and in both places, Tiberton and May Hill, they had a crop of spoiled barley. Sour. Not even fit for the brewers. Some of that land never turned a profit. They came, of course, the brewers, to see what might be salvaged and bought cheap. And then when they'd gone, the feed merchants arrived. Good enough for pigs, they said, and paid the price of the seed. There were smallholdings up on May Hill that changed hands every year. We all knew which ones they were, but the incomers never did." He smiled at the memory.

I unfastened the ribbons securing the folder.

"I had folders like that at the National School," he said.

"In London?"

"Gloucester. London Road. See how straightforward it was?"

I didn't understand him, but said nothing.

I finished opening the folder, turning the loose sheets inside until they faced me.

"I don't read music," I said.

"There's words."

"Yours?"

"Some. Though I was always better at seeing the music in the words of others." He put a finger in his mouth, feeling inside. "Got a loose tooth." He opened his mouth to show me the dark molar. "Never been lucky with my teeth. Did he do it, what they're saying?"

"Lyle? Alison West says not."

"So who says he did?"

"Cox says he saw everything."

"That's that, then. Poor old Lyle."

This dismissive and seemingly uncaring judgement surprised me. He seemed almost to take some pleasure in the remark and all it might now imply regarding Lyle's future.

"I'm going to see Osborne," I told him. "I think Lyle should leave. Soon. Quickly." I waited for his response.

"He's a good boy," he said. "Seen and done nothing and been nowhere, but he's a good boy."

"You'll miss him," I suggested.

He shook his head. "He was going to stand at the piano. Reckoned I'd be playing." He grew confused. "Is that what Marion wants? Am I still the star of her show?" He looked from side to side.

"I doubt she'll insist on anything you yourself don't agree to," I said.

"But that's what she is — an insister."

"If you say so," I said, hoping he might appreciate the small joke. But he said nothing.

"Look at the music," he told me. "It's in order, first first and last last. I played a concert in Edinburgh, same pieces. Beethoven's Sonata in D, Bach's Prelude and

Fugue, the second, a Chopin ballade, three preludes and Beethoven's 'Funeral March' Sonata, the final movement."

The ease and accuracy of his remembering surprised me. He, too, seemed pleased and gratified by the memory, and I wondered if the nurse and his thwarted feelings for her invaded the same scattered thoughts.

"Will you — they — play the same here?" I asked him, knowing this was unlikely, that Marion Scott would choose pieces he had written.

"Am I playing, then?" His mind was switched in an instant between the present and the past, between this place and others.

I looked down at the music he had given me. And I saw immediately that whatever he imagined he had given me — whatever clean and perfect transcriptions and annotation of words and music — it wasn't what I now held. Half the staves were empty, and the remainder were filled with trailing lines of words and notes which ran off the right-hand sides of the sheets. In addition, they fell from the staves themselves, curving downwards as they crossed the pages, and then dropping, as though too heavy for the faint green lines to bear. Isolated notes sat like distant birds on telegraph wires; elsewhere, whole flocks were crowded ten and twelve deep on the five slender lines.

Gurney started to hum and then to sing, " 'Come, Oh Come, My Life's Delight'."

I saw the title on the page I held, but was unable to follow any of the lyric where he had written it down.

"Can you follow?" he asked me.

I nodded.

"Thomas Campion." He went on singing. His voice was low and tuneful, and I heard the choirboy in him. He stopped abruptly. "I sang that once, at St Julien, and it brought me to tears. Me and half a dozen others. You'd think a man would hide his feelings in terrible places like that — and it was terrible, believe me — but all of us cried. Turn the page."

The second sheet revealed an even more convoluted and confusing jumble of words and notes. In some places the notes had been put so close together and one upon the other, as though written by a blind man, to look like nothing more than a ball of scribble, a dark ball in its hammock of lines, and with thicker strings trailing from it. Elsewhere, these smaller scribbles looked like waiting spiders.

" 'Tears'," Gurney said. "John Fletcher. I wrote for his 'Sleep', too. Will Harvey always preferred those two pieces over everything else. Even his own work I set to music. Know what they put on *his* medical docket when he was finally repatriated? 'Soldier's Heart'. Who do you think came up with that one? The Surgeon General?"

The Office of the Surgeon General had recently decreed that "Broken Heart" was no longer to be admissible as a valid cause of death on the death certificates of the mothers, wives and sisters whose prolonged and never-lessening grief had proved too great a burden for them to bear.

"He told me about his poetry," I said.

"Verse," he said, oblivious to how callous and unwarranted the remark sounded.

"I don't —" I began.

"Like the other Gloucester Ivor."

"Sorry?"

"The other Gloucester Ivor." He waited for me to respond, impatient at my lack of understanding. "Novello," he said eventually. "The other Gloucester Ivor. All *he* ever did was write songs for people to hum to. That's all they wanted, see, and especially afterwards — songs to hum, something to sing along to, something everybody could easy enough remember." He stopped abruptly and then grew calm, looking around him as though the raised voice had been someone else's. He pointed to the page I still held. "'In Flanders' and 'Walking Song'. They were both Will Harvey's. He said I paid him a great compliment. I doubt if Marion ever preferred them over my Shakespeares, Nashes or Jonsons, though."

I looked up from the squashed ruin of the page.

"Let me see," he said, indicating the music.

I turned it to him.

He traced a finger along the lines, and I tensed against what he would discover there.

"Here," he said. "Second verse. You see how I lifted everything? I tried that in other pieces. Soft discords, they call that, the experts. Sevenths, ninths and so forth. 'Harmonic moderation far too severe and extreme.' That was Marion again. Said I jerked things about too much. I doubt many of them could understand my true purpose. They were cycle corps, those men at St Julien. Their horses, they called them."

He continued to trace his finger along the jumbled, overloaded lines, seeing his intent and not his achievement there, his success and not his failure. He turned to other sheets, other messes, other tangled skeins of lost meaning, and there too he saw only the same inviolate perfection, the same hopeful journey.

Eventually, frustrated at being unable to find the piece of music he was looking for, he took the whole folder back from me, set it on the bed beside him and scrambled through the pages, scattering them on the floor. Unconcerned by the creased and crumpled sheets all around him, he finally held up the page he was searching for. It was almost completely blank, a few late notes hanging from the staves in the bottom right-hand corner, half-heard whispers, dying echoes, time run out. It even looked to me as though the scarce notes were the remnants of a once-filled page whose contents had been tipped and scattered from it, leaving only this stubborn residue. I looked closely at the title, the only words still in their proper place, and saw that it was a song of Robert Bridges', "I Praise the Tender Flower". I knew the poem, and this somehow made its fall from the page in Gurney's hand all the more poignant.

"I know it," I told him. "My mother used to read it to us." I asked him if he could hum the music he had written for it.

"Can you not see it on the page?" he asked me.

"Yes," I said. "Of course. But not well enough to imagine it sung."

He started to hum, and I listened attentively to him, again unable to fit his music to the rhythm of the poem I remembered. He stopped abruptly, long before the song ended. "I told you about those beech roads," he said, a look of surprise on his face.

"You did." My head was still filled with my mother's voice, reciting, precise.

"I was put in charge of some tame German boys. One of them died when we were shelled. Wounded to begin with, but bad. *He* was a singer. He tried to sing for me where we laid him out. Begged me to stay with him, and I did. Me and him and a few of his own friends. All at school together. And when he couldn't sing, they did it for him. Sat around him where he lay and sang the parts he couldn't manage. He died like that, with his friends all around him, singing. Probably even thought he was still singing himself. You could see his mouth opening and closing, see the shapes of the words he was trying to say. Stomach wound, see? Never stopped bleeding, not really. You'll know all about those. We had no clean dressings. At least not for the likes of him, we didn't. They sang so quiet, you wouldn't have heard them from ten yards away. When he died, they all stopped together, like you'll hear birds all stop on a single note when they know something's wrong. That's what they did, all those German boys, finished on the note and then just let it sit above us like the dead boy's final breath. One of them told me that he'd been lifted to Heaven on the wings of that singing. They all shook my hand when they were taken back to their cage."

"Did you see them again?"

"Next day, on the road, pinning those beech slabs. But never again after that. You might say that I saw the Hereafter myself, sitting there with them while that boy died."

At first I didn't understand him, and then I saw that he was talking about the end of the war and his own survival beyond the Armistice.

"You survived," I said absently.

He nodded and started to gather up the scattered sheets, neither noticing nor caring which ones were now folded or creased as he pushed them back into the folder.

"Will he come back here?" he said. He was talking about Lyle.

"I don't know."

"Some of those potato merchants would turn up at the farms on their rounds with a waistcoat pocket full of wireworms."

"To cheat the farmers?"

"They'd cheat their own mothers and babies, some of those men. Friends of my father's at the Conservative Club. Oi Be Gurney." He laughed. "It's where I got it from — my father. 'Get the lad up for a song, Gurney.' He told me once that he'd named me after the notepaper — Ivory Gurney Premium. 'Get the lad up for a song, Gurney.' Ronald, it was, who said I shouldn't go to his funeral. Keep things respectable. They said I was too solitary in my ways." He forced the final sheet into the folder and refastened its ribbon, pressing down on the card to flatten it. "He used to talk about her, the nurse."

"Oh?"

"He hasn't ever been with a woman."

"He won't be alone in that," I said. "Not here."

"He said he was her favourite."

"Did she tell him that?"

"I don't know what she did or didn't say to him. Not truly. I think most of it was just what he wanted her to say."

And I wondered again if he was remembering his own nurse in Edinburgh.

"None of this will go well for him," he said.

"No," I said.

"Is that why you came — to tell me what he'd done?"

"I didn't know if —"

"If I'd been with him? I wasn't. He told me to stay where I was. My uncle was the one for bees. Up at Maisemore. I never really took to them. I was badly stung on my back and legs when I was a boy. And once they stuck to the honey on my fingers and stung me through it. Vicious little creatures. My uncle used to tape a bee to a willow switch, pull its wings and legs off and then use it as a brush to pollinate his apples and beans."

"My father once told me about bees he'd seen embedded in cubes of set honey. He said they'd been held in the moulds still alive while the warm honey was poured and allowed to cool around them. He said people would eat the honey, bees and all, as cures for rheumatism."

"I heard the same," Gurney said. "Will you do what you can for the boy?"

"The Nursing Sister will help him better," I told him.

He considered the truth of this.

"You waste too much of your time with me," he said slowly, looking up at me and holding my gaze.

"Not really," I said. "I'll tell the dentist about your tooth."

He pulled a face. "No need. I'll pull it out myself when it's ready to come. Done that often enough."

I remembered my mother's collection of milk teeth, set out like jewels in a small mother-of-pearl box in her bedside drawer.

"I'll still tell him," I said.

He started to hum again, a new song, oblivious to my departure.

CHAPTER
THIRTY-ONE

It would have served no purpose attempting to see Lyle while he was being held in the isolation wing. It was customary for men to be secured there in the otherwise empty cells, often jacketed if they showed signs of attempting to harm themselves, for at least two days before they were approached and assessed. As Lyle's doctor, the responsibility for this examination would be mine.

I waited for several hours after the incident — time, hopefully, for the drama, confusion and hysteria to have died down — and then I went to see Osborne.

His room was empty and locked. A passing nurse told me she'd seen him leaving the asylum in a taxi a few minutes earlier.

I was returning to my own room when I encountered Marston, who asked me if I'd heard any more about what had happened. The news of Lyle's assault would have spread through the hospital by then, ever changing as it went, exaggerated and embellished depending on who was telling it, and why.

At first, I was suspicious of Marston and his reasons for asking, wondering if he hadn't been sent by Webster who, despite his earlier unwelcome interventions, was now staying well clear until the situation was resolved.

"He didn't attack her," I said, wondering even as I said it how many more times I was prepared to make the same vague refutation on Lyle's behalf, knowing only that I was right to do so, if only for his sake.

"Not the story Cox is still telling," he said, probing for more.

I was unwilling to indulge him, and I started to walk past him.

The gesture surprised and then angered him and he called to me as I was about to turn a corner and leave him behind.

"Osborne's gone to see Steen," he shouted, his voice dropping midway through the sentence, as though he had said something he ought not to have.

I stopped walking, and then waited as he came to me.

"Sorry," he said. "This Lyle business — it's not going to amount to anything; everybody knows that. The Steen thing, the Superintendent's position here, that's all that matters to Osborne and Webster now. Besides, who cares if he did try anything on? Stupid little bugger's probably never even had it out of his trousers." It was likely to be the most commonly held view. "Apart from which, you're his doctor. All you have to do is wait until his time's up in Isolation, get some corroborating testimony together and then pack him off to Gloucester or whatever other God-forsaken hole he's going back to."

"I know all that," I said. "What I don't understand is *your* sudden interest in it all."

"I just —"

"As far as I can see, all you're interested in now is waiting for Webster to be made Senior Clinician under Osborne so that you can tuck yourself in there with him." It was an unfounded accusation to make, and after his own attempts at conciliation, the remark made him angry again.

"Oh, that's right," he said. "Besides — you don't think it strange — Lyle attacking the same little nurse *you've* already supposedly put your marker on?" He took a step away from me as he said this. "I suppose you and her — and him, for that matter — will get your stories straight."

"He didn't attack her."

"Whatever happened, Osborne is still considerably more concerned about his own immediate future." Our argument had no true momentum, and without either of us realizing it, it had already faltered to a halt.

"Sorry," he said again.

"There's nothing between us," I said. "Not like you're suggesting."

"I think I knew that all along. I was just repeating what Webster said."

"Thanks for the warning."

"You'll have to watch the pair of them — you do realize that, I suppose? Especially when everything's made official and the corks finally start flying."

I considered what he was telling me for a moment.

Then I said, "She served in France and Belgium. The nurse. Her name's Alison West. She was over there for three years."

"Probably longer than you, me, Osborne and Webster put together," he said.

"Probably."

I'd been overseas for sixteen months; Charles for ten.

He held out his hand to me and I took it. "This thing with Steen has unsettled everyone, me included," he said. "I don't think Webster thinks *that* much of me, not really. He's just careful to lead the chorus, that's all."

"Especially in Osborne's presence?"

He nodded. "I think the Lunacy Commissioners have got big plans for this place."

"And whoever was in charge when that happened . . .?"

"Got it in one."

We descended the stairs together and walked out on to the broad path which skirted the building. The men who had been earlier shepherded indoors were back outside, on the lawns and in the garden.

A group of orderlies stood gathered by the gatehouse. I searched for Cox, hoping to talk to him before Osborne returned. It was equally unlikely that Sister Kidd would have had the opportunity to see Osborne before his departure.

"Looking for Cox?" Marston asked me.

"Osborne listens to him," I said.

"Tell me something I don't already know."

I waited to see what more he might reveal, conscious of not letting slip anything of what Lewis had already told me.

"And if you know what's good for you — and for Lyle, and for her, the nurse — you won't go pushing too hard in that particular direction."

"Cox and Osborne, you mean?"

He looked hard at the orderlies before continuing. "I don't know what's going on there — between Cox and Osborne — but what I do know is that Webster let slip a few days ago that he'd caught Cox in one of the dispensaries, where he shouldn't have been."

"Doing what?"

"Doing what Cox usually does — threatening one of the pharmacists, a new man. Apparently, Cox had a note from Osborne allowing him to draw something from the medical stores. The new man told Cox he'd have to check. Not the kind of thing Cox appreciates."

"A note for drugs, you mean?"

Marston shrugged. "Webster talked to the pharmacist after Cox had stormed off." He was reluctant to say more, forcing me to guess.

"Morphine?"

He looked at me. "Webster just said it wouldn't need a genius to work things out."

We treated men with morphine addiction with increasingly smaller doses of the drug, usually in the form of gelatine discs. Men were prescribed placebos for months after they had been weaned off. The American doctors at Netley swore by these "lozenges" and were reputed to prescribe more of the drug there, and to their own countrymen, than in all the other psychiatric wards combined.

334

"Can any of this be proved?" I asked him, aware of the seriousness of the allegation, and of the likely consequences were it ever to be made public.

"Like, can Lyle having assaulted the nurse be proved? I'm simply saying, that's all."

It was the other half of the pact between Osborne and Cox.

And both men would vehemently deny everything that was put to them, and their stories of outraged innocence would mesh perfectly and protect them both from all harm. And if that wasn't enough, then whatever Webster now knew or thought he knew would never be revealed while his own position in the unsettled hierarchy of the place remained unsecured.

"We've got a lot in common, you and I," Marston said, diverting me from these thoughts. "We're neither of us on solid ground, and certainly not here, not yet."

"I don't know what you mean," I said, but without conviction.

"Osborne and Webster, they're the ones sitting pretty. They're the ones without any . . . any baggage. They're the ones with clean hands and their faces fixed on the future. Men like you and me, we're still finding our feet, even after all this time." He smiled. "In fact, we've probably got more in common with half the poor buggers in here than we have with Osborne or Webster."

I wanted to tell him that he was being ridiculous, if only to stop him from saying any more.

"Sorry," he said again. "It's just that nothing's ever settled, is it? Not really. Not *settled* settled. Not straightforward or dependable. Christ, listen to me. I've been here too long."

"I understand what you're saying," I told him.

"Good," he said, and then, "I know you do."

"And if Osborne is appointed?" I asked him.

"Will I stay on under Webster? Probably. I'm all that's left."

I didn't understand him.

"Family, I mean. My parents both died in China, four years before the war, some kind of brain fever. And two months later, my brother and sister. I was ill, but I survived. Sent home. Two years at Cambridge, and then — well —"

It was where most of our stories ended, exhausted, untellable, never needing any corroborative detail or proper conclusions.

I'd known the man for almost nine months, and yet I'd known none of this.

"What will you do?" he asked me. "About Cox."

"I'll see Osborne, make sure Lyle isn't punished any further for what happened, and then get him sent back to Gloucester as quickly as possible. He's only here in the first place because —"

"I know — conchie. It's probably not even a dirty word any more. I saw in the paper this morning that there's a Battle Nomenclature Committee. It's true. Apparently, we're to call it 'The Great Commonwealth War'. Bit of a mouthful. Personally, I've never heard anyone call it anything but what it was."

"The War?"

He nodded.

336

At the gatehouse, a cheer went up among the orderlies there, and Cox appeared in their midst. He walked through them and then stopped and looked to where Marston and I stood.

I wondered how much of what I knew and half-knew I would be brave enough to reveal to Osborne in securing Lyle's release.

"Look at the arrogant little sod," Marston said. "He's working all this out for himself. He knows exactly where *he* stands."

"Especially now that he's seen us together and he knows you've spoken to me," I said. "Now that I might know what Webster's already told you."

We both looked back at Cox.

"The pharmacist left, by the way," Marston said. "Just in case you were thinking of talking to him. Gone to work in a shop somewhere in the East End. You won't get anywhere on that score."

It hadn't occurred to me to approach the man. My purpose now would be better served by suggestion and implication rather than by dragging any of the facts of the matter out into the open.

Before I could say anything, Marston raised his arm and waved at Cox.

Uncertain what was intended by the gesture, Cox remained where he stood, his arms by his side.

Marston lowered his arm and looked at his watch. "I'm due elsewhere," he said.

I held out my hand to him, and he took it.

Cox shouted something neither of us heard properly, and the men around him laughed.

"That's right," Marston said. "Make sure everything stays just one big joke."

He left me, and I waited for a few minutes, still closely watched by Cox, before turning and following him back into the hospital.

I went through the building to the garden, and then through this to the orchard. I'd hoped to find either Alison West or Sister Kidd there, but the land around the hives was empty. Even the greenhouses were deserted of their workers.

I went to the bench where I'd first seen Alison, and I sat there. The air was again filled with the scent of freshly scythed grass, and with that of the blossoms and flowers all around me. Bees already came and went from the new colonies, foraging for the early pollen.

Days before his collapse, my father had taken me to the meticulously cut lawn at the front of our house and we had lain together on the turf there, watching the bees walk from one clover flower to another, working closely and carefully over the same small patch of ground, no bloom visited twice, no distance ever greater than it needed to be, the bees stacking the pollen until they could hardly balance amid the blades of grass. And when one bee was unable to gather more, then another had come to take its place. My father estimated the insects were using only five per cent of the energy they were gathering, telling me that it was something neither he nor I nor any man alive would ever achieve.

We followed the bees from their gathering ground back to the hives, most of them flying barely inches

338

above the lawn, saving even more energy for their final rise to the hive entrances. And when they were too heavily overloaded for even this small effort, then they climbed the legs of the hives and queued on the sills, patient as concert-goers, as they waited to go in and be relieved of their loads.

CHAPTER
THIRTY-TWO

I attempted to visit Lyle the following morning, but was refused entry to the isolation wing by the orderly who guarded the entrance from the main building.

"Osborne's strict orders," the man told me as I shook the locked doors. I recognized him as one of the men who had restrained Lyle in the orchard.

"Me, specifically?" I asked him.

"You specifically, what?" He smiled to let me know that he understood exactly what I was asking him.

"To be prevented from seeing Lyle," I said, already resigned to abandoning the attempt.

"What makes you so special?" he said.

I wondered at the source of his insubordination. "I'm Lyle's doctor," I said.

He clearly hadn't known this, and he faltered for a second. "Nobody's getting through," he said. "Osborne's strict orders. Besides, you saw him in the orchard. He's a bloody animal. Five of us it took to hold him down."

I refused to rebut this.

"Look." He drew back his sleeve to show me a bruise on his arm. "He did that. Bit me. Probably. Hard to tell with all that struggling going on."

The bruise had not been caused by a bite.

"Cox said I should have a few days' rest."

He had been sitting on a chair against the door and reading a newspaper when I'd approached him. It was how he would spend the rest of the day. The squashed ends of trodden-out cigarettes littered the floor around him.

"Listen," he told me.

I heard nothing.

"He was howling like a bloody animal for hours."

I didn't believe him. Besides, the simple crying of men in those padded rooms was distorted beyond all recognition, especially when it did last for hours.

"Are there any others on the wing?" I asked him.

"Just him. One other when he arrived, but Cox had him taken away. Our friend Lyle's been sedated to shut him up. So even if I did let you through" — he tapped the side of his nose to suggest how this might be achieved — "you wouldn't get any sense out of him. He's getting more of the same later."

I turned and left him.

"What?" he shouted after me, his voice echoing in the high corridor. "Is that it? You coming back?" He continued shouting after me as I left the building and went outside.

It was my intention to go directly to Osborne, conscious of how much time had now passed since the alleged assault, and to ask him directly what he intended to do, calculating as I went how I might use what I believed I now knew about him and Cox to secure Lyle's transfer back to Gloucester before the fabricated details of the assault were entered into his record and his punishment was extended or his treatment adjusted. No Board had ever looked benevolently on a violent patient.

I crossed the open space at the front of the asylum, and as I was about to enter it again, someone called to me. I stopped and looked around me, surprised to see Will Harvey emerge from the gatehouse, one of the porters immediately behind him. Seeing me, the porter returned to his duties.

"I went to see Ivor," Harvey said. He took an envelope from his jacket pocket. "Marion's sorted out all the arrangements for his concert. Music, musicians, visiting dignitaries, everything. Apparently, she spoke to Osborne yesterday." He said it all in a tone of weary resignation, and with a note of disbelief at what was now about to happen. He gave me the envelope and motioned for me to open it.

It was a typed sheet of details, pinned to which was a printed invitation and a programme of the event.

"She thought it would put everything on a proper footing. Six musicians, two singers. Most of the senior teaching staff — at least most of those who knew Ivor before the war; I doubt any of them have thought twice about him since — and a couple of names to add a bit more ballast. She expects Adeline Vaughan Williams to come. And a few governors, one of whom will apparently be our new Member for Parliament."

"A useful man to know," I said.

He glanced away from me, refusing to acknowledge our shared complicity in all that was happening, of the calculated, self-serving involvement of so many others.

342

"An armaments millionaire pretending he's a patron of the Arts," he said. "He'll be front and centre."

"Did you tell Ivor all this?"

He nodded. "I showed him the list of works and he spoke about them. Trouble is, every time I mentioned the concert, he insisted on remembering when and where the pieces were written and then first performed."

I remembered my own kaleidoscopic conversation with Gurney two days earlier.

"I spoke to him myself about it," I said.

"Then you know what I mean."

"He didn't seem unduly concerned," I said.

"He doesn't seem unduly concerned about anything these days. The thing is, now that Marion's at the helm, everything is about to happen. This is her forte — or at least she likes to think it is — nurturing and promoting talent, mothering her genius boys until they receive their proper dues and appreciation." He did nothing to disguise his own suspicions or doubts.

"And you think this might conflict with what Gurney himself now needs?"

He paused before answering. "I thought — perhaps hoped would be nearer the mark — that it was what you believed, too."

But in truth — and despite my own earlier misgivings — I saw little real harm in what Marion Scott was now attempting on Gurney's behalf, especially if the musicians and the singers were to be the performers and not Gurney himself.

343

"Look at the programme," he said, indicating the running order of events. "She wants to give a brief introduction, tell everybody what Ivor has achieved, what he'll go on to achieve when he makes a full recovery. She'll probably want him standing up there beside her."

"Not if he decides otherwise," I said, knowing how unhappy Gurney would be at exposing himself like this. "I'll talk to him," I said. "Reassure him."

He blew out his breath, exasperated. "That's what I'm trying to tell you. The person who already believes she knows what's best for Ivor is Marion Scott."

"Gurney's still *my* responsibility," I said.

"I know," he said. "Forgive my outburst. But she'll make Ivor choose. She'll tell him what she wants him to do, and he'll do it. I don't doubt her affection for him, or his for her; nor do I doubt that she truly believes she's doing what's right for him, what's best for him, but —"

"But whatever she wants, she'll get?"

"All Ivor could talk about when I saw him earlier was our boating trips, the *Dorothy*, our walks along the river and in the forest, about his training camps. Every time I tried to get him to look at the programme, he retreated a few years."

"And whatever it is he's retreating from, it's what you believe Marion Scott is now forcing him to confront?"

"I doubt if it's that straightforward or simple. But what I do believe is that *she* believes she sees Ivor's salvation where no one else has yet seen it."

344

"People like me, you mean? His treatment?"

He bowed his head.

"He wasn't committed against his will," I said, knowing how underhand the remark sounded.

"I know. And *I* can't exactly take him back home to Gloucester, to Minsterworth or Dryhill, and let him live there surrounded by the people who know, love and understand him, can I? *I* can't find him a piano to work on all morning and then farm work to keep him busy and then exhaust him for the rest of the day. I can't do it, nobody can."

"But it's where *you* believe his salvation lies?"

"It's a fine word, that's all. Something for the rest of us to cling to, something to keep him human in the middle of us all."

"And men like you, me and Ivor have had enough of fine words?"

He smiled at this, my own veiled apology.

"I just don't know what to say," he said. "That I want what's best for him? That I want him to be given every opportunity to recover? I just don't know what to say." He paused. "For the first few minutes I was with him, I wasn't even convinced he knew who I was. He kept going on about that Lyle character and something that had happened. I actually asked him if he knew who I was. He looked at me for a full minute. And then do you know what he did? He laughed at me, patted my shoulder and then spent the next ten minutes reciting a succession of my poems — *mine*, not his — the best I've ever heard them read. Certainly better than *I've* ever read them, better than anyone. I hadn't thought about any of them for years, but hearing Ivor recite them like that, all from memory, well, it made me realize what I'd actually achieved with them. After ten minutes, he paused, held me again and asked me if I'd got another hour to spare so that he might recite all of the others to me. 'Of course I know who you are,' he told me. 'I know who you are better than I know myself.' " He swallowed, his voice drying. "I don't begin to understand what he was telling me, but I know it means *something*. It must do. And then he started talking about Ypres again, about how he and others had been sent to shoot a hundred mules that had wandered off the road and become stuck in the mud, weighed down by the shells they were carrying. Only crack-shots like himself, he said, on account of all that live ammunition. A hundred of the creatures. And something about summer thunderstorms and laughing at the tank crews who'd been told to name their machines after pieces of fruit. My mother wrote to me recently asking if she'd be able to visit Ivor when she next comes to London."

"What did you tell her?"

"That of course she could visit him."

"And that it would probably break her heart to see him like this?"

He considered this. "The funny thing is, it probably wouldn't. She saw him before when he was bad, when he was tramping the country and when he turned up unannounced at Minsterworth and stayed there for days on end. All *she*'d see would be the Ivor she'd known then."

It was something *I* would never see.

He was about to say more when the porter re-emerged from his small room and waved to attract our attention.

Harvey raised a hand to him. "My cab," he said.

I gave him back the programme and invitation.

"It's yours," he said. "Marion wanted me to give it to you personally. I've left others for all the senior medical staff. She said Osborne would make sure everyone attended."

"The business with Lyle . . ." I began.

But he was already leaving me, buttoning up his coat and holding out his hand to me.

"Ivor said he attacked a woman, a nurse. Bad business. He'll be kept away, I suppose — away from Ivor, I mean?"

"I suppose so," I said.

"I think Ivor felt sorry for the boy. He always struck me as being a bit pathetic." It was another of those spaces between the rest of us into which Lyle would always fall, unnoticed and unmissed. "He told me about the bees, about the new queens," he said.

I walked with him to the entrance, where the porter unlocked the door for us.

"I'll see you at the recital," I said as he opened the door of his cab.

"I think Marion would prefer 'concert'. I don't think 'recital' does full justice to what she has in mind."

He climbed into the vehicle and pushed down the window.

347

"What if she's completely right about everything, and I'm completely wrong?" he said. It was not something that had only then occurred to him.

"It's always a possibility," I said. "Like Salvation."

He laughed at this. "I offered to be one of the singers," he said.

"It might help to reassure Ivor that the concert's a good thing."

"She refused point-blank, I'm afraid. Too out of practice. I'd lower the tone." He started to sing, tapping on the glass to the driver, who turned the cab on the road and drove away.

I continued on my errand to Osborne, wondering again what I might say to him about Lyle.

He was with Webster and Marston when I arrived. Marston acknowledged me with a glance and a barely perceptible shake of the head as he rose and left us. The gesture made me cautious, especially in the presence of Webster, and I asked Osborne if I might see him alone.

"No," he said bluntly. "Doctor Webster and I have a great deal to discuss. I'd appreciate it if you could be as brief as possible."

Webster sat back in his armchair, clearly savouring my discomfort and doing nothing to pretend otherwise. "Yes, we are rather rushed off our feet today," he said. He lifted his feet on to a low table. Osborne looked at him, unhappy at the insincerity of the remark and all it implied, but unwilling to say anything in my presence.

I started to talk, and the instant I mentioned Lyle's name, Osborne held up his hand to silence me.

"No," he said. "Until a full investigation has been completed, I shall not discuss Lyle's assault on the nurse. Either he was unable to control himself, or the stupid girl did something to encourage him. Either way, I'll wait to hear."

"She wouldn't have to do much to encourage *me*," Webster said.

"Besides," Osborne went on, "I've already had that bloody Harvey man in here this morning, telling me what I have and haven't already agreed to. Him and the Scott woman are hand in glove. I sometimes wonder if these people have even the faintest idea of what we're trying to do here, of what this place *is* exactly."

"Hear, hear," Webster said, and again Osborne looked unhappy at the remark.

"Lyle attacked no one," I said. "Cox made most of it up. At worst, Lyle briefly lost his temper — possibly or possibly not at something Alison West had said to him — and then he lost his footing, caught hold of her and they both fell. That's all."

"Not according to Cox, it's not," Osborne said.

" 'Lost his footing'?" Webster said. "It all sounds a bit . . . feeble."

"Thank you, Doctor Webster," Osborne said curtly.

Webster put a hand over his mouth.

"I've said all I'm going to say," Osborne told me. "I'm also waiting to hear from Sister Kidd."

"But Cox is still the one you're most likely to listen to and believe?" I said, wondering at the extent of my bravery, and what more I might be prepared to reveal to him in the presence of Webster. Webster leaned forward at hearing me say this.

"All I'm suggesting," I said, "is that Lyle be recommended for immediate return to Gloucester. And that he sit his Board there, in Barnwood House. You know how the thinking has changed on conscientious objectors over the past few years. Most asylums would be only too happy to —"

"Too happy to absolve themselves of their responsibilities?" Osborne shouted at me. "Too happy to pass these men from pillar to post?"

"The longer Lyle stays incarcerated, especially now, then the more likely he is to —"

"'Incarcerated'? Is he still a prisoner, then? Are we his gaolers?"

"It's what it must seem like to him," I said.

"Oh, and the Board back up in Gloucester will think the same and then take pity on him? Because *they're* the ones who know best? Them, and not us? Interfering local dignitaries and businessmen — not people like me and Webster here, trained practitioners, psychiatrists?" Even he sounded uncomfortable with the word.

"Steady on, old boy," Webster said, but the remark did nothing to deflate the situation.

"No one would blame you," I said. "No one would blame any of us for letting Lyle leave all this — this pointless investigation — behind him and do exactly what he would have done if he hadn't volunteered to come here with Gurney in the first place."

"There's that bloody name again," Osborne said. "Gurney, bloody Gurney. The sainted Ivor. Christ. Who's in charge here, who is actually in charge?"

"You are, Alistair," Webster said. "Or at least you will be when all the *t*'s have been crossed and all the *i*'s finally dotted."

Osborne looked suddenly uncomfortable at this revelation.

"So is your promotion confirmed?" I asked him.

"No, it isn't. It's still only a strong possibility, that's all. A likelihood." He was lying: everything about him told me he'd secured the appointment as the permanent Director of the asylum.

"Perhaps all this Lyle business could be your first beneficent gesture," Webster suggested.

"My what?" Osborne said, and both men shared a knowing smile.

"And Cox will certainly cover his own back," I said. "You should know that better than anyone."

"Oh?" Webster said. "And why's that?"

"Cox was just doing his job," Osborne said quickly.

"Oh, come on, Alistair," Webster said. "The man's a jumped-up bloody trouble-maker. Every opportunity he gets, he's clutching at the chip on his shoulder. It's a mystery to most of us why you tolerate him like you do." He seemed genuinely not to know about Cox and his history with Osborne. Or perhaps he did know about it and he too was now flexing a muscle for the first time, establishing his position in the soon to be reshuffled hierarchy of the place. Either way, neither man was about to reveal his true position or understanding in front of me.

"Cox's behaviour is not a mystery to all of us," I said, knowing that Osborne, at least, would not misunderstand me, and that I was also at the end of my reserves of so-called bravery.

"Sounds interesting," Webster said. "Do tell."

"Cox does a difficult, often dangerous job under difficult circumstances," Osborne said.

"You're starting to sound like a diplomat," Webster said. "In fact —"

"Shut up," Osborne shouted at him, and Webster immediately held up his palms, as though to soften the blow of the words.

"Sorry," he said. "My mistake. It's obviously a touchy subject." He rose angrily from his chair.

"Where are you going?" Osborne asked him, genuinely surprised by Webster's response to this reprimand.

"I know when I'm not wanted, old man," Webster said, and then he left us before Osborne could stop him.

I, too, wished he'd stayed, knowing how suddenly exposed I now was by being alone with Osborne.

I waited for him to speak.

"If you came here with the intention of threatening me . . ." he said eventually.

"I didn't," I said. "I just wanted you to know."

"To know what?"

"That Cox will tell you a pack of lies." It was a deliberately evasive and ambiguous answer, a way of drawing apart for both of us.

352

"What, and you believe I'm stupid or blind enough to believe them?" He was already making further calculations about what I might or might not know.

I shook my head. "I just think he'll make considerably more of the situation than it warrants — to punish Lyle, and to ruin his chances of going back to Gloucester. I think there are enough things going on here — important things — for this to be an unnecessary diversion." I paused. "For all of us."

He considered what I was saying, the increasing distance between us, and my own more certain route of retreat.

Then he slapped a hand on his desk. "Your concerns are noted," he said. "It's always good to know which members of one's staff can be counted upon to offer a direct and honest opinion."

Meaning that my own position in that new hierarchy was also now established, and that my continued presence under his own all-encompassing leadership would be made swiftly intolerable. It might even have been the same realization Marston had just been made to confront.

"I'd like to see Lyle," I said.

"Then see him."

"Apparently, I need your authorization."

He looked up at the word. "Then tell whoever's preventing you that you have it." He waved his hand at me in a gesture of dismissal. As I reached the door, he said, "All this Gurney business. That woman's had official invitations printed."

"I know. It's an impressive guest list."

"Is it? I haven't really looked at the thing."

I recited the names I could remember from my conversation with Will Harvey, a further surreptitious seal to our complicity.

"So you definitely think it worth doing?" he said. What he meant was would *I* now accept responsibility in the event of a disappointing evening.

"It can only reflect well on us," I said. "Changes in regime and practice and all that." It was more than I had wanted to say, and I left him before he disappointed me further by agreeing with me.

CHAPTER
THIRTY-THREE

I went back to Lyle, where I found both Alison West and Sister Kidd being confronted by the same orderly. I heard his voice long before arriving at the locked door.

The two women sat together on a bench beside the door and the man paced up and down in front of them, telling them repeatedly to leave. Neither woman paid him any attention.

I went to him and told him to stop shouting. I told him to unlock the door and let all three of us through, and when he protested at this, I told him to go and see Osborne.

"Cox is my boss," he said uncertainly. "Not Osborne."

I told him I had Osborne's authority to see Lyle. Alison and Sister Kidd rose to stand beside me. "Them, too," I said, and the man finally took out his keys and turned to the door. In a last attempt to assert what remained of his authority, he then insisted on walking ahead of us to the room in which Lyle was being held, and then checking through the grille in the door before beckoning us to him.

He unlocked the door and held it open, preparing to lock it behind us.

355

"Leave it," I told him. The room would have been unbearably cramped with the four of us inside.

He protested again, but his argument was already lost, and so he withdrew, walking noisily back along the corridor.

Lyle sat on the sheetless bed, his hands in his lap. He looked up at our arrival. It was immediately clear to me that he had not yet fully recovered from the sedation he'd been given.

Sister Kidd sat beside him and wiped his face and neck with her apron. She brushed the hair from his forehead with her hand. Seeing my concern, she told me she'd find out from the dispensary what other drugs he'd been given.

Lyle laughed at hearing the words. He looked up, saw Alison close to him, and immediately looked down again.

"I went to see Osborne," Sister Kidd said. "He told me to put everything in writing."

I told her of my own visit, about what Webster had revealed. Both she and Alison were unhappy at the news.

"Will you stay?" I asked her, hoping to hear Alison's answer, too.

But neither woman answered me.

Alison sat beside Lyle and pulled one of his hands from his lap.

"I know you didn't attack me," she told him. She turned his arm, and then his face, to examine his bruises where he'd been restrained.

"What does it matter?" he said, his words faltering and slurred.

"Osborne will support your return to Gloucester," I told him.

Sister Kidd glanced at me, surprised, and I told her of the unspoken deal I'd just made with Osborne. She remained sceptical, however, that he would stick to his side of this bargain, especially now with his authority so close to being made complete. But I was convinced he would honour the deal for precisely the same reason.

"In all likelihood, and considering why you were imprisoned and then committed in the first instance, your Board will recommend your rehabilitation," I said to Lyle.

"Rehabilitation?" He struggled with the word.

"A convalescent home to begin with, somewhere to start —"

"I don't need rehabilitating."

"No," I said. I waited a moment and then told him I'd also persuaded Osborne not to include any mention of what had just happened on the records that would be returned with him to Gloucester. It was considerably more than Osborne himself had conceded to, and again Sister Kidd cast me a disbelieving glance.

"Will you go?" I asked Lyle.

"Back to Gloucester?"

"In the first instance."

He considered this for several minutes without speaking, looking from side to side, his head still down, as though weighing up a complicated argument.

Eventually, he looked up at me. "Will Ivor be sent back, too?" he said.

I shook my head. "Gurney needs to stay here," I told him. "For his own good."

"Why — because he's going to recover his sanity by writing music again, by becoming as famous as everybody's telling him he ought to be?" Saliva ran from his mouth at the long sentence, and Alison wiped this away with her apron. Lyle closed his eyes at her brief touch, and both Sister Kidd and I saw this. He kept them closed for a few seconds after Alison had taken her hand away.

After submitting to this, Lyle then pulled himself free of her loose embrace. The gesture surprised her, and she too leaned back from him. Neither of them spoke.

I crouched down on my heels, manoeuvring myself between them.

"Do you know what medication they've given you?" I asked him.

He pulled his sleeve past his elbow and showed me the puncture marks there. I counted half a dozen, the small pattern surrounded by yet another yellow bruise.

"You're still sedated," I told him. "It's impossible for you to think straight."

To Sister Kidd, I said, "We should come back later."

"If I abandon Ivor now, he'll never forgive me," Lyle said suddenly. "We have connections, me and Ivor."

I wondered what he imagined those connections still to be. And whatever they might have been in his own mind, they were the same ties that Gurney himself was already severing.

358

"Ivor will receive —" I began.

"What?" he shouted at me, pulling down his sleeve. "You think I'm doing more harm than good by staying with him? Is that what you think? Is that what all of you think?"

There was considerable truth in what he was suggesting.

"No," I lied, and then taking a further risk, added, "But I do believe you're thinking more about yourself than about what Ivor himself might now need to help him in his recovery."

He laughed at my transparent evasiveness.

"His recovery? So you still believe that's going to happen, do you? And you're still trying to convince me that *you* know best?"

"His stability, then," I said. "Finding a way of helping him to continue with his work, affording him some peace, some calm, ease, whatever."

He shook his head at each uncertain and unconvincing suggestion.

I thought of Gurney's scrambled manuscripts.

"He only works because I encourage him to," Lyle said. "Without me, he'll stop completely."

None of us said anything to refute this. There might have been a germ of truth in what he was suggesting, but it was far from the whole truth. Besides, it had long since occurred to me that without Lyle's encouragement — without Marion Scott's too, come to that — then Gurney himself might be content to stop struggling against this all too obvious measure of his talent, and that perhaps only then might this be finally disconnected from any notion of his retrievable sanity. It was a confused and impossible argument to make, and especially to Lyle, knowing of all that he too had endured and suffered in the name of his own lost sanity.

"If you appeal against your return to Gloucester, then Osborne will probably keep you separated from Gurney, anyway," I said, knowing how cruel and threatening the remark must have sounded to him.

Beside him, Alison said, "He's right. And if you were rehabilitated, then there would be nothing to stop you from visiting Ivor on your own accord."

Lyle looked up at her. "From Evesham?"

"From wherever you choose to live."

He was suddenly uncertain of himself. "I doubt I'd have the courage ever to leave home again if I was released."

"Then perhaps Ivor himself might one day be returned to Barnwood House," I said.

"What, in ten years? Twenty? Fifty?" He turned back to Alison. "In the orchard . . ." he said, and then hesitated.

"It was an accident," she said. "You stumbled and fell, grabbed hold of me and pulled me down. That's all."

Lyle shook his head. "I grabbed hold of you because — because —"

"You don't need to explain," she told him, all of us concerned by what he might have been about to reveal.

"Osborne already knows what happened," Sister Kidd told him.

360

"I just wanted you to know," Lyle said to Alison. "*You*."

She took his hand again and held it in both her own.

"How long am I going to be kept here?" he asked me. He was asking me if he would be returned to the room he shared with Gurney.

I told him I didn't know.

"I heard them talking about Ivor's concert," he said. "None of the orderlies wants it to happen. Too much extra work for them. The first sign of trouble and they'll call for it to be stopped. They think it's all a big joke."

"Osborne has his reasons for letting it go ahead," I said.

"And Ivor?" He raised his palm to me. "No, don't tell me. You'll only feel the need to tell me what you think I want to hear."

"What *I* want to hear," I said, "is to hear *you* talking and reasoning like this in front of your Board back in Gloucester. Once they come to their decision, things will start to move a lot faster than you imagine."

"Because once I'm considered to be sane again I'll be left to fend for myself and everyone will be able to wash their hands of me, yourself included?"

"Isn't that what you want?" Alison asked him.

Lyle considered this in silence. Then he said to her, "Did the new colonies settle around the queens?"

She told him of their progress, answering all his further questions, and happy, at last, for them to have diverted along this path.

Sister Kidd motioned to me that she and I should leave them, and we went outside into the corridor, walking away from the doorway so that we would not be overheard.

"Osborne's already made arrangements for him to be kept separately from Gurney however long he remains here," she said. "Nor does he want him back in the garden or the orchard. He thinks that one of the reasons all this happened was because Lyle and Gurney have been given too much freedom, too much leeway."

"Meaning the bees?"

"That, and the lack of what Osborne referred to as 'proper supervision'."

"Meaning me?" I said.

She smiled. "I doubt you'd win any popularity contests. How quickly do you think his departure could be arranged?"

I had little idea of the procedure or paperwork involved, but I could not imagine it would be effected as quickly as any of us might now wish.

"A month?" I guessed.

"Too long. A month of him being kept away from Gurney, from the hives?"

"You think the bees were a mistake from the start, don't you?"

"I'm not the only one," she said honestly.

"And now all those others feel vindicated?"

"It isn't what I said." She held my arm. "Perhaps if a few of the other, older, more established patients had shown some interest . . ."

"Is Osborne going to tell me to get rid of the hives, to abandon them?"

She released my arm. "I think there are going to be a lot of changes. I think the past is finally going to catch up with the present and then to change even more swiftly into the future. Isn't that what we're all supposed to be doing — looking ahead to better times? And I think that while all this happens, Osborne is going to stand tall and square at the tiller and sail us there all by himself." She saluted and then smiled again at the uncharacteristically melodramatic suggestion.

"And the open sea ahead is nowhere near as rough as it once used to be?"

"Nowhere near."

Alison appeared in the doorway to Lyle's room, spoke to him briefly and then came out to us.

We waited for her to speak.

"He'll go back to Gloucester," she said. "He wanted to know if he'd be allowed to attend the concert."

"I don't see why not," I said. "Once they stop medicating him . . ."

But neither of the two women was convinced by this, and I saw by the way Sister Kidd avoided my eyes that even if Lyle had been sufficiently recovered from his sedation to attend the concert, then she did not consider it a good idea for him to do so.

She returned to Lyle, leaving me alone with Alison.

"He said he couldn't control his anger," she said, her voice low. "In the orchard. When I suggested sending for Gurney to join us there."

"He probably wanted —"

"I know what he wanted," she said, preventing me from saying more.

We were both then surprised by the sound of crying coming from the room by which we stood. I had been told the day before that Lyle was alone on the wing. I went to the door and looked in. A man lay on the bed there, naked except for his soiled tunic top, his face pressed to the wall, sobbing. I stood aside to let Alison see him. She watched him closely for a minute and then stepped back from the door.

"You don't believe Gurney will ever recover or be released, do you?" she said, and then turned and walked away before I could answer her.

CHAPTER
THIRTY-FOUR

Lyle was taken to an open ward the following day. A room of two dozen beds, where he was placed close to the nurses' station, and where his bed was screened from the others. The beds beside and opposite him remained empty.

I insisted on ending the excessive sedation he had been receiving, and Sister Kidd told me she would keep a close watch on him during his first few nights on the ward.

I finally heard from Osborne that he had set in motion the procedure whereby Lyle would be returned to Gloucester.

The next day was the day of Gurney's concert. Osborne remained adamant that Lyle should not attend this, and despite my earlier feelings, I knew that in his current state, being kept away from the event was now better for Lyle than allowing him to be there. Osborne may not yet have fully understood or accepted what had happened in the orchard, but he knew enough of the relationship between Gurney and Lyle not to allow Lyle to do anything to jeopardize the smooth running of the concert and all he, Osborne, might now personally gain from it.

Marion Scott, Will Harvey and the musicians and singers arrived during the late afternoon, coming in a succession of cars, and carrying their instruments and music stands through the hospital and across the grounds to the designated room. It was a day room in one of the newer wings. Osborne had had it laid out with seating to Marion Scott's design, and the room already contained a low stage large enough to accommodate the singers and musicians. Vases of flowers had been set out on all the window sills and clean curtains hung. It was a warm, bright day, and sunlight fell across the oak floor and the seating in elongated blocks.

The arrival of the musicians caused a stir. A group of patients offered their services as porters, asking questions, examining cases. The young women with the party attracted the most attention, and Sister Kidd and several of her senior nurses accompanied these newcomers wherever they went.

I visited Gurney mid-afternoon and told him of Marion Scott's imminent arrival at his room. He told me he'd visited the concert room earlier.

"Will you yourself play?" I asked him. He had so far refused, but I guessed that Marion Scott would persist in trying to persuade him to perform until the last possible moment.

He shook his head.

"Perhaps read some of your poetry?"

"They showed me where I would be sitting. Behind Marion and Will. Guest of Honour. Did I show you the pieces they'll perform?"

I told him he had.

"Will you be there?"

"Along with most of the medical staff." I told him how much I was looking forward to hearing his music for the first time.

There had already been considerable discussion about which of the patients would also be allowed to attend. Few of them, I imagined, even knew of Gurney's presence among us; or if they did, then they had little notion of his involvement in the event, or what it was intended to represent. On more than one occasion during all these preparations, Osborne had said that he'd be happy when it was all over and done with.

"She wants to take me to Knowle Park," Gurney said. "Marion. In a motor car. Knowle Park, Canterbury and Dover."

"Why Dover?"

He shrugged. "To look out over the sea? She's only doing what she thinks best."

"And will you go?"

He shrugged again and turned away from me. "Is Lyle going back to Gloucester?"

"Eventually. Soon."

"Because of what happened to the nurse?"

I wondered what I might reveal to him of their two suddenly divergent lives ahead that would not now make the comparison unbearably painful for him.

"Where is he?" he said before I could speak.

I told him about Lyle's return from the isolation wing to an open ward.

367

"I don't want him to stay, not here, and not with me," he said. "He'll cling to me, hang on. I think the time has come for me to be left alone."

I wasn't entirely certain what he was telling me — whether he believed his own recovery or stability was contingent upon Lyle's departure; or if he now believed that he, Gurney, was beyond that recovery while Lyle was not.

"He'll go," I said.

"And later? Will he be at the concert?"

"Osborne thinks his presence is a bad idea. He's already hand-picked the audience. Besides, Lyle's still not fully recovered from his sedation. He won't completely shake off the after-effects for another day or two."

What I was also careful to avoid telling him was what Sister Kidd had told me earlier — that the previous day Lyle had raged at being told he was not being allowed to attend the concert, and that she had been forced to call for two orderlies to briefly restrain him while his anger subsided. Apparently, Webster had arrived with the men and had been about to administer a further dose of sedative when she had intervened and told him to see me first. Webster, apparently, had tried to push her aside, but she had stood her ground. I had later supported her in all of this.

Lyle had spent the previous night in a jacket, his ankles and arms in padded restraints. These had been removed earlier that day, when he had recovered sufficiently to apologize to her for his behaviour. She told me that he seemed to genuinely regret and feel ashamed of what had happened. She said he'd cried as he'd made his apology.

He was much clearer, she told me, more lucid. He was still angry at being kept away from the concert, but he accepted this now, and he had given her his word that he would not attempt to leave the ward and attend. He'd asked her if she would be in the audience, and having told him how much she was looking forward to the music, she then promised to relate the evening to him in every detail.

Webster had come to me after his thwarted attempt to medicate Lyle and had told me angrily that I didn't know what I was doing, and that I was deluding myself if I thought I would continue to be given such authority in the future. His parting shot was to tell me that he might still be submitting his own report on Lyle to whoever on the Gloucester Board would be interested in reading it. But it was a hollow threat, and we both knew that. I wondered after he'd gone if he'd been told by Osborne to further sedate Lyle as a way of guaranteeing that the concert would pass without event.

Gurney had heard nothing of the incident.

"He believes he deserves to be there, at the show," he said, meaning Lyle.

"I know," I said. "And perhaps he does."

"He thinks he keeps me on an even keel," he said.

"And you him?"

He considered this, but said nothing.

We were interrupted by the appearance of Alison West, who told me of the arrival of the musicians and alerted me to the fact that Osborne was again looking for me.

She came into the room and sat beside Ivor on the bed. She reassured him that Lyle was well. And whereas he might have doubted me and wondered at the purpose of my evasiveness, he did not doubt her.

I asked her if she could spare the time to stay with him while I sought out Marion Scott.

She told me about the senior nurses appointed to chaperone the women musicians.

Gurney asked her if she knew any of the musicians' names, perhaps hoping to hear one he might recognize. I told him I'd find out for him from Marion Scott, adding that he would meet them all soon enough anyway.

The concert was scheduled for immediately after the evening meal, which would finish at six. The day room would remain light for several hours after that, catching the last of the evening sun.

I left them and went in search of Marion Scott and, hopefully, Will Harvey.

I found them both in the concert room, rearranging the seating on the low stage, playing the piano and listening as the musicians tuned their instruments.

I went first to Will Harvey and asked him if he wanted to see Gurney before everything began.

He surprised me by saying that he didn't. "Better not," he said, glancing at Marion Scott and making his meaning clear to me.

Marion Scott wore her hat and her fur-collared coat, oblivious to the room's warmth, concentrating on her work with the musicians and their instruments.

"Perfectionist," he mouthed.

"Ivor was telling me of the excursions she was planning."

At first he seemed alarmed, but then relaxed when I told him of the places Gurney had mentioned.

"Dover? To look out over the Channel?" he said, shaking his head.

Marion Scott saw me from her vantage point on the stage and came over to us, waiting for the pianist to leave his stool and help her down to the floor below.

"La Grande Dame," Harvey said under his breath, sounding uncharacteristically cruel.

I rose to meet her.

"I thought Doctor Osborne might be present," she said to me. "Or perhaps others among his more senior staff."

Beside me, Harvey smiled at the thoughtless remark.

"Later," I told her. "He has other things to attend to. He'll be here with the others for the recital."

She stiffened at the word.

"Concert," I said, and again Harvey smiled at my discomfort, his face straightening the instant Marion Scott turned to him.

"I doubt any of them truly understands or appreciates the importance or significance of this evening," he said to her, feigning pomposity.

"Quite," Marion Scott said. "I imagine today will be looked back upon with considerably more interest than that with which it appears to be anticipated."

I told her how recently I'd spoken to Gurney.

"He shall sit between us," she said to Harvey.

"He thinks he's in the row behind," I said, wondering if I'd remembered correctly.

"Certainly not. Between us."

"Like a reluctant prince on his new throne," Harvey said, making the remark sound like the line of a poem.

"Quite," Marion Scott said again, uncertain of Harvey's true meaning, of whatever veiled criticism or caution the remark might contain.

She left us then, returning to the stage and the singers, who had started to practise. She told them what to sing, stopping them after every few words with a small correction.

Harvey watched her intently. "What does it matter?" he said. "Can you tell what difference she makes with all her interfering? I'm surprised they continue to tolerate it."

"Meaning that without Gurney, without it being his work they're performing, they wouldn't?"

He shrugged. "All the other bigwigs will be here later. Far too busy and important to arrive early and then sit around all afternoon at Dame Marion's beck and call. They'll arrive with a few minutes to spare — a sherry, perhaps, with Osborne and his *senior* doctors — and then they'll parade here to rapturous applause as the lights dim and as events are finally allowed to proceed."

"And Gurney will be among those applauding them," I said.

"Along with you and me. What's happening with the Lyle character?"

I told him everything I knew, making Lyle's departure appear considerably more certain and imminent than it was.

"She thinks I'm another bad influence on Ivor," he said.

"Surely, Ivor and —"

"The war. All that."

"Everything she wants him to leave behind?"

"She probably thinks he could scrub himself clean in a few hot baths."

"There are plenty who tried it." We still had our constant bathers and washers in the asylum.

"I daresay. But not now — not Ivor."

There was a commotion on the stage as one of the male musicians started to argue with Marion Scott, telling her to leave him alone, that he knew better than she did about tuning his violin. She listened to him in stunned silence for a moment and then made a mute appeal to Harvey and myself. Neither of us intervened, however, and the short, awkward impasse was eventually broken by the violinist again plucking at his instrument.

Marion Scott waited a few seconds and then she walked from the stage and the room.

I left Harvey shortly afterwards, returning to my office briefly before visiting Lyle and finding him asleep. Reassured by Sister Kidd that this was due to exhaustion, I walked in the grounds until it was time for the concert.

Just as Harvey had predicted, the remaining dignitaries from the Royal College did not arrive until half an hour before the programme was due to start, and they went first to see Osborne, where a small reception was held, and where Marion Scott joined them.

The rest of us waited in the day room.

Gurney was there, sitting beside Harvey, the two of them holding an awkward, mostly one-sided, and frequently interrupted conversation.

Ivor sat and watched the men and women on the stage closely. He recognized none of them, nor they him. Only the fact that Marion Scott's empty seat remained beside him drew their occasional glances. Alison West had taken him a clean jacket, shirt and tie to wear. The shirt was buttoned to his throat, causing him to keep his head up. The tie, presumably knotted and pulled into place also by Alison, had already slipped an inch. She had washed and shaved him and brushed his hair.

I sat two rows behind him, and he looked to me, sitting stiffly in his seat with his hands on his knees, like a schoolboy uncertainly awaiting an interview. He occasionally turned to search the faces around him, but again he appeared to recognize no one, his gaze restless and distant. I raised my hand to him, but either he didn't see me or he chose not to acknowledge me amid so many others.

A few minutes later, Will Harvey pointed me out to him, and only then did he hold my gaze. I nodded and he returned the simple gesture. He was clearly tense, his face strained.

374

Alison West sat to the rear of the makeshift concert hall with a group of other nurses and orderlies. I acknowledged her and she smiled.

At six, there was a brief piece of piano music — intended as a fanfare, I imagine, for want of trumpets — and Marion Scott returned, accompanied by eight or nine men in suits — men who either bowed slightly or raised their hands to the already applauding audience — and followed by Osborne, Webster and the others. Marston brought up the rear of the party and then remained standing at the door as the others took their seats.

A short speech was made by Walford Davies, and then another by Charles Wood. Neither Sir Hubert Parry nor Sir Charles Stanford had been free to attend.

Then Marion Scott spoke, and as she concluded her remarks she called for Gurney to stand and reveal himself. The curtains had been partly drawn against the evening sunlight, casting lines of intermittent shadow across the room.

Will Harvey helped Gurney to his feet, reassuring him. Gurney stood transfixed by the further applause which rose around him. Nudged by Harvey, he held up his arm until the clapping began to subside. On the stage, the musicians, most of them seeing Gurney for the first time, gently tapped their bows against their music stands.

Harvey sat down almost immediately, intending Ivor to remain standing, but Ivor quickly followed him and the applause finally died.

Onstage, Marion Scott continued to extol Gurney's achievements, concluding by remarking that she was certain that the rest of us would soon endorse her opinion. She thanked the others for coming from the College, making it sound as though they had had a long and difficult journey. And then she thanked Osborne for making the event possible, and for possessing the foresight, understanding and expertise which, she felt certain, would soon allow Gurney to recover his health and continue with his work. Her message, in front of all these others, was clear. I saw Osborne signal his grudging thanks to her.

The concert began a few minutes later, after thirty seconds of silence. A cellist raised his bow, using it as a conductor might use his baton. And thus made ready and counted in, the pianist started to play.

The performances lasted two hours, with only a short interval, during which only Osborne and his guests were allowed to leave the room. I left my seat and walked to the front during the break. Gurney sat with his eyes firmly closed, his hand held tightly in Will Harvey's.

Upon Osborne's return, the concert resumed.

Marion Scott announced that several short pieces would now be omitted from the programme due to the constraints of time. Among the pieces to be lost, I saw, were "Severn Meadows" and "By A Bierside". I remembered Gurney telling me they were two of his favourites. I remembered the lines Will Harvey had recited while waiting for the bus.

Marion Scott returned to her seat beside Ivor.

Harvey, I saw, released his grip on Gurney's hand at her approach.

There was a further hour of music and singing.

I understood fully, and for the first time, everything Marion Scott had spent the past weeks trying to impress upon me. And I saw, too, and perhaps also for the first time, the true and terrible nature of the chasm Gurney himself had finally crossed.

He turned to look back at me as the performance ended, bathed in the evening sunlight as the sun fell lower in the sky. A further brief silence followed the final, dying notes, and then the room was filled with its loudest applause yet. This lasted for several minutes before Osborne rose from his seat and held up his hands for calm. But the audience ignored him, and defeated by their enthusiasm and by the noise they made, he sat back down. He, too, resumed clapping.

And as this applause finally faded, Gurney turned to look at me, shielding his eyes against the light. I hardly knew how to acknowledge him. When he looked away from me, I turned to Alison West at the rear of the room. She held a handkerchief to her mouth, her thumb and fingers pressed hard into her cheeks.

As the applause ended, and as the audience started to rise and disperse, I made my way to Gurney and the small crowd already gathering around him — patients, mostly, but including nurses, orderlies and several of the men from the College.

He stood bemused at their centre, Will Harvey still beside him and answering most of the questions being put to Gurney. When Ivor did eventually speak, the people around him fell silent to listen to him, encouraging him to say more. It was something he was not accustomed to doing, at least not recently, and against all my expectations, he seemed to be actually enjoying the attention he was now receiving.

I signalled to Will Harvey that I would see him before his departure, after the remaining patients had been removed. It had been Osborne's original intention to clear the room as soon as the concert had finished, but neither he nor any of his staff had foreseen what a success it would be, and he now allowed a delay while he too basked in his own small beam of reflected glory. There were even calls for more music, for the abandoned pieces, but the musicians were already packing away their instruments and folding their stands.

Skirting the bulk of the dispersing audience, I made my way to the rear of the room and to Alison West, who now stood alone.

"He's enjoying all the attention," she said, indicating Gurney.

"Overwhelmed by it, I should imagine." I knew Gurney would be fine amid his crowd of admirers while Will Harvey was at his side.

"I cried," she said. "I couldn't help myself."

Her face was dry now, but I imagined I could see the thin tracks of her tears down her cheeks.

"Ivor — *our* Ivor — wrote all that?"

"It seems so." And again I regretted not having paid closer attention to everything Marion Scott had given me.

She nodded to Osborne, who stood with the visiting dignitaries. "He's lapping it up," she said.

"Perhaps now he'll instigate a whole series of concerts," I suggested.

She shook her head. "Whatever he did, nothing would ever compare to this."

At the main doorway, patients started to assemble in short lines, each headed by an orderly or a nurse, organizing their departure.

"I should go," she told me.

I saw the men standing close by, waiting for her and watching her closely, worried now that it was time for them to leave that they had no one to follow.

She went to them and gathered them around her.

I was about to join Osborne and the others when I saw Sister Kidd, also at the door, leave the room briefly and then return. She held the door closed behind her, searched anxiously over the heads of the men around her and then signalled to me. An orderly pulled open the door behind her. She signalled to me again, more urgently this time, and I went to her.

CHAPTER
THIRTY-FIVE

Sometimes at home, our bees had swarmed and then departed without our noticing, and when this happened we were dependent on others to let us know where they had settled. It was always a strange and disorienting time for the bees before their new worlds were established, and retrieving and returning them was not a particularly difficult task. Occasionally, my father would discover that some of his bees had gone and then make the decision to leave them where they were, allowing those that had stayed to repopulate the empty hives.

The swarm I remember most vividly occurred the summer Charles finally enlisted at the Officer Training Academy. He was accepted for training at Oxford, from where, for most of his first year, he was able to return home at least once a month. These were always great events in our family history.

I saw how my mother felt about her eldest son's decision, but she said nothing. Charles, I knew, understood her feelings, and all she was suppressing, and later, on his visits home, he was quick to remove his uniform once our greetings were over.

It was mid-July, always an unpredictable time for the bees, and any new hive would need to be populated and provisioned quickly if the colony was to be made ready for the late-summer decline in pollen. A week too late, one degree too cold, or a pound of honey too little, and everything might be lost. Another of my father's mantras.

Charles was watching as the first of the bees emerged and started circling the hive for no good reason. This apparent indecision was a sure sign of swarming. Usually, the bees came out and headed immediately for their destinations, but now they appeared to be lost, waiting to be led. Several dozen of the insects formed into a loose ball and stayed close to the hive entrance.

Charles rang the bell he had been given, and my father and I ran out to join him. I am certain my father would have been happier standing watch alone during these difficult times, but both Charles and I still insisted on our involvement and he could not refuse us. He was already suffering, tiring easily, and cutting down on his work. I could not remember a time when he had tended fewer hives.

We both responded immediately to the sound of the bell, meeting in the hallway. I pulled on my protective suit as I ran, my father donning only his veiled hat and gauntlets. I had insisted on wearing the same, but my mother had been adamant about the full suit. It was her belief that the bees were crazy when they swarmed.

My father waited for me at the first gate, already catching his breath after the short journey. In the distance, Charles saw us coming and rang the bell again to urge us on. My father told me to run ahead of him, but I insisted on waiting for him, pretending to examine my outfit for any openings one of the crazy insects might penetrate. His face was red and wet with sweat, which he wiped as he resumed walking. My mother followed behind us, carrying her small copper pan and ladle and looking vaguely ridiculous.

We all crossed the patch of fallow grass and arrived beside Charles. He, too, wore only his hat and gloves. He showed us where the bees were already congregating. The swarm had grown much larger by then, but still showed no signs of moving off to a new home. My father told us to stay where we were, and then he went forward alone, searching for the departing queen. He was careful not to disturb the bees any further and he stood back from the edge of the gathering ball, individual insects circling it in ever-widening orbits, as though protecting the gathering mass. He did not see the queen and so he came back to us. Charles and I collected poles and sacks and my father constructed the portable hive he used to gather up small swarms. There was nothing we could do now, he told us, except wait. We were in the lap of the gods, he said. I remember my mother's disarming laughter at the portentous phrase.

Nothing happened for a further hour. The number of bees continued to swell. Sometimes the swarm tightened into a darker mass, and at other times it expanded into a shapeless haze.

My mother returned to the house and came back to us with cold drinks, defusing the growing urgency of

382

the situation. But when our attention strayed, my father became angry and told us to concentrate on the bees.

My mother wore her own extravagantly embroidered hat and long gloves, and I recall looking at her and thinking how beautiful she looked, how elegant. It is how I often remember her now, veiled in white and constantly smoothing the material of her gloves along her forearms, like a bride preparing for her entrance into church.

Shortly afterwards, the noise of the bees became suddenly more insistent, and rather than congregate at the hive entrance, the swarm began to move one way and then another, until, in this state of growing agitation, it was tugged by some invisible and irresistible force directly towards where the four of us stood and watched over it. I panicked and shouted that we ought to run, but my father held my shoulders and told us all to stand perfectly still.

The swarm came quickly towards us, its centre of gravity four or five feet off the ground, rising and falling like a blown balloon, and when it was only ten feet away from us, and it was clear to us all that nothing would now divert it from its blind and urgent path, my father said quietly but firmly, "Lower your heads and close your eyes and mouths." I felt his grip on my shoulders tighten. Charles, I saw, reached out and held my mother's hand, and at the same instant he moved to stand in front of her to cushion the blow of the approaching swarm. I wished I could have done the same.

The first of the bees hit us and I felt them like a heavy rain on my head. Some struck me and rebounded and continued on their flight, and some struck me and fell to the ground, where they lay in the grass for a moment before rising back into the air and resuming their journey.

The mass of the swarm went past us and around us and over us in a liquid flow, and for a few seconds I imagined I was going to be toppled by their weight. Some of the insects that collided with us clung to our clothes and veils. I saw several crawling across my eyes. I half raised my hand to brush them away, but my father grabbed it and told me not to. He alone, I suspect, fully understood the true nature of this disturbed and agitated force. I saw the far greater number of insects crawling over Charles's veil and hat. My mother pressed herself close to him and held him around his chest. She saw me looking at her and smiled at me. I smiled back. Her hands were clasped tight over Charles's heart, and there, too, the bees were already gathering and crawling.

We stood like this for only a few seconds, though it seemed much longer, as the bulk of the swarm passed through us and around us towards a copse of trees, where it eventually settled.

My father released his grip on me and picked the last few bees from my hat. He gathered these in his palm as if they were cherries, and when he had a handful of them he threw them up into the air.

Charles picked them from my mother's arms and hands, which, despite his protests, remained locked around his chest. She pressed her face hard into his neck. My father told her it was safe for her to raise her head, but upon hearing him she pressed herself even tighter to her son for a few final seconds before releasing her grip and standing back from him. She stood with bees still on her veil, their small, moving shadows passing over her face like flickering fears and doubts. Charles picked these from her.

My father, ensuring I was free of the insects, left me and followed the swarm to the trees.

My mother made no attempt to pluck the bees from herself, content to allow her son to finish the work. I went to them, but as I too began plucking the last of the insects from her, she took my hand and lowered it. She pointed to my father and told me to follow him; he would need help with the bees. "Please," she said to me, and, obedient as ever, I turned and left them.

CHAPTER
THIRTY-SIX

I pushed through the dispersing crowd until I reached Sister Kidd, my own urgency attracting the attention of the other nurses and orderlies congregating at the doorway.

"Something's happened," she said to me, pulling the orderly who had just arrived closer to her.

"On one of the wards," the man said, coughing, breathless. "You'd better come."

"Who is it?" I asked him. "A patient?"

"Of course it's a patient. God knows who, though."

Sister Kidd and I exchanged a glance, both of us making our own unspoken guesses.

"I'm supposed to go straight to Osborne," the orderly said, attempting to push past us.

I put my arm across the doorway to prevent him.

"You'll panic everyone," I told him. "We'll come with you."

"Cox told me to go direct to Osborne and tell him," he said angrily.

"Cox?"

"He's the one who sent me."

It was all the confirmation I needed.

I pointed to where Osborne still stood with the others from the College, Marion Scott and Will Harvey beside him.

"He won't thank you for dragging him away now," I said.

The man watched Osborne for a moment, considered what I was telling him, and then grew calmer. He wiped his face with his sleeve, and for the first time I saw the bloodstain there, running from his elbow to his cuff.

Sister Kidd saw it too and she pushed down his arm.

"That's what I'm talking about," he said. "That's why I'm here. Are you coming?"

Sister Kidd gave instructions to several of her nurses, and they held their patients back as the three of us left the room.

"*Is* it Lyle?" I asked her.

"Let's just —"

"Cox never said his name," the orderly said. He walked faster ahead of us, almost running, repeatedly urging us to keep up with him.

We left the main building and followed a succession of corridors. At each of the locked doors a man stood ready with the key. These men knew no more than the orderly, each aware only of the sense of urgency passing through their own small domains.

"I thought it was meant to be the big chief coming," one of them said as he locked his door behind us.

"Ask him," the orderly told him, pointing to me.

"He was meant to fetch Osborne," the man said to me. "Cox's orders. He won't be happy at you showing up."

I was uncertain whether he meant me specifically, or anyone who might have turned up instead of Osborne.

But there was no time to respond to him; our messenger already stood at the far end of the corridor, another gatekeeper holding open his own door.

We finally arrived at the ward into which Lyle had been taken the previous day. A group of patients waited outside, some of them pacing the corridor, others standing with blankets over their shoulders.

The orderly was the first to enter, and I knew by the way he ran along the room that he was going to Lyle's bed.

Our arrival provoked a small commotion among the patients. Men asked to be allowed back to their beds; some cried; others stood in silence beside the glass partition overlooking the room.

I saw the bloody smear on the door itself, and then the scattered splashes across the linoleum floor leading to Lyle.

Sister Kidd told me to go ahead alone while she stayed with the untended patients. She began to usher the men away from the door, calming them, telling them there was nothing to see. Several nurses arrived to help her, leading the men into rooms further along the corridor.

I followed the orderly to Lyle's bed, still screened, and the instant I drew this aside, I was confronted by Cox, who had just then stepped back from Lyle's bed, and who spun to face me. His tunic was splashed from collar to hem with blood; his trousers too. He raised his cupped palms to me, showing me the blood pooled at their centre and dripping through his fingers. A mound of equally bloody sheets lay on the floor around Lyle's bed.

"Where's Osborne?" Cox said absently, looking behind me, unable to understand why I had appeared and not Osborne. "Where's Osborne? I sent for Osborne."

The messenger orderly stood a few feet away, unable to answer him, staring instead at the bed and the man motionless upon it, stepping quickly back when he saw that he too was standing in the slowly spreading pool of blood on the floor.

Lyle's sheets were red from side to side and from top to bottom. His mattress was red and his pillow was red, and the blood dripped almost audibly from the thin metal frame.

He had cut his wrists, scored both his arms in a succession of deep slashes, and he had lost so great a quantity of blood, and so quickly, that he appeared to have been painted with it, lying with his face up, his arms held straight by his sides, palms raised, the slashes clearly visible where the elastic skin and flesh had already drawn back, the wounds cut close to the bone on both sides.

"I sent for Osborne," Cox repeated. "Where is he?"

I pushed past him and picked up one of Lyle's arms. I shouted at the orderly to fetch more sheets from another bed, anything to make tourniquets. But the man was rooted to where he stood, his hands on the frame of Lyle's bed, his eyes fixed on Lyle, and uttering a succession of oaths.

I pushed him hard in his chest, told him again to fetch the sheets, and he finally did this.

But I knew the instant I looked more closely at Lyle's face, and then when I tried to lift one of his arms and feel for a pulse, that we were all too late to save him. The cuts opened wider at my touch, squeezing yet more blood from the severed arteries as I raised and then lowered his arms.

"You're too late," Cox said.

Lyle's eyes were closed. There was little blood on his face, only that which had sprayed there at the first of his cuts.

"He looks to have lost the lot," Cox said. "This could have happened an hour ago. There was nobody here. The screen was drawn. Everybody was at that bloody sing-song. He should have been left where he was, in the secure wing. I told Osborne not to move him, I told him. Leave him there until we got shot of him, that's what I said. Or at least jacket and sedate him here, I told him." He paused and then pointed at me, the tip of his finger hard against my chest. "You were the one who stopped him from being sedated. Twice. Twice, you stopped it. If he'd been sedated then this would never have happened. How could it? You were the one who stopped it. You."

I stepped back from him, leaving his finger still pointing at me, a dot of red on my jacket.

"You look in his notes," he said. "That's what I said — sedate him, jacket him — and Osborne agreed with me. You look in those notes — it's all there."

"I'm sure it is," I said.

390

"And you were the one who stopped it all. You." He spoke louder now, ensuring everyone around us heard what he was saying. Then he pointed to Sister Kidd at the door. "And *she* was the one who said she'd make sure he was under constant watch. Look in his notes. Constant watch. It's all there."

"He should never —" I began.

"Are you the only one?" Cox interrupted me. "Who else is coming? Where's bloody Osborne? He'll want this one sorted out as soon as possible. Where is he?"

"Probably still getting his back slapped by all the nobs," the orderly told him.

And Cox finally understood and shook his head, and he too stood back from the bed, leaving bloody footprints on the floor and holding out his arms to examine the extent to which Lyle's blood had soaked into his own clothes.

"He was dead when I arrived," he said, his voice lower. He pointed to a piece of glass on the mattress beside Lyle's hand. "It looks like a bit of broken bottle. Christ knows where he got *that* from, or how long he's had it." He was again talking for the benefit of the men around us. He knew as well as I did that the glass had come from the dump in the garden, and I wondered how soon after seeing the glass on the bed beside Lyle he had sent someone to retrieve all the other shattered pieces from the grass beneath the wall beside the hives.

I wiped my own bloody hands on my jacket, and then on one of the clean sheets, passing another to Cox, who took it from me and then held it without wiping himself for a moment, his gaze still fixed on

Lyle's drained corpse and on the redness all around him, watching as the viscous blood continued to thicken and spread, slowly filling in the few white spaces of the bed on which Lyle lay.

CHAPTER
THIRTY-SEVEN

I next saw Gurney two days later, standing in the garden with Alison West beside him.

The gateway into the orchard was closed, and I saw that a chain had been fastened across the door.

I went to them.

"Osborne's put the place out of bounds until everything's sorted out," Alison said, shielding her eyes to watch me approach.

"What does the orchard — the bees — have to do with any of that?" I said, but it was an unconvincing denial.

"You know how Osborne works," she said.

"Meaning he's probably already started telling whoever will listen to him that he connects Lyle's so-called assault on you with what —"

She signalled for me to lower my voice.

Beside her, Gurney stood with his gaze fixed on the doorway, oblivious to what was being said.

The greenhouses were again empty, though the noise of the mowers and the voices of men could still be heard on the distant lawn.

"Ivor?" Alison said to Gurney, and he turned and looked at her, then at me, and then beyond me.

"Ivor?" she said again.

"He wasn't at the concert," Gurney said. "He would have liked that. They should have let him come. He would have liked that." He turned back to the chained door.

"Does he know?" I mouthed to her.

She nodded once.

I put my hand on Gurney's shoulder and he flinched at the unexpected touch.

"I'm sorry, Ivor," I said.

"He said that I should make my own application to go back," he said. "Said it was where I belonged — there, not here. Said he'd look out for me."

"He would have been discharged," I said.

"I know that; we both did." There was neither anger nor despair in his voice.

"At best, he would have seen you once a month, that's all." I refrained from adding that he, Gurney, would not have been allowed to return to Gloucester, and especially not on the strength of any impossible promises Lyle might have made to him.

I looked to Alison for support, but she said nothing.

"He showed me," Gurney said unexpectedly.

"Showed you what?"

"The piece of glass." He held up his palm, as though the glass were there.

"And you said nothing?"

"He made me promise him."

"Not even to me? To Alison?"

He went on as though I hadn't spoken. "My father, towards the end, he said that if he'd had the courage to do something about his own suffering, then he would have ended his misery sooner. But my mother, see, she said he'd be going against the Scriptures, against the word of the Bible. He listened to her. She took no account of his suffering, his pain or what he knew was coming to him. All *she* was ever interested in was how things might look to others after he was gone. But he told me, told his Ivor, his misfit boy."

"And that's why you respected Lyle's wishes?"

He bowed his head.

"We came out to tell the bees," Alison said, indicating the chained door. "This was the closest we could get to them."

"Osborne wants a full inquiry," I told her.

"Only because he made sure his own back was covered from the start," she said. "And because he knows he'll be completely exonerated. He'll probably even wait until his appointment's confirmed and then insist on proving how noble and decent he is by insisting on shouldering the blame himself."

"He'll point the finger of blame at —"

"I know where he'll point it," she said. She closed her eyes briefly and turned away from me.

I told Ivor about my mother telling the bees of my father's death.

"Mine, too," Alison said, her eyes still closed.

We both waited for Gurney to say something, but he remained silent.

Eventually, he said, "My uncle up in Maisemore burned his hives. Foulbrood. Every bee-keeper in the Forest suffered from it that year. Said it was the wet autumn. Last time I was up there, this was. Bad state of affairs."

My father had once been forced to burn a dozen of his hives because of foul brood. Fortunately, the infected hives had been kept separate from the others, amid the bracken of the slopes above the river and the woodland. The whole of that part of the country had been infected, and destroying the hives and their colonies along with them had been the only failsafe method of preventing the spread of the infection. That, and then leaving the land empty for at least two years following.

"Couldn't touch the wax or the honey crop, of course," Gurney said. "They blazed so fierce, those hives. Dripping and burning for hours. We were up there with him, me and my father, helping him, watching it all."

"Lyle had no relatives," Alison said to me, her voice still low, the words more mouthed than spoken.

"That should make things easier for everyone concerned," I said. Yet another unravelled family lost unnoticed and unmourned in the deepening shadow of those empty years.

I'd already submitted my own report to Osborne on what had happened. I told him I'd also sent a copy directly to the Mental Health Commissioners. And then I'd turned and left him before he could respond to this.

"They won't need us to tell them," Gurney said, meaning the bees, and he took several paces away from us towards the orchard.

396

In the report, I'd written that Lyle had drawn the glass across his wrists and arms while Gurney's concert was in progress, and that he had waited for this and then chosen his moment carefully.

"What now for Ivor, do you think?" Alison said, turning back to me.

I told her I didn't know. We both knew that Osborne would wait until the inquiry came to its satisfactory conclusions regarding himself and the asylum, and that he would then do everything in his power to get rid of me.

"You think Osborne will want Gurney as his own patient?" she said.

"After the other evening . . ."

"He told Sister Kidd that he wished Steen had been present at the concert to see and hear what Ivor had achieved."

"He achieved none of it here," I said. "All he ever achieved here was to finally sever all those ties which bound him to the world in which he once lived — the world which supported him and nourished him, and which held him safe and secure in his proper place."

She looked to where Gurney walked even further from us.

"Come back, Ivor," she called to him, and he turned and walked back to us, grinning to himself as he came.

"What is it?" I asked him.

"I was thinking of those bees," he said. "Up at Maisemore. The brood. Covered the hives in lamp oil and stacked straw under them. Went up like beacons. Plenty of smoke to keep the bees quiet, but a fair

397

number of them still managed to get out and fly in circles around the burning frames. Broke my uncle's heart to lose those hives like that. Cried, he did. Him and my father alike. The burning bees went up in the wind and in the heat off the hives like embers from a bonfire. Seeing my own dry eyes, my uncle said that there was something wrong with me, that I had no pity left in me. All this was after the war, see? No pity left in me, not a drop. He expected my father to agree with him, but my father knew better than that and he kept his silence. He knew me, see? He knew his boy. Eventually, they had harsh words and my father told his own brother to leave off me. So what if I had no pity left? So what? There was no shame in that, not after everything I'd been through and seen. No shame at all. He was still crying, my uncle, still watching all those burning hives and bees. But he was angry by then, and he said that whatever I'd seen, it was man bringing it on man, that it was a different thing entirely, and that nothing of what I'd been through over there compared to the suffering of those poor, innocent bees. My father took me away after that. Died the following May. I doubt the two of them saw each other again or exchanged a civil word. I miss that old boy."

He stopped speaking, and only then did I realize that it was probably the most I had ever heard him say; or if not the most, then the most he had ever said with that degree of clarity or consistency.

"Where will they bury him?" he asked me, meaning Lyle.

"Back in Evesham?" I suggested. "With his parents?"

"They were certainly bound hard enough together in their beliefs and their suffering," he said.

"I'll tell Osborne," I told him.

"Good," he said. And then he closed his eyes and lifted his face to the cloud-filled sky, turning from side to side, almost as though he were a weather-vane caught in a changing wind and veering back and forth in uncertain currents until catching the first draught of its new direction and settling to its course.

The Secret Scripture

Sebastian Barry

Nearing her 100th birthday, Roseanne McNulty faces an uncertain future, as the Roscommon Regional Mental hospital where she's spent the best part of her adult life prepares for closure. Over the weeks leading up to this upheaval, she talks often with her psychiatrist Dr Grene. This relationship, guarded but trusting after so many years, intensifies as Dr Grene mourns the death of his wife.

Told through their respective journals, the story that emerges — of Roseanne's family in 1930s Sligo — is at once shocking and deeply beautiful. Refracted through the haze of memory and retelling, Roseanne's story becomes an alternative, secret history of Ireland. Exquisitely written, it is the story of a life blighted by maltreatment and ignorance, yet still marked by a flame of love, passion and hope.

ISBN 978-0-7531-8178-2 (hb)
ISBN 978-0-7531-8179-9 (pb)

Being Emily

Anne Donovan

Anne Donovan is outstanding **Melvyn Bragg**

A tender, lyrical coming-of-age narrative **Guardian**

Things are never dull in the O'Connell family. With her older brother out at work, Fiona O'Connell is often left in charge at home, dealing with the terror of her little twin sisters, Mona and Rona, and their line-dancing routines. But she still thinks that life in their tenement flat is far less interesting than Emily Brontë's, and the books that she is fascinated by.

But tragedy is not confined to Victorian novels. Following the events of one single day, Fiona's happy domestic set-up is about to change forever. Her family will never be the same again. But there remains the hope of new relationships developing, built on a solid foundation of love.

ISBN 978-0-7531-8128-7 (hb)
ISBN 978-0-7531-8129-4 (pb)

A Mile of River

Judith Allnatt

It is 1976 and England is suffocating. The long, dry spring has given way to a summer of severe drought. For the farmers, life has become a living hell — the fields are tinder dry, the earth is scorched and the rivers are drying to a trickle.

Jess and Tom live on a remote farm with their increasingly difficult and brutal father. Their mother, Sylvie, walked out years before and Jess is struggling with the role of mother figure to Tom, as well as skivvy and hired hand for her father. Jess just wants to be a normal teenager, to go to dances and kiss boys, to take her exams and plan her future. Daydreaming about her mother's return, Jess discovers Sylvie's old diary and begins to uncover the shocking truth about her disappearance.

As the drought grips ever tighter, the menace in the air builds until it reaches boiling point, with a confrontation between Jess and her father that has devastating consequences.

ISBN 978-0-7531-8152-2 (hb)
ISBN 978-0-7531-8153-9 (pb)

The House at Midnight

Lucie Whitehouse

A story of compulsion, desire, darkness and betrayal

After the suicide of his uncle, Lucas Heathfield inherits Stoneborough Manor in Oxfordshire. He imagines it as a place where he and his tight-knit group of friends can spend time away from London. But from the beginning, the house changes everything.

Soon after their first visit on New Year's Eve, Lucas risks their close friendship to declare his love for Joanna. Everyone is delighted — they have been expecting them to get together for years. But Joanna soon senses that the house is having a strange effect on Lucas. He becomes haunted by the death of his uncle and obsessed by cine films of his uncle's friends at Stoneborough 30 years earlier. Within the claustrophobic confines of the house over a hot, decadent summer, secrets slide out of the past and sexual tensions escalate, shattering the group's friendship and changing their lives irrevocably.

ISBN 978-0-7531-8070-9 (hb)
ISBN 978-0-7531-8071-6 (pb)

Away to the West

Ruth Tomalin

Away to the West describes two journeys in post-war England and two young people trying to find a way to escape.

Here the observer is a young girl, Rowan, whose eyes are on the people she meets: those with settled country homes, newcomers, men and women back from the war, "displaced persons" of all kinds.

In the first part, All Round the Moon, Ralph, whose chief interest is in the wildlife around him, begins to make his own way but realises that old ties are not so easily broken. The second part, A Wind of Autumn, takes up the story six years later, when Rowan is 15. She has always been a misfit in her clever ambitious family, but alone for a long weekend in the country she begins to find herself.

ISBN 978-0-7531-8030-3 (hb)
ISBN 978-0-7531-8031-0 (pb)